A YEAR AT THE FRENCH FARMHOUSE

GILLIAN HARVEY

Boldwood

First published in Great Britain in 2022 by Boldwood Books Ltd.

Copyright © Gillian Harvey, 2022

Cover Design by Becky Glibbery

Cover Photography: Shutterstock

A CIP catalogue record for this book is available from the British Library.

Paperback ISBN 978-1-80426-968-8

Large Print ISBN 978-1-80426-964-0

Hardback ISBN 978-1-80426-964-0

Ebook ISBN 978-1-80426-961-9

Kindle ISBN 978-1-80426-962-6

Audio CD ISBN 978-1-80426-969-5

MP3 CD ISBN 978-1-80426-966-4

Digital audio download ISBN 978-1-80426-960-2

Boldwood Books Ltd
23 Bowerdean Street
London SW6 3TN
www.boldwoodbooks.com

For Mum and Dad: Richard and Barbara

1

'Don't think of it as a dead end. Try to think of it as an opportunity!' Mark said brightly, flashing his perfect porcelain veneers. 'You'll be given a generous redundancy package: three months' salary, plus an additional lump sum to keep you going.'

'I... what?'

For a moment, time slowed. Through the slightly grubby window above Mark's head, Lily could see the shadows of cars purring by on the road; the flicker of figures walking purposefully past. Muffled snippets of conversation filtered in and out of the basement office as people outside on the pavement moved closer then further away. The sights and sounds of ordinary life seemed suddenly jarring.

'In the current climate, it's a generous package,' Mark added into the silence.

Lily looked at the executive toy on Mark's desk – a silver row of balls that, when tapped, perpetually rocked back and forth. She imagined what would happen if she picked it up and lobbed it through the frosted window – the glass shattering; balls everywhere.

'Lily? Everything all right?' said the man who'd just ripped the rug from under her entire life.

'Who said it was a dead end?' she asked suddenly, the words only just sinking in.

He at least had the good sense to blush. 'I didn't... I mean, of course,' he stammered.

But this wasn't *his* fault. The partners had brought Mark's company in to 'streamline the business'; and avoid the awkwardness of giving loyal employees the boot.

Although it wasn't the boot in the traditional sense, was it? She wasn't being 'sacked'. It wasn't that she'd messed up on a client file, or started turning up for work late. She was simply surplus to requirements, and they were trying to survive in a world where every man and his dog thought he could design his own logo.

She'd have done the same, probably, in their shoes. Not that she'd be seen dead in a pair of 'comfort brogues.'

She looked again at Mark, with his untroubled, unmarked brow, sharp, fitted suit; nails that had probably had a more recent manicure than hers. He couldn't be much more than twenty-five. Employed to deliver bad news, but with no real sense of its impact. She was just another name on his to-do list.

She wished she could say that it didn't matter anyway. Or that she'd had the chance to quit before they'd fired her, marching purposefully out of the office and leaving the partners wondering if they'd made a mistake.

And if only they'd held off till this time next year, she could have. By then she and Ben would have their house on the market and be packing for a new life in France. They'd been planning for years, but each time they'd tried to fix a date something had come up: a promotion at work, Ty getting into a new sports club and so on. Then a few months ago they had finally agreed on a definite time. 'OK,' Ben had said. 'Let's take a year to get Ty settled at uni, then we'll go for it!'

She'd leaped into his arms laughing, and he'd twirled her around as if they were twenty years younger, and she was ten kilos lighter.

It had been the culmination of a lifelong dream; and she'd been looking forward to dramatically handing in her notice next spring. Now, even that minor victory had been snatched away.

'I take it I get to go home now?' she asked, turning to face Mark as she reached the office door.

'Well, it's entirely your decision,' he said. 'There is a one-month notice period but the partners were keen to stress that if you don't feel *able* to come in, it won't reflect badly on your exemplary record.' He smiled again, delivering yet another pre-rehearsed line.

She almost took the bait. But not quite. They knew she was a perfectionist, that she always wanted to do the right thing. But she wasn't going to endure a month of working effectively for nothing when she could be out finding another job. Or finally cleaning out the kitchen cupboards. Or, if it came to it, sitting on the sofa watching reruns of *Homes Under the Hammer* while working her way through a giant pack of Pringles. 'Right, well, I'll be off then,' she said, trying to keep her voice from wobbling.

Mark's eyebrows raised slightly, but he said nothing.

She raced into the corridor and up the stairs to the ground floor, then made a beeline for the exit, hoping to escape before she started to cry. But when she was halfway across the main office, her progress was thwarted by the thwack of a door almost opening in her face. Her boss, Grahame, stepped out of the toilet; saw her, coloured and vanished back inside, a lock clicking audibly.

That's right, she wanted to yell. *You hide, Grahame. Don't want to have an awkward conversation. Or, I don't know, thank me for my decade of service. I'll just go quietly, shall I?*

Inside the bathroom, she heard the sound of a flush. She swallowed her words.

'Well,' she said, turning to the other eight employees and backing towards the reception desk, in no doubt that her face was red from the heat she could feel prickle her skin. 'I guess this is goodbye.'

The words sounded dramatic in her head, but in the office on an average Friday afternoon all she received in return were a few grunts of vague acknowledgement. As if redundancy was infectious and nobody wanted to catch it.

'Bye, honey!' said Karen on reception, looking up with an oblivious smile as she passed. 'Early finish, eh!'

'Something like that.'

'Well, have fun, honey!'

Once she was safely inside her car, Lily allowed the tears to fall. They streamed, hotly, down her cheeks – tears of anger, disappointment, fear for the future. And an inexplicable shame at finding she was surplus to requirements.

The shame came as a surprise. Redundancies aren't uncommon – she knew that. Friends, ex-colleagues, strangers on social media – she'd seen it happen frequently. Often people used the opportunity to try something new, or even took it voluntarily to make the most of a fresh start.

But nobody had ever mentioned the gut punch you felt when it actually happened. No one had ever said how it felt humiliating and infuriating and so many other 'atings' she couldn't properly find words for.

Eventually, she wiped her eyes on her sleeve – something she'd spent the last eighteen years training Tyler not to do – and started the car. Switching on the radio, she tried to engage herself with the hot topic of the day on LBC – whether raising a dog was easier or harder than raising a child. 'At least babies wear nappies!' a woman was saying. 'You don't see mums in the park picking up their kids' poop.' But she couldn't focus. Instead, she kept thinking of the meeting, imagining how she could have reacted differently. Turning over chairs, or doing a Jerry Maguire: loudly vowing to start a new firm, and taking one of the better interns with her for the ride.

Maybe she should have yanked Grahame out of that toilet and forced him to actually explain his reasoning to her. Made him look her in the eye and... well, if nothing else, *apologise*. Because not only had he used to be her boss until about half an hour ago, she'd also thought of him as a friend. He'd looked at pictures of Ty growing up; he'd spoken to her about his family. Come to think of it, she'd even helped him pick out an anniversary present for his wife, Brenda, last month – her choice of necklace had got him out of the doghouse for last year's gift disaster: a voucher for a 'nooks and crannies luxury wax' at the local beauty salon.

She felt the tears well again and shook her head. No. She wasn't going to fall apart. She'd been through worse. And it wasn't as if they were going to be in financial difficulty. Ben's job was going well; they had some savings. Ty was off to university soon and even had a part-time job lined up for when he arrived. They would be OK.

She would be OK.

She began to drive the familiar route home. Cars hummed rhythmically as they passed in the opposite direction and the larger shops began to morph into smaller stores, newsagents and corner shops as she reached the outskirts of town. Everything was the same; but everything seemed somehow different – she was detaching from her ordinary life, like a greying plaster dropping wetly from a graze.

At the traffic lights she caught the eye of the man in front in his rear-view mirror, his eyebrows knitted into a scowl. People passed on the streets as she waited for the green light, their faces intent on smartphones, their expressions distant. A woman with a buggy laden with so many shopping bags it almost tipped every time she rested, fought her way past. The scenery, while familiar, was grey and man-made and set against a backdrop of miserable sky.

Nothing much had changed in the town over the past twenty years. Sure, she had happy memories of living here, working here. She remembered delicious meals in jam-packed restaurants, drinks in bars after work. Good times.

Yet stepping back, she saw her working life for what it had been: endless pounding on a corporate treadmill: reaching for more, working harder, trying all the time to keep up with others in a race that meant nothing.

It was definitely time for a change.

By the time she pulled into her driveway, she was feeling more determined. She'd sit down with Ben and make a plan.

'Let's do it!' she'd say, dramatically. 'It's only a year early – let's just take the plunge! *Vive la France!*'

She'd been dreaming about cross channel living for at least a decade before they'd even met. She'd spent summers in *Limousin* and *Dordogne* as a child, bumping along in Dad's VW campervan, trundling from campsite to campsite, and had fallen in love with the leisurely pace of life, the fresh air, the views, the culture. 'One day,' she'd said to Ben, shortly after they'd got together, 'let's move to France and have an adventure.'

If she was honest, she was a little tired of waiting for the move anyway. Every time she'd sat with Ben and discussed it, the goalposts had seemed to move. They'd originally said they'd see Ty through his GCSEs, then his sixth form exams; now they were waiting to see Ty settled at uni. She'd been on board – for the most part – with Ben's suggestions but it had still hurt to continually put her dream on the backburner.

Last time, to make up for the delay Ben had bought her a French silk scarf for her birthday, together with a book entitled *France: Your Guide to Moving*, and a hamper containing Brie, Camembert, *escargots* and wine. 'If Lily can't make it to France just yet, then I'll bring France to her,' he'd said, giving her a kiss.

It wasn't exactly living the dream, she'd thought: munching snails at the kitchen table in Basildon. But she'd smiled and kissed him, because he'd made the effort, been thoughtful. Plus, the year before he'd bought her a saucepan set (and she'd never forget the miracle juicer he'd produced for her fortieth that came with a free 'slimmer thighs' recipe book). This, at least, had been growth.

Now, pulling into the driveway, she sat for a moment and looked at the house that had been theirs for the past fifteen years.

It had served them well; had been a great family home. Newly built when they'd moved in, small but perfectly formed, their semi was part of a row of identikit houses on an estate that was neatly built and well maintained. The red bricks had faded slightly, but it still had the appearance of something shiny and modern. The double glazing had kept them warm, the garage – too small for anything but the tiniest of cars – had provided the ideal space for Ty's drum kit during his rock star wannabe phase.

It was practical. It had been a safe choice. But wasn't a patch on the French farmhouse she'd dreamed of living in for so long.

Over the years, she'd spent hours scrolling through French property listings on the internet, flicking through *French Property News;* lusting after stone cottages in the corners of tiny hamlets;

renovation projects with potential to make your own mark. She'd drooled over stories of people moving over and living the dream: snapping up properties – mortgage free – for a song and making a forever home to be proud of.

Don't think of it as a dead end. Try to think of it as an opportunity. The last thing she wanted to do was agree with Mark, whose whole reason for existence was going from firm to firm and 'trimming the fat'. But perhaps, just on this, he'd been right.

Feeling her heart-rate increase, she stepped out of the car into the spring air. It was only five o'clock, but already there was a touch of early evening chill. The sky was a bland wash of grey and white, the sun hidden and glowing weakly beneath layers of cloud. She breathed deeply, trying to steady herself. But she could feel something beginning to take hold – excitement, a feeling that actually, just possibly, her life was about to change.

Ben worked from home on a Friday. He'd be busy at his desk, not expecting her back for an hour or so. She'd wrap her arms around him, tell him the news, then open his eyes to the possibilities that lay before them. 'Ty will be fine; we can fly back and forth. And even keep the house in England for now,' she'd say. Surely he couldn't say no to that? Perhaps, at last, this was going to be 'their' time.

The house was quiet as she let herself in. Ty's coat was missing – he'd be out playing Fortnite with friends or at the gym. She crept upstairs to Ben's office – letting out a small cough before disturbing him; the last thing she wanted to do was shock him into a heart attack just when their lives were opening up.

But as she pushed his office door open, with a lively, preparatory *'Bonjour!'* she saw that the room was empty. A jumper hung on the back of his swivel chair; his computer screensaver bounced across a black screen. Piles of paperwork were neatly stacked. He'd finished balancing other people's books for the week.

'Ben?' she called, walking down to the kitchen, almost tripping over a trail of laundry that Ty had helpfully flung in approximately the direction of the dirty washing basket. She bent and picked up the errant clothes on autopilot, grimacing as she felt something sticky on her hand. Moments later, she almost tripped over her son's discarded backpack at the top of the stairs and tumbled to an untimely death.

By the time she got to the kitchen, she felt less as if she needed an adventure and more as if she needed a full hose down and a Valium. 'Ben?' she called again, with slightly more edge to her voice.

But a coffee cup next to the kettle was the only sign of life.

She pulled her phone out of her pocket and quickly scrolled to his number in her contacts. It rang several times before he picked up. 'Hello, love!' Ben said, cheerfully. 'You on your way home?'

'I'm already here, where are you?'

'Oh. Well, I got most of my stuff done then Baz asked me for a pub lunch.'

'It's five o'clock.'

'Bloody hell, is it?' He was slurring his words slightly. 'Well, we're in the middle of some pool. You can pop down and join us if you want?'

It wasn't a real offer.

'No, it's OK. I just hoped... I suppose I hoped you'd be here so... well, I've got something to tell you.'

'I can come home... if you want?' he said, then, *Just a minute! Sorry, that was Baz. It's my turn. Do you want me to...?'

'Yes!' she wanted to say. 'Come home immediately!' But instead: 'No, I'll see you later,' she replied.

She tried to settle down with a coffee, but found it hard to concentrate. She could hardly wait for the moment when Ben would step through the door and she could surprise him with her news. That they no longer had to live out their days as a middle-aged cliché. Her redundancy money would replace any savings they'd hoped to accrue. Ty was a confident boy; plus he'd seemed so much more grown-up recently that she doubted he'd need them at all once he moved into halls. The stars had finally aligned.

She closed her eyes. In her mind, Ben would be overjoyed – released from his own stressful work and able to embrace something brand new. He'd pick her up in his arms and swing her around as he had before and they'd get the house on the market as soon as possible.

'Everything is about to change,' she said to herself.

Later, she'd look back on those words and wonder: If she'd been able to see the future in all its brilliant, frightening, chaotic and unexpected glory, would she have been excited? Or completely and utterly terrified?

It was hard to know what to do with herself while waiting, so in the end she did what she always did in a crisis – picked up the phone and dialled Emily.

2

Lily lay back on the bed, staring at the ceiling, phone clamped to her ear. She noticed a hairline crack in the plaster, dust on the lampshade. 'So, what do you think?' she asked.

'I think,' said Emily, 'it sounds amazing... And you reckon Ben will be up for it?'

'You think he might not be, because of Ty?'

'Well, yeah. I mean, that was his reason for the delay before, wasn't it?'

'Yes,' Lily said, rolling onto her front. 'But you know what? I think Ty's grown up so much in the last six months. He seems so different – I'm sure Ben's noticed it too. I really don't think he's going to need his parents hanging about.'

'Good point.' Emily was silent for a moment. Then: 'Wow, so you're actually going to be doing it,' she said, her voice quieter than usual.

'Well, yes...' said Lily, 'it looks like I am.'

'I'm going to miss you, you know,' Emily said, wistfully. 'Miss spending so much time with you.'

'Even the times when I make you pluck that wayward grey hair from the back of my head?'

'Even those.'

'Even the times I drag you to aerobics on Thursdays, despite your protestations?' Lily joked.

'Well, I won't miss the aerobics, I'll admit,' said Emily. 'Although if I end up eating myself into a state and having to be winched out of my house by a crane, it'll be one hundred per cent your fault for leaving and taking my motivation with you.'

"Ha! As if that would ever happen. You've got the dogs to drag you around, remember.'

'Ah yes. Thank god for the dogs. They have absolutely no desire to live in France, as far as I can tell.'

'Ah, but you never know. I reckon Buster would look fabulous in a beret!'

'You know what? You could be right!' Emily laughed. 'Seriously though... Now it's actually happening. Wow. I'm happy for you, obviously. But... you know – I actually hate the thought of you not being around.'

'I know,' Lily said. 'But I mean, it's been a long time coming. When did I first talk about moving to France? I was – what – about fourteen?'

'Younger than that. I remember in Year Eight, all you wanted to do was help Mademoiselle François create a French café for parents' evening.'

'But that was just... I...'

'*Ooh, Mademoiselle, laissez-moi vous aider!*' Emily mimicked. *Let me help you.*

'That does *not* sound like me,' Lily laughed.

'Admit it, you're France obsessed.'

'I wouldn't say *obsessed*, exactly...'

'Really, so, tell me. How many times have you watched *A Year in Provence?'* Emily asked, knowing already that it was Lily's all-time favourite movie.

'It's called *A Good Year* actually. *A Year in Provence* is the book it's based on. *Anyway,* you know how I feel about Russell Crowe.' Lily was a sucker for the now-vintage film; the way living in Provence changes the lead character, Max Skinner, from corporate go-getter to someone more wholly real and attractive. The fact Max Skinner was played by Russell Crowe was just a bonus. But she wasn't going to admit how many times she'd watched it – even to herself.

'Still, don't catch you watching *Gladiator* on repeat. Or *A Beautiful Mind*, do we?' Emily pressed.

'OK, you got me. I'm France obsessed,' Lily said, feeling herself smile. There was no hiding her truth from Emily. 'But you know, this isn't just me. Ben's really keen to do it too. Next year at least. It shouldn't be too hard to get him to bring our plans forward a bit.'

'It's amazing what twenty years of wearing someone down will do.'

'Two decades of nagging – and finally a result!' Lily quipped back. 'Although, he honestly does love the idea. I mean, that hamper for my birthday was really...'

Emily snorted. 'If someone bought me a packet of bloody snails for my birthday, I'd turn around and shove them up...'

'It was romantic.'

'Romantic my arse.'

They laughed.

'Seriously though, good for you, Lil. I mean, just going for it. It sounds like an amazing idea. And I know you've been a bit worried about Ty, but there does have to be a time, doesn't there, when you say, it's my turn now. Before it's too late.'

'Too late?'

'Well, what are we now, forty-two?'

Lily laughed: 'Forty-four, I'm afraid.'

'Oh, fuck off, we're not. Forty-two'll do. Anyway, we're forty-two – you want to go to another country, start a business and recline on a sun-lounger or whatever...'

'Swim in the lakes, go to beautiful cafés, learn to speak French like a native...'

'Yes, yes, all of that,' Emily continued, dismissively. 'But you know, if you'd left it much longer, it might not have been possible!'

'Hey, I'm not planning on shrivelling up any time in the near future.'

'Nobody ever is,' replied Emily darkly. 'But soon you'll be fifty, then sixty...'

'Steady on!'

'I'm not saying you're old. We're the same age, for Pete's sake. And I'm practically a foetus. But there is going to be a time when it's too bloody late to do all that. When you won't have the energy to set it all up – to do the difficult bit. I reckon you're doing the right thing.'

'Thank you.'

There was a moment's silence.

'So, what's the plan? Going over and seeing where the wind blows? Arranging some viewings? Renting for a bit?' Emily asked.

'I haven't fully thought it out.' Lily opened her laptop, which lay next to her on the duvet and, putting Emily on speakerphone, brought up a list of French country houses on Google. 'I mean France is... enormous. And I haven't been that often, when it comes down to it. Except all those holidays when I was a kid. Ben... well, we've done Nice and Paris a few times, but it's not as if we'll ever afford a house in either of those places.'

'Not unless there's a EuroMillions win you haven't yet told me about.'

'Afraid not. Anyway, city breaks are great for holidays, but living... I want somewhere...'

'Cheaper?'

'Yes. Definitely cheaper.' She laughed. 'But also quieter. Somewhere, you know, tranquil.'

'Like *Limousin*,' said Emily, in an exaggerated French accent.

'*Oui*, like *Limousin*.'

'Where even is that by the way?'

'It's kind of two-thirds of the way down France, if you look at a map. You know. I went there every year from the age of about twelve to sixteen.'

'Ah, yes. All those postcards with cows on the front?'

'That's the one.'

'Wow, so really rural, then.'

'Yes. But it's beautiful. And the houses are... well,' Lily gasped as a page she clicked on loaded. 'Wow, ridiculously cheap. There's an old farmhouse here for fifty thousand euros!'

'What's that in real money?'

'Maybe forty grand. It's within the realms of possibility: I've still got most of my inheritance from Mum. And now the redundancy money... Plus, when we sell this place, we'll have money in the bank, to live off for a bit, do the renovations. That kind of thing. We'd have no obligations, time to set up a business...' She trailed off, lost in her imagination.

'Sounds blissful.'

'And it isn't as if I have anything much to stay here for, since – well – since Mum died. And with David in Australia now.'

'Excuse me? Nothing to keep you here? Your big brother may not be on the same continent any more, but you still have an errant bestie!' Emily said, with mock offence.

'The errant bestie has a passport.'

'Good point. I forgot about the free holiday for best friends aspect. Forget I said anything.'

'I mean, Ben will see how much it makes sense to get on with it, don't you think?' Lily said, trying to still a sudden doubt. 'Strolling in vineyards, exploring the countryside, collecting fresh bread from the boulangerie each morning... What's the alternative? Sitting in Basildon, watching reruns of *Bargain Hunt* or *Real Deal*?'

'Don't knock it 'til you've tried it. I think Dickinson's growing on me.'

'Are you sure? It's probably just a rogue mole.'

'Ha. Well, look. You have my one hundred per cent support, however you decide to do it.'

'Thank you,' Lily said, pulling up a page of short-term rentals. 'There's loads of places to rent too, while we house-hunt. It'll give Ben a chance to get used to rural living – you know; so it grows on him.'

'Grows on him? You make it sound like a fungal infection.'

'Emily! I'm serious.'

'Well, I'm all for you finally embracing *your* dreams. You know that. It's about time you stood up for yourself, Lily Butterworth. You are entitled to ask for what you want – put yourself first.'

'Yes,' Lily said. 'You know what. I think you're right.'

* * *

By the time Ben arrived home several hours later, Lily was sitting on the sofa, flicking through the channels in a vain attempt to find something to watch on TV. Ty had appeared briefly in the doorway at 10.30 p.m., then disappeared upstairs with a box of Frosties.

'All right, love?' Ben said, walking up and planting a kiss on the top of her head.

'Yeah, not too bad,' she said, head full of France and countryside and endless summers.

'So, work gave you the afternoon off or something?'

'What?'

'You were home early, so I thought...'

Shit. In all her chatting with Emily, paired with three-quarters of a bottle of wine, she'd actually forgotten she'd been made redundant earlier that day.

'Oh. Yes. Shit. Well, yeah. I suppose it wasn't such a great day. I mean, not initially. I was made redundant.'

'You're not serious?' She'd seen Ben grow pale before. Once, when he was at the business end of things when Ty was born, another time when he'd come down with a bad dose of flu. But she'd never seen the colour drain so fast from his skin after such a mild stimulus. He sank onto the sofa next to her, his light brown hair – which was, she noticed, desperately in need of a cut – flopping against his forehead as if it, too, was disappointed.

'Yep. Apparently I'm surplus to requirements,' she said, shrugging.

'Oh my god.'

'Yep. My thoughts exactly.'

'Well, don't panic,' he said, gripping her hand more tightly than was comfortable.

'Actually, I'm not panicking... I wanted to...'

'We'll be OK,' he continued, not making eye contact. 'My salary will cover the mortgage and most of the bills, and we've got a bit saved, and there's your inheritance – only in an absolute emergency, obviously.'

'Yes, but, Ben, don't you see, this could be our chance!' she said, turning to him, fizzing with excitement. 'We could use the money to *do* something. I thought, you know, we're moving to France next year anyway, why not just do it now! There's nothing stopping us.'

He looked at her and she saw his eyes widen – not with excitement but something else, something unreadable. He reached up and pushed the wayward strand of fringe away from his forehead. 'Oh, I don't know,' he said. 'I mean, we were going to get the place spruced up weren't we, before we sold? The bathroom needs doing and...'

'I don't care about changing the bloody cistern... This would be changing our lives, Ben!'

He took her hand. 'I just want to wait till the time is right.'

'But can't you see? The time *is* right.'

'What about Ty?'

She nodded, feeling a familiar flash of guilt. 'I've thought about him a lot, of course I have,' she said. 'But honestly, it's not like we'll be that far away. We can even keep the house here for a bit – I'll have the redundancy money; a bit of Mum's... the inheritance. We could...'

Something in his expression made her stop.

'It's just...' he said.

She looked at him, sitting in his crumpled T-shirt, hair in disarray. Worn out from a week of work and too many pints at the pub. Imagined him instead in France, sipping coffee on a terrace – no real 'boss' to answer to. Imagined the kind of life they could have together, rather than the existence they had now.

But his face was sombre and thoughtful rather than excited.

'I'm not saying no,' he said, carefully. 'It just feels... well, too soon.'

'Too soon?' She felt her eyes fill with tears. 'But we agreed... we waited for Ty's GCSEs, then A levels... For your work to pick up. All those things. Now we're meant to be waiting for Ty to get through his first year at uni. But I've realised, there's always going to be *something*, isn't there? Even next year there'll probably be *something*.'

'Well, if there is... we'll wait. There's no point rushing...'

'Are you serious?' she asked, her stomach flipping over as if she'd just eaten another bowl of snails.

'What?'

'Well...' she said, carefully, 'you promised. We decided, didn't we, that we'd definitely do it next year.'

'I wouldn't say promised... I suppose I promised to *think* about it... But if things aren't right...'

'Oh my god.'

But his expression was firm.

'Probably better to talk about it in the morning when you're not... so emotional,' he said, standing up and reaching for her hand.

'Emotional?'

'Yes, I mean it's very... I can understand it. But you're thinking with your heart, Lily. Not your head. It's just too soon.'

Say it! her mind urged. *Either come with me, or I'm going on my own!* Or, *if you loved me, you'd come. Something!* 'Oh,' she said instead, looking at her hands and feeling a tear touch her cheek.

'Well, look. How about this,' she added, almost desperately. 'Take a month off work...'

'A month?'

'Yes, just listen,' she said, putting a hand on his leg. 'Come to France with me. We'll rent a house in a great location and try it out. It'll be a holiday at worst; at best maybe the start of something really exciting!'

He was silent.

'Can I think about it? A month is a long time... maybe... we could do something, shorter? Maybe a hotel? Or...'

She felt something inside her sink.

'OK,' she said. It was clearly pointless arguing with him. She felt some of the tears she'd held back start to sting her eyes, but blinked them away.

'Are you mad with me?' he asked in the silence that followed.

The man knew her too well. 'I'm not mad,' she said, carefully. 'I'm just...' She paused. 'Ben, tell me honestly, all those plans we made. All those conversations about next year. Is it really a case of "right timing", or is it that...' She paused again. 'Ben, are you ever going to want to come to France with me?'

He was silent for a minute. 'Yes,' he said. 'No. I mean, well, probably. Almost definitely.'

'That sounds horribly like a "no".'

'It's... Well, I suppose, if I'm honest, sometimes I wonder whether it isn't better to let a dream stay a dream? Careful what you wish for, and all that. We have our whole lives here...' he said, shrugging, his palms upturned in a gesture of surrender.

'But...'

'Look, let's go to bed,' he said, putting out his hand for hers again. 'I'm knackered, I've had too many Guinnesses. I'm pretty sure you've had a few more wines than you usually would. It's hard to think straight.'

'I *am* thinking straight.'

'Well, maybe I need to... uh, sleep on it. You know?'

'OK,' she said, not meeting his eye.

'OK?'

'Yes. We'll talk tomorrow. You go on. I'll be up in just a minute.'

The minute Ben was out of sight, she opened up her laptop and touched the mouse pad. The screen lit up and she was relieved to find that she hadn't closed down her earlier searches. Because it ended here. She wasn't going to be someone whom things happened to. She was going to be someone who made things happen.

Before she could change her mind, she clicked 'select' on one of the luxury gîte rentals she'd been looking at, and committed to, if not to a lifetime of indulging her Francophilia, then at least a month trying it on for size. Ben would probably come. And if he didn't, it wasn't the end of the world. After all, it would only be a month apart. And a step towards the life she'd always dreamed of.

Hopefully, if nothing else, it would show Ben just how serious she was.

Anyway, what's the worst that could happen? she thought, as she closed the laptop and went upstairs to bed.

3

She gradually became conscious, her head heavy on the pillow, her eyes still firmly closed, feeling a pounding in her temples. It had been a while since she'd gone past her self-imposed two glass limit, and she'd started to forget why she'd set the limit in the first place. Yesterday, when she'd been knocking back the red and waiting for Ben to come home she'd imagined they'd be leaping out of bed to make new plans this morning; now she'd be lucky if she could stagger to the kitchen for a coffee without incident.

As the daylight poked its way through the gap in the curtains and flooded her skin with unwelcome light, she felt an additional throb. 'Oh god,' she moaned, turning over and covering her face with her hands.

There was a reciprocal groan by her side. 'Oh Christ,' she heard Ben say.

'Hangover?'

'Hangover.' He half sat up, propped on his elbows, eyes screwed up against the light. 'Bloody Baz. Always tempting me with one last pint.'

'You could say no, you know.'

'That is a very good point.'

'How many did you have?'

'I sort of lost count, I think. Anyway, you're a fine one to talk, Miss *Polished-off-a-whole-bottle-by-herself.*'

'Was it a whole bottle?' she asked horrified. 'All on my own?'

'Well, almost.'

'Bloody hell. No wonder I feel like shit.' She tried opening one of her eyes, glimpsed the soft flesh of Ben's belly next to her, then closed it again.

He laughed and shuffled up the bed. 'Come on, we'll get through it. Together. You're only young once. *Carpe diem* – seize the day and all that!' She heard him breathe heavily on his palm. 'Christ, sorry about my breath. I smell like I've licked the inside of a bin or something.'

She smiled in spite of the pain. They'd been together over twenty years and still managed to make each other laugh. That had to be worth something. Then a snippet of memory returned and she was retrospectively flooded with annoyance. 'Young though? Ben, we haven't been young since 2011. We're running out of days to seize.'

He laughed briefly, then realised she was serious. 'Oh, Lily. I know. I can understand why you feel this way. But you know, we'll find a way through all this.'

'All this?'

'Well, redundancy. And... and deciding what to do next.'

She sighed. 'But we *have* decided what to do next. We've talked and talked about it. All I want is to bring it forward by a year. I mean, why wait? And now it seems like, well, it's never going to happen.'

He was silent.

'Ben?'

'Look,' he said. 'Maybe we should... well, just put the conversation, the decision on ice for a bit. I just... I shouldn't have been so quick to promise....'

'But, Ben—'

Before she could finish, a memory flashed into her mind, the way they do sometimes the morning after a big night. But this wasn't a memory of dancing on tables or kissing a stranger or doing any of the things often associated with regretful post-binge flashbacks. This was a memory of pressing 'buy now' on a property site. Had she really booked a break in France for herself? The memory was vague, hard to pin down. She couldn't remember any details – location, price. Perhaps she'd meant to but hadn't seen it through.

Either way, she had to check.

'What?' he said.

'Look, we need to talk about this,' she said, sitting up, swinging her legs over the side of the bed and trying to sound more upbeat. 'But let's get some tea first, yes?' She looked at her husband, crumpled in the bed, clearly feeling sick and felt a surge of guilt. Sure, he'd pooh-poohed the idea of a month away, but she'd sprung the idea on him last thing at night. He'd have probably at least agreed to the holiday plan if she'd waited until this morning. They could have worked out convenient dates. Then once he was there... something inside told her that he'd fall for France as much as she had. But going behind his back wasn't the right way to do it.

She imagined how she'd feel if he'd done the same. It had all seemed so simple last night. So bloody obvious. But that was what the lethal cocktail of best friend and red wine did. Gave the illusion of ease when actually even going on holiday could be complicated.

But perhaps she was worrying about nothing. Best to see what she'd actually done before panicking about it.

'Are you sure you don't want me to get it?' he said, once she reached the door, in a voice that was suddenly croaky and weak.

Ordinarily, she might have called his bluff and taken his non-offer at face value. But today her laptop was calling.

'What would you do if I took you up on that reluctant offer?' she said instead.

'I'd probably cry. But I'd do it. I just hoped you'd take pity on me,' he said, his eyes playfully puppy-like.

She shook her head. 'Idiot,' she said, with a small smile, then turned and walked her reluctant legs towards the stairs, and towards the laptop that held the answers she was looking for.

She reached the downstairs hallway and headed for the kitchen to get the kettle on. Ty had obviously been up for a midnight snack – the cereal cupboard was open and another newly opened box of Frosties had been knocked on its side. By the sink, there was a bowl with traces of cereal and a small pool of milk. Lily picked up the errant box, put it back in the cupboard, then walked to her laptop, left casually on the kitchen table, and opened it up.

She had a sudden flash of self-awareness, seeing herself in the kitchen as if from outside. There she was, tidying up after someone who didn't give her a moment's thought.

How many times had she had the 'close the cereal cupboard and wash your bowl' conversation with her son? At least once a week for the past eight years. Probably twice. So about eight hundred times. Eight hundred times she'd explained to her boy that now he was old enough to clear up his own mess, the buck stopped with him. And to have a little respect. And that cereal cupboards were a magnet for ants and flies if left open.

It wasn't such a terrible thing, having to wash someone else's cereal bowl. Some of her friends had three children, even four, and came down to sinks heaving with discarded crockery. It was just the thought of all those minutes of her life – probably at least four thousand she thought, doing the maths – completely wasted. She might as well have kept schtum and let him scatter Frosties in his wake wherever he went.

Outside, the early morning brightness had given way to a shower of rain. Water began to hit the window and, as she looked out at the view over the back terrace, with its plastic chairs and the pile of single-use barbecues left over from last summer, she was struck by the contrast between the view she'd absorbed every day for twenty years while doing the washing up, and the view she could have, displayed on her now open laptop. She tried to click on the picture to see further details, but realised the screen had frozen.

She shut the laptop down and rebooted it, hoping she'd be able to retrace her steps and find out what she'd booked, and where, and for when. As her system came back to life an email pinged.

Of course! She'd have a confirmation email of some kind. 'OK, Lily,' she said to herself, 'let's see what we've got ourselves into.'

Her inbox contained the usual offers of 10 per cent discount, strangely worded spam and confirmation that a pair of tights she'd ordered two weeks ago had left the warehouse. (Constant updates meant she knew more about the whereabouts of her hosiery than her son most days). And then another email. From eBay.

She'd known she'd looked at holiday properties on the auction site, but had no idea that she'd booked a place through there. It had just been one of a number of pages she'd had open at the time.

The title of the email was half obscured 'Congratulations!' it enthused. 'You placed the winning bid for...'

She clicked on the email, eager to find what she'd let herself in for, and crucially, for how much.

As she read the text, she let out a little involuntary yelp.

'Everything all right, love?' Ben called from upstairs.

'Yes,' she lied. 'Fine. Just... burned my finger. I'm fine.' She closed her eyes for a minute, just trying to breathe. And work out what on earth she should do.

She had no idea.

She walked to the counter and poured hot water into their two mugs, feeling herself break out in a sweat. Was this even binding? Could doing something like this really be as simple as a click? She desperately tried to calculate how much money they had in their savings, on their credit card, with her redundancy money factored in. Would that even cover it?

She shut the laptop as if shutting it away might actually delete the terrible mess she'd managed to get herself into, picked up the finished teas and made her way upstairs.

There was no way she could let on to Ben. Not until she knew what she was going to do.

When she reached the bedroom, Ben was sitting, half propped against the headboard. He'd thoughtfully arranged her pillows in an upright position so she could comfortably sip her tea in bed, proving that although he wasn't the most adventurous husband, he did actually care. As she approached, she saw his face furrow with concern. 'Are you sure you're OK?' he said. 'You look really pale.'

'Pale?' she said, trying to sound normal. 'I'm fine!' She grinned widely to prove it.

'Are you sure?' he said. 'Your smile looks... weird. You don't think you're going to be sick or anything?'

'No, it's nothing,' she lied, passing him his mug and sitting back on the bed. 'No need to call the cavalry. I'm sure I'll survive.'

He looked at her doubtfully. 'OK, as long as you're sure.'

She sipped her tea. 'Yeah. It's just this hangover. Can't remember the last time I had one.'

'Think yourself lucky!'

'Ah, yes,' she said. 'That's what gives you a hangover. *Bad luck.*'

'Ha. OK, well, I like to think so,' he said. 'Bad luck and Baz.'

'Never your own fault?'

'Never my own fault.' He grinned and reached for her spare hand. 'Look, I was thinking,' he said. 'About, you know, what you said about France.'

She felt something inside her lift. 'You were?'

She looked at his face, and instead of the reluctance and fear she'd seen last night, she saw an openness. As if he, too, was beginning to feel excited about her suggestion. Despite the dark circles under his eyes, his tousled hair and the faint smell of alcohol on his breath, he looked better than he had for a while – alive with an idea.

'Yes, and look. I'm sorry. Perhaps I should have taken things a bit more seriously. I know how much you love France, and I suppose I do owe you, after sort of... I don't know, promising things...' He smiled and reached forward for her hand.

Her headache subsided as excitement began to build in her chest. Could it be that she and Ben were on the same wavelength after all? Maybe, despite what she'd done, it could all work out!

'Oh,' she said.

'Yes, and look,' he said, placing his tea on the bedside table and taking her hand in both of his. His eyes were excited in a way she hadn't seen for years. 'I have a suggestion.'

'Yes?' she asked, her voice barely more than a whisper.

'It's about France,' he said.

'Oh, Ben!'

'Because look, I know how much you want to go.'

'I do, I really do.'

'So, let's do it!'

'What? Are you serious?' She flung her arms around him – only just keeping her tea balanced in its mug - and nestled her head onto his shoulder, her heart hammering with a kind of surreal excitement. This wasn't really happening, was it?

'Wait, you haven't heard the best bit!' he said, drawing back and smiling confidently. 'I saw an offer in the *Express* last week. A weekend in Paris, first class Eurostar, three-star hotel, just £199 per person if you collect all the tokens. It's our anniversary coming up isn't it. And what a bargain!'

'Oh.'

'France, here we come!' he said, his eyes searching her face for the reciprocal excitement he seemed sure he was going to find.

'Um. Yes.'

It was as if he'd taken the helium out of her balloon of happiness and filled it instead with shit. It plummeted messily to the ground.

But, right now – she reminded herself – the disappointment was the least of her concerns. 'OK,' she said, trying to smile as her brain raced at 100 miles an hour. She'd email eBay and say she'd made a mistake. Maybe say she had a toddler who'd clicked the button by accident. See if there was any legal wriggle room. See how committed she actually was.

She wasn't giving up on France. But this was definitely not the way she'd wanted to do it.

Because the email she'd opened just now hadn't been confirmation of a break, a receipt for money paid or information from a letting agent. Instead it had read:

Congratulations! You placed the winning bid for Stone Cottage with 3000 m^2 garden and outbuilding for renovation.

She'd scrolled down, only half understanding, then stopped when she'd seen the text at the bottom.

You have committed to buying this property for the sum of €48,601. Please contact the seller to complete the transaction.

She'd only gone and bought a bloody house.

4

'So, what's the emergency?' Emily said as Lily opened the door. She was dressed in what looked like pyjama bottoms, which protruded from underneath a long coat. Her wavy brown hair was piled on top of her head in a messy bun. 'I came as soon as I got your message.'

'I can see that,' Lily said, tucking her own sandy-blonde hair behind her ear and feeling rather guilty that she was showered and freshly washed. 'I'm sorry if I made it seem... well, *that* urgent.'

'Chrissakes, Lily! I thought I was going to have to rescue you from burglars, or, I don't know, put out a house fire. You said, your message – I thought you were crying. But you seem fine!' Emily said, stepping into the hall with an eye-roll.

'I've calmed down.'

'So nothing's on fire?'

'Nothing's on fire.'

'And I could have taken ten minutes to get dressed?'

'You could have taken an hour. Sorry. I should have been a bit clearer on the phone.' Lily grimaced apologetically.

'So what on earth is this emergency? And what exactly do you need rescuing from?' Emily said, giving her a quick peck on the cheek. 'I thought *I* was meant to be the dramatic one!'

'Shh, keep your voice down!' Lily said, glancing furtively over her shoulder.

'Why the shushing? I thought you said Ben was out?'

'Yes, he's out. It's just, Ty's still here. Asleep, I think, but you never know. And I'm just not... I don't want anyone to know about this yet.'

'Now I *am* intrigued. What on earth have you done, Lily Butterworth? Surely it can't be that bad?' Emily said, slipping off her coat, throwing it over the banister and revealing that she had indeed come out in chequered pyjama bottoms and a creased T-shirt that read 'sweet dreams, sweetie pie'.

Lily grinned. 'Nice outfit,' she said. She placed a quick hand on her friend's shoulder. 'But thank you,' she added. 'I mean, you seriously came through for me.'

'You mean I overdid it, as usual.'

'Well, maybe. But it was my fault.'

They smiled at each other for a moment, then Emily shook her head. 'You only get to cry wolf a couple of times, you know, before people don't bother to turn up any more,' she said.

'I know.'

'One more fake emergency, and that'll be it. Wolves every-where. No sheep left to be found.'

'Oh, there's still an emergency,' Lily said, making a face. 'Just not a "the call is coming from inside the house" type of emer-gency. More of... a well, I suppose you could call it a *situation*.'

'A situation?' Emily said, ears suddenly pricked. 'Tell me more!'

'Try not to sound too enthusiastic about it.'

'Ooh, have you done something bad, Lily?'

'It depends how you define bad, I suppose,' she said, walking through into the living room where her laptop flickered on the sofa. She passed it to Emily silently and watched as her friend's eyes quickly scanned the text of the email.

'Bloody hell, Lily. Is this for real?' Emily sank onto the sofa, her humour draining from her briefly.

'Yep,' Lily replied, sitting next to her. 'Told you it was a situation.'

'This is almost dashing-over-in-pyjamas worthy.'

'I know.'

'*How* much wine did you actually have?'

'Well, almost a bottle, but that's not the *point*.'

'You know, most people get involved in a bit of harmless anti-social behaviour when they're on the lash. Maybe get arrested or something. Or sleep with a stranger. Or, I don't know, have a screaming row and throw their partner's stuff out on the lawn,' her friend told her, amusement turning up the corners of her mouth despite her serious expression.

'Yep. All preferable to this, I'd say.'

'Certainly cheaper.'

'Yup.'

'And who looks at properties on eBay anyway? Whenever I buy something on there, I forget to check the measurements and it ends up a complete disaster. But a *house*!'

'I know.'

'One you haven't even *seen*?'

'I know.'

'In *France*?'

'Shh! I know!' Lily said. 'What I *don't* know is what on earth I'm going to do about it.' Seeing Emily had cheered her up, as it usually did. But the anxiety she'd been flooded with this morning raced through her again as she looked at the text on the screen.

For once it had been a relief that Ben had booked up a game of tennis for Saturday morning. Usually she'd be disappointed they couldn't spend a lazy morning together. But today she'd practically packed his sports bag for him.

'Are you sure it's OK?' he'd said. 'Sorry, I forgot to put it on the calendar. I mean, I don't feel that great, so if you want me to change it...'

'No, don't be silly, it'll do you good!' she'd said, patting his back and ushering him to the front door. 'Oh look, here are your keys!'

'I'll be half an hour early at this poin—'

'Bye then!' she'd trilled, shutting the front door before rushing to the phone to ring Emily.

'Surely it's not binding? I mean, clicking a button on eBay?' Emily said now. 'You could say your kid did it, or your dog or something. It must happen all the time.'

'That's what I hoped. I was going to get on to eBay and find out this morning. But then I got a message from the seller. An email.'

'And?'

'Well, it was all in French, so I had to run it through Google translate, but...' she reached over and flicked up another web page.

TRANSLATION

Dear Mrs,

I am delighted very that you have purchased the good-looking house of stone near to a large body of water. I will speak to the lawyer and the paperwork he will become drawn up in very shortly time I truly believe very not slowly. And it is good news for you too! I am the mayor of the local town of Eymoutiers that which means I can make quicker the time for signing. There is still of course a legal process, but one that I can influence with my powers and help to make a more quickly speed. I wish to hear from you most quickly.

Many wonderful days, *Frédérique de Breton.*

It wasn't the most accurate of translations, but it was pretty easy to get the gist.

'Oh.'

'Yes.'

'He's the mayor?'

'Yep. And I looked him up. Did you know that in France the mayor is also the chief *gendarme*?'

'The, what?'

'Head of the local police.'

'Whoops. Uh-oh, you're in trouble, Lily Butterworth!' Emily said, with a laugh.

'I know! I mean, I'm not sure how I stand legally as far as eBay is concerned, but there's all this momentum from this *Frédérique* guy now, too. And it feels so official and I'm just worried that if I... back out, I might be in trouble?'

Emily slung an arm around her friend's shoulder and shook her head. 'Darling, I was joking. I don't think he's going to extradite you to France and haul you before the courts, or throw you in the dungeon of his *château*.'

'I know that. But I want to move to France one day.'

'You may have mentioned this previously.'

'Em, it's not funny. What if I muck this guy around and end up scuppering my whole future!' Lily felt her mouth wobble with threatened tears.

'You seriously think,' said Emily, looking at her, 'that making a mistake on one transaction might blacklist you for the whole of France?'

Lily felt herself blush. 'I know, it's extreme. But it feels so serious. I mean, of all the houses on eBay why did I have to commit to buy one from the fucking chief of police? And you know what I'm like with, well... getting things *right*?'

'You mean your misplaced sense of honour?'

'I mean, wanting to do the right thing.'

'That's what I said.'

'So I'm screwed, basically, aren't I?'

Emily looked at her and put a reassuring hand on her knee. Her brow was slightly furrowed and she focused her intelligent green eyes on Lily's face. 'He's not the inspector general, sweetheart. He's just the local bobby at best. I mean, how many houses *are* there in Eymoutiers?'

'I don't know. Maybe a thousand?'

'And the hamlet the house is in?'

'Probably about a hundred, at most.'

'And by the looks of this one, half of them are derelict or for sale. So, he's not the big I am, or anything.'

'No, I suppose not. Still, I feel...'

'I know you do.' Emily said kindly. 'That's one of the things I love about you.'

'My chronic anxiety?'

'Your honesty.'

'Thank you.'

'So what are you going to do?' Emily said. 'Do you want me to help you? I can't remember much French from school, but I'm sure I could help you wriggle out of it. I can say I did it, if you want.'

Lily looked at Emily, her face earnest. 'You're such a good friend,' she said.

'So that's a yes? You want me to contact this *Frédérique*?' Emily said, with a mock French accent.

'No,' said Lily, slowly, looking at her friend. 'I don't think I do.'

'You're not actually going to go through with it, are you? I mean, I know you want to move to France and all. But buying a house this way – sight unseen – is extreme, even for you!'

'I know. And my first response was – how do I get out of this? But since then, I haven't been able to stop thinking... well, what if I just go for it? What if this is the universe's way of getting me to take the plunge?' Lily said, feeling suddenly shy.

'And by universe, I take it you mean three-quarters of a bottle of Beaujolais?'

'Well, yes,' Lily blushed. 'The wine... well, it did come into it, I think. But wine just sort of... well, releases your inhibitions, right?'

'Definitely,' Emily said, her eyes clouding a moment with memory. 'Yep. Makes you do things you probably secretly wanted to all along...'

'And, I suppose... on some level, however drunk I was... maybe I tapped into something. Something I really wanted to do but have been too... I don't know. Scared, I suppose.' Lily moved the laptop back towards her and pulled up the picture of the house again. 'I mean, *look* at it, Emily. I could do everything I wanted there. There's a huge garden, a habitable stone house and room for a whole studio in the barn if I can afford to get some works done, or even do it myself.'

'Wow, you've really thought this out!'

'Well, yes. I've just about got enough to cover it, if I use our savings, plus Mum's inheritance, or max out the credit card. Then later, when Ben and I sell this place, we could renovate the feck out of it.'

'Bloody hell.'

'Yup.'

'It sounds like,' Emily said, 'I mean, I know you feel guilty, or think that the whole of France will shut its doors to you if you so much as put a toe out of line. And that this guy you've agreed to buy the place from is some sort of super powerful politician policeman hybrid...'

'Yes...?'

'But it kind of sounds like the main reason you might be moving forward is because... is it because you actually *want* to?'

Lily looked at the property again. She imagined herself and Ben putting up curtains, tidying the garden. Painting and plastering walls. Learning how to replace the pointing in the ancient stone. Then getting quotes for a barn conversion. Networking with local practitioners and putting together a relaxation retreat for guests. And the life they could have – country walks, swims in the lake, visiting art galleries. Having, if not complete freedom from work, the freedom to be masters of their own time. To set their own agenda and report only to themselves. She nodded. 'I mean, it was an accident, committing to the place, it really was. But I want to do this so much. I am... I *am* going to do it.'

'Wow! Good for you... I think.'

'Thanks!'

'But what about Ben? I mean, you said he's got cold feet about the whole France thing... and he doesn't know you've... well, gone ahead without him.'

'I suppose I'm hoping...' Lily said, 'well, sometimes when something's kind of decided *for* you... it's easier to go along with it than it is when you have more of a choice. I mean, he was completely on-board about moving to France next year until recently. Maybe he just needs a little push.'

'Maybe,' Emily said.

'I take it you don't think that's how it'll go?'

'I mean, it's a risk, isn't it?' For once, Emily's face was deadly serious. 'What if he puts his foot down and says no. And what's he going to do when he finds out you've committed to buying a new house without even mentioning it to him?'

'Hang on...' Lily shifted slightly so she could look directly at her friend. 'I thought you were always saying I should be *more* direct?'

'Well, yes. But this is not quite what I meant. Being direct in conversation is one thing. Splurging the savings on a stone cottage in France is... well... something else entirely.'

'Oh god,' Lily said. 'You're right. He's going to say no, isn't he?' She put her head in her hands.

'Not necessarily.' Emily rested her hand on Lily's shoulder. 'You never know... it's like you said... it might be the push he needs. Who knows?'

'Yeah,' Lily said, her voice less certain than before. 'I mean, except he didn't even seem up for the holiday idea last night. Not a proper holiday. A weekend in Paris is lovely and all, but it's not even meeting me halfway.'

'Oh Lily...'

'I know he... *I believe* he loves me. It's more... does he love me enough to go against all his instincts and take a risk. *This* much of a risk?'

Emily nodded. 'Well, I suppose you're going to find out.'

'Don't think I've given myself much of a choice.'

'And what about Ty?'

Lily felt a fresh flush of guilt. 'Well, he's off to uni in a couple of months. We won't sell the house from under him. And maybe if we do release some... some equity we can help him more with his rent and things. He won't get into so much debt.'

There was a pause.

'No offence but – be honest – was this actually a mistake, Lily?' asked Emily, carefully.

'Yes! Honestly. I had in mind this idea of a holiday that might lead to more. And I'd been looking. I wasn't concentrating, I know that. And I'd had a lot to drink. It was a genuine mistake. But...'

Emily looked at her, an eyebrow raised. 'But?'

'But at the same time it's given me the thing I've been dreaming of since I was about twelve.'

Emily nodded. 'Subconscious property purchases. It's probably a thing if we look it up on the internet. There'll be support groups and everything.'

'Ha, probably.'

'A Freudian slip of the mouse...'

'Possibly... but I think this is a one-off.'

'Yes, hopefully not the start of a very expensive addiction.'

The two women grinned at each other for a moment.

'So, are you going to help?' Lily asked, looking at her friend's face. The face of a forty-four-year-old woman, but also the twelve-year-old she'd sat next to in maths, the teenage girl she'd been with when she first tried a beer. The person she'd written letters to during uni, before email was really a proper 'thing'. The woman who'd followed her down the aisle despite complaining about the pinkness of her bridesmaid dress. Other than her brother, David, who'd always been a bit reserved, Lily realised that Emily was the only person she still had in her life who remembered her as a child. Who knew her inside out.

'Help? Well, yes. But, and I'm not being rude, *how*?' Emily said.

'I need to plan what on earth I'm going to say to Ben. And I need to try to write back to this grand mayor police chief guy in French. And find out what exactly I have to do to be entitled to live in France in the first place. And work out what to do next with this place. And what to tell Ty. And well, what to do first?'

'So just a small favour then?'

'Just a tiny, insignificant favour.'

The pair looked at each other for a moment. It wasn't a real question. Both of them already knew the answer.

'Of course I'll help; you know I've always got your back. But if you accept my help, there are going to be conditions.'

'Such as?'

'Lend me a pair of jeans and a T-shirt?'

'Done.'

'Dig out some of those choc chip cookies I like?'

'Already covered.'

'And one more thing.'

'Yes?'

'If we're going to basically get you out of the shit, plan your future, write an email in fecking French to rural France's answer to Judge Dredd, work out all the tedious details of a move then...'

'Yes?'

'We're going to need a *lot* of coffee.'

5

It'd been a while since she'd cooked a Sunday roast, and having spent the morning peeling potatoes until her fingers were raw, she now remembered why. But hopefully it would be worth it. 'Fill his belly first,' Emily had suggested. 'So he's feeling at one with the world when you tell him.'

At first Lily had laughed and said it was a cliché. But the idea had started to grow on her. Ben liked roast potatoes with a passion that almost made her jealous. If she plated him up more than usual, he'd find it very hard to leap from the sofa when she broke the news. Especially as he was prone to opening up his top button after a heavy meal. He'd be forced to sit and listen properly, or risk indigestion and a trouser incident.

Ty wandered into the kitchen as she worked, so focused on his phone that it was a miracle he knew where he was going. There were laws against using a phone while driving, but sometimes she wondered whether those rules should be extended to walking as well. As if proving her right, he bumped his thigh on the corner of the kitchen table.

'Ow!' he said, glaring at the table as if it had sprung at him

Ninja-style, rather than sat there passively for his entire life, in exactly the same place.

'You OK?' Lily asked.

Her son was dressed, as always, in black jeans, startlingly white trainers and a crumpled T-shirt. His light brown hair was unbrushed and fell in mid-length waves as he leaned forward towards his phone. He looked every inch his father's son – sometimes shockingly so – and if Lily hadn't actually given birth to him, she might have wondered if he had any of her DNA at all.

Ben didn't see it. 'He has your eyes!' he'd say. 'Plus, he gets that look on his face when he's angry... you know with the wrinkled forehead... Just like his mother.'

His comments didn't always go down well.

'Yeah,' Tyler said now, rubbing his thigh with his spare hand.

'Dinner will be ready in about an hour.'

'Nah,' he said.

'What do you mean, "Nah"?'

'I'm out at Luke's. Sorry.' He glanced up, briefly, with an apologetic grimace.

'You can't stay for...' She gestured at the bubbling pans, the glowing oven with its tempting content. 'Me and your dad will never manage all this.'

'Save some?' he said, glancing up again, blue eyes taking in the feast that he was turning down.

'OK.'

'Sorry.' He dropped his phone hand to his side, walked over and gave her a brief squeeze. He smelt of shower gel and deodorant and some sort of hair product. 'Thanks, Mum.'

Lily leaned into the mini cuddle gratefully. He might tower over her now, but he was still her boy.

'Don't worry about it,' she said.

Ordinarily, she'd have tried harder to get him to stay. But

perhaps his being out of the way for this particular meal and its aftermath would work in her favour. He loped out, glued again to his tiny device, and minutes later she heard a shout of 'see ya!' and a door slam.

Let battle commence.

It was barely midday, but she opened a can of Heineken and filled Ben's favourite pint glass, before walking through to the living room where he was glued to football repeats.

'Drink?' she said, feeling suddenly like a fifties housewife.

'Oh, ta, love,' he said, reaching for it. 'Not having one yourself?'

'Better not,' she said. 'I'll wait till I serve up. Don't want to burn myself.'

Plus, I need to keep a clear head.

She kept the conversation light over lunch, watching him inhale potatoes as if he was trying to put on a layer of fat to keep him toasty-warm through the winter. They chatted about yesterday's tennis (he'd won) motor racing, (his favourite had lost). About Ty and university and whether or not it would be a good idea to get the bathroom done.

Then, 'So what do you think you'll do tomorrow?' he asked.

'Tomorrow?'

'Yes, I mean, you're a free woman, after all... First proper day off work, as it were.'

'Ha. Well, knowing me, I'll probably end up sorting out the wardrobe and doing a bit of weeding,' she said, rolling her eyes.

'I thought you ladies of leisure liked to meet up for fancy lunches?'

'I wish.' She grinned.

'Seriously though,' he said. 'Are you going to be OK? Have you thought about, I don't know, applying for jobs, or doing some training or something? You won't be happy without something to get your teeth into.'

'Um...'

She hadn't meant to say anything yet. After all, he still had three potatoes to go before he reached optimum carb overload. But the pressure of waiting and the anticipation of a conversation that might go one dramatic way or another was too much.

'Actually...' she said. 'Actually, I *have* thought about what I might do next. What... what *we* might do, if I'm honest.'

'Oh yes?' he said, innocently shoving an overlarge roastie into his mouth and looking at her with interest. The potato was clearly surprisingly hot beneath its crispy outer layer and she watched as his eyes widened and he began to chew quickly with his mouth open, letting out steam and little gasps as he tackled the unexpected burning sensation.

She wondered whether he'd be able to deal with the hot potato she was about to lob him too.

'You know, obviously. You know I've always wanted to move to France.'

'Ob lob blurbin?' he said, nodding, mouth full of white mush.

'Well...'

It was now or never. Part of her wished it could be never. But she was stuck. She felt like a teenage daughter about to tell her beloved father she was pregnant, or had had a tattoo or had been excluded from school. There he was, innocently chewing and trying to avoid life-altering burns, and she was about to throw a missile into his world that might change it forever. 'I've... I've decided to go for it.'

He swallowed and began to cough slightly, taking a slug of beer that seemed only to make the problem worse. She walked to the sink and got him a glass of water.

'Thanks,' he said, taking a gulp. Gradually, his face returned to its usual colour. 'Sorry, you've decided to go for what?'

'I'm moving to France... Well, I mean... I hope that *we* are.'

He eyed her warily, then nodded. 'Oh. I mean, we talked about this, didn't we? And I love the idea. It's just I'm worried about the timing. But we can... have you thought any more about that trip to Paris? There's still time to grab a copy of the paper for today's token...'

She waited for him to finish, fixing her eyes on his so that he knew she was deadly serious. 'No, Ben. I think we should do it now.'

'Now?'

'Look,' she said, gently working herself towards the earth-shattering bit of the conversation. 'Ty's off to uni, we've got some savings, I've been made redundant. And you've been saying work's been a bit boring recently...'

'It hasn't been *that* bad...'

'You said that we'd do it next year,' she said, her eyes tearing up slightly. 'So why not this year? Why not now? I just feel...' she paused, took a shaky breath, her voice cracking a little, 'that if we don't do it now, we might never do it. There's never going to be a *right* time.'

He looked at her, then placed his fork on his plate and reached out a hand to cover hers. 'Oh, love. I do understand. I really do. But you're reeling from the redundancy. It was a shock, right? And I think... I think you're hurt too, aren't you? Because those bastards worked you so hard then got rid of you when it suited them...'

'Well, yes, but...'

'And you know,' he said, reddening, 'I loved the idea of moving to France, you know I did. But when confronted with the – ah – reality...' He looked at her. 'I'm just not sure I can do it.'

'Are you saying, then,' she said, her voice unsteady, 'that it's not just a "wrong timing" thing for this year. But you'll feel this way,' she breathed, shakily, 'next year too?'

His mouth wobbled slightly. 'I... I'll be honest, Lily,' he said. 'I just don't know. Maybe... maybe it's just I don't feel ready... Maybe... I'll be ready next year. But...'

'Maybe you'll never be ready?' she inserted into the silence.

He nodded, confirming all her worst fears. It was like a punch to the gut. 'Oh,' she said. 'But you promis—'

'I know,' he said, sadly. 'But look, we can um, think about it for a bit, hey? Nothing wrong with having dreams.'

'I...'

'Anyway I think, when you're feeling like this – you know, low from the redundancy and everything – it's better not to make any rash decis—'

The secret that she'd been keeping since Saturday morning suddenly felt more urgent and enormous than ever. She felt it heave inside her, bursting to be released.

'Ben, I've bought a house,' she said, rather more bluntly than she'd planned.

'—ions. You've *what*?'

She calmly fixed her eyes on his. His hand, placed over hers, stiffened. She felt her heart thundering against her ribs. 'Ben, I've bought a house in France.'

'What? When? How...?' he looked at her, incredulous.

'Listen,' she said, 'I didn't mean to go behind your back. I was just... well, it was the other night. I'd had... I mean there was a *lot* of wine. And I... I was just looking at properties. I wasn't... I think I wanted to book a holiday or something, but not... Obviously not *buy* anything. But then in the morning I realised I'd clicked "buy it now" and committed to buy a place.'

'Ahh.' His shoulders relaxed and he smiled broadly. For a

moment she thought he was going to throw caution to the wind. To leap up and say, 'You're right! Let's do this!'

But instead he said: 'Oh thank *god* for that. You know you're not legally obligated to buy the place, then? It's only... I mean, eBay can't get you to... it's not exactly a second-hand pair of jeans. Just tell them you've made a mistake!' He shook his head fondly, relieved to have solved the problem, and stuck his fork confidently into a fresh potato.

'No, Ben,' she said, firmly. 'I *can't.*'

The potato crumbled under his fork. 'What do you mean?' he said.

'Well, for starters, the guy who's selling is a mayor, and the... well, he's in charge of the police in the local area. And he's written to me with full expectation that I'm going to come and sign.'

'But, Lily,' he said, his brow furrowed, 'you know more about France than anyone. You know that these little local mayors don't have any *real* power, don't you? He can't have you arrested and thrown in a dungeon for making a mistake on eBay.'

'But...'

'And I'm sure eBay will refund his listing, or relist his property or whatever. Plus, we can't afford...'

'But, Ben, don't you see? This could be such a great move. It's forty grand. We've got it... just, and we can sell this house, then fund the renovations. I can run holidays! Retreats! You can help. We'll have an adventure... we'll...'

'Lily, stop.'

'We'll grow stuff in the garden, you've always wanted to grow vegetables...'

'But I...'

'Or what about...' she said, thinking desperately. 'How about we just give it a year? A year trying out this kind of life? A year at the French farmhouse to see whether it fits us... then we could...'

'Lily, *stop*.' Ben's voice was firm. She looked at him and saw his face, pale with anger. His mouth was a thin line.

'What?' she said, feeling her stomach sink.

'This is insane. You can't just buy a house on a whim, then move countries without planning things, without working out how to open a business, or even viewing where you're going to live. You need lists and plans; to think it all through properly.'

'You're not serious?' she said. 'You know I've – and I thought *we'd* – been planning this, making lists, *thinking* about it for, what? Twenty years? Christ, Ben, I've been doing French evening classes for the last two years. OK, my French isn't perfect but...'

'Look,' he said, more gently, squeezing her hand. 'I know it's been a lot. And perhaps I haven't... maybe I haven't taken you as seriously as I should have. Maybe I've made promises without really... well, without thinking properly about the reality. It's been, well, a bit of a stressful time at work for me. But that's no excuse. I should have...'

'Yes,' she said, unbending. 'You should have.'

'OK, look,' he said, brushing back his hair. 'Maybe we could compromise. Book that longer holiday you were thinking about. For next summer, once Ty's settled. Maybe not a month, but a fortnight or something. I could take time off, or work remotely. We can... maybe we can get it out of your system that way.'

'Get it out of my system?' she said, incredulous.

'You know what I mean.'

'Ben, listen!' She pushed his arm away, not wanting to be comforted. Wanting him to understand.

He looked at her, his expression unreadable.

'You're probably right about the house. About the legal side of it. In fact, you definitely are. But it's not that... it's more...' She took a deep breath and looked directly at him. 'Ben, I think this is something I *have* to do. And maybe the bid was a mistake, but it's given me something – us something – that could change our lives forever. I'm asking you to take a chance on this. On me, I suppose.'

He was silent for a moment. Then shook his head, slowly. 'I can't.' His eyes were as wide as Ty's used to be when refusing to eat cabbage. This was a serious, definite no.

'You *can*! Come on! We can reclaim our lives... we can...'

'I just can't,' he said sadly. 'I'm not... I'm not built like you, Lily. I like travelling a bit, for holidays. And I thought... When we talked about France in the past, I wasn't lying. I sort of liked the idea of doing it. But when it became real... Lily, the thought of moving to a whole new country where we don't know anyone, don't know how things *work,* trying to start from scratch, set up a business... It's just too much.'

'Oh Ben... but I can...'

'I know I don't love my job. But I like it enough. And it pays the bills. It's steady. I suppose I'm boring, but I like things to be steady.'

'But you always...'

'And look, loads of people say they might emigrate one day, but hardly anyone does. So when we spoke about it, I suppose I was just... Well, you were so excited about the idea. It was nice to let you have your... eh, fantasy. But I just... Lily. I can't do this. I just can't.'

Lily could feel something inside herself sinking. This was really, truly a no. Not only a no for taking a leap of faith now. But no to *ever* actually moving over. All those conversations. The promises of 'next year' which always seemed to be pushed back. All those times when he'd nodded along. Had he been *humouring* her?

'And what about what *I* want?' she said, her voice unexpectedly thick with tears.

'I'm sorry,' he said, pushing his chair back. 'I just can't.' He stood up, his jaw clenched.

'But, Ben!'

He turned and disappeared into the living room. Seconds later, she could hear the sound of the motor racing on TV.

As she sat there, rigid with a combination of stress and shock, she wondered whether she'd always agreed to his delays – his promises of future dates and next years, because on some level she'd known. Known that his heart wasn't in it and been scared to hear him admit it.

Worse, she'd now discovered that, all things being equal, when faced with an ultimatum, he wouldn't be willing to make a sacrifice for her. Not entertain her idea even for a trial period.

She'd spent years and years moulding herself around him, Ty, their family. Making sacrifices – maybe not earth-shattering ones, but the everyday sacrifices that parents make. And what had helped her through the difficult times, the frustrating moments – the moments when she'd felt completely invisible or unloved – was knowing that one day it would be *her* turn. She'd have the chance to live her life the way she'd always wanted; with Ben at her side.

It was hard to know exactly what feeling flooded through her at that minute on a wave of adrenalin. A kind of heady cocktail of anger, resentment, fear, hurt, disappointment, anxiety. But as it settled into her body it filled her with an unwavering certainty. She stood up, took a breath to steady herself, then walked into the living room.

'Ben,' she said, quite quietly, fists clenched at her sides. Her breathing was ragged, her heart pumping harder than it did during her aerobics class or when she had to run for the bus.

He looked up at her warily and muted the TV. 'Uh-huh?' he said. He appeared for a minute like a wild animal, cornered.

She felt a sense of calm; a stealthy predator frozen, preparing to strike. She took a deep breath. 'Ben, I'm moving to France. I'm buying that house. I'm going to go over, sign the papers, meet the mayor guy...'

'But...'

'I'm going to live in it, do it up, find a way to make it work.'

'But...'

She felt hot tears spill, but kept her eyes focused on her husband. 'I'm going to sit in cafés and swim in the lake, and make new friends.'

'Lily...'

'I'm going to perfect my French and start building a business.'

'But, love...'

'Because it's what I've dreamed of for years. I've made no secret of that. And you've let me believe all this time that it would happen one day. You've let me plan and fantasise and imagine what my life will be like in the future when we make a go of it.'

'I'm so sorry... I really thought...'

'Sure, maybe I won't make a success of it. Maybe I'll lose money, or discover that I don't actually like France as much as I think I do. Maybe it will be an unremitting, terrible, ill-advised disaster...'

'Come on, love...'

'But at least I will have *done it*,' she said, feeling heat surge into her palms.

Say it! Her mind urged. Tell him you don't want to do it without him.

'And if I have to do it by myself, I will.'

6

With a sigh, Lily watched as the cluttered tarmac of the airport fell away and within seconds the whole area became a tiny square, covered with toy planes, model buildings; ant-like people scurrying back and forth. As the plane gathered momentum, her horizons expanded. Fields and towns and roads and houses became map-like and surreal: tiny playthings in a child's model village.

She knew that, somewhere down there, a tiny Ben was making his way to work; a pea-sized Ty was off to stay with a friend who had a pool. No doubt a mini Grahame was sitting at his desk in Banks Designs, opening the first email of the day. Everything carried on, yet she'd slipped into a different life, stepped away from the roles that had defined her for twenty years. Wife, mother, designer, she'd shrugged them off as if they were unwanted items of clothing rather than facets of her identity. It was liberating; it was terrifying.

It was a relief too in some ways, knowing that although of course Ben was as heartbroken as her, the structure of the life she'd left behind was still standing; would continue to function without her in it. It had looked, beforehand, as if everything she was involved in would crumble if she was removed from the world she'd created. But she'd gently pulled herself from the tower of responsibilities and familiarity like a piece of a Jenga puzzle, and life was carrying on as normal.

She couldn't let herself think about last night, when Ben had tried for the last time to persuade her not to go. 'Don't I mean anything to you?' he'd asked, eyes pooling with unaccustomed tears. 'Stay! Please.'

She'd cried too. 'Ben – I have to do this,' she'd said. She tried to add: *Please come with me. It won't be the same without you!* But the words had stuck in her throat.

Ty had been surprisingly understanding about it all when she'd broached the subject with him a week ago. 'Will I be able to bring my mates out?' he'd asked.

'When things are sorted with the house, of course! And you're welcome any time. Plus, I'll be back. It's only an hour and a half flight.'

He'd nodded. 'Bit weird about Dad though,' he'd said.

'I know,' she'd said, brushing his hair with her hand. 'Sorry, Ty.' Then, 'Maybe he'll come and join me in the end.'

He'd grunted and shrugged in a kind of teenage acceptance. 'It's OK. Dad's a big boy, I guess.'

She'd kissed the top of Ben's head as she'd left him that morning, when he was fast asleep and looked heartbreakingly funny and rumpled. After their late night where nothing had been achieved except the sharing and perpetuating of misery, she'd decided to resist the urge to wake him and try just once more to get him to join her.

'Don't you see,' she'd said last night. 'I *have* stayed for you. I've put off this dream for years, for you, for Ty, for the family. I've loved you enough to stay over and over again the whole time we've been together. And you promised that we would do this. It might seem unimportant to you, but believing we'd do this one day was the thought that kept me going through everything.'

It hadn't worked. He loved her, she really believed that. He just didn't love her enough. And even though there was nothing *wrong* with their relationship, realising that her husband's love was in fact, conditional rather than the opposite, had made it a little easier to walk away.

Even so, although she'd known it was pointless, she'd kept finding herself glancing at the road behind as her taxi had made its way to Stansted this morning, hoping to see him in pursuit in his Volvo estate. Then, when strolling half-heartedly around duty-free waiting for her flight to be called, had found it almost impossible to tear her eye from the passport queue – perhaps she'd see his messy brown hair over the top of the crowd and discover that, after all, he had decided she was worth the risk and prove that, in fact, love did conquer all – even worries about security, mortgage payments and work commitments. The ultimate airport movie moment.

But feeling the upward motion and hearing the ting of the seat belt sign, she knew now without doubt – and somehow for the first time – he really wasn't coming. That it really had been goodbye rather than *au revoir*. Part of her wanted to roar with frustration, another to curl up in a ball and weep and weep. She wanted to stop the flight, to rush back to him. Yet she wanted to move forward too. How many more years would he have let her wait before he'd admitted he was never really on-board with the plans she'd thought were *theirs* rather than hers?

She felt a sob well up in her throat and held it back. Then, to avoid ugly crying in front of a plane full of strangers, she put in her headphones and selected the 'guilty pleasure' playlist on her phone – a list filled with some of her out-of-date and slightly embarrassing favourite tunes: Elton John and WetWetWet, a bit of Bryan Adams and James Taylor and a smattering of songs she'd enjoyed while at uni.

Then she settled back in her seat, closed her eyes and tried to picture what it would be like to wander round her new home for the very first time. The online pictures had shown a traditional stone farmhouse with an overgrown garden. Powder blue shutters at the windows. A cherry tree in the back. A slightly neglected, uninhabited property just waiting for someone to adopt it and love it and bring it back to life.

She'd been to *Limousin* a several times with her parents, although never to the edge of *Creuse* where the hamlet she'd soon call home was situated. The weather wasn't scorching like in the south but temperatures in May would be a balmy 25 degrees on average – just the perfect weather for doing anything and everything she wanted without needing to constantly seek out the shade.

Quietly, a small smile playing on her lips, she flicked to 'Here Comes the Sun' in her playlist. As the familiar tune flooded her senses, she imagined herself opening the front door, exploring the downstairs properly. Marvelling over carved wood and tiled floors. Flinging open the shutters in attic rooms to let the light pour in. Over time, clearing the garden and renovating an old wrought iron table she imagined might be nestling under the brambles. Sitting in a floral dress and sipping Beaujolais as the sun slipped behind distant fields and stained the evening sky orange.

Another day, she'd discover a hatch to a forgotten cellar filled with dusty, delicious and perfectly preserved bottles of wine. She'd create a studio in the barn, removing a stone wall side and replacing it with glass so guests could take in the countryside views while taking classes or relaxing. The studio would be bathed in light, its interior washed white; she'd invite reiki practitioners and yoga gurus and relaxation specialists and treat her guests to the type of luxurious break that would have them coming back time and time again.

Then she imagined coffees in sun-drenched cafés, walking to the *boulangerie* for her daily *croissant*, saying cheery *bonjours* to friendly locals and living each day with the knowledge that she'd had a dream and made it happen. Even if she'd had to do it alone.

She was just musing over colour choices for the *salle de séjour*, when she felt a tap on her shoulder. 'Sorry love, captain's put the seat belt signs back on; we're coming in to land.'

She felt a lurch, which may or may not have been the descent of the plane. This was it.

'I'm so proud of you,' Emily had said when she'd called her yesterday. 'It really takes enormous balls to do what you're doing.'

'Well, maybe not enormous *balls*.'

'You're right. It takes an exceptionally large vagina.'

'Hmm, why does that sound like less of a compliment...' Lily had paused for a moment, listening to her friend laugh. 'So you don't think I'm making a big mistake? I mean, Ben...' Her voice had broken slightly as she'd said his name. 'He's... we're both... devastated.'

Emily had sighed. 'I know, sweetheart. But he doesn't *have* to be. He could come with.'

'Or I could stay.'

'You could,' her friend had said. 'But it's like you said yourself – you'd always wonder, maybe always resent him for holding you back. At least this way you're doing the thing you've wanted to do for practically your whole life.'

'I know, it's just...'

'I think you're doing the right thing, lovely. It's heart-breaking, I know. But staying would be too.'

'You're right,' Lily had said, feeling a sinking sensation deep in her stomach. 'And I just... I mean, if he *loved* me enough...'

'Exactly.'

There a silence, then, 'Do you want *me* to come?' Emily had offered.

'Are you serious?'

'Yes, I mean, not forever. I'm not going to become your business partner or anything. And the dogs haven't even got passports so I'll have to see whether Chris can cope with looking after them – I don't want to come back and find him mauled to death or covered in doggie drool. But if I can sort it all, I could come out for a week or so, if you like? Help you settle in. Help knock back that wine that you reckon might be in the cellar.'

'I think the cellar is more likely to be full of junk. But, pretty sure we can stretch to buying a few bottles if that's a deal-breaker.' Lily had found herself smiling.

'You got it. Look, I'll have to organise a few things, but I'll get myself a ticket and be over as soon as I can. Only if you want me to, that is.'

Lily had felt her eyes fill with tears of relief. 'You,' she'd said, 'are such a good friend. What would I do without you?'

There was a silence. 'You'd manage.'

'Still nice to know I'll never have to, right?'

The plane bumped onto the tarmac and screeched to a halt on the tiny runway, jolting her back to the present moment. Almost immediately, the other passengers got up, grabbed bags from overhead lockers and then queued up in readiness for the door to open and release them. Lily waited until most of them had exited, then calmly removed her own bag and made her way to the back of the plane. 'Thank you,' she said to the smiling staff.

'Have a lovely trip!' one of them said.

'Actually,' she said, 'I'm moving here. I'm getting a visa for...'

But they'd moved on to the next passenger.

She rolled her suitcase over the tarmac, already appreciating the warm sun playing on her face. She was charmed by the tiny airport, the quick exit to collect her baggage, and the fact that the foyer in the building was practically empty. The department of *Limousin* had one of the lowest populations in France, and Lily noticed a difference in density even at the airport: the lack of pushing and shoving, the amount of space and the air that, despite the planes, smelled somehow fresher and cleaner than it did back home.

'Aren't you worried you'll be lonely?' Emily had said when she'd told her that there were fewer residents in the whole of *Limousin* than there were in Basildon

'Not at all,' Lily said. 'It's not as if it's completely empty. There are still people there. Just... well, I suppose fewer of them.'

'Quality not quantity?'

'Exactly.'

'Plus, there are an awful lot of cows in that area,' Emily had added. 'You can always make some bovine friends.'

'Thanks, I'll bear that in mind.'

'See, you think I'm joking. But before you know it you and the local cattle may have formed a *moo*-tiful friendship.'

'That's awful.'

'Yes, I apologise.'

'I feel as if you've let yourself down.'

'I am deeply ashamed.'

Lily had decided to book a small hire car for the first month to get her started, so after collecting her case and making her way through passport control – which had taken just twenty minutes – she headed to the car hire building. Her on-board suitcase was modern, light and had wheels. But the enormous case she'd placed in the hold was old, unwieldy and bursting at the seams.

Rolling one while carrying the other proved no mean feat, but she developed a kind of roll-limp and drag motion that got her to the tiny administrative building with a picture of a car above the door just across the pedestrian crossing.

There was one customer ahead of her in the queue who already had his keys and papers, but seemed deep in conversation with the assistant. They gabbled together in such fast French that it was impossible for her to eavesdrop. She caught the words, *soleil* (sun), *plage* (beach) and what may or may not have been *haricots verts*.

Come on! she wanted to say. *Allez*, for god's sake. She wanted to get in the car, whizz to her B. & B., get the kettle on and make herself the mother of all cups of tea. She tapped her foot and glanced behind her at the three people now waiting in line.

But instead of looking at watches or sighing loudly, they all appeared to be waiting patiently, seemingly not in a hurry at all.

Finally, the man finished his tale of beans on the beach or whatever he'd been gassing on about and it was Lily's turn. The woman at the desk shuffled some paperwork, looked up and smiled. '*Bonjour, Madame*,' she said.

'*Bonjour*,' Lily replied. Then, glancing at the back of her hand where she'd written the word '*voiture*' (car) just in case, added. '*Je voudrais louer un voiture.*'

'*Pardon?*'

She'd double-checked the French beforehand to make sure she'd got it right, so tried again, '*Je voudrais louer un voiture, s'il vous plaît.*'

The woman looked confused. 'You are English, yes?' she said. 'You can speak English if you like.'

'Thank you,' said Lily, deflated. 'I want to hire a car.'

'Ah, *une voiture*,' the woman pronounced carefully. To Lily's ears, it sounded exactly the same as when she'd said it seconds ago.

'*Un voiture*,' Lily repeated, trying to perfect her pronunciation.

'Yes, but *une*,' replied the woman. 'It's feminine.'

Lily had never completely understood the French language's propensity to give everything from toasters to toilets a sex. 'Why does it matter what sex my car is?' she wanted to say. 'I just want to drive it, –not *shag* it.' Instead, she nodded. '*Une voiture*,' she said, pronouncing it correctly.

'*Oui*, that's it!' The woman nodded. 'May I 'ave your name?'

'Lily Butterworth.'

Finally, after about half an hour spent spelling out her name, signing something and paying some sort of deposit that hadn't been mentioned on the website, Lily slipped into a small Nissan Micra – left-hand-drive – and pressed the 'start' button. And she was away, following the satnav instructions, feeling completely out of her depth in a left-hand drive car on the right-hand side of the road, and heading towards the tiny village of *Faux la Montagne.*

'This is it, car,' she told the Nissan. 'I've really done it now.'

7

Lily looked up as the cute guy sank into the seat next to her. 'Sorry,' he said. 'Crowded today.'

'It's OK,' she replied, although in reality there were a few other spare chairs, none of which had anyone's bag on it. She propped her bag against her knees and drew out her notepad.

'Not sure what else they can have to say about Hamlet,' he whispered as their lecturer walked into the hall.

'I know,' she said, although she'd actually been enjoying the series of lectures; peeling back the layers of an age-old story, revealing truths that still applied to their lives today. She looked at him properly for the first time. Light tan skin, neat brown hair, spiked with gel. Blue or green eyes — hard to tell in this light. He smelled good too — like pencil sharpenings and fresh air and shampoo.

He glanced back, catching her off-guard and she quickly looked down at her notebook. 'I'm Ben, by the way,' he said.

On the stage, the lecturer cleared his throat and began to speak. Everything was the same as usual.

Everything was different.

* * *

Snapping back to the moment, Lily wound down the window. It was 2 p.m. and the afternoon sun had kicked into overdrive. The air conditioning in the car appeared to be faulty – something she hadn't thought to check before leaving the car park – and she could feel her armpits, elbows, knee crevices, back and arse begin to develop an uncomfortable sweat.

She'd been driving now for an hour and twenty minutes – something that had seemed easily doable when she'd planned the trip from the comfort of her PC, but that in practice was testing her driving skills more than she could ever have imagined. Driving on the right was OK, but what about roundabouts? One-way roads? Dual carriageways that moulded into a single lane at a moment's notice? She'd been beeped, given the finger – one man had even wound down the window to yell something at her in French when she'd cut him up at a crossing. '*Je suis désolé!*' she'd said, close to tears. 'I can't help it!'

Finally, she'd escaped the city and begun to drive down the D940 – a long, wide road that had none of the complications of speed bumps, roundabouts or traffic lights – and felt herself relax. That was until a tractor, loaded with so many hay bales it seemed to defy the laws of physics, pulled out in front of her and trundled along at a steady 20 km per hour.

Suddenly, as she slowed, the road behind, which had been reassuringly empty, began to fill with impatient cars, the drivers beeping and gesticulating as she glanced in the rear-view mirror, eager for her to overtake. But with little visibility around the countless corners, over hills or past unknown crossroads she wasn't able to work up the nerve. Gradually, drivers began to zoom around her, glancing at her as they passed; taking risks, which meant they were either completely reckless, drunk or incredibly important and late.

Eventually, she took a turn onto an even smaller road that seemed to decrease in width the more she drove, then began to climb alarmingly, making the little car's engine squeal in protest. To her right, a small grass verge gave away to an enormous cliff-like dip, peppered with trees and without a barrier in sight. Without realising, she began to drive more towards the centre of the road to avoid this death-drop, and earned a loud blast of the horn from a careering Land Rover.

Gripping the wheel more tightly, her heart thundering, she tried to reassure herself. Everyone got a bit of road rage when they were stuck behind a slow driver, or whizzed around the corner to find a tiny Nissan cruising down the middle of the road. People weren't unfriendly here, it was just the circumstances. The near death experiences. She'd get the hang of this weird left-hand drive, right side of road combination after a while and it wouldn't all be so stressful.

Besides, she'd spend as little time in an actual car as possible, she resolved; she'd buy a woven basket and walk to the market, filling it with fresh, locally sourced produce. She'd eat at the local restaurants and purchase her bread daily from the *boulangerie*. Perhaps she wouldn't even need a car at all. This was the storm before the calm.

With just a few more kilometres to go, she breathed in the fresh air and tried to relax. She found that if she ignored the drop of certain death on the right of her, things felt a lot better. According to the GPS, she was nearly at the *chambre d'hôtes* she'd booked – and just ten further kilometres from the house she would soon call home. Once at the B. & B. she could kick off her shoes, gulp down a cuppa and start her new life.

As if reading her thoughts, the in-car satnav suddenly went black and displayed the words 'signal lost'.

'Shit,' she said, in spite of herself. In spite of the new, stress-free, relaxed version of herself she was trying to be. But how hard could it be to negotiate the last few kilometres? From what she could remember, there was literally one road that led into the tiny village. It shouldn't be that difficult, even for someone with *her* sense of direction.

After what seemed like at least five more kilometres she felt less confident. The road weaved back and forth and signposts pointing to tiny hamlets along muddy tracks gave no indication of how far she was from her destination. If Ben had been here, he'd have brought a map, she realised. He always brought a map, no matter how much she insisted that the GPS would guide them wherever they needed to go. She was literally lost without him.

But this was ridiculous. She was a grown woman, quite capable of finding her way without electronic help. Spotting a Land Rover pulled up on the side of the road and a man in a high-viz orange jacket leaning on the bonnet, holding something in his hands, she pulled up to ask directions. It would be good practice for her fledgling French, after all. And surely nothing could be too complicated. A simple *aller tout droit* (go straight ahead) would be enough to reassure her that she was still on the right route.

'*Bonjour, Monsieur,*' she said, walking up behind him.

'*Mon dieu!*' he exclaimed, jumping almost out of his skin. He swung around, and she realised what he was holding in his hands was an actual rifle.

'*Non, Monsieur,*' she said, waving her hands in a gesture that she hoped looked apologetic. '*Je suis désolé, je...* um, didn't mean, to um, *faire un choc, une... Une surprise.*'

He nodded and smiled; his mouth only just visible under his enormous grey moustache. '*Désolé, Madame*,' he said, nodding at the gun. '*C'est pour le sanglier.*'

'*Sanglier?*' The gun was still, disturbingly, pointed at her, despite his smile. The man seemed to have forgotten it was there at all. While she was pretty sure he wasn't going to shoot her intentionally, there was every possibility she wasn't going to come out of this exchange very well. She noticed a small bottle of whiskey balanced on the bonnet of the Land Rover, just past his hand. It was three-quarters empty. The man looked a little too elderly to be trusted with a gun at all, and she noticed to her horror that one of his hands seemed to have an occasional involuntary twitch.

'*Oui, le sanglier!*' he said, pawing the ground with his foot and making a snorting noise. '*Le* pig, *le* pig of the forest,' he added in broken English. 'Wild.'

'Oh, wild boar?' she said. She'd read there was hunting in the area.

He shrugged. '*Je ne comprends pas, Madame.*'

'Right. OK. Um, *je suis... je ne trouve pas... Faux la Montagne?*'

He shook his head sadly and shrugged, lifting the gun slightly as he did so, so it pointed towards her head instead of her heart. At least death, if it came, would be quick and painless, she reasoned, trying to step away from his line of fire.

She took out her phone and typed in the name of the village into her notes, then, carefully approaching from the side, away from the pointed barrel, she showed him.

'Ah,' he said, his eyes beginning to sparkle, '*Faux la Montagne!*' Only rather than her *forks la montaGnee* he gave what must be its correct pronunciation. Which sounded nothing like what she'd said at all. '*Oui, c'est la, c'est la!*' he said, pointing to the road ahead, excitedly.

'Straight on?' she said. 'Er, *tout droit?*'

'Oui, OUI!' he said, waving his gun in delight.

'Merci,' she said, backing away, only half sure she'd been given any directions of use, but quite happy to end the conversation anyway.

'*Bonne journée, Madame!*' he continued as she climbed into her car, still waving the gun with one of his hands. '*Bonne après-midi!*'

She roared away, her heart thumping – partly because of her recent proximity to the barrel of a gun; partly because she was beginning to realise that two years of evening classes may have made her on point when it came to writing things down, but speaking and pronouncing things correctly, remembering words in the moment, was going to be more of a challenge than she'd thought.

Half a kilometre on, she saw a small sign bearing the name '*Faux la Montagne*'. Sighing with relief, she rounded the corner and drove slowly past small stone houses that increased in number as she moved towards what must be the centre. About a hundred metres along, the road opened into a tiny square with a fountain at its heart, and the smallest church she'd ever seen on the right-hand side. Just ahead, a sign pointed to '*Chambre d'Hotes*', and then suddenly she was there, parked in front of *La Petite Maison*.

Back in comparative civilisation, she began to relax. The village was charming, each house with its individual shutters – some wooden, some coloured pink, white or blue. There was a tiny *boulangerie* close to the fountain, and slightly down the road she could see the purple signage of a café. In the distance, she spotted a couple walking a dog on a long lead. 'Maybe there is life on this planet after all,' she whispered to the Nissan before climbing out and walking to the front door of the B. & B.

She'd chosen this particular accommodation because of its

French rural charm – or at least what had appeared charming from the photograph on hotels.com – and its proximity to *Broussas*, which was just five kilometres away. And she wasn't disappointed. The building was narrow, but three storeys high, with windows in the attic flung open to let in fresh air. The door was adorned with hanging baskets and each window had its own little row of flowerpots. It was, in short, exactly the sort of accommodation she wanted to create herself – welcoming, charming, beautiful, well cared for and unapologetically *French*. She put her journey out of her mind, banished thoughts of rushing home to Ben and Ty, and resolved that she'd really make a go of things. '*C'est un nouveau départ*' – a new beginning.

Lifting her hand, she rang the doorbell, and almost immediately heard the clip of heels against tiles. A tall, slender woman dressed in mustard-coloured linen trousers and a black halterneck T-shirt answered the door. Her hair was black and tucked neatly behind her ears, her eyes were carefully made up. A cigarette dangled from the corner of her mouth. On Lily, a fag end stuck to the top lip would have looked slovenly. But somehow, on this woman it looked impossibly chic. Perhaps, Lily thought for a fleeting moment, she ought to take up smoking too.

'*Bonjour*,' the woman said, after taking the cigarette out and blowing the smoke upwards, politely keeping it away from her guest.

'Bonjour, *je m'appelle* Lily,' she began. '*J'ai une chambre ici?*'

'You can speak English if you want,' the woman interrupted, her eyes twinkling with amusement.

'Oh, thank you. I *am* learning French,' she said, apologetically.

'It's fine. I am afraid I don't speak English very well,' the woman said. 'You will have to excuse me.'

'It's great. I mean, you're speaking perfectly.'

An amused shrug. 'You are *Madame* Butterworth?'

'Yes – but call me Lily, please.'

'OK, Lily. *Enchanté*. I am Chloé.'

'Nice to meet you.'

'Do you want any 'elp with your bags?'

'No, I'm fine,' Lily said. 'I'll just bring in one for now.' She walked to the back of the car, popped the boot and extracted the wheeled case, lifting it by the handle, and climbed up the four stone steps to the front door. Chloé moved back slightly, gesturing her inside. As Lily walked past, Chloé dropped her half-smoked cigarette and ground it under her kitten heel on the stone step.

'Sorry,' she said. 'I should quit thees shit.' She smiled and gave yet another shrug, indicating that she actually had no intention of doing so. Lily had never realised shoulders could be so expressive.

'It's fine,' Lily replied.

'I will give you *le tour*,' Chloé said, moving past her with a waft of perfume and cigarette smoke, her linen trousers and fitted top perfectly accentuating her tall, elegant frame. Lily, feeling tatty in comparison in her skinny jeans and hoodie, trotted after her, already planning the type of outfit she might change into as soon as she'd had a shower and settled in.

She followed Chloé up polished mahogany stairs to the second floor, where her host opened a door with '*La Chambre Bleue*' painted on it in delicate script. 'This is yours,' she said, nodding towards the interior.

Inside, the room was indeed extremely blue. The bedding was embroidered with blue silk flowers, the rug on the floor was faded – possibly antique – and patterned with violets and blue-bells. The shutters were open and the window half cracked, so a small breeze entered – enough to move the shimmering voiles at the window. Above the four-poster bed was a small decorative chandelier, its glass sprinkling jewelled, rainbow lights across the bed and onto a little dressing table.

'Oh wow,' said Lily. 'This is beautiful.'

A shrug. 'It eez OK.'

'I love the whole shabby chic look!'

'I am sorry, the... what?'

'The shabby chic, you know – faded grandeur, upcycled antiques. You must have worked hard on this,' she said, hoping that Chloé might be able to point her in the direction of a decent chalk-paint stockist.

'Non, this was my grandmother's,' said Chloé shaking her head. 'The furniture has been here since one hundred years. I have done nothing.'

'Oh.' Lily nodded, chastened. 'Sorry.'

'*De rien*,' Chloé said, 'It does not matter.'

'Well, thank you. It's gorgeous.'

'*Oui*, I think so too,' Chloé said with a smile. 'The whole house is – as you say – beautiful. I am lucky. My grandmother passed it to me from ten years.'

Lily nodded, wishing she had the confidence to accept a compliment like Chloé, whether about her house or her taste or her shoes, without arguing against it, or saying something like: *What? This old thing?*

'You would like a coffee?'

'Oh, yes please.'

'I will make. Come down since five minutes.'

'I will, thank you.'

The minute Chloé closed the door and Lily heard her footsteps clip down the wooden stairs, she flung herself on the bed and sank into its feathered eiderdown. She gazed at the window, through which, from her vantage point, she could see a light blue sky, sprinkled with small, unthreatening clouds and just the very tops of buildings and trees.

If someone as beautiful and glamorous as Chloé could run a business here and make it work and be – or at least appear to be – happy and confident, then so could she. She imagined herself wearing crisp linen and elegantly cut clothes, changing up her trainers for heels. Perhaps getting her slightly messy hair cut into more of a chic bob. And lipstick – she should be ditching the dusky pinks she favoured for something vibrant, confident and red.

She stood up and looked in the mirror. Her black hoodie hung off her, shapelessly. Her jeans clung to her thighs in all the wrong places. She rummaged through her suitcase and pulled out a clean top, which brought with it several other items. Some knickers that had seen better days, a diary and a little photo album she'd grabbed at the last minute from her bedside drawer.

She picked the album up, tempted to open it, but knew it wasn't the right time. Seeing pictures of Ty and Ben, of the three of them as a family, might tip her over the edge. She'd wait until she was feeling stronger.

Plus, she told herself, it wasn't as if she wouldn't see them again. Ty was definitely going to come over, and she still had to believe that Ben might come around.

She slipped into the top then dumped here hoodie on the bed before thinking better of it and hanging it neatly over the back of the dressing table chair.

She found a brush and ran it through her hair, tucking it a little behind her ears. Then, reaching into her washbag she pulled out her duty-free purchase – amused to remember that the perfume she'd chosen was presciently a 'Chloé' one. Her mascara was smudged, so she wet a finger and ran it under each eye. It would have to do for now. 'This,' she said to her reflection in the mirror, 'is the start of a whole new chapter.'

Then, smiling, she turned and tucked her case under the bed, pulled the eiderdown back into its original position and left the room, trotting down towards the dining room and the smell of freshly ground coffee.

8

'So, what's the house like?' Emily asked.

Lily pressed the phone to her ear, turned slightly, her head comfortably cradled by the feather pillow, and looked around the charming room again.

'Oh, Em, the B. & B. is lovely – and you should see Chloé, the owner. She's about our age, but she's so glamorous, so... so *French*.'

'Are you saying *I'm* not glamorous?'

'You have your own, unique glamour.'

'Hmph,' her friend joked. 'Anyway, I'm not too fussed about how lovely the B. & B. is – I'm more interested in the actual *house*. You know, the one you bought on a whim and left your husband for.'

'Emily!' Lily felt a pang of guilt. 'You know it wasn't as straightforward as that.'

'Sorry, sorry. Wasn't thinking.' Emily was silent for a minute. 'Christ, Chris is right, I've got to think more before opening my gob.'

'Is everything all right?'

There was a pause, then:

'Yeah. Yeah. Fine. You know me – always breezy!' Emily replied.

'Ha – that's one way of putting a positive spin on the fact you're a windbag.'

Emily let out a brief, dry laugh. 'Takes one to know one.' But her voice sounded thoughtful rather than amused.

'Are you sure you're OK?'

'Yes. Buster's hurt his paw and he was whining all night. Like having a new-born, only one that weighs more than you and farts like a trooper.'

'Sounds adorable.'

'Yep. So I'm a little sleep deprived to say the least.'

Lily felt herself relax. Something in her friend's voice had sounded off, even from the other side of the Channel. But a sleepless night would explain the slight change in her voice. 'Nightmare,' she sympathised.

'Yep. Anyway, are you avoiding the question or something?'

'No! I'm just... actually... I haven't been to the house yet.'

'What! You've been there, what, half a day already and you haven't even thought to have a peek?'

'It's only half a day, Emily – give a girl a chance!'

'Even so, aren't you curious?'

'I am... it's just the drive here was awful. I was going to drop my bag and head straight over. But I was just so tired when I got here. Then Chloé made me coffee and we chatted – she studied art in Paris you know. Then went into fashion. Then her grandmother died and...'

'Lily. You know I love you.'

'Yes?'

'But seriously, are you filling me in on your B. & B. host's life story. Because this is an international call.'

'It's included in my contract, though. It's free.'

'Still...'

'Well, yes. I suppose... It's just she's so interesting.'

'But about the *house*?' Emily said, impatiently. 'When are you going to see this place? I want pictures! Details!'

'I'm going to drive and see it in a moment, actually. It's just... I feel a bit, well, nervous.'

'Excited nervous?'

'Terrified nervous.'

'I get that, sweetie. It's a big thing. But remember you're not obligated to...'

'I know, I know. But also I sort of *am*. In some ways.'

Emily sighed. 'Lily Jemima Butterworth, what are we going to do with you?'

* * *

Driving once again along the tiny main street, a rudimentary map drawn in biro on a piece of paper sitting on the passenger seat in case she went out of signal with her GPS again, Lily found herself smiling. Emily might be a bit intense at times, but she was such a good friend. Without that call – that friendly but firm push in the right direction – she wasn't sure she'd have been able to muster up the courage to negotiate the roads again, let alone go and see the house in the flesh today.

Now she was bumping along tree-lined roads, marvelling at the view and breathing in the pine-scented air that buffeted her skin through the half-open car window. Any nerves she'd felt had been released by her chat with Chloé and her phone call with

Emily. She was going to enjoy her life here, she told herself. She was going to make it work. And with a bit of effort, she could become a completely new person to boot. The sort of person who wore linen trousers and lipstick, and while she wouldn't smoke, the sort of woman who'd look pretty cool if she did.

The roadway began to narrow again as she neared *Broussas*, and other than the odd abandoned stone house or roadside café, there were few landmarks to break up the endless green of the evergreen trees, ferns and shrubs that lined the route. Occasionally she'd meet a car – sometimes with a windsurfer or dinghy strapped to the roof – or a camper van on a corner and they'd stop and negotiate around each other before continuing on their way. Each and every time, she was convinced she was going to lose a wing mirror, or plunge into the roadside ditch. Each and every time, the other driver seemed to have no such concerns and rushed around her, their wing mirror a whisker away from hers. It was terrifying. But she'd get used to it, she told herself. Driving on new roads was always a little fraught.

Finally, she passed a little black and white sign announcing the name of the village that was to become her new home. *Broussas.* Feeling her heart pound, she carried on, eyes taking in every detail. There were two houses immediately on her right – both newish builds painted in a peach colour a world away from the stone buildings that had otherwise dotted the route. She rounded a corner, wondering what she'd find next, but to her surprise, instead of more houses or some sort of village centre or a church or a shop, she found another sign announcing that she was now leaving the hamlet.

Surprised, she drove on until she found a sizeable muddy lay-by, turned around and headed back. She must have missed something. Sure enough, in a gap between the two houses there was the start of an even smaller road with a sign that said '*lac de*

Vassivière', the lake that was apparently walking distance from her new property. She turned and bumped down the road, passing more buildings as she approached the lake in earnest. A small pottery shop, a restaurant that seemed to be closed, a sign for a campsite and finally another two houses, partially hidden by the trees.

Instantly, she knew. The overgrown garden, the stone walls, the cherry tree – albeit now in leaf rather than blossom. The blue shutters, some open, some firmly closed. And to confirm it all, a handwritten sign that read '*Vendu*' – sold. This was it. This was her new home.

She pulled up outside,, bumping up the kerb slightly to ensure any other cars would be able to pass her and make their way to the lake. Then she got out of the driver's seat and looked at the property that had led her to leave her husband, and the country she'd grown up in to take a chance on a completely new start.

It was beautiful. Traditional stone walls, pointed with a beige mortar, a front garden that, while in desperate need of a trim, boasted roses, blackberry bushes, elderflower berries and what might or might not be grape vines towards the back. The front garden was walled, and a tiny metal gate – slightly open on its hinges – revealed a little path to the front door, almost entirely obscured by the foliage. Measured against some of the houses she had seen en route, it was small, but compared to the identikit houses on her estate at home, it was enormous – two storeys plus an attic that, according to the spec, was ripe for conversion. The advertised 3,000 square metre garden at the back was barely visible, and the little she could see was thick with brambles.

Next door, the house was similar in style, but in a better state of repair. The shutters were made from varnished wood, pinned neatly back against the walls. Each window had its own floral display just below the sill. The front garden was orderly, the path leading up to the front door a patchwork of stone. A cat sat on a small front terrace and, as she peered more closely, Lily could just make out that some of the back garden had been set up as an allotment, with vegetables planted in orderly rows – even what looked to be melons growing from the rich soil.

It was more remote than she'd thought – other than her soon-to-be neighbour's property, there were no other houses along the route. And she wasn't sure where the nearest *boulangerie* was, or where a market might be held in the tiny village, if at all. All things she might have researched had she taken more time, or consumed less wine. But as she breathed in and smelled the scent of myriad flowers and the surrounding trees, looked at the well-kept house of her new neighbour and took in the utter silence, she felt as if she'd made exactly the right choice.

She lifted up her mobile phone and took a snap, messaging Ty immediately. She wrote:

Look! New house.

Then, with slightly less confidence, she sent the same picture to Ben. She said:

House is beautiful.

Then, 'It's not too late,' she added, before deleting it.

Looking behind her, wondering exactly where she stood legally in terms of entering a property she'd promised to buy but hadn't yet signed for, she moved towards the gate and slipped through the gap. Stepping over thick, snake-like brambles and avoiding nettles and weeds, she made her way along the almost obscured path. Thorns snagged her T-shirt, and at one point in the epic five metre journey, she wondered whether she might end up trapped. But she managed to arrive at the front door somehow, hair in disarray and nursing nettle stings in at least two places, but triumphant, nonetheless.

Feeling a little like an intruder, she tried the handle of the front door. But it was locked. Which was good, she told herself. You didn't want any Tom, Dick or Harry – or perhaps Jean, Jacques et André – strolling in off the street.

Instead, she sidestepped carefully into the flowerbed, wincing slightly as she crushed plants under her feet but reminding herself that: (a) most of them were weeds and (b) this would soon be her garden to trample as she pleased. On tiptoe, she tried to peep through the open shutters of a ground floor window and glimpse the room inside, but it was just out of reach to her five foot four height. She looked around, desperate to see inside now she'd got this far, and found an abandoned metal watering can half buried in the undergrowth. After testing its strength slightly with her foot, she moved it under the window, gingerly stepped onto it and raised herself up, grabbing hold of the sill to hoist herself just a little...

'*Excusez-moi?*' said a voice.

She turned to look and, as she did, lost her footing and fell heavily onto a cushion of weeds and thorns and mud and what appeared to be broken bricks.

'Ow!' she yelled loudly, feeling her shin start to throb.

'*Je suis désolé, Madame!*' the voice called. '*Ça va?*'

She carefully got to her feet and looked in the direction of the voice. A man with short brown hair and a goatee beard, dressed in blue overalls and carrying a paper-wrapped *pain* under his arm – looking almost as if he had taken on the role of Random Frenchman in the movie of her life but was trying a little too hard

– was standing by the outer wall, looking at her with a mixture of concern and confusion.

'*Je suis...*' she said, feeling her face flush and wondering what the man must think having seen her peering into the window of an empty house, teetering on a rusty watering can. How exactly did she stand legally in doing this? Would he report her to the mayor? Surely the fact that she'd made an offer on the house would stand her in good stead during any court hearing?

Realising she'd been staring silently at the bemused man over the top of the tangled garden for at least two minutes, she tried to smile. '*Je suis désolé,*' she said, desperately reaching for enough French to explain the situation and failing miserably. '*Je suis... je suis anglaise...*'

'Ah, *Madame!*' said the man, then added in perfect English. 'You do not have to apologise for being English, eh!' He chuckled at his own joke. 'Although I quite understand, huh?'

Despite not exactly having the moral high ground in this situation, Lily felt a bit put out. Sure, she looked like she'd been breaking and entering, or at least spying or something, but she'd just fallen because of this man and here he was laughing at her language. Or her nationality. Or a combination of both.

'Very funny,' she said, attempting to wipe mud from her jeans and spreading it further in the process.

'Ah, but I am sorry!' he said. 'Are you all right, *Madame*?'

'Yes,' she said, 'thank you.'

'Zen can I esk,' he continued, 'what you are doing at zis 'ouse?'

'I'm just...' she said, then, tired of half-yelling over five metres of garden, she said, 'Just a minute,' and began to negotiate the pathway again.

This time the thorns seemed thicker, the nettles stingier, the stone under her feet more uneven and precarious. The fact that she was trying to move more quickly than before didn't help matters and she tripped a couple of times, ripped her now ruined T-shirt on a thorn and had an altercation with the biggest hornet she'd ever seen.

All the while, Random Frenchman stood and watched with twinkly amusement rather than trying to part some of the brambles for her, or give her a hand over the tangled mess towards the end.

She emerged feeling an odd mixture of guilty and angry, and half glared at him.

Seemingly immune to or unaware of her anger, he reached forward and gently pulled a twig from her hair. His brown hair was flecked with natural highlights from the sun when viewed up close; his eyes green and earnest and crinkled around the edges. As he leaned forward, she smelled a mixture of fresh bread, coffee, soap and aftershave. It was a heady cocktail.

'*Madame*,' he said, 'you realise zat thees is preevate property?' He smiled, curious rather than annoyed.

Despite still feeling a bit irritated at the fact he'd watched her struggle up the path, she found herself instinctively smiling in return.

'*Oui*, yes... I was just...'

'And I am afraid zat if you are interested in *la maison*, it's solds,' he said, shrugging as if fully giving in to the stereotype. All he needed was a beret to complete the picture.

'Yes, I know. I'm... in fact, it's sold to me. I was just...'

'To you? You are zee purchaser? Zee buyer?' he said, his eyes widening.

'Yes. I am... I'm going to sign the *compromis de vente* tomorrow, *demain*. I just thought...'

'You are Mrs Buttercup?'

'Butterworth. But... yes.'

'Zen I am very pleased to meet with you!' he said, placing his *pain* down on the wall, seemingly not worried about the grubbiness of the stone or the proliferation of insects. 'I am Frédérique – zee vendor.'

'Frédérique? You're the mayor, er, *le maire*?'

'*Oui, Madame*, at your service.'

9

Lily bit into the warm, buttery croissant and closed her eyes.

'Iz everything OK?' a voice asked. Chloé appeared at the side of the breakfast table, holding an espresso cup filled with strong black coffee.

Lily felt her cheeks flush slightly. 'Yes, yes, it's fine. It's just so... well, it's the dream, isn't it?'

'What iz?'

'Fresh croissants for breakfast, coffee on the terrace. I feel as if... well, I've just fantasised about this life for so long,' she said.

'You do not 'ave croissants in *Angleterre*? And *café*?'

Lily reddened, realising how ridiculous she might sound. 'We do,' she said. 'It's just... somehow it's not the same when you're eating them in the kitchen before work, instead of looking out over...' she gestured to the view that tumbled away from the B. & B.'s small terrace '... all this.'

Her host looked at the view and shrugged modestly. 'It iz OK, I suppose, eh!' She set the cup down next to Lily. 'Your coffee.'

'Thank you.' Lily eyed the tiny cup suspiciously. 'Do you have any milk?'

'You want milk?' Chloé looked surprised. 'But you said *un café*?'

'It doesn't matter,' Lily said, lifting the tiny cup to her lips and sipping the bitter liquid. 'Mmm, lovely.' She smiled, trying not to grimace. Next time she would remember to ask for *café crème*. Or perhaps tea.

Chloé was looking at her, amused. 'It iz too strong per'aps?'

'No, no, it's lovely. Thank you.'

She looked again over the view and thought about yesterday's encounter with Frédérique. It had been a bit embarrassing at first, but somehow his easy manner had meant she'd soon relaxed and stopped feeling a bit like a would-be burglar caught red-handed. Once they'd cleared up any misunderstanding, she'd explained that she had just been trying to take a little look inside. 'But I can come back wiv *les* keys?' he'd offered. 'I 'ave them all *chez moi* – at my 'ouse?'

In her usual fashion, she'd refused, not wanting to be any bother – then kicked herself for being so pathetic as soon as he'd left. She would have loved a look around. Still, the fact that he was so chilled out about it all suggested there weren't any nasty surprises lurking inside.

She was still the only guest at the small B. & B. and was beginning to feel as if she wasn't a guest at all, but just a woman who'd moved in with her glamorous friend, albeit for eighty euros a night. Last night, they'd enjoyed dinner at the same table – a three course feast prepared by Chloé, who'd behaved as if it was perfectly ordinary to enjoy duck à l'orange on a Monday evening. They'd chatted about the house, about Lily's appointment this morning. About Frédérique.

'Ah, be careful weeth that one, uh?' Chloé had said. 'I 'ave known 'im a long time.'

'Careful with Frédérique? Why?'

'You will see,' Chloé had said darkly, sipping her red wine.

'But isn't he the mayor?'

'Ha. He thinks he is the king, *non*?'

Lily hadn't mentioned the watering can incident, or the fact she'd been caught peeking through the windows. Chloé would *never* do something like that. She was far too elegant, too put-together. Lily had found herself trying to copy some of her mannerisms, correcting her posture when she was in Chloé's presence. She'd even slipped on her smartest trousers and blouse this morning in an attempt to summon her inner chic.

'Do you want me to come to 'elp you today?' Chloé asked now. 'For your *rendez-vous* wiv the lawyer?'

'Oh, thank you. No, I'll be fine.' She wasn't sure whether turning up with Chloé, who clearly had some sort of grudge against Frédérique, would be a good idea. Plus, the *notaire* had insisted she employ a translator as part of the transaction; so she'd be fine with the nitty-gritty.

Chloé shrugged. 'As you want.' She looked a little put out.

'I mean, it's really kind of you to offer. I'm sorry. I don't want you to think... I mean, it's so generous of you to... and I know my French isn't... well, great...' Lily trailed off, noticing that Chloé was looking at her, an eyebrow raised in amusement.

Lily couldn't operate her eyebrows individually. She resolved to start practising in the mirror. She tucked her wayward hair behind her ears and vowed, too, that she would find a local hairdresser in the next few days to cut it into a neater style. 'What's funny?' she asked at last.

'You Engleesh and your "I'm sorrys",' said Chloé with a smile. 'You do not 'ave to apologise to me. If you do not need my 'elp, it iz fine.'

'You're right. I'm sorry...' She felt herself blush. 'I mean...'

'It iz OK,' Chloé said. 'You do not 'ave to be sorry for being sorry, uh!' She smiled.

Lily suppressed the urge to apologise again, with some difficulty, and sipped from her coffee instead, this time ready when the thick, bitter liquid hit her mouth and managing to keep a neutral expression.

* * *

Half an hour later, she was in the car, a rudimentary map on the passenger seat and her GPS loaded with the *notaire*'s address. Only she was beginning to wonder whether she'd programmed it correctly. She seemed to be heading deeper and deeper into nowhere, and unless the *notaire* was actually a cow, or worked from a barn, she wasn't sure he could possibly have an office in such a rural and uninhabited location.

Just as she was about to give up – and her GPS had once again lost signal – the road opened up slightly and a cluster of stone houses appeared to her right. They curved around a small grassy area that looked a little like the shape on the map that Chloé had drawn. But Lily couldn't see anything that resembled an office among the ramshackle buildings, and, with no visible signposts, had no idea exactly where she was.

But relieved at least to see signs of human life rather than just bovine, she pulled up, determined to either find the place, ask for directions or simply turn back and give up. She clambered out of the car gratefully, feeling the cool morning air against her sweaty skin. Sadly, rather than being fresh, the air smelled strongly of cow, which was hardly surprising given that the field to her left was full of brown *Limousin* cattle, who walked up to the flimsy wire fence with interest and regarded her sadly over their wet, pink noses. 'Do *you* know where the *notaire* is?' she asked them and they looked at her solemnly.

Then she jumped, hearing laughter behind her.

Turning, she found Frédérique, who had appeared seemingly out of nowhere. For a moment, she didn't recognise him. He was dressed smartly in tailored trousers and a short-sleeved shirt, revealing – to her surprise – pretty impressive biceps previously invisible under his shapeless overalls. His brown hair was brushed and had clearly benefited from a little gel, and his beard seemed tidier than it had yesterday – perhaps he'd trimmed it? He flashed his annoyingly infectious smile at her again and, again, she found herself grinning in return.

'Oh! Hello!' she said. 'I mean, bonjour, I didn't... *vous êtes un surprise!*'

'*C'est* une *surprise,*' he corrected. 'Surprises, they are feminine.'

Seeing as he'd made her jump out of her skin twice in two days, and was unequivocally male, she wanted to dispute this. But she knew better than to argue with the strict rules of French grammar.

'Oh, *une surprise,*' she said. Then, 'What?' she asked as she saw his eyes still twinkling with amusement.

'It iz nothing. Just... *en* France we do not ask le cows for the directions,' he said, with amusement. 'Zey are not so good weeth the map reading, huh?'

'Very funny,' she said, feeling completely out of her depth. She wondered what this man – head of the police, top official of the local town – must think of her. First trespassing and now speaking to a herd of cattle. 'I was just...' She trailed off, unable to explain exactly what she *had* been doing. 'Is this the right place,' she said instead, 'for the *notaire*?'

'*Oui, c'est là,*' he said, gesturing to one of the houses.

By the ordinary-looking front door, she now noticed a tiny plaque, flashing gold in the sunlight. A business premises.

'Oh,' she said, feeling, as usual, on the back foot. She wanted to ask him where he'd come from and how he'd managed to appear out of nowhere on a seemingly deserted country road just seconds after she'd pulled up. But as he already thought she was either a criminal or completely mad, she decided to leave that particular question for another time.

They walked together over the half cobbled, half muddy ground and as they approached she could clearly see the lettering on the plaque which read:

M. Jean-Jaques Berger, Notaire

They pushed open the black-painted door to find themselves in what looked like an ordinary house and she was glad, then, that Frédérique was at her side. Without him, she'd have assumed she'd come to the wrong place, despite the plaque, and that she'd walked accidentally into someone's hallway.

Frédérique then opened a door to their left which revealed a small, cluttered room with a woman sitting at a desk. Its surface, the surrounding floor and several of the chairs that lined the room were covered in manila files and the room smelled suspiciously of cigarettes.

'*Bonjour, Florence!*' Frédérique beamed, and, seeing him, the woman stood up and held both of his hands as they kissed each other's cheeks.

He introduced Lily and the pair of them were directed to sit on two of the chairs, which spilled their foam filling through cracks in the leather. Minutes later, a man entered, clutching a backpack under his arm.

'*Bonjour,*' he said to Florence, then took his place on a chair next to Lily without being directed. 'Sorry I'm late,' he said to Lily. 'Always get lost around here. I'm Chris.' He put out his hand and she automatically extended hers for a shake.

'You're the...'

'The translator, yes,' he said. He placed his backpack heavily on the floor, then removed his glasses and cleaned them on a corner of his shirt. 'Sorry,' he said again, 'had another signing this morning already over in Eymoutiers, and barely made it.'

'Thanks for coming,' she said, not knowing what else to say. 'You're English?'

'Welsh.'

'Right. Well, nice to meet you.'

'You too,' he replied. Then, 'So, do you know what happens next?' he added in a low whisper.

'Not really,' she admitted.

'Well, there's a lot of legal jargon, of course. The *notaire* will see us in a minute and we'll read through all the paperwork. He'll go through a number of clauses, and I'll explain anything you don't understand. Then you'll sign...' He leaned his head close to hers as if imparting state secrets, his hair, fashioned in too spiky a style for his age, drooping in response to the additional gravity.

'And that's it? It's all done?' she asked, incredulous. It certainly seemed more straightforward than when they'd bought the house back home.

'Well, for now,' he said. 'Then there's the reports and the waiting, and you'll get another call in about two or three months for the completion. Less if you're lucky.'

She felt her heart somersault. 'The completion? So this is...?'

'This is the *compromis*. You're promising to buy. It's legally binding, subject to any clauses we insert. You'll pay the deposit, which, if you back out, will be lost I'm afraid.'

'But the house won't be mine?' she said, feeling goose bumps sprinkle her skin.

'No.' He looked at her with a mixture of confusion and amusement. 'Has nobody explained the process to you?'

'Well, it's all a bit... sudden, really,' she said. 'I just...' She couldn't for some reason tell this man that she'd bid on the house by mistake on eBay. 'I suppose it was a bit of an impulse purchase,' she finished weakly.

'It's—' But before he finished his sentence a door opened and a small man with dark hair and a well-groomed beard appeared in front of them.

He greeted Frédérique like an old friend and then turned to look at Lily. '*Madame* Butterworth?' he said, his brown eyes crinkling as he smiled.

'Yes,' she said, offering her hand for a shake. 'Nice to meet you.'

He looked at her hand for a moment as if confused then shook it briefly. '*Et Monsieur Chrees!*' he said, his face breaking into a wide smile as he looked at the translator. 'We meet again!'

Chris stood up and awkwardly exchanged air kisses with the *notaire* followed by a brief handshake with Frédérique.

Lily wondered at the need for a translator when everyone seemed to speak such good English, but didn't say anything. Surely it was better this way than trying to work out legalese in a foreign tongue, even if it was costing her €250.

Moments later, she was sitting in a chair in front of Jean-Jacques, half nodding off and half drowning in a sea of terminology, as Chris quietly translated by her side. Rights of way and boundaries and the location of the septic tank and the sheer amount of clauses made her head spin. According to one document, the house was rated 'D' on a scale of A to E for its environmental credentials. 'Is it not double-glazed?' she asked Chris, who was in the middle of telling her what modifications she might need to make.

'Well, no. Surely you noticed when you viewed?' he said, confused.

'I haven't actually... I mean, I've seen the outside, but...'

Chris looked genuinely surprised. 'You're signing for a property and haven't yet seen the inside?' he asked, concerned.

'Well, I've seen pictures... so...'

'Did the agent not...?'

'I'm not actually using an agent... it was... advertised online.' The ridiculousness of her situation made her blush again. What exactly was she *doing*?

Chris held up a single finger towards Jean-Jacques who obediently fell silent. *'Je suis désolé,'* he said to the *notaire. 'Un petit moment, s'il vous plaît.'* Then to Lily. 'Do you really want to sign the *compromis* without a proper viewing,' he said. 'It's legally binding, you know. And you have every right... We can view today and come back tomorrow. I'd really advise...'

Lily felt the eyes of the room on her. 'It's fine,' she said, feeling embarrassed. 'I've seen... I mean, I know it needs work...' She trailed off.

'If you're sure?' Chris asked. doubtfully.

'I am,' she said, feeling uncomfortable and slightly doubtful herself. Was she sure? Her stomach dipped slightly as she considered the risk she was taking. The property was cheap, but it was still a lot of money to spend on something sight unseen. In normal times she'd probably have stopped, taken a viewing, made sure.

It was just, she'd already left her husband – at least for now – crossed the Channel, committed in every way to a life in France. Signing a *compromis* seemed almost insignificant when she'd made a promise to herself that she'd see this through.

* * *

Eventually she was released back into the sunshine, her hand aching from initialling each page in a series of documents that she didn't completely understand, despite Chris's efforts. She wondered if this was how they kept the property market moving in France. Just literally kept talking to you about clauses until you'd sign anything just to escape?

Before she could say anything else, Chris appeared in front of her. 'Well, thank you,' he said. 'See you at the completion.'

'Yes,' she said. 'Thank you.'

'No questions before I rush off? I'm afraid I'm rather booked up today.'

'No, it's fine.' She smiled.

'OK. Well, nice to meet you,' he said. She noticed a line of sweat beading on his forehead. 'I'd better...'

'Yes, that's fine.'

'Right. Goodbye, then.' He disappeared, half running towards a Renault Clio before clambering inside, his too-tight trousers revealing a cheeky glimpse of buttock as he climbed into the driver's seat.

Left alone for a second, she suddenly felt quite tearful. The transaction, even with Frédérique green-lighting it through the local council, might take up to eight weeks or even more. Eight weeks in which she'd thought she'd be in the property, doing it up. Starting a new life. Eight weeks when instead she might find herself having to rent or stay with Chloé, which although wonderful would be expensive in the longer term.

It wasn't as if she could go home though, was it? She had every right to live in the house in the UK that had her name on the paperwork. But she couldn't make a dramatic exit then scuttle back for an eight-week wait. She'd have to find another way, if only to save her pride.

She had only been here a couple of days and already she'd started to feel as if the puzzle pieces of her life were falling into place. But suddenly, standing in the unfamiliar hamlet, fifteen miles from the B. & B., twenty from the property she'd committed to buy and at least five hundred from everything normal and familiar in her life, she felt suddenly and completely alone.

10

'Do you want me to come weeth you to see *la maison*?' Frédérique said, appearing beside her, an enormous set of keys jangling in his hand.

'Sorry?' she said, turning to face him and trying to smile. She could feel her mouth wobble slightly with emotion and hoped it wasn't too obvious that she was on the verge of tears.

He peered more closely at her, and for a moment she wondered whether she had a stray facial hair she needed to whip out with the tweezers. Then, 'Are you all right?' he asked, his brow furrowed with concern. '*Pleurez-vous*? You are... raining? Your eyes?'

'Oh. No. *Non, je suis... je suis bien*,' she said, forcing out even more of a smile. 'I am fine.'

'*Je* vais *bien*,' he corrected.

'Sorry?'

'It doesn't matter,' he said, shaking his head. 'Are you sure you are all right, *Madame Buttercup*?'

She didn't bother to correct him. 'Yes, yes, I'm fine. *Bien*. I just... buying the house, doing all this. It's a bit overwhelming.'

'Ov-er-whel-ming?' he said, slowly.

'Oh. Um, it's... *c'est trop pour moi... um... parfois,*' she said, desperately reaching for the right words. *It's too much.*

He nodded. 'The new 'ouse? It eez... you are scared?'

'Yes. Scared. Sort of, anyway. It's just, I'm on my own and... well, it seems...'

'Do you want not to buy it, per'aps?' he said, putting a hand on her arm. She looked up and saw his eyes clouded with concern. 'It eez not too late. The *notaire*, Monsieur Berger, 'e iz *mon ami*, my friend? If you have made a mistake, we can rip.' He mimed ripping up paperwork. 'The ink is not dry, huh?' He smiled. 'It eez not a *problème.*'

'No, no. It's not that,' she said, shaking her head and looking away. It was something about his smile – the friendliness and openness of it – seeing someone smile at her like that when she felt so alone might actually break her. 'I want the house, it's just...' She trailed off. How much detail of her life did she actually want to share with this stranger? She decided to keep any thoughts about Ben close to her chest, but said: 'I suppose I was hoping I would be able to live there now; I didn't realise it would take so long for it to be mine.'

He nodded, understanding. 'But you can move in, eh?' he said. 'There izz no one living in de 'ouse. It izz empty!'

'But it isn't mine? I haven't... the paperwork.'

He shrugged. 'In France, it 'appen sometimes. You can move in, if you want? After all, I am zee owner and I say it's OK!' he said, smiling. 'You can start today, if you want? The water, he is still turned on. And I can telephone for the électricité if you want?'

'Oh! Thank you,' she said, not sure how comfortable she felt with the idea, but grateful for the offer nonetheless. 'Are you sure that's all right? I mean, legally?'

'*Mais oui!*' he said. 'I am the *maire*, yes! I am – ow you say – the law.'

'Like Judge Dredd?'

'Who?'

'Never mind.' She smiled and saw his mouth turn up at the corners reciprocally. 'Just... well, thank you. I might do that. If you're sure.'

He held out the enormous set of keys. 'You can take zem now,' he said. 'But if you want I can come weeth you to 'av a proper look? Per'aps save you from *le jungle*, eh! There are no tigers, but maybe a wild boar, or *un chat*, huh?' He mimed an animal peeping over long grass. 'Maybe it is not safe for you!'

She grinned. 'Thank you,' she said, taking the keys. 'If it's OK though, I think I'd like to have a look by myself. 'Um... *par moi-même.*'

He nodded, understanding. 'But if you are sure,' he said. 'And I am sorry for *le jardin*. It is not in a good state, eh? But the plants they grow too fast *en été*, um, in le summer. And the 'ouse, it has been on sales for many years. I forget for a month or more and poof! *Le jardin devient une forêt!*'

'Yes, *j'imagine*,' she said, worried at the fact that apparently, there had been no other interest in the property. Which didn't bode well. But then, renovation projects weren't for everyone, she reassured herself.

'But, I can 'elp, yes?' he continued. 'My friend, he is a farmer. He can come wiv eez *tondeuse* – the machine for le grass cutting, yes? He will come and you will 'ave no more jungle, huh?' He smiled, mimicking someone chopping down excess foliage with a scythe. Or at least, that's what she decided he was doing, after feeling slightly confused at his dance-like movements.

'Thank you,' she said.

'*De rien*, it iz nothing,' he said, with yet another upward lift of his shoulders. 'It is *normale*. I weel speak to 'im today and tell you when he come.'

'Thank you. And I can pay, of course. I have... it's no problem.'

He shook his head. 'No, it is good.'

'Well, thank you.'

'And don't worry. It iz a good house, yes? It was my grand-mother's.'

'Oh. I'm sorry, I...'

'No, she is still 'ere,' he said. 'She is not died. Just... she go to an 'ome.'

'Right.'

'And it iz not... this was 'er second property,' he clarified. 'She live in Toulouse, but when she come to see uz, she stay in de house.'

'Ah, right.'

'She does not come for many, many years now. Her 'ealth is not good. So, the 'ouse... it is crying... It – how you say – needs some 'elp to be better? And then since three years she ask me to sell it for 'er. But it is not easy. Then I try *l'internet* and 'ere you are. Someone to give the 'ouse a new life, eh? I tell my grand-mother and she iz very 'appy.'

'Well, that's good,' she said. 'I'm glad.'

He nodded at her. 'I 'ope you will like it,' he said. 'It is not perfect, huh? But the price, it is good.'

'Yes.' She nodded. 'Yes, very good.'

'I will go to work now, but if you need... my number iz 'ere.' He pulled a piece of paper from his pocket and scribbled down a mobile number. 'You call, yes? If there is a *un problème*?' That smile again.

'*Merci, oui,*' she replied, then carefully added: '*Si j'ai une problème...*' If I have a problem.

'*Un problème,*' he corrected. 'Problems, they are male, yes?'

She smiled. 'OK.' At least, she thought, the French had got that one right.

'And *les solutions*, in French they are female,' he said, smiling.

She laughed. 'Well, not always,' she said.

They stood for a minute in companionable silence, which suddenly became awkward. She jangled the keys purposefully. 'Well,' she said. 'I'd better be... you know.'

'OK, *Madame Buttercup*.'

'It's Lily.'

'OK, Lilee. I weel see you later. And call me, yes? For any *problèmes* you need?'

'I will.'

* * *

It took twenty-five minutes and two wrong turns to find her way to *Broussas* again. Once in the small hamlet, she quickly found the house that she'd just deposited her redundancy money on. She'd have to clear her savings account to cover the rest of the cost; the remainder of the small inheritance her mum had left when she'd passed. 'Well, I hope it's going to be money well spent, Mum,' she said quietly as she pulled up in front of the house and looked again at its overgrown garden.

Not for the first time in the eight years since her mum had died, she wished she could pick up the phone and get some advice. Mum wouldn't have had much to say about France – she'd been a homebody like Ben and had never felt the urge to up sticks and move somewhere completely different. But she would have known what to say in the moment, how to bring Lily's determination to the fore.

She thought about calling David – but a quick check of her watch and a mental calculation put paid to that idea. It would be early evening in Australia and her brother would be busy putting the twins to bed. They rarely called each other; she didn't have the right to ring for advice out of the blue during the busiest time of his day.

And, of course, she no longer had Ben to talk to.

She sat for a moment, looking through the windscreen at the pair of stone cottages. The day had become unseasonably cloudy, and the location looked less appealing under shadow. She wondered, suddenly, what it would be like in November, and January. She'd only ever really pictured it in the summer.

But, she thought, unclicking her seat belt, sitting here feeling sorry for herself was not going to help matters. This – or a version of it at least – had been her dream for over half her life. She owed it to herself to see it through for better or worse.

She climbed out of the driver's seat, clutching the set of keys – there were about twenty of them, all different sizes and she wondered whether they were all still relevant. Or whether, in fact, Frédérique had given her the wrong set and this ridiculous bunch fitted the locks at the local church or town hall or something.

She brandished them before her as she tackled the overgrown path – slightly easier this time after the partial gaps cleared by her venturing down there yesterday. Still, she ended up with more than her fair share of stings and leaf stain by the time she reached the front door. *Her* front door.

Then, swallowing hard, she put the key in the lock.

Five minutes later, she was still at the front door, sweating and swearing as she rotated the set of keys again and selected another candidate. 'Come on,' she said, shoving it into the lock; more like the lock on a prison door than a house, she thought. But finally, it slid into place and turned and suddenly she was able to push the heavy wooden door forward and step into the house for the very first time.

* * *

Ten minutes later, she was leaning against a wooden dresser in the kitchen, phone clamped to her ear.

'How's it going?' Emily said, cutting to the chase.

'I'm not sure, actually,' she said, her voice thick with tears once again. The phone felt sticky against her hot face.

'What's up, Lily? Has something happened?'

'It's... well, I've signed for the house,' she said with an enormous sniff. 'Paid the deposit and everything.'

'Right?'

'And now... I mean, I'm in it for the first time... and...'

'What's wrong?'

'Oh, nothing. Well, everything. I don't know... *des problèmes*...' she said.

'Lily, you're not making sense,' said her friend. 'What's the matter?'

She explained to Emily how she'd walked through the house noticing dangling wires and peeling wallpaper, smelling the damp and neglect and forlorn emptiness. How the parquet floors that had shimmered in the online photographs were scuffed and in need of polishing when inspected close up. How the kitchen simply consisted of a dresser and an enormous porcelain sink that was chipped and contained a pool of rust-coloured water. How she hadn't been able to set foot in the back garden for fear of getting lost in the tangle of brambles and weeds. 'Some of them are about six foot tall,' she said. 'How am I meant to even begin to tackle that?'

Upstairs, she'd found one old, tired metal bedstead that looked like an ancient (possibly haunted) relic, and three empty rooms, each of which needed more than a little TLC to make them passable. The windows were old, and several panels were damaged or cracked.

'So it's a shithole?' Emily said. 'You've bought a dud, is that it? Because I'm sure we can... there must be recourse, even if you have paid a deposit... there must...'

'No, it's not that,' she said. Because despite the musty wallpaper and dangling wires and curiously plumbed in toilet, the cracked windowpanes, missing roof tiles, scuffed wooden floors and pretty much absent kitchen, she was utterly in love with the place – or the place it *could* be, given a little time, money and elbow grease. She'd *expected* renovations, plumbing issues, faulty shutters. And she was able to look through these problems, to see the house underneath that could be stripped and repaired and polished and refitted and brought back to life.

It was all doable.

'Actually, it's beautiful... I mean, it's not a château, and it's certainly only just habitable, if that, at the moment,' she said. 'But I'm not completely insane...'

'Well, that's debatable.'

'Hey! Well, I'm not. I'm not crazy enough to believe that you can snap up a house for forty k and discover it's a fully renovated dream home. I've bought a shell. But it's a good shell. I mean, there are parquet floors. Real parquet floors, Emily!'

'That's... very impressive.'

'It's just...' She sniffed loudly. 'Standing here, I can see everything that needs to be done, I can see just how beautiful the place will be when the work's complete.'

'Right...'

'I can even imagine what it's going to be like living here in the interim. I mean, not perfect, right? But doable. Even an adventure if I look at it in the right way.'

'The right way being after several glasses of rosé?'

'Ha. Well, yes.'

'So what exactly is the problem?' her friend asked, an edge of impatience creeping into her voice. 'Don't tell me you've got a rat infestation? Or squatters? Or, I don't know, the place is balanced on the edge of a cliff or something?'

'None of that. It's... I mean, it could be – will be – great. I just didn't... I don't know how I'm going to even begin to do it all by myself. Whenever I imagined starting again, having an adventure, it was with Ben. Encountering problems together. Working out what to do together. Here on my own, well, I just feel completely... stuck. Alone. As if I've bitten off more than I can chew in every possible way.'

'Oh sweetheart...'

'It's like I've stepped into a dream, just I've left part of it behind.'

'Oh Lily...'

'And I know I'll get myself together and start, well, to *tackle* everything. But right now I'm just completely alone.'

'Bullshit,' Emily said decisively.

'What?'

'You, my darling, are *not* alone. At least you won't be for more than another day or so...'

'No?'

'No. I was going to tell you tomorrow, but I've persuaded Chris that he can actually manage to pick up a bit of dog shit for a couple of days, and that try as the boys might, he won't actually get licked to death.'

'And...?'

'And I'm coming.'

'Oh!'

'Yep. Flight booked, suitcase almost packed. Husband pacified. Job... well, they owe me about a month's worth of leave so they basically don't have a leg to stand on.'

'Thank you,' Lily said, feeling tearful again, but this time with relief.

'Yes. So you can dry up those tears, dust off that parquet and buy an inflatable mattress. I'm on my way.'

'Thank you,' Lily said again. 'I really appreciate it, you know.'

'Hey, what are friends for? I'll ping over the flight details if it's OK to pick me up?'

'Of course!'

'And Lily?'

'Yes?'

'For god's sake buy in a case of vino. Emily is *en route*!'

11

'Well,' he said, 'what do you think?'

'What do you mean, what do I think?'

'Which one would you like?' he asked again, colouring slightly.

She looked at the jeweller's window he'd stopped in front of. 'Are you serious?'

'Yes. Pick one. Go on!' His face broke into a smile and he nodded at the window. 'Within reason, obviously.'

'Ben Butterworth, are you saying you want to marry me?'

He laughed. 'As if you didn't already know.'

Later, she'd have fun regaling friends and family with his lacklustre, unromantic proposal. But right then, she couldn't have asked for anything more.

* * *

At first, on waking, she wondered where she was. Her back ached and her limbs felt heavy and unrested. Turning over, she could feel the mattress beneath her sink onto a hard surface below. As her eyes adjusted to the gloom, she remembered. She was on an airbed on the floor of the largest bedroom in her new house.

The sun streamed through gaps in the shutters and shot across the room onto the back wall – highlighting air that was thick with dust particles. Outside, she could hear the cheering sound of birdsong and the rumble of a car or two on a distant road.

It hadn't been a restful night. As evening had come on and the area around the house had fallen into silence, she'd suddenly felt more aware of her isolation; of the fact that she was alone in an unfamiliar house in the middle of nowhere. Darkness had set in by the time she'd pumped the mattress – purchased quickly from the supermarket where she'd driven to buy a few provisions yesterday afternoon – and as she'd settled down to try to sleep, she'd felt as if she was seven years old again and afraid of the dark.

With no other furniture, her bags sat in the corner of the room, spilling their contents onto the dusty floor. She'd collected them from Chloé's but hadn't had the energy to do much more than rifle through for the few bits she needed.

She'd never lived alone. Sure, she'd had her own small room in uni halls when she was eighteen, but it was on a corridor filled with similar rooms, each with its own occupant. Nights had been filled with the sound of voices passing on the street outside, the purr of traffic, drunken students stumbling back to bed after a night out. She'd known that if she'd opened her door at any time, there would have been someone within easy reach.

Then she'd lived with Mum for a while, before moving in with Ben. A few years later, Ty had come along and filled any empty spaces with noise and activity and a variety of different smells – some good, some not-so-much.

Now, entirely alone in a place where passers-by were rare and genuine silence fell once local residents went to bed, she'd realised what it was to be isolated, what darkness – unpolluted with the constant flicker of streetlights – really looked like. It had fallen across the house like a blanket over a birdcage at around 11 p.m. and she'd felt suddenly as if she might be the only person left in the world.

Some of her fear had melted away when she'd stepped outside to deposit a rubbish bag on the front step, in an attempt to rid the kitchen of its stench. She'd glanced up, then stared, her mouth open like a caricature. The stars – distant flickers in the night sky back home – were bright and close and enormous and magical. There were thousands of them, their glow uninterrupted by light pollution, making them seem both beautiful and alien. They'd shed a dull light onto the scene and somehow made her feel that, despite being alone, she was part of an incredible universe. That she could do anything.

She'd stood for a minute, rubbish bag in hand, and gazed upwards, drinking in the unfamiliar sight. And realising that when humans are removed from the equation nature is able to step into the breach and show itself fully.

It had been somehow reassuring.

The thought of the stars, the evenings she might spend gazing upwards in wonder, had faded again later as she'd laid on her uncomfortable mattress under a thin blanket and willed sleep to come. The house had settled as the temperature had dropped, each creak or click making her hyper-aware. Childhood fears of monsters and ghosts she'd thought she'd left behind had resurfaced, and it had taken every ounce of rationality she had left to ignore the urge to get up and switch on the light; to get in her car and seek out safety. The door was locked, she'd reminded herself as she'd closed her eyes.

Sleep had finally come, to her relief. But now, lying in the semi-darkness she wondered whether she'd benefited at all from the rest. Everything ached, from her head down to her feet. Her back was sore and every time she turned, her elbow would sink into the half-deflated bed and bang the wooden floor beneath.

She sat up, then gingerly stood, stretching out her limbs and feeling her muscles ache with relief. One thing was for sure, if she was going to stay in the house while the transaction went through, she was going to have to invest in a decent bed.

She'd managed a rudimentary wash in what passed for an upstairs bathroom last night. The water had been cold and slightly rust-coloured, but she'd quickly flicked herself over with a flannel, trying not to think of the hot shower and fluffy towels that were waiting in Chloé's perfect bed and breakfast. 'I 'ave not so many bookings this year...' her new friend had shrugged when Lily had told her she planned to move into the house early 'so if you want to come back, it is possible, yes?'

'Oh, thank you,' she'd said, quite positive that she wouldn't need to take Chloé up on her offer.

Now she wasn't so sure.

Her phone, plugged in to a two-pin socket courtesy of her one and only travel plug, showed a message and she opened it up with a smile.

House looks cool. Miss you. Ty.

It was short but, by his teenage standards, heartfelt.

Come and visit whenever you can!

She replied.

There was no message from Ben, although she could see from

the blue tick next to her photo that he'd seen the picture she'd sent.

Dropping her phone on the mattress, she pulled on her jeans and a T-shirt, socks and shoes and walked down to the dusty kitchen. The box with some of her provisions was on the counter – packing it away into cupboards peppered with ancient mouse droppings had not seemed like a good idea – and she poured some cornflakes and milk into the cereal bowl she'd bought, which still had a stubborn label on the underside. Leaning against the counter and looking out at the ragged mess of the back garden – still somehow beautiful in the morning sunlight – she resolved that while today she'd crunch down this British breakfast on the go, by tomorrow she'd have located the *boulangerie* and would go all out on crusty *pain*, *croissants* and bitter black *café*.

Suddenly, some movement in the long grass caught her eye, perhaps a cat was stalking through the garden, or a large bird was flapping its wings amongst the stray branches? She put down her bowl and stood on tiptoe at the window, looking out, but could see nothing except the endless green overgrowth stretching away.

When the back door creaked, she let out an involuntary cry. Had she left it off the catch last night? She watched, frozen to the spot, as it continued to groan, praying it was a stray cat rather than a feral Frenchman intent on robbery. Not that there was anything to rob, she thought, desperately. Unless he had a particular penchant for cornflakes.

To her relief, in what seemed like minutes but was probably only seconds, the door opened enough for her to see the reason for the creaking. A small woman was standing there, holding what appeared to be a plastic bag.

'*Bonjour!*' said the woman, stepping past her as if walking into a stranger's kitchen was completely normal.

'*Bonjour,*' Lily replied, desperately trying to find the words, *Who the feck are you and what are you doing in my house?* in French, but finding she was unable to locate them in her brain. Instead she went for an unsatisfying: '*Comment vous appelez-vous?*' What are you called?

'Bonjour,' the woman said again, '*je suis votre voisin,*'ermione.'

Her neighbour. Lily knew there was a woman living next door, but hadn't glimpsed her so far. She tried desperately to think of something to say. 'Ah! *Une belle nom. Comme* Harry Potter!' she said, at last.

The woman looked confused. '*C'est* 'er-mion-e,' she said slowly.

'*Oui,* Hermione, you know – like from le Harry Potter?' Lily said. 'Oh, for heaven's sake!' she continued, doing her best Hermione impression. 'Um... expellimarus! Um... J.K. Rowling...' She trailed off.

The woman regarded her with a confused stare. '*Je ne comprends pas, Madame,*' she said, sadly. Her hair was short and tousled and a big, army-green wax jacket enveloped a body that could have been any size under its enormous folds.

'*Désolé,*' said Lily, feeling like a complete idiot. '*Je m'appelle* Lily.'

The woman nodded; her face serious.

'*Je suis anglaise,*' Lily felt the need to add, with an apologetic grimace. I am English; sorry about that.

'*Oui, oui,*' the woman replied without smiling, stepping unceremoniously across her kitchen in wellies that were almost certainly covered with chicken poo. '*J'ai un petit cadeau pour vous!*' She finally smiled, revealing a set of coffee-stained teeth. She held the plastic bag, bulging with something, up as proof.

'A present?' Lily said. 'Oh, thank you!'

She watched as the woman rummaged in the bag, finally

pulling out what appeared to be a glass bottle filled with cloudy urine. '*Jus de pomme,*' the woman said, grinning and nodding enthusiastically.

'Oh, lovely. Did you... is that yours?' Lily said, holding up the too-brown liquid.

The woman looked at her in confusion and Lily felt embarrassed to have fallen into the all-too-British trap of assuming that everyone could understand your language if you spoke loudly and slowly enough. '*Vous l'avez fait?*' she said. You made this?

The woman nodded, then returned to the plastic bag, this time producing something that looked at first glance like an old white rag, but actually – to Lily's horror – turned out to be a chicken, fully feathered, muddy footed and completely and utterly lifeless. Its head hung limply to one side, eye open, regarding Lily with a fixed stare.

'*Pour le pot!*' Hermione said, brandishing it towards Lily's face. The chicken dangled, silently, just inches from Lily's nose. Hermione mimed putting it into a saucepan, then did a chef's kiss on her fingers. '*C'est délicieux.*'

'Oh, thank you... but I'm not sure...' said Lily, resisting the urge to back away. 'I mean, *merci beaucoup, mais...*' She paused. What was she going to say? That she didn't eat meat? Because that was absolutely not true. She could chow down a Sunday roast with the best of them, and never said no to a chicken korma.

What she objected to, it seemed, was having a dead, unplucked bird wobbling in her face. But why? Because it made her feel squeamish? Because she couldn't bear to eat it because it actually looked like a living creature? She was so divorced from what she ate, all packed neatly into supermarket plastic, that when confronted with reality she felt complete revulsion. This chicken, God rest its tiny soul, had probably had a better life than half the shrink-wrapped organic chicken breasts she picked up from the chilled aisle. She looked deep into its eye, and couldn't help but feel judged.

With few neighbours nearby, it was important to get off to a good start with this one. Her heart thundering, she gingerly took hold of the chicken's soft, feathered neck. Hermione released her grip and the full weight of the bird swung in Lily's hold. Trying not to gag, Lily laid it quickly on the kitchen counter. Almost unbearably it was still warm – her neighbour must have snapped its neck on the way over. '*Merci, Madame.*' She smiled. '*Vous êtes tres gentille.*' You're very kind.

'*C'est vraiment frais!*' the woman said.

'You can say that again.'

The woman stood and smiled at her for a moment.

'Um, *voulez-vous un café?*' Lily asked.

'*Non, merci,*' said her neighbour, still standing there.

'*Un thé peut-être?*' *Maybe you want a tea?*

'*Non.*' The woman abruptly turned to go. '*À plus tard!*' See you later. She lifted her hand in a wave without looking round and disappeared back into the foliage.

'OK, a... *oui, à plus tard,*' Lily replied, feeling slightly sick. Hopefully the woman wasn't going to come over for dinner and help her polish off the poor chicken. She was quite willing to accept that when it came to meat eating she was a hypocrite, but admitting you had a problem and actually plucking a chicken were two very different things.

Just as she was wondering whether she could get away with sweeping the bird into a bin bag and depositing it in the street-side bin without being spotted and causing terrible offence, there was a knock at the front door.

Tentatively, hoping it wouldn't be yet another neighbour

waving a dead animal or a jar of pee in her face, she moved forward to open it.

Outside, she was greeted by the smiling face of Chloé, who stood – miraculously immaculate in a white trouser suit and red scarf, despite having somehow negotiated the weed-infested path – with a gift bag.

'Bonjour,' said her former host, holding the bag. '*Félicitations!*'

'*Merci beaucoup*,' Lily said, her face breaking into a genuine smile at seeing someone familiar. 'Come in.'

'Thank you,' Chloé said, stepping into the hallway, her eyes scanning the dusty floor, faded wallpaper and hanging wires. 'I cannot stay, but I want to bring you thees gift, for your moving in – 'ow you say, 'ouse 'eating, yes?'

Lily didn't correct her, partly because she would have felt like a hypocrite – Chloé's English put her French to shame – but also because she quite enjoyed the little nuances and mispronunciations Chloé came out with. Plus, she loved the idea of calling it a house heating rather than housewarming. Especially as this particular house didn't seem to have any decent heating at all.

Chloé held out the gift bag that contained the unmistakable weight of a bottle of wine. Now *this* was more like it. '*Merci!*' Lily said, accepting the bag and walking through to the kitchen to put it on the dresser.

'*C'est votre poulet?*' asked Chloé, noticing the dead bird on the side and looking completely unfazed. 'It's yours?'

'My *voisin*, my neighbour gave it to me. *Un cadeau*,' Lily replied, unable to disguise the slight turn up of her lip.

Chloé laughed. '*Quel est le problème?* You are not *végétarienne?*'

'*Non, non*, it's not that. It's just...' Lily felt suddenly embarrassed. 'I haven't, I don't know how... I don't think I can...'

'Ah, you do not know what to do weeth it?' Chloé said, picking up the bird as if it wasn't a newly dead, feathered murder victim, but a simple kitchen ingredient. 'It is a big bird, no? You want that I 'elp?'

Lily paused. She wasn't sure she wanted a tutorial in chicken plucking. Now or ever. Perhaps becoming a vegetarian might be a good option. 'I'm not sure I can...'

Chloé laughed, seemingly reading all of this information on Lily's face. 'Then you want that I take him? And cook him for you?'

'Would you?' Lily coloured. 'I just... I can't...'

'It iz not a *problème*. I will cook 'im and we will eat 'im tomorrow, if that work for you. I 'ave guest tonight but tomorrow, *un pot-au-feu!*'

When Chloé had gone, somehow sauntering up the tangled and hazardous garden path in her heels and fitted suit, bloodied chicken dangling at her side and still managing to look enviably chic, Lily realised she was smiling. She'd only been in the country a few days, but had already met someone who'd become a friend. Plus, she'd met and conversed with the *maire*. Plus, she seemed to have a nice – if a little rustic – neighbour.

Yesterday in the *notaire*, she'd felt as if she might have made a terrible error.

Yet now, just for a moment, she felt a flicker of recognition. As if somewhere inside she sensed that this strange, rural corner of France could indeed become her home.

As if on cue, her phone beeped. When she saw the name Ben, her heart turned over.

Ben:

Looks nice. Come home. I miss you.

She felt a pang: but reminded herself that, once again, Ben

seemed just to be asking her to do what *he* wanted, without considering her.

Come here, she typed. But deleted her words.

I can't,

she wrote instead.

There was no answer.

12

What was it about Emily? Lily wondered as she began trying to cut tough-stalked weeds with a pair of shears she'd acquired at the supermarket. She absolutely couldn't wait to see her friend, knew that having someone here would cheer her up; she knew that Emily was coming with the best of intentions – to be supportive, to help make her feel more settled.

But when she cast a critical eye over her property, imagined *Emily* being here, looking at the dusty rooms and the wallpaper and the kitchen; taking in the garden, or the tangled overgrowth that passed for one, Lily felt a sense of rising panic.

Emily was not one to hold back an opinion. And Lily couldn't help but worry that the scathing remarks she'd probably make about the state of the house and garden – humorously, and well meant – would shatter the romantic haze she'd managed to create whenever she looked at anything negative in the place.

She'd spent so long fantasising about what life in France would look like, she could see past the wreck that the property had become through years of neglect and visualise what it could become with a little money and a lot of work. In all honesty, it was this ability to visualise, to dream, that was keeping her sane; that was keeping her from panicking that she'd made a terrible mistake.

With Emily's flight arriving this afternoon, she had no hope of carrying out the full renovation the house would need before it passed muster with her lovable but opinionated friend. But she'd decided to at least clear the path at the front so that Emily could make it to the door unscathed... and, hopefully, unscathing.

After an hour of being stung, of jumping whenever the loud buzz of an insect got too close to her ear, and swearing at the shears, the weeds and anything else that got in her way, the path was at least visible through the overhanging shrubbery.

The final few brambles close to the gate were thick and, rather than clip them neatly, the shears seemed just to break the surface bark but barely dent their tangled, stringy green interior. Lily tried again, and once again the bramble resisted. 'Come on,' she hissed at the unyielding stalk. The shears slid slightly to the side, and closed around the tendril, pinching it between the blades but barely making a mark.

She just wanted to finish. To actually achieve something.

'Come. On. You. Stubborn. Bastard,' she hissed, opening and closing the shears against the resistant stem with each coughed out word.

Then, suddenly, she heard laughter.

Slowly turning, she saw a man standing behind the wall, looking down at her as she waged war on the stubborn tendril. She felt her face get hot, and stood up, brushing bits of bark and grass and weed and plant from her jeans.

Why, when anything was going wrong in her life, did she have to endure the additional shame of being laughed at by a random stranger?

For once, at least, it wasn't Frédérique.

The man was tall, with dark brown eyes and brown hair that sprung from his head in curls. He was casually dressed in khaki trousers and a jumper. As she rose, enough to see over the small wall, she realised he was holding a lead, which led to a small, brown dog that was sniffing the lower half of the wall and depositing little drops of pee while it waited patiently for its owner.

She glared at the man, affronted that this stranger could literally stand and laugh at someone he'd never met, when she was clearly having a terrible time trying to tame this beast of a garden. '*Qu'est-ce que c'est?*' she asked, haughtily. What is it?

Rather than looking abashed, he grinned widely, clearly finding her French, or her accent, or something else about her, highly amusing. She felt her nostrils flare. '*Vous riez!*' she said. '*Pourquoi?*' Why are you laughing?' She longed, suddenly, to be in England – speaking her native language. Then she'd know how to be cutting, yet non-aggressive, to make it clear that she was angry, without resorting to name-calling or violence. She would be able to send him on his way chastised but not angry or insulted.

Here, she was left with no choice but to ask him why he was laughing.

'You are Lily, yes?' he asked. 'I am Claude, a friend of Frédérique.'

'Oh,' she said, feeling less inclined to be angry. 'Hello.'

'I am sorry to laugh like thees. But to see you curse at that plant, it – how you say? – tickles me.'

'Yes, well,' she said, still not feeling entirely Zen. 'It's hard work.'

He laughed again. 'Yes, it iz le hard work with a pair of *ciseaux*, er – how you say? – skissers.'

'Scissors?'

'Yes.'

'These are gardening shears.'

'Yes, they are shears, *cisailles de jardinage*, I see that. And per'aps in your English gardens, they are the right solution, yes? But 'ere in *Limousin*, they are no better than *ciseaux*. Things in Limousin, they grow, *oui*? They are tough, like the *Limousin* men.' He gave her a wink and flexed an admittedly sturdy bicep – she wasn't sure whether he was making a joke or starting to flirt.

'Oh,' she said, looking at the small space she'd hacked into the weeds over the course of an hour. She suddenly felt completely exhausted. 'It's just,' she said, 'my friend is coming and I want it to look...' She felt tears prick in her eyes and blinked them away. What was it with all this crying recently? She was tired, that was all.

'I do not mean to be cruel, eh!' Claude continued, his brow furrowed with concern. 'I – how you say – I would like to 'elp you, if you want?'

'No, it's OK,' she said stubbornly. 'I'll manage.'

He laughed. '*Madame*,' he said, 'you can curse at *ces plantes* all you wish, but I am afraid they do not speak English!'

She looked at him, aiming for a glare, but found that when their eyes met, she smiled instead – a reluctant smile, the sort a child uses when he's determined to stay cross, but can't quite manage it. 'Well, what would you suggest?' she said. 'And it's Lily,' she added, a little annoyed that he'd gone straight for the *Madame*. It made her feel ancient. Then again, playing the *Mademoiselle* card would have embarrassed them both.

'Sorry, I no understand "suggest"? You want to know what would I do?' he queried.

'Yes, what would you do, *Claude*?'

He grinned. 'I can come later, if you like. I 'ave a tractor. I am – how you say? – *un agriculteur*, a... a...'

'A farmer?'

'Yes, a farming. I can come wiv my *tracteur* if you want. Frédérique, 'e tell me you might need some 'elp and 'e waz not wrong, uh?'

She imagined tossing the shears aside and watching as a tractor with a cutting attachment mowed down the stubborn brambles front and back. She thought about how she had been intending to buy a strimmer to hack through the undergrowth. She thought about the ache in her arms just from clearing the tiny path.

'That,' she said, 'would be amazing! Thank you!'

'*De rien*, it iz nothing,' he said, as if literally saving her life, or garden at least, was the most natural thing in the world.

'And I can pay of course,' she said. 'How much?'

He shook his head. 'We are *amis*, friends now,' he said. 'We do not charge for our friends, I think?'

'Well, thank you,' she said.

'Then as we are friends, you must forgive me for laughing?' he said, his eyes twinkling.

She nodded.

Moments later, she experienced a sudden jolt after realising she'd been lost in thought, while looking at his eyes that seemed to flicker hazel in a certain light. 'Well,' she said abruptly. 'I'd better get on.'

'Yes, you 'ave to tackle that terrible *plante*, oui?'

'Not any more!' she said.

'Well, I will get this little *Madame* back 'ome, I think,' he said, rattling the lead slightly and receiving a bark for his trouble. '*À tout à l'heure* – see you later.'

'*À tout à l'heure*,' she replied.

* * *

An hour later she was driving the long, field-flanked road to Limoges. She'd finally managed to find a radio station that played recognisable music without too much incomprehensible – to her at least – chatter, and sang along with bits of the hits she recognised. She'd been tempted to link up her mobile and stream one of her playlists – perhaps 'upbeat' or 'summer tracks' – but seeing as she'd yet to sort out a French mobile contract, she'd decided for once to be sensible and stick to something that wasn't going to put her into her overdraft.

When she'd visualised moving to France, she'd definitely glossed over the admin side of things. As well as the bureaucratic nightmare that would come with applying to stay here full-time, moving house and countries simultaneously had thrown up a great deal of additional paperwork. Or online form-filling work, if you were being entirely accurate.

For a start, she didn't yet have the internet. In fact, she wasn't sure whether she'd be entitled to install internet at the house until she'd actually signed the final completion papers. She'd yet to speak to Frédérique about how she should pay, and who, for the electricity – had he put the account in her name, or was it still in his grandmother's? And she desperately needed to sort out a new phone, which, in the absence of internet, she'd have to do in person, and eventually a car – this one had been on special offer to hire for four weeks, but she couldn't afford to rent one forever.

When was she going to have time in between planting out the garden, patching up a leaking roof, getting basic facilities like a proper kitchen sink, signing phone contracts and sorting out the internet to actually sit in the frickin' sun and drink red wine? That was the problem with moving to a holiday destination, she realised. Part of you expected that living there would be like a holiday, whereas in reality all the messy details of life still accompanied you. Other than with her dinner when staying with Chloé, she hadn't had a sniff of alcohol at all so far, and although she was far from dependent on the substance, it would be nice if she was able to put her feet up and relax just once in a while.

She also felt a little guilty about this evening. When she'd gratefully accepted Chloé's offer to cook the murdered chicken, she hadn't considered that would mean she'd have to cook for Emily too. But Chloé had been fine when she'd called her earlier to check it was OK. 'How you say? The more the merrier!' she'd said. 'Yes, to bring your friend.' Still, Lily hated the lingering feeling that she was putting her new friend to too much trouble.

The journey passed quickly, and soon she was weaving her way through the city centre, sweating slightly around the one-way system, and then picking up pace as she made her way along the long, straight route to the airport. Parking in the short stay car park, and remembering for once to tuck her ticket into her purse and save herself the panic of trying to find it in a couple of hours' time, she walked the short distance to the little terminal.

The building was fairly empty; with only one flight due in this afternoon. A few people were milling about with suitcases, or queueing at the flight desk, and there was a rumble of quiet conversation, but she could see the arrivals door clearly, and there was space in the café in which she could sit and read her book.

A member of staff had opened the large glass doors at the back of the seating area, and customers spilled out onto a terrace which overlooked the runway on one side, and the car park on the other. It wasn't exactly the dream location, but it was a chance to sit and feel the warm sun on her face – even if the air was fragranced with fumes.

She ordered a tea at the counter – having not had one for a few days – and remembered for once to request '*thé au lait*' (tea with milk). She chose a *tarte aux fraises* from the mouth-watering selection of pastries and promised herself she'd walk it off later.

The server nodded then, moments later, produced a tray with the glistening *tarte* and a cup filled with warm, steamed milk.

'I'm sorry,' Lily said. 'I ordered *thé au lait.*'

'*Oui,*' he said, 'you can choose the tea, 'ere.' He opened up an embossed box which housed teas in every conceivable form – green, herbal, rooibos and, thankfully, English breakfast – for her to select from. She reached in and took an English breakfast, before pointing again to the tray. 'But the milk... you've put the milk in the cup already,' she said, patiently.

'*Oui, pour le thé au lait,*' he said, seemingly confused.

'But we don't...' she began. A cough in the queue behind her alerted her to the fact there were about five other people waiting to be served. 'Never mind,' she said, handing him a ten euro note and heading over to the terrace. There, she set down her tray on a small, vacant table and unwrapped the tea bag, then placed it in the milky cup, hoping beyond hope that something resembling tea might emerge if left long enough.

She busied herself while she waited by listening in to snippets of conversation around her. Usually, she craved quiet, but now she lived in practical silence, it was nice to hear the murmur of others talking. Some conversations sped past in French and she was only able to grab on to the odd word. Others were in English. One woman was telling her son how he should behave when he got to his grandmother's. A couple discussed the price of air travel. One man, on the phone, seemed to be talking about computer software, and might as well have been speaking another language entirely.

She scrolled pointlessly through her phone, and re-sent the message she'd sent to Ben last night, hoping to prompt a response. It looked a bit heartless in the cold light of day. But what else could she say? If he didn't love her enough to come, she wasn't going to try to force him.

Then, trying her best to put thoughts of 'home' or the place she'd used to call home, out of her mind, she drew her book from her bag and began to read, feeling the sun playing lightly on her face, and breaking small forkfuls from her *tarte* as she read. Eventually, she gave up on the tea and went to get herself a coffee instead, making sure to order a *'grande crème'* rather than simply assuming she'd be offered milk if she didn't request it.

The time passed quickly and she was taken by surprise when a plane screeched onto the nearby runway, practically skidding to a halt. Did they always look so haphazard when they landed? Or was it only the budget airlines that went for a white-knuckle finish?

Tucking the book away, she got to her feet and walked to the arrivals door to greet her friend.

13

'OK, so promise you'll use your imagination,' Lily said again as they turned down the road that led to her new house. 'It's not perfect, and I didn't expect it to be.'

'You really have no faith in me at all,' Emily said. 'Besides which, after *that* drive, I'm too travel sick to complain about *anything!*'

When Emily had walked through the double doors from passport control two hours earlier, Lily had had to fight the urge to leap into her arms. Her friend had been her usual dishevelled yet beautiful self: sporting tracksuit bottoms, a hoodie, dark glasses and a messy bun. But in that moment, she'd seemed so familiar, reminded her so much of home, it had thrown the experience of the last few days into sharp relief. Lily had been lonelier than she'd realised.

'You get used to the roads, honestly,' Lily said hurriedly. 'They are a bit twisty, but you learn to sort of go with it.'

'I know – I'm kidding. I'm just traumatised from looking out the window and seeing we were driving on the edge of some sort of death-drop.'

'Yes, that freaked me out at first,' Lily admitted. 'It's a long way down, huh?'

'At least it holds the promise of certain death,' Emily said. 'You don't have to worry about life-altering injuries.'

'Always a bright side.'

'Precisely.' Emily grinned. 'But please do try not to veer sideways, won't you?'

'I'll see what I can do.' Lily smiled.

There was a moment's silence before she began again. 'Look, in all honesty, the property does need serious attention. The garden is so overgrown – some of the grasses and weeds are taller than me. And there are repairs needed. And I haven't really had the chance to clean it properly...'

'You really *do* want me to like this place,' said Emily, placing her hand briefly over Lily's. 'Seriously, don't worry. You've told me about it and it sounds beautiful.'

'Well, it has potential at least.'

'It'll be fine. I won't judge. I promise.'

'I guess we'll find out,' Lily said, bumping slightly up the small, gravelled kerb. 'This is it.'

'What, this one?' Emily said, pointing at her neighbour's cottage.

'No, that one.'

'Oh. But you said... overgrown?'

Lily looked up properly and gasped. In place of the tangled mess that had filled the entire front garden, was a plot of flattened, slightly grassy, slightly muddy, ground. The path was clearly visible and from the looks of it had even been swept.

'Oh, my god,' Lily said. 'It must have been Claude.'

'Who's Claude?' Emily asked as they got out of the car.

'Oh, he's a friend of Frédérique's – you know the guy who's selling me the place? He said he'd bring his tractor over and –

well – sort out the garden. But I didn't realise he was doing it today.' She glanced at her watch – it had been four and a half hours since she'd left, but even so the progress was astounding.

'Wow, that's nice of him.'

'Ridiculously nice,' Lily said, taking one of Emily's bags from her as they walked up the path to the front door.

Inside, she inspected Emily's face closely as her friend made positive comments about the I, the size and the potential of the place. 'Really?' she asked repeatedly. 'You really like it?'

'Darling, I like it *for* you,' her friend said at last. 'It wouldn't be my bag, but I'm a lazy cow – you know that. If you say you can transform this into your dream property, I believe you.'

'Thank you.'

They finally walked through to the kitchen, after she'd explained to Emily in probably too much detail, exactly what to expect. 'I know I said it was a kitchen, but it's really only a work in progress...' she was saying, as they pushed into the room. 'And you'll see the back garden from the window and it's a complete and utter... oh.'

She stopped so suddenly that Emily bumped into her and almost sent her flying.

'Oops, sorry,' her friend said.

'No, I'm sorry,' she said. 'It's just... I saw...' She gestured to the window.

Rather than the tangled greener' she'd used to view whenever she was at the back of the house, the back garden too had been flattened. The job was rudimentary – clearly done with a tractor that had left the grass cuttings in its wake and scored lines in the newly revealed ground. But for the first time Lily was able to see the 3,000 m^2 of garden that stretched away from the back of her cottage. A line of fir trees signalled the end of her plot giving way to a wooded area through which – wherever there was a small gap – she could glimpse the lake beyond.

Propped in the corner, uncovered during the job no doubt, was a rather rusty cast-iron table and chairs.

'Oh my god,' Lily said again, 'it's beautiful. This is my garden. This is...'

Emily draped an arm around her friend's shoulders. 'It's absolutely perfect,' she said.

They were mid-coffee when there was a knock at the door. Lily went to answer and found Claude standing on her doorstep, smiling.

'I just come to see if it is OK?' he said in his broken English. 'I know it is not pretty, yes? But there were many – how you say – sticks and trunks and it is very hard to cut. So I 'ave to use my biggest *tracteur*.'

'Oh, it's wonderful!' she said, just managing to resist the urge to jump into his arms and give him the thank you hug of his life. 'It's... I don't know how I would have managed.'

'It is nothing,' Claude replied, modestly.

'Are you sure you don't want me to pay? I really don't mind. I...'

Claude shook his head. 'It is – how you say? – what *les amis*, the friends are for.'

'Oh, well, at least come in for a coffee?' she said, then, hoping that coffee wasn't quite the euphemism for sex in France that it had become in England, quickly added, 'My friend, Emily, is here and I'm sure she'd love to meet you.'

'Well, for *un petit moment* per'aps,' he said, stepping into the house and pulling off his boots.

'Emily, this is Claude,' Lily said, as they walked back into the kitchen.

Emily, who'd been leaning against the kitchen sink, sipping a coffee, straightened up. 'Ah, the farmer!' she said, nodding in his direction. 'Nice to meet you.'

'It is my pleasure.'

Lily quickly poured out another coffee and set it down on the small shelf close to where Claude was standing, placing a bag of sugar and bottle of milk there too for him to personalise his drink as he pleased. 'Sorry it's a bit messy,' she said.

'It is what?'

'Um, messy – er a bit *négligé*?'

'*Désordonné? C'est normale!* You have just moved, oui? It take time,' Claude said, adding several spoonfuls of sugar to his *café* then grimacing as he took his first gulp.

'Lily,' Emily said quietly, sidling over to where Lily stood leaning against the sink. 'Did you seriously just talk to that man about negligees?'

'No, *négligé* means untidy – neglected – or at least I hope so,' said Lily. She looked at Claude who was studiously staring at his coffee, recognising they were having private words, and felt guilty. 'Désolé, Claude,' she said. '*C'est* her... um *langue.*' It's her language, nodding at Emily to ensure he understood.

'*Sa langue?*' he said. 'She 'ave a problem with er mouth, um, her tongue?'

'No, no,' Lily said. 'Her language, she doesn't speak much French – even less than me.'

'Oh, I don't know! I understand you're talking about negligees and tongues. Do you want me to leave?' quipped Emily.

'Emily!' Lily chastised, feeling her face get hot. She barely knew Claude, and the last thing she wanted to do was to make him feel uncomfortable, or give him the wrong idea.

To her relief, Claude laughed. 'Ah, she is a joker, yes!' he said, grinning at Emily. 'She 'ave the Breetish humour.'

To Lily's surprise, Emily flushed slightly. '*J'essaie,*' she said, *I try*, then glanced at Lily. 'You're not the only one who listened in French lessons at school,' she said.

'So I see.'

After answering a few questions about what farming life was like in the Limousin – 'Yes, it is a lot of work'; 'No, I don't kill the cows myself"; 'Yes, I grow sweetcorn'; 'Yes, I have three dogs but the little one is my favourite' – Claude finished his coffee and left, with the promise of coming to help if Lily needed anything else.

'My word,' Emily said, when the front door closed. 'No wonder you're enjoying the scenery around here.'

'Emily!'

'What? The man is bloomin' gorgeous. And he seems to like *you!*'

'Don't be silly, he's just being nice. People are... well, the ones I know so far, they seem really lovely. And it was Frédérique who suggested he came. You know, the owner. If anything it's a favour to *him.*'

'If you say so.'

'I do say so,' she said, grinning over her lukewarm coffee.

'Still, those eyes.'

'I know.'

'That accent.'

'Well, you'd be surprised, but lots of people have the same accent around here.'

'That body...'

'Em! You didn't see his body.'

'No, but I've imagined it and believe me, it's to die for.'

Lily shook her head. 'God, I've missed you, Em.'

'Glad to hear it. And you too, actually.' Emily looked suddenly teary.

Lily looked at her friend's eyes, at the unfamiliar shine of threatened tears. It wasn't the first time she'd felt something was different about Emily since her arrival. The moment in the car when she'd looked wistful, the slight sadness at the edges of her smile. 'Are you OK?' she said.

'Oh, yes. I just keep tearing up at the moment. Chris reckons it's peri-menopause, but I'm obviously far too young for that in reality.'

'*Far* too young.' Lily reached out and squeezed Emily's shoulder. 'You know, if it's not... I mean if it's anything else... if something's wrong. You know you can...'

'I know.' Emily nodded.

There was a silence, but clearly Emily wasn't about to fill it.

'Sorry about the lack of furniture by the way,' Lily said.

'It's cool. I like the minimalist look.'

'Pah! Yes. But it would be nice to sit down occasionally.'

In the end, they spent the next thirty minutes dragging two of the extraordinarily heavy garden chairs in from the newly mowed garden. 'Let's leave the table,' Lily puffed when they were heaving one of them up the single step into the kitchen. 'I'd rather have to eat on my lap than go to hospital with a hernia.'

'That sounds like a plan,' Emily said. 'But should we drag in a third just in case your *boyfriend* comes around?'

'Frédérique?'

'No,' Emily said, but raised a quizzical eyebrow at the conclusion Lily had jumped to, 'although let's talk more about *him* later. I was talking about the ridiculously dishy Claude.'

'Dishy?'

'I'm trying to expand my vocabulary.'

'Fair enough. Well, first of all, Claude might be dishy, but he's really not my type.'

'Lily, that man is *everyone's* type.'

'Well, he's easy on the eye, I'll admit. But seriously not the type of man I usually go for.'

'Yes, you prefer them slightly more rotund with more of a receding hairline, right?'

'Ouch!' Lily said, giving her friend a nudge. 'That's a bit mean.'

'Sorry.'

'Plus, as far as I'm concerned, I'm not single. Ben and I have been together for over twenty years. You don't just walk away from a commitment like that.'

'Um, you kind of have, sweetheart,' Emily said, plonking the chair down and sliding into it. 'Fuck, these are uncomfortable.'

'No, I haven't,' Lily said, feeling her throat constrict slightly. She sat down in her own uncomfortable and slightly damp chair. It was heaven to take the weight off her feet, even if it was torture to sit on the hard, metal surface. 'I know you think I'm mad, but I still think Ben will come round. I just need to show him I'm serious. And maybe show him how great life in France can be...'

Emily's eyebrow raised once again.

'What?' Lily asked.

'Nothing.'

'You're doing the eyebrow thing.'

'Oh, bloody hell. I need to train myself to keep them still like a normal person. Talk about wearing your heart on your sleeve. Mine's on my bloody forehead.'

'Yep. And you've obviously got something to say...' Lily said. She tried not to let her impatience show – not wanting to fight with her friend – but it wasn't easy.

'OK,' Emily said, sitting forward, her forearms on her thighs, hands clasped together, like an interrogative interviewer. 'I just feel there has to be a point when you decide you've given that man enough chances. You've got to give him an ultimatum.'

'But...'

'I know. You love him. And he loves you. But are you a

hundred per cent sure that he knows how much you still want
him to join you?'

'Of course he does – he must do!'

'But, sweetheart... have you actually laid it on the line – said it
openly?' Emily said kindly.

'Well, not exactly...'

'Oh, Lily.'

'I know. I suppose I'm just clinging on to the hope that he'll
kind of *wake up*,' she said, feeling her face get hot. 'That he'll
come and we'll be together because he wants to – not because I
begged him to.'

'There's no shame in begging, you know,' Emily said, eyebrow
arched. 'It can work wonders...'

'I know... Well, I know what you mean. It's just... I can't
explain it...'

'You have every right to tell him what you want. Tell him it's
now or never.'

'Ah, I don't know, Emily. I suppose I'm deluded. I just haven't
given up on it all working out yet without, well, without me
forcing anything.'

'Good! You shouldn't. But you also need to be realistic. You
know?'

'I know. Just, maybe not just yet.'

'Well in the meantime if a gorgeous French bloke decides to
make a move, maybe you should consider it. Whether it's Claude
or the mysterious *Frédérique*,' Emily said, using a French accent.

To her surprise, Lily felt her face flush even more hotly.

'Ooh,' said Emily, not one to miss a trick. 'Lily loves
Frédérique!'

'Stop it!' Lily retorted.

'I'm only joking, but out of interest, if you had to choose out of
the two.'

'Of Frédérique and Claude?'

'Yes.'

'Well, neither, obviously.'

'But who's more your type?' Emily pushed. 'Go on. I quite fancy Claude, there – see, it's just a game. I'd never do anything, obviously. But wow, if Chris dumped me I'd hunt him down immediately. So... hypothetically...'

'Hypothetically,' Lily said, carefully. 'I'd choose Frédérique.' Her cheeks were burning so brightly she wondered whether the house needed air conditioning rather than heating. 'But that's all it is – hypothetical.'

The conversation moved on to dinner at Chloé's and paint colours and where they might get second-hand furniture to make the house more habitable.

But when Lily was making tea later, Emily having dragged her chair back into the garden, and rolled up her trousers in an attempt to attract some sun to her pale skin, Lily couldn't help dwelling on the question a little more. It was OK to be a little attracted to someone else, especially in her situation. But she couldn't shake off the feeling that she ought to keep Frédérique at arm's length.

At least for now.

14

'Yes,' he said on the phone. Then, 'I understand. OK.'

Next to him, Lily strained to hear what was being said, but it was impossible.

He hung the phone up, quietly, and looked at her.

'Well?' she said, almost bursting. 'What is it? Has it fallen through? Do we have to wait? Don't tell me the sellers have pulled out again?'

'Lily Butterworth,' he said. 'We got it.'

'We got the house?' she almost screamed.

'We are the proud owners of number 32.' He grinned as she launched herself into his arms.

* * *

'What are you smiling about?' Emily's words broke through her day-dream and she snapped back to reality.

'Oh, nothing,' she said. 'Just thinking.'

They rounded the final corner, crossed the bridge over the lake and turned onto the main road through *Faux la Montagne*. The evening was cool, but it was light and there was no threat of rain. The Nissan bumped up the now familiar road, passing the café with its purple sign. The lights were on and as they passed Emily glimpsed people inside.

Seconds later, they were pulling up outside *La Petite Maison*.

'Oh god, I feel like I'm intruding,' said Emily dramatically.

'Don't be silly. Chloé's happy you're coming – and she's got plenty of *pot-au-feu* apparently.'

'As long as you're sure.'

'Yes, she literally said the more the merrier.'

'That was nice of her.'

'Mind you, eating that poor chicken,' Lily added, with a grimace. 'Not sure if I have the stomach for it.'

'I hate to break this to you, but you're a carnivore, my love,' said Emily, 'you had a chicken sandwich for lunch!'

'Yes, but that was some random, anonymous chicken,' said Lily. 'This is... well, it feels different.'

'The chickens you usually eat are probably scrawny little mistreated things. At least this one had a proper life...'

'Yes, but isn't that worse somehow? She was probably *happy*. Fantasising about the many years of pecking ahead...'

'You know that's irrational, don't you?' Emily said. 'Especially as you, *Madame*, have chosen *la* French country life, eh!' she continued, dropping into a faux French accent. '*It iz what zey do 'ere.*'

'I'm proud of my irrationality. It's what makes me mysterious and unpredictable,' joked Lily.

'Idiot.'

When Chloé answered the door, somehow managing to look elegant and well-dressed despite wearing ripped jeans and a simple black blouse, the smell that followed her from the kitchen was delicious.

'*Bonjour*, welcome!' she said. 'It iz almost ready.'

'Hi, Chloé, this is Emily,' Lily said as she entered.

''ello, Emily,' Chloé said, with a smile. 'It iz nice for to meet you.'

'Yes. You too.' The pair of them went through the small dance that sometimes happens when people aren't sure how to greet each other; leaning in for a kiss, but abruptly changing course; sticking out a hand for a shake, then retracting it. In the end, Emily just leaned forward and gave Chloé a hug and they both laughed.

'See,' she said. 'We're friends already.'

Chloé smiled. 'Yes, so it seem.'

She showed them through to the dining room, where she'd set the table with a burgundy tablecloth and a porcelain centre-piece, fashioned into the shape of delicate flowers.

'Oh, it looks beautiful!' said Lily. 'You needn't have gone to any trouble.'

'It iz no trouble, just dinner, uh? We 'ave to eat, and it iz better together. And if we do it, it is just as well to make it look beautiful, *non*?'

'And look, thanks for having me,' Emily said. 'It's really nice of you.'

'*Pah!*' said their host, flicking her fingers as if swatting a fly. 'It iz nothing.'

They took seats at the table, and Chloé poured them each a tiny glass of purple liquid which turned out to be a kind of black-currant alcoholic drink.

'I weel be with you soon, *oui*?' Chloé said, once they were settled. 'I just go to poke le chick.'

'Wow,' said Emily, leaning forward across the table once the door closed. 'You didn't tell me she was so...'

'So what?' Lily prompted, feeling strangely protective as she noted her friend's serious expression.

'Gorgeous? Friendly?' Emily said.

'Which is good, right?' Lily replied, still unable to read Emily's tone.

'Which is brilliant. Seriously.' Emily took a swig of her blackcurrant drink and made a face. 'Woah, strong! But yeah, it's brilliant. I'm seriously happy for you. You've already found a new friend – and she's a definite upgrade from the old model.' She grinned.

'What?'

'Yes,' Emily continued. 'I used to wonder what you'd do without me... you know, in France I mean. But now... well...'

'Don't be daft. You're irreplaceable and you know it!' Lily smiled, putting a reassuring hand on Emily's arm – not sure if she was joking.

'No,' said Emily firmly. 'No, I'm not irreplaceable.' Then, 'And it's *good*. It's a *good* thing,' she added hastily. 'Emily 2.0. Version *Française*.'

'You are so...'

But Chloé entered the room, carrying a casserole dish in carefully gloved hands and Lily lost what she was about to say. 'Wow,' she said instead. 'That smells amazing.'

Chloé smiled at them both then, placing down a trestle, set the dish in front of them.

Lily found, if she suppressed any images of the forlorn murdered hen that popped into her mind, she quite enjoyed the casserole, which was very similar to the ones her mum had used to make. 'Thank you for this,' she said to Chloé. 'It's delicious.'

'Mmm, yes,' agreed Emily, forking a large piece of chicken into her mouth. 'Tasty.'

'*Merci beaucoup*,' said Chloé, pleased.

* * *

Two hours later, they were negotiating the winding route towards *Broussas*.

'I cannot believe I went for seconds of that mousse,' said Emily. 'You should have stopped me. You're going to have to roll me out of the car at this rate. I almost definitely can't walk.'

'You should have stopped *me*,' Lily countered. 'Honestly, if I carry on like this I'm going to have to buy a bigger house.'

They both laughed.

'Diet starts tomorrow,' said Emily.

'Always.' Lily smiled.

'And tomorrow never comes!' they said in unison.

'God, but it was delicious though,' her friend sighed.

'Yep. Puts my attempts at chocolate brownies to shame,' Lily replied.

They both sat in silence for a second.

'I meant what I said though,' Emily told her. 'I'm really pleased you've found a friend already.'

'Yeah, I guess I'm lucky.' Lily smiled. 'Although it's early days, isn't it. I'm not sure how long you have to know someone before calling them a friend.'

Emily snorted. 'I think for us it was – what – five minutes?' she said, referring to the time they'd been paired up on the first day at their new school.

'Probably,' said Lily. 'I think you wrote "BFF" on my hand within about the first thirty seconds.'

'Marking my territory.'

'I guess I was lucky you didn't pee on me or something.'

'There's always time…'

They both laughed.

'If someone had told me in Year Seven,' Emily said, 'that one day we'd be in our forties and driving around France, it would have completely blown my mind. That we'd be friends that long. Do all this together.'

'It blows my mind, now,' said Lily. 'I still have to shake myself to believe I'm actually here. That I've done it. That I'm not just on holiday but... well, this is permanent.' Her voice wobbled a little on her last word – as if it had somehow put the last nail in the coffin of her life in England, of her relationship. 'I mean, you know. It's not *quite* as I'd dreamed it.'

'Ah,' said Emily. 'Give it time.' She reached over and patted Lily's knee. 'I have a feeling everything's going to work out OK.'

'You think?' Lily wanted to ask Emily what she meant. What 'working out OK' would really look like. But she stopped herself.

'Yeah. I really do,' said Emily, looking at her with a surprisingly watery smile. 'You are going to have a wonderful life here.'

'Hang on,' said Lily, veering slightly into the middle of the road as they rounded an unexpected corner. She slowed the car down. 'Where's the sarcastic comment?' She glanced briefly at her friend's face.

'What do you mean?'

'Well, the Emily I know would say it was going to work out OK, but then – I don't know – make a quip about my fashion sense, or my chances of landing a handsome Frenchman, or... something,' she said, with a smile. 'I'm just waiting for the punchline.'

'Suppose I'm just feeling sentimental,' said Emily. 'Usual service will resume shortly, I promise.' She rubbed her nose with the back of her hand.

'Glad to hear it. It's very disconcerting, all this positivity,' joked Lily. 'Although remind me to write down the name of that drink Chloé gave you – perhaps it has some sort of magic powers.'

She waited for Emily's snort. But her friend remained silent. 'Em?' Lily said.

'I'm sorry,' Emily said, after a moment.

'What do you mean?'

'Oh, you know. I'm sorry that I'm such an arse. That I always joke about everything. You know it doesn't mean anything, don't you?'

'Of course! I...'

'Because it doesn't. Lily, you're my best friend. And I think you're, well, bloody brilliant, if I'm honest.'

'Steady on.'

'Well, I do,' said Emily firmly. 'Whatever stupid stuff I may say, I... well, I love you, Lily Butterworth.'

'OK. Well, thanks. You too.'

They fell into silence, neither quite knowing what to say next. Then Emily put the radio on and managed to tune it to a station playing some sort of cheesy medley from the eighties and nineties.

By the time they arrived at Lily's house, their voices were hoarse from singing along to everything from Wham! to Steps, and all the melancholy they'd felt on the journey seemed firmly and safely in the past.

* * *

'What the hell is *that*?' a voice in the darkness hissed in Lily's ear.

'Wha—?' she said sleepily.

'Lily, wake up for god's sake. The house is haunted and we need to get out *now*.'

This was enough to make her sit up, her bottom lightly touching the floor beneath her airbed, which had deflated under her during her first hours of sleep.

'What are you talking about?'

Emily snapped on the light, her face pained.

'Ouch!' Lily's vision blurred as her eyes adjusted to the sudden brightness.

'Sorry,' Emily said, 'but something is in the house and you need to wake up and get the hell out of here before we're both eaten alive or something.'

'Are you sure you haven't just had a nightma—'

'Shh,' said her friend.

True enough, a banging and scratching sound could be heard above their heads.

'It's probably mice or something,' Lily said sleepily.

'That,' said Emily, her face pale as a loud bang and thud combination made them both jump, 'is not a frickin' *mouse*.'

Her body protesting, Lily stood up and cocked her head to the side to hear. 'It's definitely something in the attic,' she said, trying to stay calm, although the savage way she'd been woken up had done nothing for her blood pressure. 'Maybe the neighbour's cat has...'

'If you think that's just *one* animal,' said Emily, 'then you're insane. There's a whole zoo up there. Or some sort of poltergeist party.'

More thundering above their heads seemed to support the first hypothesis. 'Oh,' said Lily. 'Well, maybe I could call someone in the morning, you know, to take a look.'

'Are you actually mad? Look, I watched this documentary about poltergeists and there was a family in Norfolk who had an old house – not much different from this one – and they began to hear banging in the night. Over the course of a week it got worse, then crockery started flying through the air. One of the children got hit on the nose by a teacup! It was carnage.'

'Emily, you don't believe in ghosts, let alone poltergeists.'

'Nor did they, Lily. Nor did they,' Emily said darkly.

'I'm sure we could...'

'You know me,' Emily said, 'I don't want to be melodramatic...'

'God forbid.'

'But I haven't slept in two hours. And now, until I know exactly what we're dealing with up there, I don't think I'll be able to settle at all.'

'Right.'

'So either we call someone *now*, or you investigate what's up there, or we get the hell out of here and sleep in the car.'

'In the car! It's a Nissan Micra!'

'He was hit on the nose, Lily. On the nose. With a teacup.'

'Right.' Lily knew better than to challenge Emily on zero sleep, a shed load of alcohol and what seemed to be the beginning of a nervous breakdown. Instead, the quickest route back to her much-needed rest seemed to be for her to poke her head through the hatch in the attic, confirm that they had mice or rats or birds or something else non paranormal, and put her friend's mind at rest.

Not that the idea of sticking her actual head into a room full of rodents appealed in any sense. She'd watched enough *I'm a Celebrity Get Me Out of Here!* to know that rats, mice and other vermin had no qualms when it came to clambering over faces, or putting little claws into entry-points.

But her need to sleep seemed to override everything else. As she wearily pulled on her dressing gown she was reminded of nights with a younger version of Ty when she'd have to chase moths out of the window, or deal with a wayward wasp. The need to actually get her body back into bed overrode any fear she had herself.

It was similar now. Deal with the problem, back to bed. If a rat decided to perch on her head, so be it.

The main problem was the lack of furniture. She certainly didn't have a ladder, and although there might be one inside the hatch of the loft, she had no way of getting to it without a chair to balance on or a pole to knock it open. Eventually, they dragged the end of the ancient (and probably haunted) iron bedstead out of the spare room, turning it on its side to fit through the doorway, and half wedged it on the landing. 'That'll be fine,' Emily said. 'You can use the struts as a kind of ladder! And you've got a torch on your phone, right?

'I take it *you're* not going to climb up and investigate?'

'Er, no. I'll one hundred per cent support you though,' Emily said, giving her a thumbs up and sheepish grin combination.

'Thought as much. Well, if I get murdered by a poltergeist, or eaten by some sort of giant rat, it's entirely your fault.'

'Agreed.'

Sighing, Lily clambered up the wobbling bedstead, pushed open the hatch, cautiously, and shone the torch light from her phone into the interior of the attic. The scrabbling stopped.

Raising her head into the gloom, she moved the light around and was suddenly met with a tiny pair of round black eyes. The animal froze in terror, then performed a sudden leap to the left, whisking what looked like an enormous feather duster behind it. Then all at once, it was as if the movement had provoked some sort of rodent riot, as several other small animals began darting around, their shadows looming large in the light from the torch. The tiny animals jumped and scratched and skittered and panicked around, and a fluffy tail whipped the side of Lily's ear as one creature passed.

As the soft hair of the tail touched her, Lily let out a cry that was somewhere between a shout and a scream and drew her head sharply back through the opening, banging it for good measure and letting the wooden hatch fall back into place. The sudden movement caused the bedstead below her to wobble and she slipped and fell heavily onto the floor at Emily's feet.

15

It was impossible to sleep.

Nothing was broken, they were fairly sure, but Lily ached from head to toe.

'I'm so sorry,' Emily had said. '*I* should have climbed up the fucking bedstead.'

'No,' Lily had replied. '*Neither* of us should have.' Their eyes met briefly and they'd exchanged a smile. 'But no harm done,' she'd lied.

'Today's disaster is tomorrow's brilliant anecdote,' her friend had added, giving her a squeeze. 'You'll be dining out on this one for years.'

'Well, in that case, thank you for your help.' Lily had replied.

Then, after Emily had helped her back onto the unforgiving mattress, she'd disappeared to her room leaving Lily aching in the dark. The noise of rodents overhead seemed twenty times louder than it had before, and she pictured them, scurrying, their enormous tails flicking behind them; their black, beady eyes shining in the slivers of moonlight that shot in between the tiles.

Eventually, she fell into a light doze, but awoke each time she tried to turn. By seven, she gave up any hope of proper sleep. Instead, she dragged herself up from the floor, slipped on her dressing gown and went to wake Emily, who'd apparently now found the ability to sleep no matter how many poltergeists or rats were making merry above her head. Lily gave her prone figure a poke with her slippered foot.

'Eh?' Emily said, blinking blearily.

'Come on,' Lily replied. 'We're getting out of here.'

'What time is it?'

'Just after seven, but I've been up since, well, you know.'

'Ouch, how are you feeling?' Emily grimaced.

'I've been better.'

'I feel completely responsible.'

'Good!' Lily said, with a wry smile. 'You *are!* But... look, it doesn't matter. I've decided: why don't we spend a couple of nights on a decent bed, and get someone to deal with the squirrel things before we come back? Might see if I can't pick up a couple of proper mattresses before we do too – those air things are bad enough when you haven't fallen from height, but believe me when your body is one big bruise, they are seriously uncomfortable.'

'Again, really sorry,' said Emily, patting Lily's leg from her prone position. 'But decent beds? Sounds lovely. Where were you thinking? There was a hotel I saw in *Eymoutiers* when we drove through that looked relatively habitable...'

'I thought we'd go to *La Petite Maison*.'

'Of course! Chloé's place. Do you think she'll have rooms?'

'Hopefully.'

Leaving her friend to gather an overnight bag and stick on some clothes, Lily went down to the kitchen and filled the kettle. Then she drew out her mobile phone and, after checking the time – half past seven: Chloé served breakfast from seven, so surely it was OK to call? – she went to dial Chloé's number.

Before she did, she noticed a missed call from late last night. It was from her old home number and the sight of it there, still displaying as 'Home' on her screen, made her heart flip. She clicked quickly on the icon for her answerphone and listened as the automated voice told her she had one new message. Then she heard Ben's voice: 'Look, Lily. I need to ask you one more time. Please come back home. I know you have this dream or whatever, but what you're doing is crazy. We can buy a holiday place, maybe? Or travel a bit more if you like – to all sorts of places. But you need to come home. I miss you. Tyler misses you. Surely that should mean something?'

Lily felt her eyes fill, first with tears of guilt and worry, then with anger. Had her husband just called her crazy and suggested she didn't love her son, or him? Could he literally not see things from her perspective? All those promises; years of dreams, shattered.

She'd spoken to Ty yesterday evening and he'd seemed fairly upbeat. He'd finally sorted his accommodation for uni and had opened a student bank account. If anything, not having his mum constantly looking over his shoulder would be a chance for him to stand on his own two feet – he was, after all, an adult now. She'd told him she missed him, and he'd said 'you too' but it had sounded simply affectionate rather than desperate. Meaning Ben had just used their son as a pawn in his guilt-inducing game.

Then she looked at the time of the message. One o'clock in the morning. It wasn't like Ben to stay up late and she felt a sudden pang for everything she was putting him through. Perhaps he hadn't been thinking straight, she told herself.

She decided to try to put it out of her mind and called Chloé, who confirmed that she still had one room available that she and

Emily could share. Lily wondered what it might be like sharing a bed with her oldest friend. The last time they'd done it was aged twelve at a sleepover, when Emily had been all kicking legs and sleep-talking, had stolen the duvet and woken her up at 3 a.m. because she thought she might have seen a spider.

Hopefully, at least some of her behaviour had been caused by teenage hormones and too many midnight snacks. If not, she was jumping out of the frying pan into the fire.

After several coffees and the dry end of a French loaf, she called Frédérique.

'*Oui* 'ello?'

'Frédérique? It's Lily.'

'Ah, *Madame Buttercup! Comment ça va?*'

'*Oui, ça va bien merci, et vous?*'

'*Tutoie-moi.*'

'Sorry, what?'

'*Tutoie-moi*, we are friends, no? You can say *tu*, not *vous*.'

'Oh.' For god's sake, was this really the moment for a grammar lesson? 'OK, well, in that case *tu as un problème.*'

'I do?'

'*Oui, dans le grenier... il y a beaucoup des... des...*'

'I think,' Frédérique said, with a touch of amusement, 'it is per'aps better if we speak English for now, yes?'

'Fine,' she said, starting to feel cross. 'There's a bunch of rat things in the roof.'

'Rat fings?'

'Yes, *le rat...* but not a rat, something *like* a rat. With a bushy tail.'

'Ah, a soft tail – like *un écureuil*? A squirrel?'

'Yes, just like a squirrel.'

'Ah, *c'est un loir*! But they are cute, yes?'

'Yes, but, Frédérique, they are not cute at three in the morning when I am trying to sleep.'

There was a brief silence. 'I understand,' he said. 'Then I will come and bring some poison for them. They will not be noisy when they are dead, uh?'

'Poison! Oh, no! Can't you just, well, sort of *take them away*?'

Frédérique laughed. 'Well, it is possible, yes. But it take a long time. You trap them, you take them away, they come back. Or you drive them to a ten kilometre of distance and maybe they don't come back, eh.'

'OK, can you do that?'

There was a brief silence. 'You want me to take the *loirs* for a trip in the countryside?'

'Would you?'

He was silent again for a moment. Then, '*Madame*, I will try.'

'Thank you.'

'But if it was just me, I would prefer some poison on an apple, and the *problème* it is no more, eh?'

'Sorry,' she said. 'I just can't...'

'I understand. It is done. Please do not worry.'

'Thank you.'

She ended the call, then dialled Ben's number, but hanging up before the call connected, anxiety suddenly flooding through her. Instead, she went to her messenger service and recorded a voice note: 'Ben, I got your message. And I miss you too – of course! But you know this is something I just have to do. And you know, I do wish you would... oh, never mind.'

Please come, she wanted to add.

She knew it was a bit pathetic to use the 'leave a voice note' option rather than speak to Ben properly. But she was too tired to have another argument, to talk around in circles again. And if she was honest, on zero sleep, in a considerable amount of pain and with the memory of a rodent flying past her head, she might have ended up bursting into tears if she'd heard his voice.

By the time Emily finally appeared in the doorway everything was sorted. 'OK, so we're off to *La Petite Maison*; I booked us a room –but we're sharing for now, I'm afraid. Hopefully we'll still get some decent sleep, Frédérique's coming to sort the *loirs*...'

'The what?'

'Oh, the rat things, you know, furry poltergeists.'

'Hope he's going to poison the damn things.'

'Actually, he's going to trap them and drive them ten kilometres away or something.'

'Wow, he must be a real animal lover.'

'Something like that. Anyway, I thought we could take a breath – you know, have a mini break within a break and go to the market – there's one in *Eymoutiers* today apparently.'

'That lovely little town we drove through?'

'That's the one.'

'Count me in.'

* * *

Luckily, the room was already free and Chloé had told them they could turn up before the usual check-in time of eleven.

It was nine thirty when they arrived, and the downstairs smelled of coffee and fresh bread. Through the door into the breakfast room, Lily could see a man and a woman munching *croissants* and smiling at one another. She imagined for a moment she was looking at herself and Ben, how things might have been.

'But you are hurt!' Chloé told her, as they brought their bags into the hallway. She looked at Lily, who was stooped and limping, with some concern. 'You want that I call the doctor?'

'No, honestly. I just need... I mean, I'll be fine.'

'Then at least you will let me put some arnica in your room to rub. For the bruises?'

'Thank you.' She wasn't a big fan of alternative medicine, but it seemed rude to refuse.

''Ow did this 'appen?' Chloé said, taking her bag for her. 'You 'av *un accident*?'

'It's a long story.'

'Then you tell me, uh? And I will make coffee.'

An hour later, having showered, taken advantage of the readily available and bitterly strong coffee and filled an incredulous Chloé in on their night-time antics, Lily and Emily drove into the small town of *Eymoutiers*, just twenty kilometres along the windy road, now nicknamed 'Death-fall Heights' by Emily.

As they approached the town, endless green gave way to small houses, some inhabited, others clearly empty, which increased in frequency until they were driving down a small high-street, dotted with shops fitted out on the ground floors of three-storey antique stone buildings, each adorned with a hand-painted sign. It was busier here, and people strolled along the pavements individually and in pairs, carrying fruit and vegetables from the market; or sat outside cafés sipping coffee with friends. Some walked, carrying French bread under their arms, others stopped to exchange kisses and greetings.

'God,' said Emily, 'it's like every stereotype of French life all packed into one bite-size piece.'

'To be fair, I haven't seen anyone wearing a beret yet.'

'Good point.'

'And I'm not sure I've noticed a poodle.'

'There'll be one along any minute.'

Laughing, Lily pulled the car into a small space between a van and a motorbike outside a tiny convenience store and they both got out, grateful to stretch their legs again and enjoy the gentle

warmth of the morning sun. Lily's back protested as she straightened, but the stiffness was already easing.

'How you feeling?' Emily asked, noticing her grimace as she
stood.

'Think I'm on the mend.'

'Thank god for that. Does that mean I can stop feeling guilty?'

'Let's say you pay for lunch and we're even,' Lily said, linking
her arm through Emily's as they stepped along the sunlit road.

The market was small, but sold a variety of fresh produce:
fruit and vegetables, freshly roasted chickens, olives glistening in
ceramic pots, handmade leather bags and a huge array of fresh
cheeses, the scent of which could be detected in the air from
quite a distance. People milled in front of stalls, chatting, queued
for oranges and apples, sat drinking coffee on small tables
outside the café, smoked elegantly in tiny groups. Everyone
seemed to know everyone else; eyes were caught, waves and
kisses and snippets of gossip were exchanged.

Although they weren't part of the small town's inner circle,
Lily and Emily were welcomed by smiling stallholders, or wished
a *bonne journée* by passing locals. People seemed to have the time
to notice one another; there was a sense of calm and contentment
and togetherness that Lily had never felt in the rushed, frantic
melee of the markets back home. Perhaps it was just that the
town was small, meaning the residents had come to recognise
each other. But it felt like more than that.

'It just feels friendly here, doesn't it?' Emily remarked.

'Yes! That's the word I was looking for,' Lily said. 'As if we're
part of things, even though we're not.'

'Yes. Yes, exactly that.'

'No sarcastic comments?'

'Lily, I can't think of one. I think maybe I've been cured.'

'Well, that I can—'

'Hey look,' Emily interrupted. 'It's *Monsieur le Dish*.'

'Who?'

'Claude, you idiot, look!' Emily pointed in the direction of the café-bar where Claude was sitting at a table on his own, sipping a coffee and reading a book. 'We should go and say bonjour, or something.'

Claude looked up and smiled widely when he saw them both approach. '*Bonjour!*' he said, half-standing in greeting. '*Comment ça va?*'

'*Oui, ça va,*' said Emily. '*Et toi?*'

'*Oui, oui, ça va.*' He nodded, folding the corner of his page over and tucking the book away in his jacket pocket. 'You are 'ere for a drink? You can join me if you like, I am waiting for my friend and 'e is not coming I fink.'

'You've been stood up?' Emily said, removing her jacket and hanging it on the back of a chair.

'What is this "stood up"?'

'Your *date* hasn't arrived?' she said, slipping into one of the chairs and giving an elaborate wink.

'Ah, no, 'e is not a date,' Claude said. ''e is just my friend, the vet. Per'aps 'e is called away, for an emergency wiv a cow?'

'She's just joking,' Lily said hastily.

'Ah, yes. The Breetish humour. I know this,' he said, shaking his head. 'You say one thing, but it mean something else, *oui?*'

'Something like that.'

Claude smiled. 'Now I understand. It is funny, eh. That I have a date with my friend.' He laughed, politely. 'You make it sound like my friend, 'e is my lover, *non?*'

'Coffee?' Lily asked Emily, standing up to go to the counter inside.

'OK. Large and black, I think, for me.'

'No problem. And, Claude, can I get you another coffee?' Lily asked.

He looked at his watch. 'Ah, it eez almost twelve – *midi* – *oui*? Per'aps an *apéritif*?'

'A drink? Now?' Lily said.

'Go on then,' Emily interrupted. 'What do you recommend?'

16

'Pull over!' Emily cried, grabbing at Lily's arm as she drove.

Her tone was so urgent that Lily did as she was asked without question, bumping slightly up a grass verge near an old stone cottage. The minute the car came to a halt, Emily scrambled out and vomited copiously into the undergrowth.

An old man came out of the front door of the cottage and stared at the car in confusion. Lily couldn't see his expression from where she sat and hoped that meant he couldn't see the stream of orange-flecked liquid lurching out of her friend's mouth and was simply wondering why a car was parked close to his drive.

'Sorry,' Emily slurred, climbing back into the car, wiping her mouth with the back of her hand.

'Are you all right?' Lily said, making a face.

'Not sure,' her friend replied, belching slightly into her balled fist. 'What was that drink? Eighty per cent proof or something?'

'To be fair,' Lily said, 'you did have four of them.'

'But it tasted like strawberry,' Emily said. 'I kind of... I don't know. Forgot.'

Looking at her dishevelled friend, Lily couldn't be angry. Although a few minutes ago she'd been close.

Emily wasn't an aggressive drunk, she wasn't one of those people who started picking arguments the minute she was a couple of units down. Instead, she simply got louder, drink by drink. And, even by her standards, she'd excelled herself this afternoon.

* * *

Things had started fairly innocuously. Once it was clear that Emily was getting a little tipsy, Lily had gone into the bar and ordered some pizza to soak up the alcohol.

'Probably best stop now,' she'd told her friend quietly when she'd asked her for a top up.

'Ah come on, you only live once,' Emily had said. 'Plus, I'm on holiday!' And she'd filled her little shot glass to the brim.

'So, you two have been friends for many years?' Claude had asked, his eyebrows raised slightly in amusement as Emily had tried unsuccessfully to spear a piece of pizza with her fork. 'You – how you say – go back to the childhood?'

'Yes,' Lily had said, smiling. 'We met at school actually.'

'But that is wonderful,' Claude had said. 'To know someone for so many years and to still be close.'

Emily had glanced up when Lily had mentioned school, and looked wistful. 'So many years,' she'd said. 'So many memories.'

They'd fallen silent for a moment, but then Emily had continued. 'Hey do you remember Raquel's? That club we used to go to when we were – what – eighteen or something?'

'God, yes,' Lily had said. The venue had been quirky and niche, and they'd often gone along to its eighties-night midweek

– purely in an ironic way, of course - and also because that was the night cocktails were two for one.

'Do you remember that night we danced to "Fame"?' Emily had said, referring to the famous eighties hit.. 'You know – it goes like this!' She'd then started to belt out the lyrics.

A couple at the next table had turned to look, either amused or annoyed.

'Ha, oh yes,' Lily had said, remembering their late teens when they'd spun around the dance floor, not caring who was watching or how completely insane they looked. 'I'm just glad they didn't have phone cameras in those days.'

But Emily hadn't finished.

She'd continued to sing, in a loud, off-key voice, still apparently lost in the moment. Then, to Lily's horror, she'd stood up, knocking her chair back, and tried to clamber onto the table.

'Emily! What are you doing?' she'd said, as Claude had watched, amused.

But Emily hadn't listened. She'd managed to get both feet on the table and had straightened up, her arms flung asunder. She'd been just about to belt out another line, when a table leg had given way and, with an enormous crash, everything on its surface – the cutlery and plates and glasses and forty-four-year-old woman – had smashed onto the paving stones below.

After the crash, Lily had kept her head down as much as possible, but she'd known without doubt that all eyes in the market square, at the café, probably in the shops and residential apartments above, were looking as she'd gathered her friend up. She'd helped her into a chair, handed money to Claude so he could pay for the food and the table and the embarrassment, then – once she'd ascertained Emily was more or less in one piece – had dragged her to the car.

* * *

Lily was relieved, when they finally arrived at *La Petite Maison*, that Chloé had gone out. After parking outside, she opened the front door and then helped a staggering, bruised and slightly more sober Emily into the house and up the stairs to their shared bedroom.

Now, sitting opposite her, drinking a mediocre tea that she'd made using the travel kettle and teabag from the room, Lily looked at her friend's face as she slept. They'd been out time and time again over the years, and she'd seen her in pretty much every state from sober to blind drunk to hungover and regretful.

Maybe some of her memories had faded with time. Perhaps things they'd done had seemed funnier when they were both drunk. But she didn't think she'd ever seen Emily like this. Drunk, yes. Vomiting, definitely. But never at midday, in a place where nobody else was putting away the booze. Never like this.

'What's wrong, Em?' she said quietly, knowing her friend wouldn't hear.

While she waited for Emily to sleep it off, Lily sat by the window, listening to her snores and scrolling through her mobile phone, as if somewhere in that tiny portal to the entire world she could find an answer to explain why Emily's behaviour today – and, when she thought about it, since she'd arrived – had been... well, different.

But that was the problem, she realised. Usually, when things went wrong, it would be Emily whose advice she'd seek out. Or Ben's. Ben had always been there to listen to her.

The only other person she'd usually speak to was Mum. *I'd give my right arm,* she thought, *for one more phone call with you, Mum.*

Looking out of the window at the view with its myriad greens and yellows, dotted with ramshackle stone houses and topped with a blue sky, she knew she was exactly where she wanted to be. The problem was she felt utterly alone.

With her friend unconscious and unable to tell her whether or not this was a Bad Idea, she decided to ring Ben.

'Hello? Lily?'

It was the first time they'd spoken properly since she'd left. Text messages and voice notes had passed between them. But she hadn't directly heard his voice, or directly responded to it. It felt strangely intimate.

'Hi, Ben.'

'Hi.'

A silence.

'I just wanted to call to say... well, I wondered how you were, I suppose.' Her whole body suddenly ached for him; she wanted his arms around her, wanted him to be on her side again. She sniffed, determined not to cry.

'I'm OK. Well, not really OK. You know how it is.'

A silence.

'I do. Look, Ben, I am sorry. I really am. I never... it was never in my plan to leave you, to break us up. But...'

'I know. But you did leave.'

'I know, but I suppose I could say... you let me?'

His voice became harder, more guarded. 'So you're not calling to say you're coming home.'

'No. I'm just... I suppose I just miss you, that's all.'

The line went dead.

She wished she'd never called. Sipping the last of the tea, she tried to close her eyes, to focus her thoughts on something else. But it was almost impossible.

Half an hour later, the lump on the bed began to groan.

'Coffee?' Lily asked.

The lump made a sound that seemed a bit like a yes, so Lily tore open a small stick of instant coffee and poured it into a mug. Then, she boiled the little kettle, filled it and added two sugars for good measure.

She walked to the side of the bed, sat on it, and placed the coffee on the bedside table. 'Here you go,' she said, looking at Emily's ashen face. 'How are you feeling?'

'Bloody awful.'

'Physically? Or...?'

'Oh god. Physically,' Emily said, gingerly sitting herself up. Then, 'Hang on. I didn't... the table... the café. I – my singing. Oh my god, I'm so sorry.'

Lily smiled gently and passed her the mug. Clutching it, Emily carefully blew steam from the top before sipping it and placing it back on the bedside cabinet.

Then: 'Emily, what's wrong?' Lily asked.

'It's a bit hot is all. I'll drink it in a minute. Unless you could put a splash of water in...'

'Not wrong with the coffee! What's wrong? With you?'

'What do you mean?'

'Well, I've known you for more years than either of us can bear to count. But I've never seen you like this.' She sat on the edge of the bed and put her hand gently on Emily's arm

'What, drunk?' Emily said, squinting against the sunlight.

'No, you know what I mean. Since you arrived. You're just not... you. You know?'

Emily was silent. 'It's probably just all this French stuff,' she said. 'I'm not in my natural habitat so I stand out.' She pushed her curls away from her face and gave a little shrug. 'And that strawberry stuff, whatever that is, is strong. I'll go easy next time. And I'll pay for the table obviously. So...' She shrugged again. But her eyes told a different story.

'Come on, Em. You can tell me anything, you know? Are things OK with Chris? Has something happened?'

Emily picked up the coffee mug again, went to sip it, then seemed to remember that it was too hot, and put it back down. She placed her hands together on her lap, and began examining one of her nails.

'Emily?'

'OK,' she said. 'But don't be mad.'

'What, madder than I am already?'

'Good point.'

*　*　*

'You want that I make you *un café*?' Chloé asked an hour later as Lily walked out onto the terrace.

'Oh, no. I'm fine thanks. Just thought I'd get a bit of air.'

'And Emily? Is she joining you?'

'No, she's just... she's not feeling very well. I've left her to sleep for a bit.' Lily smiled. She wanted to ask whether Chloé had heard anything about the café incident on the local grapevine, but thought it better to keep it to herself rather than risk opening that particular Pandora's box unnecessarily.

Instead, she slipped off her trainers and walked over to the large cherry tree at the back of the garden. Clearly decades old, its trunk and bark were weathered and twisted, but the fruit that hung from its branches was fresh and juicy, shining in the afternoon sun. Wasps buzzed around, attracted to the sticky juice, or crawled on half-eaten cherries that lay on the grass.

Lily sank into one of the sun-loungers, after brushing it free of stray leaves and stalks, and closed her eyes. The sun gently shone through tiny gaps between the leaves and dotted her face and body with spots of light. She tried to breathe deeply, her thoughts racing at a hundred miles an hour.

Here, at least, she could take a moment to be alone, to digest what her friend had said. To take stock of everything that had happened in the last few weeks. She could...

'Ooh, Reg, is that a hornet?' a woman's voice asked loudly.

'Don't be daft, it's just a normal wasp.'

'Did you see the size of it? It was bigger than my thumb!'

'You need your eyes testing.'

Lily opened one eye to see the couple she'd noticed at break-fast, both wearing navy shorts, walking across the grass towards the three other sun-loungers spaced out close to the tree.

'Grab up a couple of those chairs, love,' said the woman.

'But what if she's reserving them? For friends?'

'I doubt it. Don't think anyone else is staying here.'

'Still, it'd be rude.'

'Well, ask her!'

'You ask her! You're the one with all the French.'

Lily sat up slightly on her elbows, about to tell them that they could take any of the other recliners they liked – she wasn't waiting for anyone. And that she could speak English. But before she could open her mouth, the woman – whose deep tan and bright red hair both fought for her attention – crouched down and said, '*Bonjour, je m'appelle* Dawn. *Vous besoin er... les* chairs?'

'Take them, it's fine.' Lily smiled.

Hearing her English, the woman visibly relaxed. 'Oh, you're English! That's a relief. My French is so rusty at the moment. We're just back from a couple of weeks in Manchester, aren't we, Clive? And I've just lost all me verbs.'

'Ha. Yes. So do you live over here?' Lily asked, confused.

'Yes, been over here four years now, haven't we, Clive?'

Clive confirmed with a nod that yes, they had.

'We're just spending a couple of nights here while we wait for our guests to go.'

'Guests?'

'Yes. Oh, not proper guests. I mean, rental guests. We rent out our property for a month each summer and it pays for tickets back to see family and the like. Win-win.'

'Oh, I see.'

'Only muggins here booked the flights for the wrong day. So here we are! Still, it's nice to have a little break before getting back to it all.'

'Oh, what do you do out here?'

'Oh nothing. This and that. We're retired really. But you know how it is.'

Lily had no idea how it was, but nodded anyway, leaning back down and closing her eyes. 'Well, nice to meet you,' she said, to signal the end of the conversation and regain the space she needed to try to work out what to do to help her friend.

But the signal was lost on Dawn. 'You on holiday then?' she asked.

'Oh, no. I'm... I've just bought a property over here, actually.'

'Oh, right? Whereabouts?'

'Broussas.'

'Ooh, lovely. Right by the lake?'

'Yes.'

'What you doing staying here on your tod then? Had a fight with yer fella?'

'No. Actually I'm here with a friend. Just while we get the *loirs* problem sorted in the attic.'

'Oh, bloody *loirs*. Noisy little beggars. We've got 'em too, but nothing really stops me sleeping. And they're harmless enough.'

'Oh right.'

'Clive's always saying he'll put some poison down, but I'm

worried about the dogs. And don't like the idea of them all up there... you know, rotting away.'

'No,' said Lily.

'Anyway. Look, love, if you're here to stay you should come over for a drink. We're having a little do at ours in a few days. You can get to know some new faces.' Dawn smiled, revealing a set of patchwork teeth – four white crowns at the front, juxtaposed with the slightly more yellowing ones at the edge of her grin.

'Well, thanks. I'll... well, I'll definitely try to make it,' she said, only half meaning it.

Dawn finally straightened. 'Right, well, let's get these chairs shifted and give the girl some space,' she said to Clive. 'Looks like she needs a rest, that one.'

'Nice to meet you,' Lily said as they lifted their chairs to another part of the garden.

She assumed that the invitation meant she'd be meeting other British people. A kind of expat community. When she'd dreamed of living in France, it was with the aim of integrating properly, learning the language fluently and adopting a different culture.

But, after having spent a few days feeling a little out of her depth, the idea of meeting others in a similar position appealed too. The more she tried to speak French, the more she realised how far she actually was from being 'fluent'. She'd get there, sure, but it would take months. In the meantime, she had to admit that it would be good to have people she could chat with without worrying about the sex of her verbs.

Feeling slightly more at one with the world, she lay back again in her shady spot and began to replay her conversation with Emily.

17

The breakfast room at *La Petite Maison* had a pleasing smell of coffee mixed with the faint aroma of pastries. As she sat at a small oak table in the cool, silent room, Lily lost herself in her drawing. Acquiring the house, despite its faults and rodent infestation, had inspired a long-dormant desire in her – to take something and truly make it her own. She smiled as she began to sketch the perfect window dressing for the front room, then sat back to...

'What's all that?' asked Emily behind her, making her pencil skitter across the page.

'Bloody hell, Em!' Lily said, reaching for her eraser.

'Sorry.' Emily sat down beside her. 'Just wondered what you're up to?'

'Sketching,' Lily said, pushing the pad towards her. 'Just a few ideas – you know – for the house.'

'You're really good, you know?' Em said, flicking through the pad, her brow furrowed. 'You should be a designer or something.'

'Ha ha. Well, it makes a change from designing logos for solicitors' firms and hairdressers' websites.'

'I'll say,' said Em, turning a page and screwing up her eyes.

'This is the kitchen, right?'

'What gave it away? The sink? The fridge? The island of cupboards in the middle?'

'Sorry. I mean, I know it's the kitchen. Obviously. What I meant to say was – wow. I love it.'

'You do?' said Lily, self-consciously taking the pad back and looking at her own design with new eyes.

'Have I ever held back when I *haven't* liked something?' Emily said, arching a slightly dishevelled eyebrow.

'Very true.'

Lily reached her hand out and touched Emily's arm lightly. 'How are you feeling?'

'Better. Bit hungover. But it's sort of wearing off.'

'Good. Although, I meant about the other thing.'

Emily shrugged. '*C'est la vie,*' she said. 'What will be, will be, I suppose.'

'Isn't that *Que sera sera*?'

'Depends what country you're in. Anyway, you have to agree with me, remember? I'm the one in the midst of a health scare.'

'Oh, Em.'

'I'm not joking. It's one of the few perks of being potentially very ill. People have to be nice to you. It's the law.'

'Shh, let's talk about something else.'

When Emily had told her that she'd hopped on the plane after having an out-patient biopsy at a private clinic, Lily had been horrified. 'Shouldn't you have been resting?' she'd said.

'Well, maybe a bit,' Emily had admitted. 'But then I thought – how exactly does one rest one's cervix? And I thought I'd be better off, well, keeping my mind off the results.'

'Which you'll get...'

'Which should have arrived yesterday, only they didn't.'

'Oh.'

'Yep.'

Like most women, Lily had been going to smear tests for years – complaining about the discomfort, both emotional and physical, of having someone peer at her nether regions, open up an enormous speculum for a better view, then scrape off cells to send to some unfortunate scientist in the post.

She and Emily had shared anecdotes with each other over the years – the time Lily had lost her knickers when the doctor had inadvertently kicked them under the radiator, the time when Emily had coughed, only to see the speculum fly out of position. They'd laugh, and dread them, but neither had ever missed one.

But, Lily realised, for all their talk of vaginas and speculums and knickers and examination tables, they'd never spoken about what might happen if a test result came up positive. She realised she'd had absolutely no idea what might happen next.

Now she knew. Emily had had a call from her GP, who'd told her there had been some abnormal cells, and booked her in for a biopsy as an outpatient procedure. Only she hadn't been able to wait the three weeks for that appointment so had paid privately, without telling Chris.

'I just wanted to get it over with,' she'd explained. 'Didn't want him going through all the stress if there was nothing to get stressed about.'

'So you took it all on yourself.'

'Yes.'

'Which, as it turns out, wasn't the best idea.'

'No.' Emily had told her how she'd argued with Chris the night before she'd flown to France. 'He knew something was wrong,' Emily had said, 'but by that time it seemed almost worse to admit that I'd kept it all from him. So I came here to get my mind off things.'

'But you couldn't...?'

'Turns out, my mind is pretty focused when it comes to people snipping samples off my body for analysis and then taking an inordinate amount of time to produce the results.'

'Well, yes, I can imagine. And drinking the stress away didn't exactly work out.'

'Not really.'

'Oh, Emily, you're such an idiot.' Lily had said, leaning forward and gathering her still alcohol-breathed friend into her arms. 'You should have told me sooner.'

'I know.'

Lily had pulled free of the hug and had taken her friend firmly by her upper arms, looking into her eyes. 'Well look. You've told me now. And whatever comes next, I'm here.'

'Thank you,' Emily had said. 'Sorry. I thought I was stronger than this.'

'It's not about being strong, Em. You're the strongest woman I know...'

'Coming from you, that's an enormous compliment.'

'Is that a joke?' Lily had said. 'You know as well as I do that I'm a complete and utter mess half the time.'

'No, for once, sweetheart, I am *not* joking. You are one formidable woman.'

'Oh.'

'Well, how much strength does it take to walk away from your husband, move to another country and start some sort of brand-new life?'

'Try not to confuse strength with being completely and utterly mad.'

'Ha. Well, there is that.'

'Anyway, OK, let's change the subject,' Lily said now, pushing an interiors magazine across the table. 'I was thinking dove grey for the hallway – what do you reckon?'

'It's a bit... well, grey.'

'Well, grey does tend to come up a bit on the grey side.'

'It's quite a *loir* colour, isn't it?'

'That,' said Lily, crossing her pen through the colour swatch, 'is a very good point.'

'Well, look. How about we go for a walk, or something. Up at the lake? Check out how that French mayor guy is doing ridding your house of vermin on the way?'

'Sounds like a plan.'

'Great. I'll go and de-hangover in the shower, and then...?'

'Perfect,' Lily said.

Emily left the breakfast room, her feet tapping on the hall tiles then coming to an abrupt halt.

'*Bonjour, Madame*,' came a familiar voice.

'*Bonjour*,' Lily heard Emily reply.

Then there was the sound of two sets of footsteps, one heading away, the other drawing nearer. The door swung more fully open to reveal Frédérique, his face and hands peppered with small red wounds.

''ello?' he said. 'Ah, *Madame* Buttercup!' His smile was wide, despite his evidently sore face.

'Oh my god,' Lily said, turning to him and forgetting to even try to speak French. 'What happened to you?'

'These little '*mignon*' loir, they are not so sweet when you try to catch them, uh?' he said, with a shrug as if it didn't matter he'd clearly been set upon by a family of rodents. 'And then when you try also to release them, he is even more angry, I think.'

'I'm so sorry!' Lily stood up, hand over her mouth. 'I didn't realise they could be so... well, vicious.'

'*De rien*, you are welcome,' he said. 'You can sit, eh? I have put some treatment on zem and I will live, they say.'

'Well, that's good to hear,' Lily said, sinking back into her chair, still feeling guilty. Should she have let him use the poison after all? Or just been a bit more relaxed about her loft-invaders, like Dawn seemed to be? After all, she hadn't even noticed them until the night of the fall.

Still, it was done now, and she looked at him gratefully. 'Well, thank you,' she said. 'It is appreciated.'

'*Pas de problème.*'

Lily had read many times about how the French were more relaxed, how stress rates in France were far lower than in the UK. One of the reasons she loved the culture here was that so many people seemed friendly and easy-going.

But could he be for real? She couldn't imagine being completely calm about being set upon by a pack of snarling mini squirrels. Especially if her initial instinct had been to get rid of them in a much less humane way.

But Frédérique's smile seemed to be genuine. He walked over and peered over her shoulder, looking at her sketches.

'This iz nice,' he said, pointing at the kitchen sketch, his arm just inches from her ear in a way that felt strangely intimate. She could smell the antiseptic he must have used to treat his wounds, the faint scent of coffee on his breath and underneath, the aroma of soap and aftershave.

She wondered for a second whether he could smell her in return. After spending a couple of hours on the sun-lounger, she was probably slightly less fragrant than she'd have preferred.

'Thank you,' she said. 'It's the new kitchen for the house, or at least I hope it will be.'

'It iz very nice. I like it with the modern *placards et bar Améri-cane*,' he said. 'The cupboard, eh? You 'ave a good eye.' He slid into a chair next to her unasked. 'And these are your other plans, yes?' He picked up her sketches and flicked through them. 'Zey are, how you say, very stylish.'

'Thank you,' she said.

'When you 'ave finished, I think my grandmother will not recognise it, eh?'

'No, maybe not,' she said, not quite sure how to answer this without accidentally insulting an elderly woman's taste in decor. She could hardly say 'Let's hope not!' and laugh her head off, could she? 'Can I get you a drink or something?' she said instead. Chloé had said that she could help herself to the room and make use of the coffee maker in the corner if she wished. She was sure that her host wouldn't mind her getting Frédérique a cup.

'Fank you, but *non*, I am fine,' he said. He looked at her for a moment, his eyes intensely green in the afternoon light. 'But I want to ask... I 'ear you 'ave a *problème*,' he added quietly, 'in ze town wiv your friend, *aujourd'hui* uh? Is it all OK for you?'

Lily nodded. 'I hope we didn't upset anyone?'

Frédérique made a face and shook his head. '*Non*, I do not think people are very easy to offend, *tu comprends*? But some people, they find it *très* funny. They say, look at the English ladies, uh? But I tell them, *Madame Buttercup*, she is my friend; she does not be'ave like that *normalement*.'

'Thank you,' Lily said.

'But your friend, eh?' Frédérique added, raising an eyebrow. 'She like to 'ow you say, she like a drink a little too much, per'aps? She is a bit crazy?'

'I know. But... *c'est compliqué*,' she said. 'It's complicated. She is... *un peu malade*.'

'She is sick?' Frédérique looked concerned. 'From the drinking?'

'No. Well, yes. But no, I mean... She's not sick exactly. It's more that she's *triste*, sad.'

'She 'as *une dépression*?'

Another female word, Lily thought. Great. 'Well, a bit. At the moment,' she said. 'She...' But she couldn't find the words to explain without betraying Emily's confidence. And she wasn't sure whether Frédérique would cope with the mention of a cervix over the breakfast table.

Frédérique nodded sagely. 'I understand,' he said. 'You want that I tell people this?'

'Oh no! Please don't tell everyone she's depressed!'

'I mean,' he said, leaning forward slightly, his face only inches from hers; eyes earnest, 'I mean to tell them that she is not well, that it is *pas normal* for 'er to, how you say, drink the piss?'

'To get pissed,' Lily corrected, with a grin. 'And yes, please. I mean, if people say anything about it.'

'OK, I tell them,' he said. 'But I tell them for *you*. Because you are my friend, *oui*?' He held her gaze for a moment and she found herself looking away, face flushed.

'Yes. Yes, definitely,' she said.

Frédérique stood up decisively. 'And now you can go back to the new 'ouse, without *les ravageurs*, the little pests!' he said with a grin.

'Yes. Thanks for that again. And sorry about... the bites. Do you want me to... do I owe you anything?'

'No, you do not need to pay me,' he said. 'After all, it iz still my 'ouse *pour l'instant*, eh. Zey were my *petite* pests, *oui*?' He smiled. 'But maybe when your friend goes back to *Angleterre* you can buy me a beer? Tell me about your *dessins et* your plans'

She looked up at him, his earnest, injured face so open and friendly and found herself smiling.

'Definitely,' she said.

He reached a hand out and gently touched her shoulder. 'And perhaps, *Madame*, you will solve another mystery for me – eh? 'Ow such a beautiful woman end up coming to zis small place alone?'

It had been a while since she'd been touched. She wanted to say something, to say that she wasn't available – not like that. But perhaps he didn't mean anything by it. It was just a friendly gesture.

She wanted to say something modest, like, *Pah! Beautiful! You need your eyes testing.* Or something Emily might say, such as, *Do you mind taking your hand off my shoulder.* Perhaps even, *Unhand me, sir!*

But actually, it was quite nice to feel his hand on her shoulder. And she didn't know what she wanted to say about it.

'Well, yes,' she said. 'I'm not sure when Emily's going. But yes. That would be *très bon.*'

There was a clatter from the hallway and, as Lily lifted her head to look she saw Emily peeping around the doorway – invisible to Frédérique from her position. She made a little face at Lily, unsure whether or not she should come in.

'Hey, Emily!' Lily said loudly. 'Frédérique, this is my friend, Emily. Emily, this is Frédérique, the *maire*, the man who is selling the house to me.'

'Bonjour,' said Emily, walking up to them and sticking out her hand for a shake. She eyed Frédérique with interest. She'd changed into a pair of white jeans and a red, flowered blouse and looked so fresh and groomed from the shower that Lily suddenly felt sweaty and inadequate in comparison.

'*Rebonjour, Madame,*' Frédérique said, briefly touching his fingers to hers. 'I 'ear you 'ave quite an experience *au marché* this afternoon, huh?' He grinned.

'That's one way to describe it, I suppose.'

'It is OK, I now, I know your *secret* ah? I will tell all zat this woman, she is not like this *normalement*. She does not mostly like to drink like the *poisson*, eh? All will be well.'

'Well, thank you,' Emily said, looking at Lily with eyes that told a different story.

'Well, I'd better go,' Frédérique said, looking at them both with a wide smile. '*Bonne soirée, Mesdames.*'

'*Bonne soirée*,' they chimed in unison as he left the room.

'Right, missy,' Emily said, grabbing Lily's arm and pulling her into a chair. 'You have got some explaining to do.'

'I have'

'Yes, first of all, what secret of mine is that man going to tell to the entire *Limousin*?'

'Oh, it's nothing to worry about... it's...'

'And didn't you think to tell him that I'm quite able to fight my own battles?'

'Well, I probably should have but—'

'And,' interrupted Emily with a grin, 'much more importantly, why didn't you tell me that the man you were buying the house from looked so much like Max Skinner?'

'Max Skinner?' the reference was briefly lost on Lily. 'Who's—'

'"This place does not suit my life",' said Emily, with a dramatic flourish. '"No, Max, it's your life that does not suit this place."'

'Oh god, you're right,' Lily said, her mouth dropping open.

'"Pardon my lips",' began Emily.

'..."they find joy in the most unusual places",' finished Lily. 'Oh, bloody hell.'

'Lily, I hate to break this to you. Yes, the house is a bit smaller and you don't have a vineyard. But other than that you've pretty much just stepped into the set of your favourite film.'

Because behind the beard, behind the bites, when you imagined him in a cream linen suit and with slightly longer hair, Frédérique was the spit of a younger Russell Crowe.

18

'It doesn't matter,' he said, wrapping his arms around her tightly. 'We can try again.'

'But what if it doesn't work?'

'Then we'll try again... again.'

She felt her heartbeat calm as she lay against his chest. Then, 'Ben,' she said, 'what if it never happens?'

He was silent for a minute. 'Then,' he said at last, 'I will still be the luckiest man in the world. Just to have you. Anything else, well, that would be the icing on the cake. But you know what? The cake's pretty damn good just as it is.'

She laughed then, despite the tears. Despite the tenth negative pregnancy test in a row. 'Who are you calling a cake?' she said.

* * *

The house smelled musty and damp when they arrived and Lily spent the first twenty minutes grappling with blinds and old window catches to try to air things out a bit. 'It's funny how it had started to feel like home, but now it doesn't,' she said to Emily. 'It's like it's reset itself while we've been away – reverted to its original form.'

'I can always get some *loirs* to move in again, if you think that's the problem?' said her friend, giving her a squeeze.

'No, thanks. I think I'll do without.'

'Come on, cheer up. I know what you mean. But it'll soon feel like yours again. We'll get some coffee on and blast out that musty smell for a start.'

'Thanks, Em.'

'Hey, it's what I'm here for,' Emily said, with a wry smile. 'To lift your spirits.'

'Well, that and because you're running away.'

'Well, yes. That too.'

'Are you... well, how are you feeling?'

'Absolutely shitting myself, darling.'

'Oh, Em. Not long now.'

It was 9.30 on Monday morning and although they'd packed up their things and come to the house early to keep themselves occupied, it was impossible not to think about Emily's imminent call to the clinic. She'd rung up yesterday at Lily's insistence to chase the errant result, only to be told that – although the clinic was open at weekends -there was nothing new in her file and her consultant wouldn't be in until the next morning.

'Don't worry,' the receptionist had apparently said, 'these things take a little more time to go through the system sometimes.'

'She sounded as if she expected me to laugh and say: "Ah, don't worry about it" – as if it was a pair of knickers I'd ordered that had got lost in the post, or a library book I'd reserved. Not an actual medical result that might change my life forever,' Emily had fumed afterwards.

'I suppose when you work with that sort of thing day in, day out, it becomes very ordinary,' Lily had suggested. 'You can't *feel* it all the time or you'd go mad.'

'Yes, but surely she should understand a bit more about what people need to hear in this situation,' Emily had said. 'She was just so... breezy. She could at least have made a sympathetic noise or two.'

'What kind of noise?'

'Well, hmm, haaa,' Emily had said, tilting her head to the side and fluttering her eyelashes.

'That is very impressive.'

'Yes, maybe I should see if they have any jobs going.'

As the evening had worn on, Emily had become more nervous. They'd taken a walk about ten o'clock at night, in an attempt to drive the restlessness from her body. But it hadn't worked.

It had been a difficult night. Their bed at *La Petite Maison* was a neat, small double and even sharing it with an intimate partner might have been a challenge. Sharing it with a wriggling best friend and a mind full of worries had not led to the most relaxing night and Lily had woken early, her back aching more than it had after her fall from the iron bedstead.

At least being back at the house might mean a better night's sleep, Lily told herself now. Despite having failed to buy anything to replace the two airbeds in the upper rooms, she was looking forward to at least being able to spread out a bit in bed again, even if her bottom would be grazing the floor at the same time. And, of course, there would be no rodent riots above her head in the wee small hours.

Earlier, over yet another pastry filled breakfast at Chloé's, she'd introduced Emily to Dawn and Clive who'd promptly invited her to their party too. 'It won't be anything much,' Dawn had reassured her. 'Just a few mates and a few beers, you know? Come along and meet the gang!'

'Thanks,' Emily had said, with a smile.

But the minute the couple had left the breakfast room, her face had changed. 'Meet the gang!' Emily said. 'You're not going to go, are you?'

'Why not?'

'Well, they're old enough to be your parents, for a start.'

'Not that I *have* any parents,' Lily had reminded her.

'Sorry. But you know what I mean.'

'Anyway, I hate to break it to you, Emily, but they're only about ten years our senior,' she'd added. 'Old enough to be siblings; aunt and uncle at a push. But not parents, I'm afraid.'

'I wish you'd stop that.'

'What?'

'All that maths. It's bad for the brain. I stopped counting once I reached thirty-five and I'm much happier for it.' Emily had winked.

'Still, doesn't stop you celebrating your birthday each year though?'

'That's different.' Emily had grinned. Then, 'Sorry,' she said. 'I just thought they seemed a bit... you know.'

'What?'

'Well, a bit "expatty". You know, when Clive bent to tie his shoelace, I'm pretty sure I saw a glimpse of Union Jack boxers.'

'Expatty? Is that even a word?'

'It is now.' Emily had grinned. 'Look, I just mean, they seem like they're a type.'

Lily had been silent for a moment. 'I know what you mean,' she'd said. 'But I've come to realise the idea of properly integrating with my smattering of evening class French, well, it isn't going to happen right away. And it wouldn't hurt to have a few friendly faces in my camp. They seem nice. And I suppose, when it comes down to it, I'm an expat too, whatever that is...'

'Posh immigrant.'

'Ha. Well, less of the posh.'

'Sorry. You're probably right. I'd go mad if I didn't have anyone I could talk to properly.'

'Exactly. I can't integrate with people if all I can do is ask directions to the tourist information centre.'

'Or buy a train ticket to Paris.'

'Or order coffee and a *croissant*.'

'Exactly. I mean, I'm going to get more lessons like, yesterday. But I've realised – even if I study day and night – I'm pretty sure it's going to take longer than I'd thought.'

'Although *Monsieur Crowe* has a pretty good command of English.'

'*Monsieur Crowe?*'

'*Russell* to you,' her friend had told her with a wink. 'Or *Frédérique*.'

'Oh Em, will you stop!' she'd said, feeling her face go red. Ever since Emily had pointed out the likeness between Frédérique and the heartthrob from her favourite movie she couldn't shake off the image. Now she was in danger of either flinging herself into Frédérique's arms and calling him Max or asking to see his vineyard next time she saw him.

'Shall we sort the beds while we're waiting?' she said now to Emily, picking up the rather pathetic foot-pump that she'd bought from the supermarket.

Luckily both beds needed repumping – something that was ordinarily a chore, but got both their minds off the imminent call. When they finally finished – legs aching – it was time. 'I'm so fucking nervous,' Emily said just before she dialled.

'I know you are, love,' Lily said, putting an arm round her. 'But it's better to know.'

'I know. Sorry if I've been a bit over the top. It's the nerves.'

'Over the top? You? Never.' Lily smiled.

Emily put the phone to her ear. 'Do you mind if I?' she said, gesturing to the next room.

'Sure.'

To give her friend some space, Lily stepped out of the front door into the garden, but, restless with anxiety, found herself walking down the road that led past the campsite to the beach-side lake. Although she'd driven by and given it a quick look when she'd first arrived, she hadn't since taken the time to explore it properly, and never on foot.

The morning still had a nip in the air, but the sun was breaking through, gently shining on the road ahead of her. After passing the entrance to the campsite, set in between a canopy of trees, the road started to open out, and soon she'd reached the wooden walkway that led to the lakeside sand.

Other than a couple walking their dog a little along the beach and a couple of campervans parked in the small car park, she was completely alone. The lake stretched out to the distance and, had she not known, she could easily have imagined that she was on an island, surrounded by the bluest of seas. Later, she knew, the car park would begin to fill as holidaymakers and locals made the most of the chance to swim, take out one of the canoes for hire, or sit at the ramshackle beach hut and order white wine and a *crêpe* or *barquette de frites*. But for now, at this hour, it was all hers.

She slipped off her trainers and walked across the soft sand to the lake's edge. The shallow water was clear against the sand but became murkier as it stretched away and deepened. She spotted a tiny shoal of fish – each no bigger than her smallest fingernail –

darting and moving together as she dipped her toes into the water for the first time.

In England, they'd visited some relatively remote places, but wherever they'd gone she had always been able to hear the faint hum of traffic on a distant motorway, the purr of cars on nearby roads, music emanating from vehicles or houses or tiny speakers tucked into oblivious ears. Here, other than the odd bark of a dog, she realised she was enveloped in a peaceful silence, with no throbbing undertone.

She stretched her arms up, spreading her fingers and luxuriating in the sensation of releasing tension from the furthest part of her. Perhaps she could come and do yoga on this beach, meditate, do all the things she hadn't had time for before. Actually practise self-care instead of sharing quotes about it online. Bathe her eyes in the beauty of a landscape that was entirely natural as far as her eyes could see.

This is why she'd moved here. The tranquillity, the silence, the sense that time was hers to stretch, shape, seize or drift along with as she wished. Yes, there was work to do, bills to pay; there would be difficulties no doubt with admin and renovations and setting up a business. But as long as she could walk to this lake, look out over the expanse of deep, calm water, ground herself somehow in the nature her body had craved more than she'd realised, then she could find the strength for anything else that came her way.

The thought brought her back to herself – Emily would be finished with her call by now. Feeling a tingling sensation in her fingers, she walked back over the sand, which covered her skin with a rough, uneven coating. As she stepped onto the wooden decked path, she felt the sand begin to crumble away, and by the time she was at the edge of the tarmacked road, she felt clean enough to slip her trainers back on.

She half walked, half jogged to the edge of the parking area; breathing heavily and resolving to improve her fitness now she had the time to do so. Then suddenly a small figure appeared where the road curved.

It was Emily.

'Em!' Lily called, waving a hand. She felt suddenly guilty – why had she come so far from the house? The figure stopped and then started moving more quickly towards her. Lily began upping her pace in turn, wanting to reach her friend quickly and apologise for not being there when she'd received the news, whatever it was.

She'd been caught up for a moment, and it had been wonderful, but thinking about how Emily must have stepped outside and been unable to find her and share whatever she'd learned made her feel guilty. She dropped into a light jog.

As Emily's features came more into focus, she could see her friend had been crying; her face was red and blotchy, her mouth turned slightly down. Like Lily, she wasn't a natural jogger, but between them they managed to cover the distance that separated them quickly.

Looking at her friend as she approached, seeing her face so unnaturally streaked with tears, Lily felt the years fall away. They were two children on a playground, one running to pick up the other who had fallen. Two teenagers at a club, helping each other get home safely. Two women supporting each other through marriages, pregnancy, with bereavement, sadness, joy and all the ups and downs of life.

In that moment, everything else Lily had been striving for or worrying about fell away. She knew instantly that if Emily was ill, she'd drop everything else to care for her. In that moment, nothing else mattered but the friend who'd been at her side for almost her entire life.

They raced into each other's arms like long-lost lovers at the end of a romantic movie, Emily burying her head in Lily's shoulder, hot tears on her cheeks. 'I...' she said. 'I...'

'What is it?' Lily said, gently pushing her friend's shoulders so they were standing face to face. 'Whatever it is, we are in this together. No matter what.'

'Oh god, Lily,' Emily said. 'It was so... they kept me waiting for ages, and my heart was just...' She looked at her friend, her eyes wide and frantic.

'It must have been awful,' said Lily. 'But you got the result?'

Emily nodded, her messy bun flopping forward on her head almost comically.

'And...?'

'It's... well, it's actually... it's nothing.'

'Nothing? You mean it's small? Early stage? Pre-cancerous cells?'

'No,' said Emily, shaking her head. 'I mean absolutely one hundred per cent nothing at all,! Basically, as much as I usually hate the word – they said that my sample was... normal.'

'Normal! So you don't have...'

'Nothing to see here, guv'nor,' Emily replied, giving a little watery smile.

'Oh my god, Em, that is brilliant!' Lily gathered her in for a squeeze.

'And I called Chris. I called him straightaway,' said her friend. 'And I told him everything. And he was so cross, but so happy for me too. And I realised that I should have shared it all with him. He said that's what he's there for. To share it all, no matter what.'

'Oh, Em. I'm so happy for you.' They separated and began to walk slowly towards the house.

'And, look, I was thinking – and I'm so sorry – that I'd really,

really like to go home and see him,' Emily said, looking at Lily guiltily.

Lily's heart turned over in her chest. 'Yes,' she said. 'Of course you must.'

What she actually wanted to say was, *Don't leave me*. Despite the drunken display, the 3 a.m. *loir* emergencies and the fact that her friend had now pointed out Frédérique's resemblance to a noughties Russell C., she'd become used to having Emily around. She had made things feel, if not relaxing exactly, then more like a holiday.

But when Emily left she'd be alone with the house.

Still, she smiled, and hugged her friend and did all the things a grown-up person was supposed to do. And reminded herself how incredibly, incredibly lucky they both were that the biopsy had been the end of the story.

Yet Chris's words had struck her: that he was there 'no matter what.' It was exactly how she'd felt about Ben until just under a month ago. That certainty. Suddenly and so viscerally it took her breath away, she was reminded just how much she missed him.

As soon as they arrived back at the house and she was alone in the kitchen, she slipped her phone from her pocket and messaged Ben.

Thinking about you.

His reply came almost instantly.

You too.

Can't we do anything to make it work?

She ventured.

I can't.

He replied.

His words felt physically painful to read. She felt both hurt and embarrassed and wished she could pluck her message straight back from cyber space. That was the problem with being truly open. You were exposed, vulnerable. She hated feeling that way.

'You'll be all right, you know,' a voice said behind her.

She spun around, hiding her phone like a guilty teenager. 'Oh, Em. I was just—'

'Let me guess... texting Frédérique and arranging a hot date?'

But Lily couldn't join in with the banter. 'Honestly, that isn't something that's going to happen, Em. I'm still married, and I still *want* to be.'

'I know, love.'

'I was actually texting Ben.'

'Oh.'

'Said I was thinking about him. He said the same. So... for once I said it – I asked if we could make it work. But... no.'

'The man's an idiot.'

'Maybe,' said Lily.

'Hey, don't cry!' Em stepped forward and wrapped an arm around her shoulder.

'I'm not... not really. I'm just. You know what I'm like. It takes a lot to...'

'Ask?'

'Well... yes. I don't know why. But it does.'

'I know.'

'And hearing what Chris said about you, about going through it all together, just brings it home that Ben doesn't seem to feel that way about me. At least not any more.'

'God, I'm sorry, Lil—'

'No, don't be... I'm just feeling sorry for myself.'

'You have every right to, you know? I think you're being incredibly strong,' said her friend loyally.

'I've just got to accept it,' Lily said, straightening up and taking a breath. 'I've got to accept that he doesn't love me enough.'

19

The airport entrance was packed with people, rolling suitcases or sitting on the shiny plastic seats in the waiting area. The queue for the check-in desk had already started to form – a mixture of visitors returning home or expats taking a trip to the motherland. As soon as they'd walked through the sliding doors, Lily felt a lump in her throat.

Emily was her family. All the 'real' adult family she had left. And she didn't want her to go.

But it wasn't about her. Emily had her own life to lead too. So she swallowed the feeling as best she could and masked it with a smile.

'Love you,' she said, giving Emily a squeeze.

'Oh god. You too,' her friend replied. 'And look, I'll be back to check up on you in a few weeks. It's less expensive than hopping on a train into town.'

'Thank you. I'd love that. And bring Chris, maybe?'

'Thanks. Maybe. Hey, maybe we can double-date with you and Freddy.' Emily's eyes sparkled with mischief and Lily was struck suddenly by the fact that this was the first time she'd seen her friend's genuine, cheeky smile since she'd arrived. 'Only joking. And, look. You'll be OK,' Emily added, rubbing Lily's shoulder. 'I think you're going to have a brilliant adventure.'

'Thank you.' She'd promised herself she wouldn't cry. After all, it wasn't as if she'd moved over with Emily or expected her to stay long term.

'And you're going to that party, right?' Emily said, looking at her insistently.

'I thought you said it would be a complete bore?'

'Ah, but you don't want to listen to anything I said during this trip. Most of the time I was either drinking too much or hungover,' Emily quipped. 'Seriously, though, I think you should go. It'll be good to meet some new people – make some proper connections.'

'I'll try.'

'Atta girl.' And with that, Emily gave her quick peck on the cheek then joined the small queue leading to passport control.

Lily waved her hand when Emily was in the queue and her friend raised a reciprocal palm.

It felt wrong to disappear before Emily made it through security and into the waiting area, but the queue moved painfully slowly, meaning they were stuck performing an embarrassing scene: Lily playing the patient waver-offer, Emily rummaging in her bag, checking her passport, glancing up occasionally to grin and do another mock wave. It was excruciating, this need to be polite and do the right thing. They both knew it, yet they both played their parts to perfection until at last Emily disappeared through the glass double doors and Lily was able to turn and make her way home.

Six hours later, she was parking down the side of a country road, tucking the Nissan alongside ten or so other cars – muddy Land Rovers, battered Clios, and several cars that still had

English plates. She'd opted to wear one of her summer dresses – something she didn't often get the opportunity to slip on – and had taken the time to properly blow-dry her hair. The shampoo she'd used smelled of apples and she caught a whiff from time to time as she walked.

It had taken a while to find the right place. As in *Faux la Montagne*, none of the houses had numbers and it was a case of taking careful directions, looking out for landmarks such as 'a field of cows' or 'the barn with all the solar panels' in order to find what looked to be the right place. Even now, she was only half sure she wasn't turning up to another party altogether.

The house looked gorgeous from the outside as she walked up the muddy, half-gravelled path. The shutters and front door were newly painted in a pale green, and a table and chairs sat under an enormous oak tree, its twisted trunk marking it out as at least a couple of hundred years old.

As she approached, she could hear the gentle hum of conversation, and saw to her right a group of people gathered together, wine glasses in hand, standing by an in-built pool. A couple of children were in the water, splashing and calling to one another. It was an idyllic scene, but she felt suddenly shy – not able to see Dawn or Clive among the guests and unsure how to introduce herself.

'Hello, love.' The voice in her ear was so sudden that she couldn't help but jump. She turned and found herself face to face with Dawn, red hair backcombed into a resplendent bouffant, eye-liner slightly smudged and wearing a bikini top and sarong. She grinned and shoved an enormous glass of wine into Lily's hand. 'You found us then!'

'Yes, oh, thank you. I shouldn't really, I'm driving...'

'Oh we don't worry about that around here!' Dawn said with a conspiratorial nudge and grin.

'We don't?'

'No, well everyone else seems to just get in their cars after a long lunch. You see them weaving around the streets come two o'clock. All the farmers, and the like. No-one ever seems to stop them.'

'Oh. But...' Lily was going to suggest that being caught was only one of the risks of drink driving, but Dawn marched off ahead towards the group and she found herself hurrying in her wake like a young child chasing her mother.

'Right,' said Dawn, letting her catch up on the edge of a small cluster of people. 'This is Lily. Lily, this is Pat, Kenneth, Wilbur, Sharon, Conor and Bob.'

'Nice to meet you,' said Lily, lifting her glass slightly and realising that while Dawn might only be a decade her senior, the small group she'd been introduced to were definitely old enough to be her parents.

'Lily's moved over all on her own,' Dawn continued, making a sad face. 'So I thought it would help her to see a few friendly faces.'

There was a chorus of murmurs and nods. Her job done, Dawn clapped her hands. 'Right,' she said, 'better get back to me sausage rolls.'

Lily took a tentative sip of her wine, which was pleasingly cold although a tad on the vinegary side, and looked around the group. She could feel her body tense under the soft folds of her dress. She wished more than anything she had Ben with her, or Ty. Or ideally both. Without them she felt exposed – not knowing what to say. And despite the crowd of people, terribly lonely.

The man to her left, who'd been introduced as Bob, caught her eye and gave her a grin.

'So what brings you to these parts then?' he asked.

'I'm hoping to do up a property, start running retreats,' she said. 'What about you?'

'Me? oh we've been here for about a decade. Me and Sharon over there. Both retired now, thank god.' He took a gulp of his wine. 'Takes a bit of getting used to, mind.'

'Yes, I can imagine.' She smiled. 'But you're settled in now.'

He shrugged. 'It has its moments,' he said.

She noticed a bead of sweat at the top of his bald head begin to tremble slightly, before it snaked its way along his forehead and glided down to the tip of his nose, at which point he wiped it off with the back of his hand.

'So,' she said in the slightly awkward silence that had formed between them. 'What do you do?'

'You're looking at it,' he said. 'Meet up with mates, have a wine. Maybe a pizza night sometimes.'

'Oh, right.'

'Course it's harder in this weather. It never used to get this hot until August.'

'That'll be global warming then,' she said with a wry smile.

'Yeah, right,' he said, shaking his head. 'Global warming.'

'What?'

'You don't seriously believe all that stuff, do you?' he said, leaning forward slightly. 'Tell me this, then. How can we have global warming when it's freezing cold come September? Could do with a bit more global warming if you ask me.'

'Eh,' she said. She'd heard this argument before – the odd Facebook forum nutter online – but never had someone voice it to her face. 'Well,' she said, 'it's not all about things heating up, it's—'

'Global warming,' he continued, not really listening to her, shaking his head, almost fondly, as if she was a small child talking about Santa.

She used the pause in conversation to make her escape and drifted over to two women in sundresses and hats standing by the water. One of the women had clearly been wearing a strappy dress the day before, and white lines of a cross-strapped back were clearly visible against the red of her sunburned skin.

'You all right, love?' one of them said. 'Been talking to Bob, have you?'

'Yes,' she said, tentatively, not wanting to make a comment in case she'd accidentally stepped into some sort of climate-change deniers' expat drinking group.

'Was he giving it all that?' the other woman asked, moving her hand like a bird's beak.

'Well, maybe a bit.'

'Just ignore him,' the first woman said. 'He's harmless enough. But... well, getting on a bit.'

'Right.' Lily felt flooded with relief. 'I did wonder...'

'Anyway, I'm Kelly and this is June,' said the first woman, whose red complexion was topped with a startling blonde quiff.

June smiled. 'Hi,' she said. She was younger than Kelly by a few years, and had softly curling brown hair that hung neatly around her face. She'd accessorised with the sort of chunky jewellery that a kind person might describe as 'individual'.

'So, out here all alone?' Kelly said, making the same sad face that Dawn had made during her introductions.

'Yes,' she said, not really wanting to go into details. 'But it's great... I'm looking forward to getting to know people, settling into the area.'

The pair nodded. 'I was like that at first,' June confided. 'Thought I'd be fluent in French within a month! Now look at me – I can barely ask where the bogs are!'

'Oh, how long have you been here?'

'Twelve years.'

'And you don't—'

'It's all those verbs,' June said, solemnly. 'We get by quite well without those in English.'

'Ha,' Lily said, then wondered whether June might actually be serious.

'Anyway,' she said, moving the subject on to safer ground. 'What brought you to France?'

'Oh, it's lovely here. We sold up in the UK and bought a property outright, so no mortgage. Meant we could retire at fifty-five,' said Kelly. 'We run a B. & B. in the summer to get a little bit extra in, but we use the rest of the time to relax or go on holidays in the campervan.'

This was more like it. 'So you enjoy living here?'

'Oh yes, nothing like it.' Kelly smiled.

'And where have you travelled to? You've probably done a round-the-world tour by now.'

The women exchanged a look and Lily had to review her words to find out if there was something wrong. She didn't think she'd said anything insulting.

'Yeah, right,' June said. 'All the way round the world, right, Kelly.'

'Yep. A *round*-the-world trip!' They both laughed, almost affectionately.

'Sorry,' Lily said, unable to take the weird feeling of tension stretching in her stomach. 'Did I... Was it something I said?'

'Oh, don't worry about us,' June said. 'We're just not used to meeting... well, globe-heads.'

'Globe-heads?' Lily unconsciously raised her spare hand and placed it on her head. Was it rounder than the average head shape? And if it was, why had she never noticed? And even if it was, it wasn't very nice of them to laugh at her for it. She began to feel a little as she'd used to at school when walking past the popular crowd on her way to lunch.

'Yes.' June nodded. 'I mean, don't worry. It's not your fault. I was one until I met Kelly.'

This sounded even more alarming. 'So...?'

'I think most people are moving away from the round earth theory,' said Kelly, leaning forward conspiratorially. 'People in the *know* I mean.'

'You mean, you think... you believe the world is flat?' Lily said, trying to keep her tone light.

'Well, it's not really a case of believe, love. It's fact.'

'But...?'

'I tell you what,' June said, putting an arm around Lily's back. 'Give me your email address and I'll send you some links...'

Lily couldn't help wonder, as she backed away smiling after promising to read and really 'take in' the information June was determined to send her, what Emily would have done in the same situation. And really how far against her own beliefs she'd go just for the sake of politeness. So far she'd appeared to agree that it was fine to drink-drive, so long as you didn't get caught, that global warming was, at best, a ridiculous joke. And now she was well on the way to being brainwashed into a flat-earther's cult.

Emily would have flattened each argument and still managed to somehow make friends and become part of the crowd. She'd simply smiled and scuttled away.

Why couldn't she ever speak up?

Noticing a spare deckchair by the pool, she sank into it, almost spilling her wine as she went down. The glass was still perilously full – she'd only had two tiny sips as she definitely wanted to drive home sober. She took the opportunity to tip a little onto the grass next to her, hoping that Dawn wouldn't notice.

'Oops, see you like the wine then?' said a voice.

A woman with red hair tied back in a ponytail was sitting in the deckchair a metre or so away from her.

Lily grimaced. 'It's not that, it's just—'

'Seriously, it's horrible.' The woman grinned. 'Save it to sprinkle on your chips instead. I accidentally spilled my glass. Got myself a few Cokes for me and the kids. Want one?' She reached down beside her, then waved a can in Lily's direction.

'Oh, yes please,' Lily said, reaching for it.

They lapsed into silence. She wasn't sure whether she dared start another conversation at this particular party. But then the woman said, 'I'm Sam, by the way.'

'Lily.'

'Nice to meet you. Dawn said you're new?'

'Well, yes. Just moved over.'

'I've been here a couple of years now,' Sam said, leaning forward slightly, her hair brushing against her cheek. Then, 'Derek, give him the ball back *now*!' she barked so suddenly that Lily almost spilled her new drink to boot. 'Sorry,' she said. 'Never bring kids to a party, is my advice.'

'Sounds like a sensible plan,' Lily said.

'You got any of your own?'

'Just one. Tyler. He's eighteen now, off to uni.'

'So you took the chance to move?'

'Yes. Something like that. How about you? What brought you here?'

'Oh, love, I suppose. Met Gabriel, got married. Now stuck speaking French for most of the day,' she laughed.

'Ah OK, is he here, your husband?'

'No, I'm giving him a day off,' she said. She leaned forward. 'A few people here are a bit of an acquired taste.'

'Flat-earthers?' Lily ventured, keeping her voice low.

'They're the ones.'

'Then why—?'

'Ah, they're harmless enough, unless you're particularly susceptible to conspiracy theories,' said Sam. 'And I don't know. It's nice. I don't get to see my parents that often. And hearing voices from home... It's ... I need it sometimes.'

'Even if they are trying to convince you that global warming is just a phase?'

'Even then.' Sam grinned. 'And you know, don't let the conspiracists put you off. There are a few normal people lurking about if you know where to look. And I like to think that I'm one of them. Here.' She leaned over and rummaged in her bag, producing a piece of paper and pen. 'Take my number,' she said, scribbling rapidly. 'You know, in case you ever need anything.'

'That,' said Lily, taking a swig of Coke and feeling her eyes water slightly from the fizz, 'is really kind of you.' She took the paper from Sam's outstretched hand, and was just about to key the number into her phone, when it began to ping and vibrate in her hand.

Three messages from Ben.

Lily, I'm not sure what else we can say.

I miss you, but I can't come to France.

Maybe it's better if we don't message any more.

20

The grey early morning light gave way to the first proper rays of sun as she sat in her kitchen nursing her third cup of tea. After an evening spent on the phone to Emily, followed by a call to Ty during which she'd pretended all was well and tried to sound upbeat, she'd spent a restless night lying alone in the silent house, waking what seemed like every five minutes only to find the clock hands had barely moved.

Lily hadn't realised how much she'd been clinging to the hope that Ben would come round. That whatever it was that was holding him back wouldn't seem so important once he started missing her.

But his message to her had been so stark, so final, that it had felt almost like they had broken up all over again. Her text messages, pictures of the house, lake, local town, which had been met with thumbs up or the odd smile emoticon had not had the effect she was hoping.

Around five o'clock, when she'd given up on sleep and come downstairs to the kitchen, her bare feet shocked by the cold, tiled floor, misery had given way to a kind of indignant rage. Rage that

she'd spent so long with a man who clearly wasn't in it 'for better
or worse', but should have added to his vows 'within a thirty-mile
radius of Basildon'. Rage that she'd put off her dream for so long
when perhaps she could have saved herself a decade of wasting
her designs on local shopfronts and been running retreats in the
French sunshine – perhaps with a little bilingual Ty by her side.

Rage that she'd allowed herself to miss Ben so much, to feel
lonely without him, to – she realised now – put off some of the
things she wanted to do to the house in the vain hope that they
might be able to do them together.

She knew that underneath the anger, the devastation she'd felt
was still lingering. But for now, she was determined to embrace the
energy that came with being furious. It was still weeks until she'd
be able to sign for the house entirely, but Frédérique seemed
perfectly relaxed about the idea of her living here. Surely he
wouldn't mind if she started some of the work? After all, it wasn't as
if she was knocking anything down. Simply making improvements.

Having the house project firmly underway would give her
something to think about if any other sleepless nights came her
way. It would give her something to bang and hammer at when
she felt angry. It would harness her creativity and keep her
whirring brain occupied.

In short, it would be something to do.

Returning to her bedroom, she slipped on a pair of skinny
jeans, a T-shirt and trainers, and pulled her hair back into a
rough ponytail. Some of her outgrown layers were only just long
enough, and several strands fell forward around her face. But it
would do. Then, armed with her list of potential jobs to run past
Frédérique, she was about to exit the house when she realised it
was only 7 a.m. and suddenly felt completely exhausted. Was it
even worth driving into town at this hour?

But then, she resolved, she simply couldn't stay around here a minute longer with all this on her mind. Besides, she knew that the *boulangerie* opened in the early hours and possibly the café too. Frédérique wouldn't yet be installed in his office, but could well be chatting with locals over coffee. If not, she'd read her book, watch and wait for 9 a.m. – and at least see a bit of life around her to get her mind off Ben's message.

To her surprise, when she'd rung Emily last night, her friend had been sympathetic, but not as outraged on her behalf as she'd expected. 'Poor Ben,' she'd said at one point. 'He must be feeling completely devastated.'

'It wasn't exactly a fun message to receive either!' Lily had said, a little put out.

'Oh sweetheart, I know. I'm just... I suppose I'm just feeling a bit sentimental about things.'

'Well don't,' Lily had said decisively. 'You should be completely on *my* side.'

'I thought you said there weren't sides?'

'There are now.'

When she arrived in Eymoutiers at 7.30 a.m., Lily was surprised to see that the small town was already relatively busy. There was a queue outside the *boulangerie*; dog-walkers chatted in the town square; lights were on in the two small cafés and people milled around holding bread and talking and seeming in no rush whatsoever to get to wherever they ought to be.

She pulled up in a small side street and squeezed the Nissan into a tiny space between a van and some sort of classic car. Then, climbing out, she wandered over to *La Consolante*, a pretty café decked either side of the door with hand-painted murals of whimsical women strolling in grassy fields.

One or two of the outdoor tables had been set up, but it was clearly only just opening time. Inside, ten or twelve people were dotted around, most at individual tables or on bar stools in front of the main counter. Other than two men sitting opposite each other, tapping on phones, most seemed to be alone. She pushed open the door and the murmur of conversation suddenly halted as she entered. A few faces turned to look at her; there was the odd nod or acknowledgement, then the conversation resumed.

Perhaps they were all locals, unused to seeing a stranger in their midst? she thought, wondering why her entrance had seemed to garner so much attention. She walked to a small table in the corner, with a menu written on a chalkboard at its centre. She smiled at the waitress as she came over. '*Café crème, s'il vous plaît.*' The woman, her black curly hair falling softly to her shoulders, nodded with a slight smile and disappeared behind the counter. The screech of a milk frother could soon be heard, and Lily felt herself relax a little.

Gradually, more people wandered in from the *boulangerie*, some taking *croissants* from paper bags and dipping them in their morning coffee, others propping enormous *pains* on the table while they took their first caffeine hit of the day. A few people on the outside terrace began to smoke, and the smell drifted in every time the door opened. Lily had never smoked, but didn't mind the vague scent of cigarettes in the air – a smell that transported her back to nights out in her twenties, or – earlier still – watching football matches at the local club with her dad before his illness, munching on salt and vinegar crisps and breathing in what was probably a toxic mix of chemicals, but at the time had seemed grown up and exciting.

Dad had never been very adventurous and she wondered

what he'd make of her current situation. He'd probably have thought she was mad, but would have been quietly supportive in his own way. Furious at Ben, too. And Mum would definitely have come over with her to help her out.

Emily barely saw her parents, and Lily understood why. She'd had a difficult childhood and although nothing terrible had happened, she'd never felt completely loved, completely nurtured at home. Not for the first time Lily felt angry that her kind and loving parents had been taken too soon, while others who seemed disinterested in their children appeared not to appreciate what they had.

Even her brother, David, who was still alive and kicking and doing very well in finance, lived so far away that she barely saw him from one year to the next. They spoke occasionally on the phone, but he was someone who never quite seemed comfortable on the end of the line. She ought probably to update him about her split; he'd want to know – he wasn't completely useless. But she wasn't really ready to relate it all to someone from scratch. It was too new, too raw. She'd email him soon.

Her coffee arrived, placed before her on the little coaster set out for the purpose.

'*Merci, Madame*,' she said to the waitress.

'*De rien*,' the woman replied. Then, in broken English: 'You don't want anything else?'

'No, that's great. There's sugar there, so...'

'Not ready for *le vin* yet, this morning?'

'Wine? Oh. No, thank you.'

It seemed like an odd thing to offer, although she had heard rumours that a few of the locals liked a little morning snifter. Surely it wasn't common practice though? She lifted the coffee and breathed in the rich scent before blowing gently on the top and taking a sip. It was good, and she earmarked the café for future visits. Just the right amount of milk, a professional swirl on the foam, two sugars and – bonus – a tiny wrapped square of 70 per cent chocolate on her saucer.

She was just peeling the corner of her miniature treat, when the door opened and a slightly smarter version of the Frédérique she was accustomed to walked in. He was wearing light, linen trousers and a pale blue shirt, had combed his hair and – if she wasn't mistaken – even given his beard a trim since they'd last spoken. He carried his suit jacket over his shoulder like a model in a catalogue, and seemed very aware that he was looking his absolute best. She tried not to think about Max Skinner or idyllic French holidays in inherited mansions but to remind herself Frédérique was simply someone she was buying a house from, not a rom-com love interest.

The woman behind the counter beamed at him when he approached and exchanged *bisous*. Then he collected a tiny espresso and looked around for a table, stopping when he caught Lily's eye and flashing her a smile.

'*Madame Buttercup*! Eh, Lily!' he said, walking over to her as if they were old friends. 'Do you mind if I...?' He gestured to the seat opposite her.

Once again, a few of the customers turned to look.

'No, that's fine,' she said, feeling herself flush.

'And your friend, she is not coming?'

'She's gone back to England.'

'Oh, but this is a shame. So you are all alone?'

Usually this phrase wouldn't bother her, but after the finality of Ben's messages yesterday, the word 'alone' stung a little. 'Well, yes, I suppose I am... for now,' she said and tried to smile.

'Ah, but then you are not alone, not here. There are friends to be made,' he said, gesturing around.

From behind the counter, she caught the woman who'd served her looking at her with a slightly stern stare.

'Well, hopefully,' she said. Then, leaning forward. 'Is... are people normally so... I don't know, *interested* when someone new comes in?'

''ow do you mean?'

'Well,' she said, trying to keep her voice down. 'I don't know if this is a café more for local people. But when I came in, it was as if... I don't know, everyone stopped and looked.'

Frédérique took a sip of his coffee with a grin. 'I fink you will find zat you are becoming quite *une célébrité* 'ere.'

'Me? What, because I'm a woman, moving over and starting a business on my own?' she said, feeling quite affronted.

'*Non, Madame*,' he said, looking at her kindly. 'Because you 'ave made quite an impression at the *marché*, eh?'

'Oh.' The Emily incident. 'You think people remember...'

'Not much 'appen 'ere,' he said with a shrug. 'You 'ave made some entertainment, eh?'

The waitress's question suddenly made sense. She said, 'The waitress—'

'*Oui*, Sophie,' he interrupted.

'Yes, well, she offered me some *wine*. Was she being...?' She didn't know how to fill in the gap. Was it a joke at her expense? Was it a mean jibe? Was it normal?

'Ah, please not to mind Sophie. She is a little strange, I fink. With new people. But she will be OK.'

'Oh.' Lily dropped her gaze, not wanting Frédérique to see that it bothered her. 'So she was being... it was a joke?'

'Well, per'aps. She 'ave...'ow you say – she always *cherche la petite bête*.'

'She looks for a monster?' Lily said, brow furrowed.

'She like to find something to be angry for,' he said. 'She like to pick for the nits.'

'Oh.'

'But don't worry, she is OK. Give her time.'

'Right.' Lily sipped her coffee, feeling a little nervous. Behind the counter, she could see Sophie glancing in her direction. She tried to shake off the feeling of being unwelcome. She was sitting with the mayor; things really couldn't be that bad. 'Look, I was hoping to see you, Frédérique.'

'*Oui?*'

'*Oui, j'aimerais faire des travaux à la maison?*' I want to do some work on the house.

'*Oui?* You would like to *obtenir une autorisation?*'

This was the trouble with starting out in French. She quickly got out of her depth. 'Um, well, yes. Authorisation. Permission – from you?'

'Ah,' he said. 'But I cannot... I mean, I will need to get the forms. It is not simple, the process.'

'Oh.'

'What did you want to do?'

'Just... well, paint the kitchen. Um... maybe put some wallpaper up.'

'Oh, to *faire de la decoration?*'

'Well, yes.'

'I thought... *les travaux*... we say this for bigger things... *Par exemple*, you knock down the wall, yes?'

'Oh. No. Just *la decoration*,' she said.

'Well, this is not a *problème* for me! You do what you wish. It is your property, eh?'

'Well... almost.'

'Yes, yes,' he said, flapping his hand as if the matter of the actual legal ownership wasn't really important. 'But yes, of course!

And listen, I will introduce you to *mes amis, oui*? Zey can give you a good price for *la peinture*, if you wish? *Et les matériaux?*'

'Oh, thank you. That would be *très gentil*. Very kind.'

'It is no *problème*,' he said again, before sipping the last of his coffee and standing up. 'Come with me, *Madame Buttercup*, eh? I will love to 'elp.'

Standing up and walking out of the café next to Frédérique, Lily felt suddenly optimistic. With his help, and by making connections with some of his friends, she'd find her feet. She'd only been here a short time, but she already felt less alone.

As she passed Sophie, she thanked her, put a ten euro note on the counter and refused change.

Sophie thanked her and gave her a short smile. But as she left the café with Frédérique, his hand resting gently on the small of her back, Lily turned, only to find the waitress regarding her with a fixed, unsmiling stare.

21

As his key turned in the lock, she had to hold in a little shriek. He walked into the front room, ruffled but smart in his day-old work clothes and she rushed towards him. He dropped his briefcase and pulled her to him.

'Wow, what on earth have I done to deserve this?' he joked.

'Ben,' she said, waving the plastic stick close to his face. 'We've... I'm...'

'Really?' He pulled back and looked at her, his eyes shining. 'You're really...?'

'Yes, Ben. Really.'

* * *

Lily plonked the heavy bucket onto the dusty floor, slopping some of the contents out in the process. '*Le seau*,' she said to herself, trying to memorise some of the words she'd learned for her shopping trip. She unwrapped the sponge (*éponge*) she'd also picked up at the *bricolage* and dropped it into the soapy mixture. Then, tucking the scraper (*grattoir*) into her pocket out of the way, she looked for one last time at the dated wallpaper.

The wallpaper looked back menacingly.

It ended here.

'OK, here goes, wall,' she said, taking a picture of the wall for posterity before slipping the phone back into the pocket of her old jeans. 'Flock wallpaper out, neutral tones in.'

Using warm water, she began to soak the wall, seeing the faded colours darken as the water seeped through the thick paper covering to dissolve the glue beneath. She'd always enjoyed decorating – transforming a room from dull to beautiful, or changing the feel of a place by altering a colour scheme. One of the things she'd looked forward to about owning a 'fixer-upper' was being able to put her mark on a property properly.

In the UK, her house had been a cardboard cut-out of pretty much every other house in the street.

This house, for all its issues, had plenty of personality.

After soaking three panels, she began to peel the wallpaper off, using a scraper to loosen edges and pulling them as far as the paper would allow before new water needed to be applied. It was satisfying watching the wall change from faded flock to a sort of green, undercoated surface. And she could hardly wait for the moment – admittedly probably a couple of weeks in the future – when she'd be able to roll the first satisfying coat of paint across the darker tones and bring the house up to date.

It was only a bit of wallpaper, but each time she pulled on a piece and felt it gather traction and lift easily in her hands she wanted to wave it in the face of any incredulous person who'd doubted she'd be able to cope with this place alone. Because here she was; hair tied back, sweat forming on her brow, clothes covered in splashes of water, tiny pieces of sodden backing paper and glue. But doing it. And – even to her surprise – loving it.

'See, Ben,' she said, starting on the second panel, reaching for a particularly large corner, where a strip of wallpaper had begun to wetly peel itself off the wall, promising an especially easy race to the bottom when pulled. 'I *can* do it on my own.' She tugged at the paper, feeling it yield effortlessly in her hands. But just as she began to feel confident in her DIY skills, it decided to stick. She tugged, then a piece of plaster that had attached to the back of the sticky sheet dislodged with it, and flew out – hitting her in the face. 'Ow,' she said, rubbing her cheek, and then attacking the wall with a little more venom.

But worse was to come: as she continued to pull, it seemed that the glue on the paper was actually stronger than the plaster, and even some of the stone beneath. Great chunks of wall crumbled as she tugged, revealing – instead of an improved, flat blank canvas of wall – a mottled, ruined surface. 'Oh shit,' she said as she looked at the pitted plaster, the loose crumbling mortar and the chunks of wall that had somehow stuck to the wallpaper strip in her hand and dislodged with it, like hair on a strip of salon wax.

Perhaps it was just that one panel, she thought, feeling herself begin to sweat. She pulled at another strip of paper, but the wall beneath was even worse, crumbling and uneven and damp beneath its colourful disguise.

'No...' she said. 'Please, no.'

Her heart beating hard, she stepped back to observe her work. One clean, smooth strip of wall, then a mess of stone and rubble and broken plaster. Crumbled chunks of loose mortar and tiny rocks at her feet. And a wall that looked not only unsightly, but actually downright dangerous to her untrained eye.

'Oh no,' she said to herself, close to tears. 'Oh no, oh no, oh no.'

Was it *her* fault? Had she done something wrong? Soaked the paper too much? Pulled on it too enthusiastically? Or – worse – was it the house? Was it that her little piece of paradise was actually not all it promised to be?

Wiping her face roughly with the back of her hand, she pulled her phone from her pocket, thumb scrolling instinctively for Frédérique's number. But before she could dial, she noticed a text message from an unknown French number. She clicked on it, wondering who it could be from.

Hi Lily, we're in your neck of the woods this morning – off to the lake. Fancy joining us? SAM

She and Sam hadn't spoken for that long at the party; then after she'd left abruptly, holding back the tears brought about by Ben's break-up messages, Lily had assumed she probably wouldn't hear from her. But it seemed she had made a friend after all. Or at least had the beginnings of a friendship with someone who'd seemed wonderfully normal.

She replied:

Having a nightmare but I'd love to escape.

What's wrong?

Decorating disaster…

Shall I pop over on the way – sure it can't be that bad. You live right by the lake, right?

That would be brilliant. I need a second opinion. I may have accidentally demolished a wall!

Oh dear.

* * *

'Ah,' Sam said, half an hour later when she arrived with two
excited children in tow. Derek, three, was already running up and
down the hallway, laughing loudly. And Claudine, four, was
hiding shyly behind her mother's legs.

'Yep,' said Lily, looking at the mess she'd created again, but
somehow feeling less devastated than she had at first. Just having
someone there with her helped her to see it in more practical
terms. She could get it fixed. And the damage wasn't a result of
her lack of DIY skills. The wall beneath the paper had already
been in a state. She grinned. 'I guess I'm not quite as good at do-
it-yourself as I thought.'

'Oh, don't beat yourself up,' Sam said. 'There's DIY in the UK.
But in France? In one of these properties? DIY is a whole different
beast.' She rubbed her hand lightly on the bare wall, loosening a
tiny sprinkle of debris and dust, which crackled as it landed on
the wooden floor. 'Oops. Sorry.'

'No problem.'

'Yep. If you'd told me beforehand you were doing this... well,
I'd have advised you to stay well clear. Every job we've ever
done in our stone ruin has just revealed seven more jobs underneath. You learn to approach everything with caution after a
while.'

'Oh really? So it's not just me?'

'Nope, we've all been there,' said Sam. 'Plus, worse. We had
exposed wires and all sorts coming out of the wall. Someone had
literally shoved wallpaper over an electrical nightmare.'

'Really?'

'Really. Anyone who's bought one of these stone houses... I

mean they're beautiful. But... well, put it this way. There's a reason why they're for sale.'

'Ah.'

'And often there's a reason why the wallpaper's still in situ. Or covered up with more wallpaper, rather than stripped.'

'I can believe it.'

'Lots of the younger French people I know live in those little new-build houses. They leave the stone wrecks to idiots like us.'

'Oh.' Lily had seen the peach-coloured houses dotted around. Little rectangles of brick and mortar, devoid of personality. 'Aren't they a bit... well, bland?'

'Well, maybe. But bland is underrated,' Sam said, gesturing to the wall. 'Gabriel was desperate to buy one when we got married. He was all, *We do not wish to be a slave to our home.*'

'Well... yes.'

'But I insisted we went for something more traditional. And you know, I'm glad I did. But there were moments when I totally saw his point too.'

'Oh.'

'I think,' Sam said, 'we see the beauty in the houses like this because we haven't grown up living in one, and we're looking to come out here and live a completely different kind of existence. But local people want to get on with their lives, their careers. They can't spend hours working on a house as it crumbles around them.'

That didn't sound good. 'Crumbles around them?'

'Sorry. I'm prone to exaggeration. This is... well, it's pretty standard.'

'You don't think it's a complete disaster then?' Lily said, feeling a little lighter. 'In your professional opinion?'

'Ah, you'll be OK,' Sam said, prodding the wall with her hand. 'It's not terminal, I don't think. We had a couple of walls like this –

and it's just a case of ancient or non-existent plaster, strong glue and wallpaper that's been left in place since the dark ages.'

'Thank god for that.'

'You'll need someone in to give it a proper look-over and fix-up though. Unless you're a dab hand at pointing and plastering as well as demolition?' Sam gave her a sideways glance.

'Yeah, think this might be a bit beyond me right now.' Lily nodded. 'Although, you know, I'd love to learn how to do all of those things eventually.'

'Oh, you will.'

'Thanks.'

'And you know,' Sam said, 'these houses drive us all mad – I don't know anyone who's actually *finished* all the work that's needed. They come with a lifetime of projects.'

'Really?'

'But,' Sam said, 'once you get a bit further down the road, you become... well, sort of attached to the house. And you learn about how to cope with the various hiccups. And you also learn what to touch and what to leave to the experts.'

'Right.'

'And, you know, I say a lifetime of projects, but they're not all patching up and making good. Some of the projects are fun. Once you're a bit more confident that you've uncovered all the nasty surprises, they're the kind of projects with less effort and a bigger payoff.'

'Sounds more like it.'

'And it is worth it! A bit of work and this place will be gorgeous.'

'You think?'

'Definitely.'

'So,' said Lily, looking at the wall again. 'What did you do when it happened to you? How did you... fix things?'

'Well, budget version? What we did was get the bit of disaster wall repaired, then left the rest of the wallpaper in situ and just covered it with about twenty coats of paint.'

'Oh!'

'Yeah. I mean, I know the wallpaper is not to everyone's taste – and it's quite an undertaking to cover it up – but in *Limousin*, some of this sixties wallpaper is load-bearing.'

Lily laughed. 'I can imagine.'

'Yep. More important than some of the beams in keeping the house together, I reckon!' Sam winked. 'Derek! Come here. No. Don't touch that. No! Not the stairs...'

'Right, perhaps I'll follow your advice,' Lily said. 'And thank you. You've really saved my life.'

'Don't be silly.'

'I mean it. You hardly know me, and you've no idea how much better you've made me feel,' Lily said with a watery smile. She tried not to think about how many times she'd already welled up in front of this practical stranger, and was astonished that Sam still seemed to want to know her despite her seemingly constant misery.

Sam smiled and touched her arm briefly. 'Don't worry, we've all been there.'

'Really?'

'Yes. That's one of the reasons I go to those expat gatherings. Almost all of us are out here, away from family. We're all missing that sort of backup – parents or sisters or uncles we can call. So we sort of step into the void for each other.'

'Oh.'

'Yeah. I suppose that's why I excuse the flat-earthers and the conspiracy theorists. Because they're like sort of great-uncles, or crazy aunties. They're family. You tolerate it at least, tackle it sometimes. And you stay in touch. You stay around for each other.'

'That sounds... well, it sounds really nice,' Lily said, warming to the idea of a sort of substitute family, especially as even back in the UK she had few relatives to call her own.

'It is... I mean, we're all completely different. But we have that in common. That need for someone to call on. It's not something anyone talks about. But you'll find out – people do a lot more for each other than they might do for neighbours or friends at home. Because we're all in it together in a strange way.'

Lily smiled. 'Thanks, Sam.'

'Ah, this is nothing. Wait till you try to do anything with the electrics or plumbing.'

'Call in the experts?'

'Definitely.'

'Anyway, what do you reckon?' Sam said then, gently brushing down a few of Claudine's loose curls. 'Want to help us build a few sandcastles?'

'I'd love to.' Lily smiled. 'Just got to make a couple of phone calls first.'

'Join us in a bit?'

'Definitely.'

'I'll get you a coffee.'

'Thank you – see you in five.'

As soon as Sam had bundled her children back up the garden path and into the car to drive to the lakeside car park, Lily scrolled through her phone to find Frédérique's number. After all, the property was still *his* she reasoned. She ought to tell him what had happened. And he'd probably know someone trustworthy to make the repairs.

She waited for the number to connect, then listened to it ring out before going to answerphone.

'Hi, Frédérique. It's Lily. Can you call me when you have a moment?' she said. 'A wall in the house has... well, I think it needs to be repaired.'

As she hung up, a thought struck her. That, rather than needing to speak to Frédérique, she'd *wanted* to.

Of course it was sensible to inform the homeowner when you'd ripped half a wall down by mistake. It was just, she realised, that wasn't the only reason she'd raced to dial his number. Although the wall looked unsightly, it wasn't going to actually fall down. There was no *urgency* in having to call him. She'd calmed down talking to Sam and knew what she needed to do.

In reality, she probably should have downed tools and gone to the beach with Sam immediately. Switched off for a bit. Built a sandcastle if the urge had taken her. And embraced some of the calm that came with being close to the still, cool water and lush green trees.

She didn't even need to ring Frédérique to find a suitable artisan to help her make the repair. There was Sam – who'd literally been right there – and Chloé. Each probably knew one or two people. All things being equal, a rational decision might have been to leave Frédérique alone – after all, he'd already tackled a rogue gang of squirrels for her, and was trying to manage the reputational damage from Emily's drunken exhibition.

But she'd wanted to hear his voice, she realised. She'd wanted him to come around and look and laugh about it, and make her feel better.

At the heart of it all, she'd just wanted to see him.

22

'So you're a plasterer *and* a farmer?' Lily said to Claude as he removed the loose bits from her wall and began to mix up some filler. They were standing in the hallway, the front door open to let in the light, which cruelly revealed not only the mess she'd made with the wallpaper, but the millions of dust particles that floated in the air, every chip and dent on the skirting board and probably every single one of her wrinkles.

'*Mais, non.* I am just *un agriculteur*,' he said with the obligatory shrug. 'I'm a farmer, just a farmer. *Mais, j'ai aussi une maison* – I have a house too, uh? You learn to care for *la maison.*'

'Right.' Lily nodded. 'Well, *merci beaucoup* for your help... *votre aide.*'

'Ton *aide*,' he corrected. '*Et de rien*, it is nothing.'

She'd tried to hide her disappointment when he'd knocked at the door this afternoon, complete with bucket, box of plaster, some sort of mixing tool, wearing a navy-blue pair of overalls. 'Frédérique, 'e say you need some 'elp?' he'd said by way of greeting. 'You 'ave... 'ow you say – made the wall *tombe*? It fall down?'

'Er, yes. Well, sort of,' she'd said, standing back to let him in.

When she'd finally spoken to Frédérique and explained the situation on the phone last night, he'd seemed really concerned. 'I will fix this,' he'd said. 'Don't worry.'

He'd clearly outsourced the job to Claude, but if she was honest, she'd been hoping he'd be the one arriving at her front door. It was probably for the best though, she told herself. It was fun having a little crush on someone, but she wasn't in the market for a relationship, or even a bit of fun. Not yet. Things were too raw.

'Would you like a coffee?' she asked now.

'*Oui, bien sûr,*' Claude said, keeping his eyes on the battered wall and starting to fill the gaps with white paste.

'So,' she said, handing him a steaming mug a few minutes later, 'you must be very busy at the farm.'

'*Oui,* all the time.'

'And you don't mind Frédérique, well, outsourcing things like this?'

'Sorry, *je ne comprends pas* – I don't understand. What is this "hout soursy"?'

'*Je suis désolé.* You don't mind helping Frédérique as well?'

'Ah, non. We 'elp each other,' he said with a shrug. 'We are *amis.* And he pay for *les matériaux.*'

'Oh. Well, that's kind.' Lily wondered whether it was her poor French, or the need for Claude to concentrate on his work, but she couldn't help feel there was a bit of an atmosphere between them. Perhaps it was the incident with Emily. Or maybe he really was very busy and this was a terrible inconvenience.

'I'm sorry,' she said then, 'for *Samedi dernier* – last Saturday. My friend, she is not usually... so...'

'*Tellement soif?* She is thirsty, *pour le vin?*' he said, with a raised eyebrow and a smile. 'It is no problem. Frédérique, 'e explain.

Mais, pour moi, for me it is just – 'ow you say – *très drôle*. It was funny.'

'Oh good... I mean, *bon*,' she said. 'I mean I am glad – *je suis heureux* – that you are not... um... um... *vache*.'

Claude paused his trowel and gave her a quizzical look. 'You say that you are glad I am not a cow?'

'No, no...'

'*Une vache, c'est une* "cow" oui? *MEUH!*' He lifted his fingers into the shape of horns and pawed the ground slightly, then grinned at her.

Lily laughed. '*Non*,' she said, 'not a cow...'

'Per'aps you mean, you are happy that I am not *fâché* – annoyed, *non*?' He smiled.

'Yes, *fâché*,' she said. She felt more relaxed after his cow impression for some reason. Ironically, he seemed more human.

He laughed. 'I am not a man who make anger very often,' he said. 'Life is too short, iz it not?'

She nodded. 'Definitely.'

'And your friend,' he added, his brow furrowed slightly. 'She is not well, Frédérique *m'a dit*, 'e say?'

'Oh, she's fine now. Er... *elle va bien*,' she said.

'That is good.' He turned back to the wall and began smoothing the paste with his trowel.

'And Frédérique – will he be coming later?' she found herself asking.

He looked at her.

'To see the work, I mean. *Pour voir les travaux*?' she added hurriedly.

He nodded. 'Per'aps,' he said. 'But 'e trust me, uh, so per'aps not.'

He seemed to be wrestling with something, and she hoped for

a second that he didn't think she was suggesting his work wouldn't be up to scratch.

'*Tu sais*,' he began, 'You know... Frédérique, 'e is my good friend, *non*? But you are also my friend, now, I think?'

Lily nodded. '*Oui*,' she said. It was nice to hear him say that.

'So,' he said, 'as we are friends, I should say zat *pour les femmes*, Frédérique, he is not always such a good friend, uh?'

'Oh,' she said. A memory stirred. Hadn't Chloe said something similar? But Frédérique, seemed so nice – so open. It was hard to understand what could be so terrible about him.

He nodded. 'Just, er, be careful... *fais attention*, uh?'

'*Merci*,' she said, feeling slightly awkward. She'd only just worked out that she might have a little crush – a tiny attraction – for Frédérique. How was it possible that Claude had seen through her already? She could feel her cheeks getting hot. 'Anyway, I better... um...' She waved vaguely towards the kitchen, indicating that there was an important job to be getting on with.

He nodded, and returned to his trowel. 'You will not say to 'im?' he asked as she turned back to the kitchen.

'Oh, no. Of course not!' she said.

'*Merci*,' he said. 'As I say, 'e is a good friend for me, yes?'

'*Oui*,' she said. 'Don't worry.'

* * *

An hour later, when she was scrolling on the local selling site hoping to source a decent sofa or two, Claude popped his head around the kitchen door.

'It is all done,' he said. 'You 'ave now a wall in your 'ouse, *madame*.'

'Oh, *merci beaucoup*!' she said. 'Thank you so much, Claude.'

'*De rien*,' he said again. 'And I will tell Frédérique that you wish to talk to him?'

'Oh, no,' she said, hurriedly. 'No, I think it is OK.'

He nodded. '*À tout à l'heure*,' he said. 'See you later.'

'Bye.'

Nervous about placing bids online, she sent a message to the seller of some second-hand furniture in *Eymoutiers* and hoped the online translator she'd used hadn't let her down. Then, slipping on her trainers, she packed up a few essentials and took a walk to the beach.

Spending time at the lake with Sam yesterday had made her realise how much she'd already missed out on. To live within a stone's throw of such a beautiful spot and barely spend a moment there seemed ridiculous. She'd moved in part for the beautiful scenery, but had spent more time than she'd care to admit since arriving staring at four stone walls.

Not that she'd want to spend too many afternoons building sandcastles – something she remembered fondly doing with Ty in years gone by, but that had seemed quite a slog yesterday when she'd been handed a bucket and spade by Derek and given her orders.

'You don't have to, you know?' Sam had laughed when she was turning out her fourth.

'It's fine,' she'd said. And it had been. She hadn't minded.

But now the idea of spending some time on the beach just reading a book or – if she felt brave – perhaps having a little swim seemed much more appealing.

It was Friday afternoon and the beach was busier than she'd seen it before. Families sat on spread-out blankets, children paddled in the shallows. There were a few swimmers making their way up and down a marked-off area. The bar was busy too – people sat on the wooden terrace chatting with one another, drinking coffee or beer. People smoked. There was a general hum of noise – a background of chatter, with screams and shouts of children played intermittently over the top.

It was nice to see the place come to life a little more, but noticing all these people so obviously gathered in groups made her more aware of her solitude than she'd been last time.

She flapped out a towel and made herself a little base from which to operate – book, water bottle, sunscreen, beach bag - then sat for a minute, feeling the sun play on her skin. Looking around, she noticed several faces she half recognised – the woman from the *bricolage*, one or two people she'd seen at the supermarket. A man whom she'd spoken to briefly with Frédérique, resplendent in his Speedos.

She'd always been quite self-conscious about being in a swimming costume in front of people she knew. When she'd lived in England, she'd drive twenty miles to a slightly further away swimming pool rather than risk parading in what was basically underwear in front of people she worked with, or might bump into in her professional life.

Now she lived so close to such a gorgeous location, she was going to have to get used to it. Nobody else seemed in the slightest bit self-conscious – whatever their body shape – stopping and exchanging greetings with other beach users, standing and having a chat, or striding into the water with confidence.

After a surreptitious but undignified change under a towel, she emerged triumphantly in her bikini and, for the first time, prepared for a lake swim. She walked down towards the water's edge, smiling at children making sandcastles, nodding at their parents, feeling generally at one with the world and if not part of things, then at least on the periphery.

The water was warmer than she'd expected, and despite the 'sea-like' appearance of the lake, was perfectly still. She walked in to waist height – gasping when the water hit her thighs, then lower stomach – then, first checking she was in the cordoned off swimming area and that nobody was in her way, she plunged forward and began a gentle breaststroke.

Lily had never been much of a swimmer. She loved the idea of swimming, loved being in water. Loved the sensation of moving forward, kicking her legs and gaining momentum. The problem was she wasn't actually very good at it, which meant that she expended the kind of energy that an accomplished swimmer might expend in an hour just navigating a length.

The water was not her friend.

But if she was going to be living in a lakeside paradise, she ought to try to get to know it a bit better. Feeling herself just inching forward with breaststroke, she changed, diving under the water slightly and kicking her legs. She gained momentum and – briefly coming up for air – dived below the surface again, enjoying the sensation of being submerged briefly in her own little world, hearing only the gentle rhythm of her heartbeat.

Her vision was clouded by debris stirred up from the lake bed and – resolving to buy goggles – she closed her eyes. Then she kicked forward, enjoying the added meditative quality that shutting off one of her senses brought – of being alone, underwater, focused just on herself, on her movement. She kicked again and... collided with something soft.

Hitting the thing sent her reeling and she stood up, slightly unbalanced, gasping for air. Only to see a man doubled over in front of her. His back was covered in a thin sprinkle of hair, and his skin was lightly tanned. His hair, a blonde mop, flopped forward as he bent down, clutching himself.

'Oh god. I'm so sorry,' she said. 'I was... I had my eyes closed and...'

The man straightened up; his face slightly flushed, his mouth contorted. 'It izz OK,' he said. 'I em fine.'

'But you...' She wasn't sure quite what to say. 'I've hurt you.'

'I will be OK in a minute,' he said, a single tear rolling down his cheek. 'Please, continue your swim.'

She awkwardly, but gratefully, turned and disappeared under the lake's surface. This time keeping her eyes open despite the cloudy water, she pushed herself forward once again, then turned and swam back. The man had hobbled into the shallows and she now had most of the area to herself. Gaining a little momentum, she completed another length, and kicked back to her original position – only to find herself now confronted with a set of extraordinarily hairy legs and a pair of orange Speedos that only became visible through the cloudy water when she was a little too close for comfort.

Seeing the orange beacon-like glimmer of Lycra, she came up abruptly, not wanting to repeat the horror of her earlier collision, only to find herself standing in front of a person she recognised.

What was he doing here, in the water, when she hadn't seen him at all on the beach?

'Lily Buttercup!' Frédérique said, laughing. 'I did not know you like to 'ave a swim 'ere.'

'Oh,' she said, feeling suddenly embarrassed at her sodden hair and half-nakedness. '*Oui, j'aime*, I like the water. It's my first swim here though.'

'Ah, but I like to come often in the summer after my work is done,' he says. 'But not so much the winter, eh. *Mais il y a une association* – a club you can join, if you wish. They like the water all the year.'

'Er, thank you,' she said, trying to keep her gaze on his eyes. It wasn't as if she hadn't seen a male torso before – the beach was littered with them. But having involuntarily imagined what

Frédérique might look like under his shirt in the past (in her defence, notary appointments are *long*) she felt as if somehow he might be able to read that in her eyes. As it was, her imagination hadn't been far off – he was just as tanned and toned as she'd imagined, albeit with the hairiest chest she'd ever had the pleasure to peruse up close.

'Anyway, I will let you get back to making your sport,' he said.

'Thank you.'

'And your *casse* it is looking good, eh?'

'My what?'

'Your *casse?*'

Had he seriously just told her she had a nice ass? 'I'm not sure you should...' she began... then thought better of it. 'Sorry, I don't understand,' she said.

'Your *casse*. The breakage – you damage the wall, yes? And it is now good?'

'Oh, yes, thank you,' she replied, feeling herself blush. 'It's perfect.'

Then in a move that was almost too French to be believable, he took her hand and kissed it. 'Then I am 'appy,' he said, seemingly oblivious to the swimmers that had joined them in the little enclosure and were trying to wend their way around them.

'Thank you,' she said, desperate now to plunge back into the water and hide her blushes.

'And,' he said, finally, 'I fink we 'ave to celebrate that it iz fix, yes? Do you want to join me for a drink tomorrow to 'ow you say, *faire une célébration?*'

'I'm...' There were thousands of reasons why she should say no. Not least that she was still married and – against all odds – still held a tiny thread of hope that Ben might yet get himself on a flight. Then there was Claude's warning – that Frédérique wasn't such a good friend to women. And the fact he was selling her a house. And that he was the local mayor, so someone who would probably be in her life going forward whatever dating disasters might happen.

But before she could let her rational mind step in, she found the words 'I'd love to,' coming out of her mouth.

23

'You agreed to go on a *date*?' Emily's voice on the phone was incredulous.

'Well, I'm not sure if it's a date, exactly,' Lily replied. 'But I suppose I'm open to it being one. I mean, why not?'

She was sitting on the front steps of the house, looking across the front garden and, beyond it, the road that led to the beach, coffee in hand. The air was cool, but the shards of sunlight that broke from behind the puffs of cloud held the promise of warmth. She took a sip of her hot coffee and felt it shiver through her.

Emily was silent for a minute. 'But I thought you said you weren't going to do anything until you were sure...?'

'I *am* sure! Emily, Ben told me he didn't think we should contact each other – surely that's enough evidence that it's over between us?'

'I know,' Emily sighed. 'But I suppose... I mean, haven't you ever sent a text message in haste? And regretted it? Or,' she added pointedly, 'clicked a button you didn't mean to click after a few drinks?'

Touché.

'Well, you know the answer to that.'

'What if Ben's desperately sorry? Has he tried to contact you since?'

'Well, no. But I blocked him, obviously. I didn't want to be tempted to call him if he isn't interested in hearing from me.'

'So for all you know, he's been trying to get hold of you.'

'Seriously, Emily. If he has, he hasn't been trying that hard. I'm still on email...'

'Lily, he's a man. You have to be realistic about what he's capable of...'

'Ha. Well, yes. But seriously, Em, I thought you were all for my embracing a new life over here and anyone else who might come along?'

'I know...' Emily paused. 'I suppose, well, don't tell anyone, but things with Chris have been so good since I've been home. I mean, they were good before, you know? But since... we're so much closer. I think we'd drifted apart a bit – like you do.'

'I get it, I do...'

'And I couldn't help but think how much closeness and togetherness you build up over the years. And how awful it would be to throw it away.'

'But I'm not throwing it away. He is. Or rather, he has.'

'I know. Just... well, if anything happens with Frédérique, it kind of makes it final in a whole new way.'

'I know,' Lily said. 'But I suppose... I mean, I can't keep waiting and hoping forever, can I? I can't... Well, I don't want to be alone forever.'

'I know, chick.'

'I'm not even a hundred per cent sure it's a date, so...'

'Well, there you go then. Enjoy his company. Get to know him. Just maybe... I don't know... Maybe take a breath before jumping into anything else. Life is short, and I just... I suppose I don't want to see you making a mistake.'

Once she was off the phone, Lily tried to get her mind off Emily's words. It wasn't as if she'd had any intention of rushing into anything with Frédérique – for starters, the idea of it being a date at all might be entirely in her head. But she'd expected her friend to be her usual, enthusiastic self. To tease her and encourage her and make her excited for the evening ahead. Now she just felt... well, flat at best.

And the thought of a possible reconciliation with Ben – something that she'd kept at arm's length as much as she could recently – was back at the forefront of her mind.

For twenty years, they'd been everything to each other. Sure, they'd probably gone through periods where they'd taken each other for granted, or snapped at each other, or not spent enough time together. But underneath it all she'd always had a feeling of safety and permanence. She'd felt that, for better or worse, it was Ben she wanted by her side. And she'd been convinced he'd felt the same way.

But now she'd had to question everything she'd assumed, everything she'd felt. Because she was here, and he was there. And there didn't seem to be anything she could do about it without making one of them desperately unhappy.

And Frédérique – not only did he look like the man in a movie she'd drooled over for the last decade or so, but he was also funny and kind. And actually *there* in a way Ben refused to be. Sure, she'd love to wake up and find out the breakup had all been a bad dream – to find Ben by her side. But even if he turned up now, begging forgiveness, she wasn't sure what she'd say. In letting her go so easily he'd revealed how he felt about her. Maybe she couldn't ruin any chance for their future, because there simply wasn't one.

The hot water spat and hissed as she filled the old ceramic bath, added some shower gel – making a mental note to get some bubble bath next time she was out – and sloshed her hand in until a few bubbles formed on the surface. Then she slipped off her dressing gown and sank into the warmth.

Her shoulders stung where she'd been lightly sunburned the day before, and she washed herself quickly, then sat up a bit to allow them to cool in the air of the tiled room. Originally, when she'd walked home yesterday, overjoyed at the idea of going out for a drink – just actually having something to *do* in the evening – she'd thought she might slip on one of her favourite dresses.

But Emily's words had dampened her enthusiasm. Instead, she pulled on a pair of jeans, paired them with a light green blouse and applied just a little bit of makeup. Inspecting herself in the mirror, she nodded. She didn't look like a woman expecting to be romanced. But at the same time, she'd scrubbed up pretty well – had made an effort.

What she was doing wasn't wrong, surely? Yes, she had blocked Ben, but only after the stinging finality of his text messages. And if he really wanted her back, or had had any sort of change of heart, he would have found some way to contact her. It was time to move on – it was the only healthy thing to do.

* * *

When Frédérique arrived at her door, she was doubly glad she hadn't opted for a dress. He was wearing navy jeans and a short-sleeved, light-blue shirt, with three buttons undone, showing a hint of tan and skin but stopping short of the forest of hair she now knew lay beneath. The outfit suited him – he looked more

Russell Crowe than... well, than the actual Russell Crowe looked these days, but casual at the same time.

'You look *très belle*,' he said to her when she answered the door.

'Oh! *Merci*,' she replied. 'Um... *toi aussi*?'

'Ah, yes. I am beautiful, *non*?' He grinned.

She smiled – it was hard to tell whether he was simply agreeing with her, which while a touch arrogant was kind of cute, or whether he was laughing at her French.

'I 'ave brought my vintage *voiture*,' he said, nodding behind him to where a light blue 2CV was parked. 'We can ride in style, huh?'

'Oh, that's great,' she said. Although bearing in mind the state of some of the 'vintage' cars she'd seen on the roads since moving here, she couldn't help wonder if it would be a rattling death trap. Still, it would be impolite to offer to use her hire car instead.

Typically British, she thought, as he opened the passenger side door for her – I'd rather risk life and limb than be thought of as rude.

Luckily, her fears were unfounded. The Citroën had clearly been well looked after – the interior was immaculate, and while the seats weren't exactly comfortable, the engine purred smoothly and the ride felt relatively safe.

'So, where are we going?' she asked, once she'd clipped herself in and they'd turned onto the slightly wider road that curved around the edge of the lake.

'Ah, I know a little place – they serve drinks, yes? But food if you want? And it is perfect tonight for the balcony?'

'Sounds lovely.'

'You 'ave the date, too, today yes?'

'Pardon?'

'The date – I receive the date for signing of the 'ouse?'

'Oh. Yes.' She'd received an email earlier arranging the date for final signing – in just a few weeks' time. 'It's all becoming very real.'

'Sorry, I don't understand? It is not real?'

'No, I mean. It feels amazing that it's happening.'

'Oh. Well, I am glad.'

'It must be nice to complete the sale after so long.'

'Ah, bah, *non*! It eez not a problem, eh? But I am pleased that I am completing the sale for to you, Lily,' he said. 'That you will stay, huh?'

'Oh. Thank you.'

'And pleased too of course for my grandmother,' he said. 'She is not well, so she worry about things all the time.'

'Oh, I'm sorry to hear that.'

'Yes, but this is what 'appen when we get old, *non*?' he said, trying to keep his hands on the wheel and shrug at the same time. Which only partially worked.

'Well, I'm happy about it too,' she said. 'It will be nice to feel... Well, that things are falling into place.'

'But not falling down, uh?' He grinned.

'No, hopefully not.'

They arrived in *Auphelle*, a small village at the far side of the enormous lake, and Frédérique parked his car in an almost-empty car park in front of a grassed area. A small path led down to a restaurant, set right on the waterfront, its balcony extending almost to the water's edge.

'This is lovely,' Lily said, accepting Frédérique's hand as he helped her negotiate the rather uneven stone steps that led to the entrance. It had been a while since she'd worn heels and she was already regretting it a little. They might make her legs look longer, but the aesthetic was lost when she started to walk – she could barely balance.

'It izz just a little place that I like to come,' he said. 'Zey are very nice 'ere. And we can sit, in the sun, eh? And look at some of *les* boats?'

'Yes, perfect,' she said.

The waiter showed them to a table on the corner of the balcony that offered uninterrupted views of the water. Despite the parasol over the table, she could feel her shoulders start to heat up in the direct sunlight. She shifted along and tried to shade herself as best she could.

'You are all right, Lily?' asked Frédérique.

'Oh yes. I'm fine.' She smiled.

They ordered wine and Frédérique spoke quickly to the waiter who came back with a board covered in different cheeses and a basket of bread as well as a carafe of house red. Frédérique poured her a generous glassful and she took a sip, feeling herself start to relax.

'This,' she said, 'is what I came to France for.'

'You come to the country for wine? Zey don't have wine in England?' He grinned.

'Oh, there's definitely *no* wine shortage in England.' She laughed. 'It's this.' She gestured around her. 'Sunshine, scenery...'

'And of course the good company, yes?'

'Well, yes,' she said, finding herself blushing.

He laughed. 'It is joking,' he said. 'I am sure you have lots of friends in England? And lovers?'

The word caught her off-guard. 'Well, sort of,' she said. 'A husband. Well, I did have one.'

'Yes, but you 'av not brought this 'usband wiv you.'

She shook her head, desperately holding back a swelling tear. 'No. It's... we're over.'

'I am sorry,' he said.

'Yes, me too.' She shrugged – perhaps the habit was rubbing off. 'But *c'est la vie.*'

'Yes. *C'est la vie.* And to new beginnings in France,' he said, clinking his glass with hers and fixing his intense gaze on her. 'I wanted to ask you...'

But at that moment, Lily spotted a familiar face over Frédérique's shoulder. 'Oh,' she said. 'It's Chloé!'

Her new friend had walked in with two other women, all dressed casually but exuding the kind of effortless glamour Lily hoped one day to emulate. Chloé glanced around the terrace then caught Lily's eye and smiled.

'Yes? She is 'ere?' Frédérique said, turning to look.

When Chloé saw Frédérique, her face took on a stonier expression. She seemed to say something to her friends and then walked over to their table.

'*Bonjour*, Chloé,' Lily said standing up and exchanging a brief air-kiss. '*C'est une surprise!*'

'*Oui*,' she said. '*Bien sûr.* You are 'ere for dinner?'

'Just a drink,' Lily said. 'Frédérique... we wanted to celebrate the house sale.'

Chloé nodded, her face uncharacteristically expressionless. 'Ah, ze house it is done?'

'Well, no. But we're getting there,' Lily said, realising how weak an excuse that sounded, then wondering why she felt the need to have an excuse to be with Frédérique in any case.

'*Bonjour*, Fred,' Chloé said, and exchanged a quick kiss with Frédérique. It sounded odd to hear him called 'Fred' – such a plain, normal name. Even so, the way Chloé said it, with her accent, it sound much prettier than the version Lily was used to.

'Well, I 'ope you enjoy,' she said, after a brief silence. 'It is a good evening, yes?'

'Thank you.' Lily smiled.

'*Oui, merci. À bientôt!*' Frédérique added as Chloé walked back to her friends. She said something when she arrived and they all glanced at them for a moment.

'Did Chloé seem OK to you?' Lily asked.

'*Oui*, she is always like zis wiv me,' he said, making a sad face. 'I fink she does not like it when I 'ave a drink wiv a woman, eh?'

'Oh. Why?'

'Ah, it is nothing. We used to date, many years ago. And she, I think she maybe like me still.'

'Oh.' Lily made a face. The last thing she wanted to do was to upset Chloé.

'It iz OK, she will not 'ate you for speaking wiv me though!' he said, with a grin. 'She is *juste*... it is – how you say? – a bit uncomfortable, awkwardable.'

'Awkward?'

'Yes. That is it. We are friends, I think.'

'OK.' Lily took a sip from her glass, feeling slightly uneasy. But then if Chloé *was* an ex of Frédérique's it was always going to be a bit odd for her to see him on a date. Or something that looked like a date.

She took a deep drink from her glass and wiped her hand over the back of her mouth, only to look up at a pair of amused eyes. 'What?' she said.

'It iz nothing,' he said. 'You like the wine, huh?'

'Oh, yes,' she said. 'Just nervous. It's difficult, being somewhere new. With new people. Being... I suppose being *alone* for the first time in ages.'

'But, Lily,' he said, taking her hand, 'you do not 'ave to be alone.'

* * *

Two hours later, when they left, Chloé was still there, sipping after-meal coffees with her friends. She looked up as Lily passed, giving her a small, polite wave. But when her eyes rested on Frédérique, Lily saw her expression change and her mouth form a hard, straight line.

24

'Just breathe,' he said, nodding his head. 'Like at the class.'

'Fuck off,' she said. 'You breathe.'

'OK, OK,' he said looking over her at the midwife and making a 'help me' face.

'Hubby's right,' said the midwife. 'You need to...'

She trailed off as she caught Lily's eye. 'Let me just give you a quick check,' she said, snapping on a glove. 'Maybe we're ready to push...'

Lily was just slipping the first pansy plant from its plastic pot when she heard a shout behind her. 'Working hard, I see?'

She turned to see Sam, who'd pulled up quietly in her car and wound the window down. In the back of her Fiesta, Lily could see Derek and Claudine both slumped over, asleep in their car seats.

'Oh, hi!' she said, slipping the plant back in for a second and wiping the soil from her fingers. 'Just trying to brighten up the front a bit.'

'I assume this means the interior is fully renovated?'

'Of course!' Lily joked. 'I'm not trying to avoid doing the hard work at all!'

Sam laughed. 'We're just off for the obligatory "get them out of the house they're driving me mad" excursion,' she said. 'Thought I'd pop by to see whether your house is still standing while they're snoozing.'

'Thanks.' Lily grinned. 'Actually, I've had the wall fixed. And slapped some paint on the rest, like you said.'

'Oh, brilliant. I'd pop in and see, but I daren't leave these two or they'll be screaming,' Sam said. 'But I'll stop by next week for a tour if you're around?'

'Definitely.'

When Sam had driven off, Lily continued with her planters, enjoying the afternoon sun and making the most of the easy, rhythmic work. She'd actually planned on making a start on the kitchen today – she'd taken delivery of a second-hand dresser this morning and had earmarked the afternoon for cleaning it up and giving it a lick of paint.

But to her surprise, she'd woken up with a hangover. Laying in her makeshift bed, head throbbing, she'd thought back to the evening before. She hadn't been drunk, but realised that she'd probably put away half a bottle of red. Perhaps that was all it took in your forties?

Either way, the idea of inhaling paint fumes didn't appeal. Instead, she'd driven to the local supermarket and picked up the pansies, along with a few essentials. It was a reason to get out in the garden, and something she could cope with despite feeling less than on form.

She thought back to the night before. Frédérique had been a gentleman – insisting he paid for the drinks and nibbles, ferrying her back home and making no attempt to come in for coffee. They'd got on well, despite the odd language hiccup, and she'd been surprised how much they had in common. He loved drawing – 'it iz an 'obby' he'd said, and was so interested when she told him about her work in graphic design.

She'd told him, too, about her idea to run relaxation retreats, once her renovations were finished, and he'd loved the idea. 'But it will be such a success for you!' he'd exclaimed. 'I can feel it, uh?'

In fact, the only downside of the evening – other than the slightly strange encounter with Chloé – had been the fact that she wasn't sure whether she was on a date at all for most of it.

Luckily, though, that had also been cleared up. Just as he was about to leave, Frédérique had given her a hug then, pulling back, held his gaze on her face. Instinctively, she'd tilted her lips up to meet his and he'd kissed her softly – with enough intensity and tongue to leave her in no doubt that they'd made a leap out of the friend zone.

She touched her lips now, unconsciously, remembering how gentle his kiss had felt, how fresh and soapy his aftershave had been. How his beard had felt soft against her skin. His arms, tight around her back.

She was reliving the moment when her phone pinged.

So – how'd it go. Spill!

Good, thanks.

And… was it a date? Call me!

Yes. But don't worry. Nothing happened.

She didn't add how much she'd wanted it to.

She repotted the last of her plants and picked up the watering can – not the relic that she'd clambered on the day she'd first met Frédérique, but a new one purchased from the *bricolage*. It was made of metal, painted blue, and once filled was heavier than she'd imagined in the shop. Using both hands, she tilted it towards the planters and flooded each with probably too much water. Then, straightening up, she made her way back into the house to wash her hands and make a coffee.

She'd never been very good at keeping her mind off her problems – *Just think about something else!* her mum had used to say. But Lily found it impossible. Her mind kept drifting back to Emily; she knew her friend would either worry or be offended if she left it any longer before calling and talking to her properly.

In an attempt to keep herself busy and delay the post-date post-mortem that no doubt Em was desperate to conduct, she picked up her phone and dialled Ty instead. It had been a few days since they'd spoken, and it would be nice to catch up.

'Hi, Mum,' he said, after a few rings.

'Hey, Ty,' she said, feeling both happy that he'd answered and sad that she was so far away from him. She reminded herself that he was an adult now – he wouldn't have been at home with her for much longer even if she had stayed in the UK. 'How's it going?'

'Ah, OK,' he said. 'You know.'

'Well, I don't... really. Did you get your room in halls sorted?'

'Yeah, it's all right.'

'Seen any of the gang? Gone to the pub or anything?'

'Yeah.'

'And how is everyone?'

'You know.'

'Right... Well, I'm doing OK here too.' She wasn't offended that he hadn't asked; phone calls weren't her son's strength. 'Getting some of the house fixed up.'

'Uh-huh.'

'And...' She wondered, for a moment, whether she should say anything. But then she had nothing to be ashamed of. 'I'm thinking of going on a date.' She couldn't quite bring herself to tell him she'd already done it; somehow it felt easier to introduce it this way.

'What?'

'Yes. A lovely French gentleman has asked me to go out with him. And I might say yes.'

Her heart began to thud. She realised for the first time how much she needed Ty's ... well, not his *support* or *blessing* but just to know that he wasn't completely aghast at the idea.

'But, Mum,' he said, 'what about Dad?'

'Ty, you know me and your dad... well, we're not together any more.' She felt a pang of anxiety as she spoke the words aloud. 'We... I mean, I'm here, he's there... I know it's difficult... but...'

'What? You've actually split up with Dad?' he said, an edge to his voice now.

'No, Ty. Dad split up with me. He sent... well, put it this way, he doesn't want to be in touch with me any more. And it's hard – I know, it's hard for me too. But I can't sit and mope forever.'

There was silence on the line.

'Ty?'

'Yeah. Sorry. I mean, I get it. I do. But I think you should talk to Dad.'

'But...'

'I know you said he said not to. But I think you should, Mum.'

'I just don't think...'

'He misses you, you know. I mean, loads, right?'

'Oh Ty. I'm sure he...'

'And he's in a right state. The house is a shithole.'

'Ty!'

'Sorry. It's very messy,' he said. 'He needs you, I think.'

'Oh, Ty... it sounds like he needs a cleaner.'

'Nah, it's not that... he's just... He's sad, I guess.'

She wished now that she hadn't brought the subject up. 'OK, Ty. I'll, well, I'll see what I can do.'

This seemed to satisfy him. 'Thanks.'

In a way she was proud of him – an eighteen-year-old trying to save his parents' marriage. But at the same time she was angry at Ben, for not filling Ty in on all the details and leaving him to assume she was the 'bad guy' in all this.

Angry, she dialled the one person who she knew would say the right thing.

'Hello, stranger,' Emily said, a smile in her voice.

'Hey, you.'

'So?'

'So, what?'

'So spill. About the *date*?'

'It was. Well, it was really lovely,' she said, feeling herself begin to blush.

'That's great, Lily.'

'Really?' Lily's face relaxed. 'Because yesterday you seemed to think it was a mistake to be going at all.'

A beat.

'Look, honey. It's your life – your choice what you do with it. It was just... I suppose I wanted to make sure that you're sure, about Ben.'

'Well, I am.'

'Well, then I'm happy for you.'

'Thank you.'

'And now it's your duty to tell me *all* the details!'

Lily told her about the restaurant, the wine, the drive back home. And the kiss.

'Wow, romantic!'

'Very.'

'And you're not rushing into anything.'

'Would it matter if I did?'

'Well, no. I just...'

'Look, Em... you know I love you. But you seem to be siding with Ben in all this. He let me go. He. Let. Me. Go. He didn't want to come, he didn't even want to *try*.' She heard the wobble in her own voice. 'What am I supposed to do? Sit around and wait forever? Live alone somewhere where I know no one and not leave the house?'

'I'm sorry,' Emily said. 'And I am your friend. Always. It's just... I don't know. I want things to work out for you, I suppose. And it's hard with you over there... I just worry about you.'

'I know. But honestly, I'm fine. Well, most of the time.'

'Good. Well, I'm glad to hear it.'

'Thank you.'

There was a silence.

'But Lily, just... just don't rush into this thing, OK? I mean, it's your life and I don't want to interfere...'

'Yes, Mum.'

'Ha. You know what I mean. I care about you... is all. And... I just... Look, don't give up on Ben, Lily. Not yet. Not completely.'

'OK,' she said. Because it seemed like the thing she ought to say.

But when she hung the phone up minutes later, she wondered why Emily had said that. Had Ben actually been going round convincing everyone she was the one in the wrong? Had he bad-mouthed her to Ty? Painted a tragic picture of his suffering to Emily? Surely Emily would have said if she'd seen him, heard from him.

For years, she'd been going to work, coming home; feeling

completely invisible and unimportant. Now it seemed the world and his wife wanted to tell her how to live her life.

She debated whether to call Emily back and challenge her. But it was easier to leave it. It wasn't as if she even had another date with Frédérique sorted yet. Any more conversations about what she should or shouldn't do with the attractive, kind Russell Crowe doppelgänger (circa 2006) would ruin things entirely. Just when she had been feeling upbeat and excited and attractive and all the things you feel when someone new comes into your life.

Instead, she decided to search online for a few more pieces of furniture. She'd seen a wooden bedstead on sale recently, and needed to research what kind of mattress might fit it. And sitting down and scrolling was all she was really good for right now.

Just as she was about to fire up the laptop, there was a knock at the door.

Perhaps it was someone else, ready to stage an intervention on her love life, she thought as she went to answer it.

'Bonjour.' It was Chloé, clutching a *pâtisserie* box.

'Oh, bonjour, Chloé.' Lily said, feeling her heart turn over.

'It is OK for me to come in?'

'Of course,' Lily said, stepping back and smiling nervously. Then 'Thank you,' as Chloé handed her the box. Inside were two *tartes aux fraises*, glistening with sweetness.

'I want to tell you for last night,' Chloé said, settling herself down rather uncomfortably on one of the metal garden chairs. 'I did not mean to be unfriendly, uh?'

'It's OK,' Lily said, putting spoonfuls of coffee in her new cafetière and pulling a couple of plates from the cupboard. 'Frédérique explained everything.'

'Oh, he explain?' Chloé said with a delicate raise of the eyebrow.

'Yes, don't worry. I understand.' Lily smiled, passing Chloé her coffee before sinking into her own hard, metal seat.

'Well, I am not sure what he say, but maybe I say what I think too?'

'Yes, of course,' Lily replied, her heart sinking.

'Because Frédérique and I, we were lovers many years before.'

'Yes, he said.'

Chloé shot her a look. 'Yes? But did he tell you zat I don't approve of 'im much?'

'Well,' said Lily. 'Sort of. That you find it... difficult.'

'*Difficile? Pourquoi?* Why?'

'Because,' she felt herself going red. 'Well, he said you feel...'

'Pah! I feel. That I am in love with him, yes?'

'Well, sort of...'

'That I cannot 'elp myself to feel *amour* for 'im,' Chloé said, shaking her head. 'Bah.'

'So you don't...?'

'Not for many, many year. But I watch him, huh? He did not treat me well, he – 'ow you say – three-time me.'

'Oh.'

'And he say he love me, and want to marry. And then, pouf!'

'Oh, that's horrible.'

'So, he is a friendly man. Kind. But not a nice man for boyfriend, I think,' Chloé concluded.

'So you don't mind if we... if I...?' Lily took a sip of her coffee and looked at Chloé intently.

'But you wish to date him still? If he is not a good man?'

'Well...' Lily shrugged. It was hard to know how to reply without causing offence. It wasn't great that Frédérique had form – perhaps this was what Claude had been referring to too? But she didn't want to judge him on past misdemeanours. 'Maybe not. But we're just getting to know each other.'

'As you want.' Chloé took a bite of her strawberry tart, a little custard escaping over the side of the generously filled pastry, and wiped her mouth delicately with the serviette from the *pâtisserie* box.

'You don't mind?'

Chloé smiled. 'I don't mind for me. But maybe a little I mind for you, huh?'

'Well, thank you. It's nice, that you care.'

'Well, we are friends, I think?'

'Yes. Yes, we are friends.'

* * *

An hour later, after Chloé had disappeared into her car and driven off into the early evening air, Lily sat on her front step, head spinning.

She'd woken up with a headache dampening her mood. Now the headache had lifted, but her mood remained sombre. Because although it was nice that everyone seemed to care so much about her, there was a big part of her that wanted to tell them all to mind their own business. She was an adult, she was alone for the first time in two decades. And while it was kind of them to try to spare her from hurt, surely taking a risk was part of actually living?

The phone beeped, interrupting her thoughts. Frédérique.

Vendredi soir? You are free to come to a restaurant?

She typed:

Oui, bien sûr.

You bet I am.

25

The second-hand furniture store wasn't quite what Lily had expected. When she turned left, as instructed by the GPS on her phone and bumped down a potholed lane she was certain she'd made a mistake. Passing a wood yard stacked high with *cordes* of wood for winter burning, and some sort of industrial unit, she was just about to turn around when she saw a ramshackle barn, the space around it filled with old garden ornaments and toys, a leaning stack of metal gates and a few rusty bikes.

She parked up at the side of the road and got out of the car, feeling the kind of sinking sensation you get when reality doesn't quite meet with your expectations. Still, the interior of the barn might be well stocked and organised for all she knew, she told herself, as she made her way across the outdoor area, careful to avoid the piles of rusty garden tools, makeshift planters and decomposing garden furniture that littered the yard.

Inside, she was met with the smell of mustiness that you get in a charity shop or National Trust property – a sort of polish meets dust meets benign neglect. A memory popped into her head of walking around Wimpole Hall in Cambridgeshire with a then five-year-old Ty. 'Mummy,' he'd said, 'this place smells of *old*.'

She exchanged bonjours with a bored-looking man at a trestle table who was clearly overseeing the enterprise while scrolling through his phone, then began to inspect some of the second-hand bargains she'd been promised by Sam would help her to plug her furniture gaps for the time being.

She'd been thinking about having some sort of house-warming party once the ink was dry on the contract. Partly to mark the occasion, partly to thank those who'd been around to help – Sam and Claude and Chloé, as well as Dawn and Clive and anyone else they wanted to invite along. It wasn't as if the renovations were finished – they'd barely started. But she'd slapped a bit of paint around and gradually the house had started to seem more like it was 'hers'.

She'd need to do a lot more work before she could welcome visitors to any sort of relaxation retreat – at the moment the would-be studio remained untouched. She'd barely ventured into the outbuilding, which was in dire need of some proper attention from an artisan builder to plug the gaps in the pointing and make sure nothing was about to fall down. And she'd have to do something about heating it if she wanted to run retreats in the autumn or winter – perhaps a wood-burner would need to be installed, and electric points, and probably a toilet.

She'd begun to realise that the house would never quite be finished in the way she'd envisaged. But if she rebranded her thinking and considered the quirks of the house as being 'charming' rather than annoying; if she sold her accommodation as rural and 'shabby chic' rather than luxury, then she was pretty sure she'd be able to keep a few guests happy.

She'd thought she was ready to immerse herself in a project – to transform a house from ramshackle to state-of-the-art and gorgeous. But she'd found the longer she lived in the property, and the more local buildings she'd ventured inside, that it was her who needed to change. She'd detested the straight lines and lack of personality in her UK house, yet her mind had initially wanted to impose the same neatness on a French property.

Instead, now, she'd begun to see the beauty in the house's flaws – not so much the bits that were falling down, or the need to burn lorry-delivered oil in order to heat her water, which she'd have to do something about. But the wonky walls and rickety stairs; the unusual design of the brick-decked fireplace and the mismatched furniture she'd assembled to use in the kitchen had begun to grow on her. The house had personality, was quirky and fun. And perhaps if she overdid the renovations she'd lose some of that.

In the end the trip to the barn wasn't a complete disaster. She found a pair of comfy armchairs – wooden framed, the kind her grandmother used to have, but somehow charming. She even discovered a small table with chairs that would definitely make an improvement on the garden table she'd dragged into the kitchen as an interim measure. She managed to communicate with the man behind the till – despite his only speaking French – that she'd like them delivered tomorrow if possible, and given her address and brief directions.

He was friendly, patient with her fledgling French and more than happy to help her out. For €200 all in.

With the bedstead she'd bought on LeBonCoin – a second-hand selling site – now delivered and a mattress on order from a shop in Limoges, these extra additions would feel like the height of luxury after putting up with airbeds and metal chairs, propping her dinner on the edge of a dresser or balancing a plate on her knees. An actual real-life table. Who'd have thought?

* * *

Since agreeing to go for a meal with Frédérique, she'd been worrying on and off about how it might go. About what it *meant*. So it was a relief when the hands of the clock finally crawled to 5 p.m. and she could legitimately begin to get ready rather than thinking about whether she should be going out, whether it was OK that – despite her half-promise to Ty – she hadn't been able to bring herself to ring Ben.

She turned on the taps and left the bath running and walked into the bedroom, where she'd laid out a couple of outfit choices on the airbed. A black dress seemed too much – it wasn't as if she was going into Limoges; he'd told her it was a local restaurant – but she wanted to look nice. In the end she selected a light summer dress, in a dusky pink, patterned with tiny white flowers. Not too much, but definitely more date-like than the leggings and jeans that had become her at-home 'uniform' while she patched up the house.

Smiling, she drifted back into the bathroom, ready to add a slug of the bubble bath she'd picked up earlier to the tub. Only, when she stuck her hand into the water to test the temperature, she found it was freezing cold. The oil in the tank must have run out.

Now she was left, stubbly legged, slightly sweaty, greasy-haired with a dilemma; to brave a freezing cold arse, or to go on a date looking like a yeti. She chose the former, grimacing as she stepped into the cold water, stood and washed herself as best she could.

At least, she thought, as she towel-dried her hair, she'd probably burned about five hundred calories in the process.

* * *

Finally it was 7 p.m. and she paced the living room waiting for a knock at the door. It came.

Frédérique was there, his normally floppy hair brushed back and gelled. It didn't suit him as well as his usual style, but the sweet effort he'd gone to made her smile. He'd trimmed his beard, and was wearing a white shirt and light blue trousers that showed off his tanned skin. He was holding a flower, clearly plucked from his – or someone else's – garden and handed it to her.

'For you, *mon amour*,' he said with a little bow.

'*Merci beaucoup!*' she said, smelling the bloom before placing it on a stepladder in the hallway and hoping he wouldn't mind.

He reached for her hand and she stepped down the path with him, pushing thoughts of Ben and Ty and Emily, plus anyone else who wanted to interfere in her life and her feelings, to the side. It was easy for people to judge from the side-lines. To want everything to go back to normal because it suited them. The only one who had even a tiny bit of a right to feel that way was Ty – she ached for any hurt she might be causing him. But she had every right to happiness, and was going to embrace it fully.

The restaurant was a short drive away, down a seemingly empty country road, which eventually opened out to reveal a stone building set on its own, with a few cars scattered in an enormous parking area behind. A sign – '*Le Bistro*' – hung in carved wood over the entrance was the only indication that this was anything other than an old farmhouse, half-forgotten in its isolated position.

She climbed out of the car, her heels sinking slightly into the soft ground and, gratefully taking Frédérique's hand, made her way to the entrance.

Once they were seated at a small mahogany table next to a window, a woman in a white shirt and jeans came over with a menu. They were one of just three couples in the small room, and the venue felt intimate and charming – the sort of place that tourists would never stumble across; authentic and rustic and ridiculously *French*.

Frédérique looked at the menu, his eyes flitting back and forth, and she waited patiently for it to be passed to her.

But to her surprise, before she'd even been able to glance at the starters, he clicked his fingers in the air – something that seemed rude, but that she assumed was a custom in France – to summon the waitress. Then, in rapid French, he said something about steak and frites and red wine and bread. It was straightforward, but the speed of the language meant she was only able to grasp on to the edges of the meaning. Was he asking what cuts they had? Or for the wine menu?

She waited patiently, then was surprised when the waitress thanked him and walked away with the menu in her hand.

'Is something the matter?' she asked, once the waitress was out of earshot.

'*Bah, non?*' Frédérique said, his brow furrowing. '*Pourquoi* – why do you think this?'

'It's just... she took the menu. Did she do it by accident? Or is there a different one or something? When do we get to order?'

'*Non, tout va bien!*' he replied. 'I 'ave ordered you the steak, *oui*? It is the best.' He performed a chef's kiss with a flourish and smiled at her.

Lily felt a bit affronted at his ordering on her behalf. She tried to tell herself that he wanted to treat her, to show her the best the restaurant had to offer. But it was difficult for a moment to smile. 'Oh,' she said. 'Thank you.'

'Ah, you are welcome!' he said, completely missing any change in tone and fixing her in his gaze. The gaze had the desired effect and she was soon melting into his green eyes, all offence forgotten. After all, his motive had clearly been to ensure she had the best meal – there was nothing wrong with that.

The steak arrived more quickly than she could have anticipated and her stomach growled hungrily – luckily not loudly enough for anyone else to hear. The cut was thick, seared and smelled delicious. The frites were chunky and home cut, and they'd added a tiny salad in a bowl with vinaigrette in a nod towards making it healthy.

'Mm,' she said, as the waitress placed the laden plate in front of her. '*Délicieux!*'

'*Oui,*' said Frédérique. 'Zey do the steak to perfection 'ere.'

She picked up her knife and cut into the dark-brown meat, only to find it yield easily beneath the blade. Blood began to seep out of its red interior onto the plate.

She'd tried a steak rare before, but this was something else entirely. Other than its browned crust, the inch-thick chunk of meat was entirely raw. 'Oh,' she said.

'Is something *le* matter?'

'Yes... well, no, but I prefer my steak a little more cooked.' Or actually cooked at all.

Frédérique looked momentarily surprised, but before she could tell him not to make a fuss, clicked for the waitress who appeared instantly at his side. He said something to her in low tones, as if discussing something delicate or troubling. The waitress snorted briefly then, with a glare, snatched Lily's plate away.

'Is everything OK?' Lily asked, sensing the shift in atmosphere.

'*Mais oui!*' he said. 'She weel cook it more for you!'

A couple of minutes later with a '*Voilà – bien cuit,*' the woman reappeared and shoved Lily's plate rather roughly in front of her. The meat on it was steaming from the griddle.

'*Merci*,' Lily said. '*Et désolé!*' she called after the woman's retreating back.

'Are you sure I haven't done something wrong?' she said to Frédérique with a grimace.

'Do not worry about it,' Frédérique replied, chomping on a chunk of what was basically raw cow arse, 'they are very precious about their cooking, eh? The chef, 'e is insulted a bit I think?'

'Oh,' she said, her heart sinking. 'Well, I didn't mean...'

'It is nothing, we are the customers!' Frédérique told her, his smile a little spoiled by the small runnel of blood seeping from mouth to beard. 'We come first, zey say this?'

She nodded, then cut into the steak, which – after an initial millimetre of cooked meat, was still entirely raw.

'It iz better, yes?'

'Much better,' she lied, reaching for her wine and taking an enormous gulp before forcing a bit of raw meat into her mouth. 'Yummy.'

They began to talk about her plans for running retreats, about Frédérique's hope that he could introduce a new market day into the local town. They spoke about family – carefully avoiding anything about ex-husbands or divorces – and life in the local area.

The conversation flowed, the wine kept pace and soon Lily was relaxed, happy and tipsy enough to chow through her dinner without too many issues.

After the steak came dessert, paired with a rosé, then coffee and a small shot of something sticky and sweet. She offered to pay, but Frédérique refused. '*Mais non*, you are my guest,' he said, handing his bank card to the waitress, whose look in Lily's direction showed that she still hadn't been forgiven for rejecting the steak.

After this, her memory got a bit blurry. She remembered

stumbling back to the car with Frédérique afterwards – who clearly hadn't filled his own glass as much as hers – laughing as she almost broke her heel on a rogue stone, climbing awkwardly into the passenger seat and beginning the journey back to *Broussas*, with Frédérique at the wheel.

But when she found herself in a strange room the next morning, she couldn't really remember much about what had happened after that.

26

The curves in the road towards *Broussas* were car-sick inducing at the best of times. But this morning Lily definitely couldn't be described as 'being at her best'. As the driver signalled to turn into the road leading to her house, Lily asked him to pull over. '*C'est bon*,' she said. '*Je veux marcher*... I'll enjoy the walk.'

It was partially true, partially a complete and utter lie. Although the walk wouldn't be completely unwelcome, she was more worried that navigating the bumpy road in the back of a taxi might wreak havoc on her stomach, which was already grumbling worryingly after its overdose of *vin rouge*, raw meat and whatever they'd had for dessert. The last thing she wanted to do was vomit in the back of a cab – not only because it was pretty disgusting, but because the driver was a local guy, one of only two taxi drivers around.

As it was, she was already a bit embarrassed at the fact she'd called a taxi to pick her up from Frédérique's house. She'd woken at 8 a.m., to find a note telling her he'd had to go to work, but to help herself to coffee. He'd put the card for the taxi firm next to the note, and €20 for her fare, which she hadn't taken.

It was kind of him not to wake her, but in some ways she wished she'd seen him this morning – if only to reassure herself that the magic that she'd felt the night before hadn't just been caused by having too much wine. As she'd drunk her coffee, memories had began to flood back and she'd relived the last couple of hours of their date, piecing everything together. Frédérique driving them back along windy dark roads, laughing when she'd been convinced that a log on the verge had been a deer about to spring in front of the car.

Then she'd come back to his, sat on the sofa while he'd made them both a nightcap. They'd talked a little more, before he'd leaned in for a kiss – a deep, passionate embrace that had left her fizzing on the inside. But then, as she'd laid back and pulled him towards her, he'd broken off and told her it might be time they went to bed – separately. 'I fink it will be better for us when per'aps you have not had quite so much to drink?' he'd said. At the time, she'd felt a bit put out, but this morning she felt grateful that they hadn't rushed into anything. Instead, he'd shown her to a guest room, where she'd crashed – fully clothed – on top of the feather duvet.

After drinking the rest of her coffee and resisting the urge to explore some of the closed-off rooms, she'd called the number of the taxi firm and given Frédérique's address, which had luckily been written on a couple of letters that were sitting unopened on the kitchen counter.

As soon as she'd hung up, she'd regretted it though; she should have arranged for the taxi to meet her on the corner – somewhere anonymous. Now, whatever had or hadn't happened between them last night was going to be public knowledge and she wasn't sure she was ready to be the subject of speculation – after all, the talk of Emily's escapades had only just died down.

Once she stepped onto her road from the taxi, she also wished she'd remembered about the heels she'd chosen to wear the night before. Because walking the kilometre to her front door was going to be quite a challenge on the uneven surface. Rather than risk a broken ankle, she removed her shoes and held them in her hand by the straps; but walking was still uncomfortable at best. She wondered what she'd look like to anyone glancing out of their window – would they be able to tell she'd been out all night? Or could she just be going for a morning stroll in a rather flimsy summer dress?

By the time the roof of her house came into view, she'd started to wish she'd actually worried less about the taxi driver's sensibilities and more about the effect of the stony, bumpy road on her bare feet. She'd trodden on at least three sharp stones, her feet were aching and dirty and to her horror she'd stepped on something cold and slimy on route, only to find that she'd flattened an enormous slug, lying black and sticky on the edge of the pavement.

As soon as she arrived home, she resolved, she was going to have the bath to end all baths – even if she had to boil a thousand kettles to warm it to the right temperature. She wasn't sure whether she'd damaged the slug, or whether she'd simply made it slightly flatter with her tread, but whatever was on her foot, she longed to scrub it off, before also attempting to wash away the horrible feeling of being hungover. Next time they went out, she resolved, she'd stick to one glass, whatever stomach-churning delights were on the menu.

She hoped so much that there would be a next time.

Finally, her house came properly into view and she was on the home stretch. Just a couple of hundred metres and she'd be able to let herself in the front door, strip last night from her body, pop a couple of paracetamol, scrub herself clean then see if she couldn't get an hour or so's nap.

Then she stopped, feeling the blood drain from her face as she took in the sight of a figure standing close to her front gate. Someone who looked incongruous in his surroundings, but achingly familiar, even from this distance. But it couldn't be, could it?

Since moving in, she'd come to like the occasional knock at the door – the way people popped around on their way to the lake, or dropped in to help out with something. She'd even enjoyed a coffee with her next-door neighbour last week – although her thick accent had been hard to understand, it had been a pleasant enough experience that had left her determined to pick up the pace with her online French lessons and find a local class as soon as possible.

But this wasn't her neighbour, or Claude, or Frédérique, or any of the people she'd encountered in her time on French soil. It was someone else entirely, someone from a completely different world.

Even with his back to her and from this distance, she felt a flood of recognition taking in the chequered shirt, the tousled hair, the way he stood, one shoulder leaning slightly.

She began to run, her heart pounding, her whole body longing to get closer to him, to fling herself into his arms. All the missing him she'd repressed suddenly rushed to the fore. She hadn't stopped loving him; hadn't given up hope that this might happen. It was Ben! Perhaps he loved her after all? Perhaps he'd decided to make a go of it.

But as she approached, the man turned towards her and fixed his eyes on her, lifting his hand in a small wave of greeting and she felt a flush of heat on her neck. Her feelings raced from elation to disappointment to another sort of elation altogether. It wasn't Ben at all. Just someone who looked incredibly like him from behind.

'Ty!' she cried, as she raced towards him, no longer worried what her poor bare feet might encounter and stumbling over a particularly pointy stone, before flinging herself into his arms. 'What are you doing here?'

He embraced her briefly before standing back, slightly horrified at her enthusiastic greeting. But she'd missed him so much over the past few weeks, despite their phone calls and texts, that seeing him out of the blue had made her momentarily forget that although he was still her boy, he was also a teenager standing in front of a mother, asking her *not* to hug him.

'All right?' he said, picking up the bag at his feet.

'Yes. Oh, Ty, it's so good to see you!' she said, feeling slightly dizzy. It was wonderful to see him, but the merging of one of her worlds with the other made the whole experience feel surreal.

She saw his eyes take in her appearance and suddenly realised how this must look. Flimsy dress, shoes in hand, messy hair, smudged mascara. It was a classic 'walk of shame' only in reverse – she, the wayward mother sneaking in after staying out all night, he the disapproving teen waiting on the front doorstep.

'It's not what it looks like,' she said, instantly regretting the words, surely one of the most incriminating phrases in the world.

'I've been here for two hours,' he said, frowning.

'Oh, I'm sorry. I just didn't... Why didn't you call?'

'I wanted to surprise you.'

'I'm really sorry, Ty,' she said, rubbing a hand on his arm.

He nodded, looking again at her dishevelled appearance but not saying anything – probably in fear of unleashing the most awkward conversation in the history of awkward conversations. You didn't ask your mum where she'd been all night, did you? Especially if you were afraid of the answer.

'Come on,' she said as brightly as she could, hoping to distract him from her appearance. 'Let's get inside and I'll give you the tour.'

Half an hour later, she'd slipped on some more respectable jogging bottoms and a loose T-shirt, given her face a rudimentary wash, made a quick call to the *bricolage* to arrange an oil delivery and made him a cup of tea with a side order of pretty much all the biscuits she had in the cupboard. At last she no longer felt on the back foot (although one of her feet was still suspiciously sticky under its clean sock).

'So,' she said, sitting down opposite her son and taking a grateful gulp from the mug of tea she'd made. 'What made you decide to come?'

He shrugged. 'Dunno.'

'I mean, I'm *delighted* you're here. You can stay for as long as you want – forever if you want. But it's a surprise, is all.'

He looked at her over the top of his mug. 'Where did you go last night?' he asked.

The question was unexpected. 'Well, I was out for a meal with... well, with a friend. I'd been drinking, so I crashed at... hers,' she said, feeling a little guilty. But it was less complicated than admitting she'd been with Frédérique. Plus it was private and new and something that was – for the moment at least – just theirs. The moonlight shining on the edge of crystal glasses, the softness of his lips against hers. The way in which he'd made her feel attractive, wanted in a way she hadn't felt in years.

Tyler nodded, his eyes dark.

She tried to smile.

'Well, I came for... I wanted to come for Dad,' he said.

She felt something inside her sink. Guilt rose up. But what could she do? 'Oh, Ty.'

'What?'

'I'm so sorry we're putting you through this, sweetheart. And it's so lovely that you love Dad so much and want to come and fix things for us. But...'

'No, wait,' he said, 'I'm not...'

'Not what?'

'I don't think I'm going to fix things for you, I'm not stupid,' he said, frowning. 'I'm just... you don't know everything and I thought you should know everything before you...' He trailed off, his eyes pleading with her not to make him say it.

'Before I... move on?'

'Yeah,' he said, comfortable with her choice of words.

'Oh, Ty,' she said again, reaching over and covering his hand with hers. He let her, briefly, before moving his away. It wasn't a gesture of rejection, just an automatic teenage reflex. 'I know Dad loves me. I love him, too. You know? But...'

'It's not that.'

'Then what?' She felt a lump in her throat. 'Is something wrong?'

'Well, not exactly. Dad, he's... A couple of nights ago, I came in and he was kind of...' He paused and looked at his nails, finding a dirty one and lifting the grot out of it with another fingernail.

'He was *what*, Ty?'

'I dunno.'

She sighed. 'Angry?'

'No, not that. More... you know like, sad, I guess.'

'Oh.'

'And like he doesn't normally talk to me about stuff like this. But he kind of said some things to me.'

'OK?'

'He... he's got... He's not well, kind of...'

Her stomach heaved slightly. 'Oh my god, Ty, what is it?'

'He's... He said he feels anxious. He's... Well, he feels anxious about coming here, or really doing a lot of things. He says that's why he can't come. He just... Well, he can't.'

'Oh.'

'Yeah.' Ty shrugged. 'I thought you should know, in case you want to...'

'In case I want to...?'

'I dunno. Come home and look after him.'

'Oh, Ty.' She reached for his hand again but this time he pulled it away before she got there. He stared down at the table, the back of his neck red. For a boy who'd barely admitted emotions existed for the past five years, to fly out here to tell her Ben had anxiety was nothing short of incredible.

'I don't know what to do,' he said, at last. 'I mean, I'm meant to be going to uni... but I can't leave Dad in this state can I?'

'Ty, look. I realise this is hard. It's hard for me to hear too. But your dad... I mean there's help out there. People can... well, get through these types of things.'

'But...'

'And there's no way you're going to delay going to university. You've worked hard for that. We'll find a way – we'll sort it. Dad will be OK, I promise.'

He grunted.

'I mean, he's eating? He's going to work? There's food at home for you?'

Ty nodded.

'And do you know if he's getting any help?'

A shake of the head.

'OK, well, how about I ring him. I'll ring him and check he's OK.'

'And if he's not?'

It was so hard to have this conversation with her son. And even though it wasn't directly Ben's fault that Ty had taken it upon himself to come out, she felt angry that once again she'd been put in this position – the last thing she wanted to do was to use her son as a kind of envoy between them.

'If he's not, we'll find some help for him.'

'But you won't come?' He looked at her then, and she saw something in his eyes.

'Ty, did Ben... did your father send you?'

'No.' He flushed. 'I mean, he knows I've come to see you... He paid for the flight, and that. But he doesn't know why.'

She nodded. 'Right,' she said.

'You're not mad at him?'

'No. Not mad.' She lied. She was a little bit mad. A little bit worried too though. Ben had suffered from anxiety on and off in his twenties – panic attacks, sleepless nights. They'd worked through it together, but there had been a few dark days. Eventually, he'd learned to manage it. If it had flared up again, then she felt wretched for him. But at the same time, she couldn't put her life on hold to help him; she'd give what help she could, speak to him, help him find proper support.

But anxiety or not, he must have known what Ty intended to do. He'd driven him to the airport, paid for his ticket. In an attempt to – what? Get her to come home? Make her feel guilty for being here without him?

The mix of elation at seeing Ty, anger at Ben, worry for Ben and the churning in her stomach from last night made her feel suddenly nauseous. She took a sip of tea and tried to calm herself down. It would be OK; she'd find a way to make this OK.

'Anyway, I'm so glad you're here,' she said, changing the subject. 'How long have I got you for?'

'Four days.'

'Well, that's brilliant. I can't wait for you to see everything, to meet some people; I've got loads to show you and tell you about,' she said, smiling.

She didn't like the fact that Ben was trying to manipulate her. But on the plus side, it had given her a few days with her son. And she was determined to make the most of them.

27

It was 10 p.m. and the sun had begun to set, bleeding red and orange across the horizon, and the trees stood in contrast, black against their coloured backdrop. It was the kind of scene that, if she'd seen it in an oil painting, might have made her assume that the artist had got a bit carried away with creating the perfect canvas. *Good effort, but too idealised – B+.*

'So what do you think?' Lily asked as they sat together on the wrought iron chairs that had now been returned to their rightful place in the back garden. She'd invested in a couple of cushions for them and for the first time she'd been able to settle comfortably into their curved shape, without her back or neck complaining.

Ty sipped his lager, looking out over the enormous grassed area, then through the scattered trees to the lake beyond.

'It's all right,' he said.

'All right? Ty, this is paradise!' She poked his leg with her finger. 'Come on, tell me this isn't the most beautiful view you've ever seen!'

'Yeah, maybe.'

She grinned at him and he caught her smile, the corners of his mouth turning up adorably. An all right from Ty was actually a pretty good score.

This morning, after she'd shown him around the house, they'd gone into *Eymoutiers* to pick up some bread and a few essentials from the *bricolage* – she'd found she was getting through paint at a rate of knots, but at the same time wasn't making the progress she'd have hoped for. The paint was thin and the wallpaper was strongly patterned, meaning each wall took several coats and a plethora of different swear words to cover. But she was gradually getting there – dipping a paintbrush into a tin whenever she had the chance, and gradually transforming the walls from dreary and overly patterned to neutral and bright.

She'd watched Ty as he'd taken in the surroundings of her new hometown – the ancient stone buildings with old-fashioned sash windows, some with bars across their lower half. Each building with its individual quirks: a wall that narrowed almost to a point, a door leading from the second floor without a balcony to make sense of it; an ancient wooden archway with a curving staircase just visible inside. Seeing it all anew through his eyes, she had to pinch herself that she was actually here. That she actually *lived* here.

It was wasted on him of course, for the most part. He'd made the right noises, but she could see that it wouldn't be his first choice of places to live right now. He was set on London, the UCL halls, the life and buzz and mixture of people he could meet. She was glad, on reflection, she'd waited until he was eighteen to move, if they'd moved over when Ty was eight – something she'd fought for at the time – he might have been completely at a loss. Now she could establish a life here, and make a home for him to come to whenever he chose – somewhere he could feel completely safe and nurtured and have a bit of sunshine to boot.

He'd perked up a bit when they'd visited the new pizza restaurant opposite the car park. It was run by a young couple who made each pizza to order in a corner kitchen then brought it to the table on a wooden board. The *menu du jour* consisted of a starter of tomatoes in vinaigrette – which he wolfed down quickly, scowling slightly at the bitter taste – and finished, post pizza, with chocolate torte.

'Well,' Lily had said, watching him lick the back of his spoon. 'What do you think?'

'It's all right,' he'd said.

The restaurant had been full and the rumble of conversation had made the place seem friendly and vibrant. Most of the tables had been taken up with people on their lunch-break from nearby businesses – she'd recognised a couple of faces, although she hadn't yet been able to put names to them. She'd nodded and exchanged 'bonjours' on the way out, feeling pleased that she could show how she was settling in and getting to know people.

On their way out, they'd bumped into Chloé who was coming in with an older lady. '*Bonjour*,' Chloé said, exchanging *bisous* with Lily, then nodding at Ty. 'This is my mother,' she said, gesturing to the woman, who was tall and slim and looked to be in her late fifties.

Once they'd gone through the formalities of the introduction and Chloé and her mother had disappeared into the interior of the restaurant, Ty had turned to Lily, his eyes sparkling for the first time since he'd arrived. 'Who was *she*?' he asked.

'Chloé? She's the woman whose B. & B. I stayed in at the start.'

'She seems... like, really nice. Like, you know... fit.'

Coming from a boy whose highest compliments seemed to be

either 'all right' or 'pretty good' this was an amazing endorsement.

'Ty! She's old enough to be your mother.'

'Yeah, but she's not like you, is she? She's kind of...'

'Careful how you finish that sentence,' she'd said, not minding in the least.

'Well, she just looks kind of cool,' he'd said, with a shrug.

In the afternoon they'd taken the obligatory trip to the lake, where Ty had waded in up to his waist and swum lengths, his strong arms driving swathes of water out of his way as he'd raced along. She'd sat and watched – not keen on taking a dip herself – feeling proud of her son who had grown up more than she'd realised. Something about him being here had made everything seem doable, permanent. She'd imagined the holidays he might take; that he might choose to come here to revise in peace or decompress after a difficult term.

'So,' she said now. 'You don't think I'm completely mad to have moved here.'

He stiffened slightly and she wished she could grab the question back and reframe it. It sounded as if she was asking him to take sides, to tell her she'd done the right thing in leaving Ben behind. But it wasn't like that at all.

'I just mean,' she added hurriedly, 'that it's not such a bad place, huh?'

'No,' he said. 'It's actually all right.'

Praise indeed.

They sat in silence for a few more minutes, her looking out over the view, him scrolling on his phone. Then she got up. 'Just going to make a call,' she said. He nodded, and she made her way into the house, and took her phone up to her bedroom to make sure she wasn't overheard.

Emily answered after a few rings. 'Hi, Lily, how's life *en France*?'

'Surprising.'

'Oh, do tell?'

So she told Em about Ty's visit, and how he'd seen her come back from her night out looking dishevelled and holding a pair of shoes.

'Talk about bad timing!' Emily said. 'But it must be nice to have him there.'

'It really is,' Lily said. 'I mean, I don't feel so... lonely now. I'm OK living on my own, but I've missed him so much. I didn't realise how much until I saw him.'

'Must be difficult knowing you're so far away from him?'

'Well, kind of. But then he's off to uni in a few weeks – I probably wouldn't have seen him much anyway if I'd stayed.'

'So,' said Emily, 'why do you think he surprised you? Why not just book a trip and tell you to pick him up from the airport?'

'I'm not sure. I think maybe because he came to talk about Ben.'

'Oh?'

'Yeah. Apparently, Ben's anxiety has flared up again.'

'Oh shit.'

'Yeah, poor guy. And I do feel sorry for him. I want to help. But I kind of feel a bit angry too, because he must have known that Ty was going to mention it to me. And I can't help but think he might be trying to work the situation in his favour.'

'Really?' Emily sounded incredulous.

'Well, yeah. It just seems... well, Ty seemed to think I'd come running home once I knew.'

'Oh bless him... But I doubt Ben was thinking that way.'

'You don't think?'

'Well, no. I don't know how Ben is when he's feeling low, but you know I've had my moments over the years...'

'Uh huh,' Lily nodded. When Emily had had a series of miscarriages in her thirties, she'd experienced such a slump in mood that she'd barely been able to get out of bed. It had taken six months and antidepressants to get her back on her feet.

'Well, I can tell you from my perspective, that when I was down, all my energy was focused on just trying to cope. Just trying to get through the day. I didn't have the energy or willpower, or even presence of mind, to really try to manipulate anyone.'

'True...' Lily thought back to Ben's last episode over a decade ago. He'd managed to keep working, but really struggled just to keep himself on track. Perhaps she'd judged him too harshly. 'You're probably right,' she said.

'Darling, I am *always* right,' said Emily, sounding more like her usual self. 'So what are you going to do?'

'Well, I'll call him, or try to at least. And maybe if I think he needs me to, I'll ring Baz or his mum or something. Make sure someone's keeping an eye.'

'Do you want me to pop over and see him?'

'Oh.' Lily hadn't thought of that. 'Well, actually yes. If you don't mind?'

'Not at all. I can make up some sort of excuse for being there if you like? So he doesn't feel too... well, exposed?'

'If you can think of one.'

'You forget who you're talking to. I am the queen of excuses!'

'Thank you, Emily. I think I'll feel a lot better with your take on the situation.'

'No problem. It's weird but when I had those horrible months, what surprised me most was the people who came through for me, and the people who didn't. It turned my world upside down –

friends I thought were... well, proper friends turned out not to be quite so reliable. And then my neighbour – do you remember? – Pat. She was round most mornings for a coffee. We never really spoke about it, but we both knew why she was there.'

'Yes, I remember. She was great.'

'Exactly. So that's who I'll be, for Ben. If he needs me that is. His weird but present neighbour.'

'Thank you.' Lily felt a weight lift from her. It would have been hard to call Ben's mum at the moment, and she'd never really seen eye to eye with Baz. Having someone on her team to check up on Ben would work wonders putting her mind at ease.

'Anyway, I have to ask. How did the date go? And, come to think of it, *why* were you walking back on your own, wearing last night's clothes?'

Lily blushed, although there was no one to see her. 'It's not what you think,' she said. 'He was a proper gentleman. I mean, we kissed. But nothing else. I was too drunk, he said.'

'So he's a good guy.'

'A very good guy.'

'Or maybe just worried that you might vomit on him or something.'

'Well, that's always a possibility...'

'Ha. And the kiss was...?'

'Kiss-*es*.'

'Ooh, and they were...?'

'Heavenly. Honestly, I felt about eighteen again – I'd forgotten how exciting it was to be in the beginning of a relationship, the kind of thrill of not really knowing how it's going to go.'

'I think I remember. Although to be honest, it's been a while.'

'Well, only for good reasons.'

'True. Then coming home to see Ty! You must have died!'

'It was weird, though,' Lily said. 'For a minute, when I noticed him standing there from a distance, I thought he was Ben. He had his back to me, and he's grown, even in these few weeks. He looked just the same as his dad from the back. I ran up to him and nearly threw myself at him, until he turned around and I realised just in time.'

'Eek, nothing like a full-on snog from your own mother.'

'Quite.'

There was a brief silence, then Emily took an audible breath. 'But, Lily, what do you think that means?'

'What do you mean?'

'Well, bear with me, but don't you think it sort of *means something* that you had that reaction when you thought it was Ben? Running towards him with bare feet? Flinging yourself into his arms? It's like a scene from a bloody Richard Curtis movie.'

'Ha. Well, I suppose. Although to be fair, it wasn't raining.'

'That's true.'

'And neither of us were about to board a plane, or had just ducked out of our own wedding.'

'Good point. So not very Curtis-esque after all.'

'Except for the running.'

'Except for that. But seriously, Lily. What if it *had* been him? What would have happened?'

'I'm not sure... I mean, I suppose, well, in that moment I was just so happy to see him. Like I'd been missing a puzzle piece and it had finally turned up. But maybe once the initial... thrill had died down, things wouldn't have felt so straightforward.'

'But what would you have felt like,' Emily said carefully, 'if it *had* been Ben, but you'd actually slept with Frédérique?'

Lily was silent for a minute. She imagined coming home one day to find that Ben had actually decided to join her. Whatever she told herself, she knew deep down that her dream of living in France had always included him. And admittedly, had she slept with Frédérique, despite the fact she and Ben were separated, it would probably scupper any chance that they might get back together.

But what was she meant to do? She couldn't wait forever. Be alone forever.

'Thing is, Emily,' she said firmly, 'Ben isn't coming.'

'You don't *know* that,' said her friend. 'Maybe he will. It's only been a few weeks, and he's dealing with god knows what. Maybe think about giving him a bit more time.'

'I don't know, Em,' she said sadly. 'I can't help but feel he'd be here by now if... well, you know.'

Once they'd said their goodbyes, she padded downstairs to find Ty in the kitchen, opening a packet of crisps. 'All right, love?' she said.

'Yeah, not bad. Want one?' He offered her the packet.

'No, I'm OK.'

'Did you call Dad?' he asked innocently.

'No, not yet. I was just chatting to Auntie Em.'

'Oh, right.'

'But I will. Call him.'

'You will?' Ty's wide-eyed look made him seem about five years old again, looking at her when she'd said she was taking him to the fair, or going to buy a packet of his favourite sweets.

'Yes,' she said, wanting to please the ghost of her little son who'd suddenly flickered in the face of the man he'd become. 'Tell you what, I'll do it now.'

He nodded and wandered back outside, pulling the door softly behind him in order to give her some privacy.

She'd done it now.

She looked at the mobile phone in her hand and scrolled through to the number that she'd blocked. Her thumb hovered for a moment over the button before she pressed, restoring the connection between them. She wondered whether any messages, stored somewhere in cyberspace, might appear when she did so. But there was nothing.

And then, because there was very little else to do but get it over with, she pressed the 'call' button and rang her husband.

28

When he found her on the bed, he pulled her into his arms. 'Oh Lily,' he murmured into her hair.

'I'm sorry,' she said. 'I know I'm meant to be happy about this... and I am. I love our baby, I really do. It's just...' She looked at him, her eyes wide, pleading. 'Ever since the labour I've been feeling... Everything just seems wrong.'

'Shh,' he said. 'I know. And we'll get through this.'

'You promise?'

'I promise.'

* * *

'Um... *deux crêpes au fromage avec salade, s'il vous plaît.*' Lily smiled, handing the menu back to the waiter.

'*Oui*, of course,' he replied in English, tucking the menu under his arm and scribbling in a notepad. 'I 'ope you will enjoy.'

Yet again, she'd been rumbled the minute she'd opened her mouth. It seemed no matter how impressive she thought her French accent was, the locals could spot her Britishness a mile off. She'd start conversations in French only to have them reply in flawless English. It was helpful, and she knew that many of them enjoyed the chance to practise their English, but it would be nice if they could humour her occasionally.

'Wow,' said Ty.

'What?'

'I didn't know you spoke French well. I mean, I knew you'd gone to classes or whatever.'

'Oh, Ty, I was only ordering a couple of pancakes,' she said with a shrug.

'Still...' he said. 'You kind of *sounded* French. You know?'

She decided to let him be impressed – after all it was a rare occurrence. 'Well, I've been practising,' she said modestly. '*J'essaie.*'

'Which means...?'

'I'm trying...'

He nodded, his mouth turned down at the corners – impressed with her for probably the first time since birth. She resolved not to speak too much more French today if only to leave him with the illusion that if she wanted to, she could.

They were sitting in *Le Potron-Minet*, a restaurant and *crêperie* she'd discovered close to the church in *Eymoutiers* and had earmarked as the kind of place to bring any visitors who might come her way. It served an array of *crêpes* and waffles, as well as larger meals such as *boeuf bourguignon* and *coq au vin*, all of which looked delicious. But the main draw for her was the beautiful building the tiny restaurant nestled in, the atmosphere and – if she was honest – the fact that the place, to her at least, seemed authentic and French and like somewhere only a local would visit.

The door into the building was small, but the restaurant inside opened up into a modest eating area, with exposed stone walls and a small wooden bar to one side. If you continued through the door at the back of the room, you'd find yourself in a tiny walled terrace which, unless you ventured into the eatery, you'd never know existed. The tables were small, mismatched and wooden, the floor tiled, and when the restaurant area was full, the rumble of voices made her feel somehow as if she was in the heart of things.

And it was always full – something that never failed to astound her. They'd had four or five restaurants within easy walking range in Basildon, but they'd rarely been full on a weekday night, much less at lunchtime. She'd mentioned it to Chloé during her second visit at the B. & B. 'Everyone seems to have so much time to eat!' she'd said. 'And the lunches – surely people can't afford to eat out every day?'

'Ah, but it is their boss, he 'ave to pay for their lunch if they work for 'im,' Chloé had explained. She explained how workers were given vouchers with which to buy lunch, a scheme that kept workers happy and restaurants thriving.

'I'm surprised you aren't all overweight,' Lily had joked. 'I don't think I could eat a three-course meal for lunch without ballooning.'

'Yes, but you English, you don't respect your food.' Chloé had laughed. 'We take time, yes? We enjoy. We know when we are full. And we are satisfied. We – 'ow you say – we are in time with our bodies.'

'In tune?'

'Yes, that is it. We don't just sit and work and eat. Eating is important. You do it right,' Chloé had said.

Since then, Lily had been taking a trip into town fairly regularly to fill up at midday. She thought back now to her hurried sandwiches over a work keyboard in the UK – stuffing down food without thought – and tried to take her time over her meals. Even now, she'd still finish way before the other punters, but it was fun practising and gave her the chance to nod and smile at familiar faces.

When she'd suggested to Ty they eat lunch in town, she'd wondered at first whether she'd made a mistake. The chance of bumping into Frédérique was high – and *Le Potron-Minet* was literally a stone's throw from his offices. In the end, she'd decided to avoid potential disasters by sending him a text.

Ty and I are coming into town today for lunch. I'm so sorry, but I'm not going to come and introduce you – just because I think it's too soon. It will be hard for him.

He'd replied:

But of course!

She'd been glad he hadn't pushed for an introduction and replied:

Thank you.

Her body flooded with relief and Frédérique was awarded another gold star in her mind.

She hadn't added that she was also unsure whether they should have another date just yet; whether it was too soon for her to get properly involved. That was more of an in-person conversation, and one she'd have when she'd thought about it all properly.

In what seemed like seconds, the waiter returned brandishing two plates with enormous *crêpes*, chunky fries and a tiny lettuce leaf nestling in the corner. 'Bon appétit!' he said.

'Thanks, mate,' her son said.

'*Merci*,' she added, her stomach rumbling as she took in the gorgeous meal in front of her. Ty, she noticed, had already manoeuvred a forkful into his mouth.

'Good?' she asked.

'Mm humm,' he said.

Last night, when he'd asked her how the phone call with his father had gone, she'd felt his disappointment. 'OK,' she'd said. 'You know, I think he'll be all right, Ty.'

'You're not...?'

'No, I'm sorry, love. But I'm going to speak to him. We're going to... well, be more adult about the whole separation thing. We're still friends, and more importantly we're still parents.'

The speech had sounded good in her head, but Ty had seemed unimpressed.

The call itself had been awkward at first. Ben had answered, but his gruffness had left her feeling immediately on the back-foot.

'Hi, it's me,' she'd said.

'Hi.'

'Sorry, I know you said you didn't want me to call...' she'd added, before feeling annoyed at herself for apologising.

'Uh-huh. So, everything all right with Ty?'

'Yes. He's fine. Having fun, I think.'

'Good.'

A silence.

'Ben, he said you weren't doing so well. Are you OK?'

'Well... been better.'

'Ben, look, I know things aren't exactly easy for us right now. But we've got Ty to think of. And I'd like to think that we can be friends... eventually, at least. And look, I went through it all with you last time. You can still talk to me, you know?'

'I know,' he'd said, his tone more friendly than before. 'It's just... I dunno. I feel stupid, I suppose.'

'Stupid?'

'Yeah. You know. Weak.'

'That's ridiculous. Come on, you know that, Ben. It's a medical condition. It's nothing to do with not being strong.'

A silence.

'So is it like last time?' she'd ventured.

'Pretty much.'

'And how long...?'

'About three months.'

'Three months!' She was genuinely shocked. 'What, you mean before I... before we...? Before the whole French thing?'

'Yep.'

'Why didn't you talk to me?'

'I dunno. I just thought. I mean, you were busy. And I just wanted... I thought maybe I could beat it by myself, you know? I thought after last time, all those... strategies and things, I could kick it to the kerb without, you know... bothering you.'

'Oh, Ben.'

'Yeah. I know. I'm an idiot.'

'Well, I wasn't going to quite say that...'

'Yeah, but you were thinking it, right?'

'Well, maybe. But seriously, I wish you'd said something.'

'Well, so do I now. But then all the French stuff happened and it kind of – I suppose everything began to feel out of control.'

It was funny how, as the conversation had gone on, it had felt more natural. And yet of course it made perfect sense – because he was the person she'd talked to more than any other over the last two decades. Despite their separation, the familiarity had crept quickly back.

He'd told her how he'd woken up one morning feeling

panicked out of the blue, but had been determined to shake it off. How it had proven harder than he'd thought. How he'd begun to catastrophise – what if he crashed his car? What if something happened to Ty? What if he got lost his clients at work?

'Then I got made redundant,' she'd said.

'Yep. And you know what, it wasn't so bad. I mean, it happens all the time. But for me, just then, it felt like the end of the world. I began to worry about paying the mortgage, getting Ty to uni OK. But I didn't... I couldn't say because the rational part of me knew I was being over the top... I was just kind of... don't know. Frozen. Like a rabbit in headlights. Trying to keep going. Trying to... well, trying to keep everything the same. You brought up the whole France thing... and...'

'And?'

'Lily, I just didn't know what to do. What to say? Like how could I tell you then because it would have seemed a bit too convenient... You'd have thought I was putting it on to make you... well, stay, I guess.'

'I wouldn't have!' she'd protested, but felt something shift inside. She might have, she'd realised.

After promising to stay in touch, they'd ended the call on a good note.

'You know, what I said. About not contacting me for a bit. I mean, it seemed sensible. Everyone says, don't they, when you're trying to get... over someone, that you should cut all ties. But maybe... I mean, if you do want to call again, I think I'd be OK with that,' he'd said, awkwardly.

'Well,' she'd said. 'I might just do that.'

* * *

The waiter arrived to clear their plates just as she was lifting the last bit of lettuce into her mouth, and offered them the dessert menu.

'Dessert, Ty?' Lily said.

He nodded. 'Always.'

Afterwards, as they wandered back to the car, they began to talk about his uni course and what he was looking forward to. He seemed to have very little knowledge of the reading list and she resolved to look up the information and send it through.

'I can find out when I get there!' he protested.

'Ty, if you read the stuff now, you'll feel more prepared,' she said, sounding so much like her own mum that it was both annoying and heart-wrenching. She remembered a similar conversation with her mum back in the day, and she'd probably reacted more or less the same way. Evidently, it was a mother's lot, it seemed, to be appreciated more posthumously – like Van Gogh or Edgar Allen Poe. The Cassandra of the family dynamic, cursed to utter truths and for no one to take them seriously.

She was just pondering this when a voice interrupted her thoughts. '*Bonjour!*' it cried loudly.

She looked up, across the road was Frédérique – dressed in a short-sleeved shirt and linen trousers. A slight purple stain at the corner of his mouth revealing he'd had a couple of glasses of red over lunch. He was grinning widely.

She lifted her hand to wave at him before walking on, but he waited for a car to pass then strode determinedly towards them.

Merde.

It wasn't that she didn't want to see Frédérique. In fact, she'd been checking her phone for text messages like a lovelorn teenager since their date. It was seeing him with Ty – not knowing how to introduce him and not wanting to upset either of them in doing so. Plus, she'd told him specifically that she didn't want the pair of them to meet, not yet.

'Sorry,' he said. 'I know you say it's too soon for us to meet, but I cannot resist to stop and say hello when I see you walking.'

'It's OK,' she said, embarrassed that he was revealing she'd asked him to stay away. 'Um... This is Ty – my son. Ty... this is my *friend*, Frédérique.' She made wild eye contact with Frédérique in the hope that he'd pick up on the fact that she wasn't ready to come out as anything more.

'Ah, we are friend, yes!' Frédérique replied with an elaborate wink, before leaning forward and kissing her proprietorially on the mouth. 'Very good friends, eh!'

Was he actually doing this on purpose?

'*Enchanté*,' he said, reaching a hand out to Ty, who studiously ignored it. 'But wait, this cannot be your son. He is a man. You are not old enough to 'ave a child who is grown. Maybe he is a lover, eh? Maybe I should be jealous?'

The humour didn't land well with either of them. 'Oh, thank you,' she said, blushing. 'But... we'd better...'

'She's forty-four,' said Ty, sullenly. 'She had me when she was twenty-six.'

'*Mais oui*, but she look so young!' Frédérique continued, not really sensing the tone. 'She is beautiful, your mother, *non*? You must be very proud!'

'Um.' Ty seemed lost for words.

'Anyway, we'd better...' Lily said again, pushing past him slightly and grabbing the sleeve of Ty's shirt to keep him at her side. 'We're... well, I'll call you – OK?'

'*Oui*, for our next date, per'aps?' Frédérique called after her. 'The last one, it was perfect. I cannot wait.'

She felt her shoulders stiffen. But resisted the urge to turn and glower at him. It would only make things worse.

They walked to the car silently then slipped in.

'So who was that?' Ty said, his tone flat.

'Frédérique? Well, he's... he's a friend, I suppose. A new friend.'

'A friend you're *dating*?'

'Well, yes. Sorry. Someone I've been on a date with. But a friend, too.'

'Right.'

'Which is OK, Ty. I mean, I'm single now, right?' she said, giving him a worried sideways glance.

'Yep,' he said, shortly.

She didn't push him. It was always going to be difficult for him to think of his mum as someone who could go on dates. Especially as he was clearly clinging to some sort of hope for her and Ben.

What had Frédérique been playing at? After her message explaining the situation, to plant a kiss on her mouth, and mention dating in front of Ty – it was as if he was forcing her hand. But surely Frédérique wasn't like that? Perhaps it was the wine, she told herself. Wine at lunch was never a good idea. Or maybe his lack of subtlety had been a language issue?

As the drive continued in silence she wondered whether she ought to tell Ty that she and Frédérique hadn't slept together yet. But after constructing the words in her head in several different ways, she concluded that any mention of – or even allusion to – sex was not going to help matters much.

'I wondered if you might help me this afternoon,' she said instead, trying to sound bright and cheerful. 'I've found a second-hand car on LeBonCoin and thought maybe you could come and see it with me.'

'Yep, no problem.'

There was a few minutes' silence, then she tried again. 'You know, Ty, I'll always love your dad.'

He was silent.

'And Frédérique and I... well, we only went for a meal. It was nothing... really.'

'It's OK, it's none of my business.'

'Well, it kind of *is* your business though. And I don't want you to feel... well, you know.'

'So,' he said, 'what kind of car is it?'

29

'Don't forget these,' Lily said, handing Ty some underwear she'd washed for him.

'Thanks, Mum.' He stuffed them into his bag where she suspected they'd be mixing with dirty socks and other sweaty garments and would need another good wash once he unpacked them – probably in a month or so's time. But it was the thought that counted.

The four days had flashed past, and she was yet again getting ready to take someone she loved back to the airport – to facilitate their flying hundreds of miles away from her.

'I can't believe you're actually going already,' she said, looking at her son as he emptied the bag out again and began rifling through the contents, probably looking for his passport. 'It's flown by, hasn't it?'

'Yeah,' he said, only half concentrating. She wasn't insulted. Over the past few years, she'd got used to teenage communication – one-word answers, grunts and shrugs. She knew they had more to do with the particular combination of lethargy, hormones and distraction spinning in the teenage brain than a desire to be rude.

'Want anything from the *pâtisserie*? I'm going to pop there in a sec,' she added. 'Give the new wheels a spin.'

'Just get me whatever,' he said. By which he meant a selection of all available pastries, preferably in duplicate.

Yesterday, they'd gone together to look at a second-hand car at a garage just north of Limoges.

She'd seen an ad in the paper for a small Clio at a reasonable price had rung the garage and made an appointment to go and see it. But as the original car they'd showed up to see had proved to be more battered and bruised than she'd imagined, she had instead picked up a second-hand Micra, very similar to the one she'd hired. It had felt good to have Tyler with her – it was the first time she'd bought a car by herself and although she knew what she wanted, having a second opinion gave her the reassurance she needed to part with a few more thousand of her inheritance. She felt a little sick as she punched in her pin code in at the garage – she'd have to get this retreat up and running soon; or maybe talk to Ben about her share of the equity in the UK, or she'd be struggling.

Later, she'd be able to drop Ty and the hire car off at the airport and take the train back from Limoges afterwards.

Yesterday evening, Frédérique had called her to see if she'd fancied going out again later in the week and, despite his over-the-top behaviour in the town, she'd been over the moon to hear his voice. 'Tyler's going back tomorrow,' she'd said, and told him about her plan.

'But of course you must not go home in the train,' he'd told her. 'My love, I will give you a lift.'

'Oh no,' she'd said, thinking how Ty would probably not appreciate his accompanying them to the airport. 'But thank you.'

It had been nice of him to offer.

Emily had called briefly too. She'd popped in to see Ben.

'He cottoned on straightaway that it was an intervention,' she'd moaned. 'In spite of my brilliant excuse.'

'Which was?'

'I said I thought I might have left my sunglasses at yours a couple of months ago.'

'That's a pathetic excuse.'

'So it seems. He rumbled me immediately.'

'Whoops.'

'But in a way it was nice, because it meant I could ask him about the anxiety and that. I mean, he knew what I'd been through, so I think it helped.'

'And...?'

'And I think he'll be OK. He's missing you of course.'

'Well, yes,' she'd said. 'I know, but...'

'Sorry, I didn't mean anything by it. I just felt sorry for him I guess. I mean, if he'd told you he was going through all that, you'd have understood why he didn't want to move right then – maybe things would have been different...'

Lily had been silent. 'Well, maybe,' she'd said at last. 'But you know... everything's changed now.'

Then they'd changed the subject and spoken about Ty, and decorating the house and Lily's idea for a house-warming party.

'I hope I'll be getting an invite?'

'Well, of course, if you want to come all that way just for a little gathering.'

'You know me – never say no to a party,' Emily had joked.

'You're on then,' Lily had replied. 'And you know what? I might even have a proper spare bed by then.'

'Oh, I was so hoping to sleep on that leaking airbed again.'

Lily made it to and from the *pâtisserie* in record time and was soon sitting opposite her son watching him put away pastry after pastry with a combination of fascination and envy. Oh, for a teenage boy's metabolism – he had no need to eat slowly or concentrate on his food. He simply shovelled it in with no thought of the bottom line.

'Nice?' she asked once or twice.

'Glub,' he replied, nodding.

She tried not to get emotional as she watched the clock count down the time until her son would have to leave. After all, he'd be back at some point. Perhaps for longer next time. Even so, she could feel the tug on her heartstrings as each minute went past and his flight approached.

At 10 a.m. it would finally be time to start the trip to the airport. With ten minutes to go, they began to gather things together and do the obligatory passport, ticket, phone, wallet checks that precede each trip. It would only be the second time Ty had flown by himself and she was determined that it would go smoothly. She wanted him to want to come back; wanted to minimise any stress.

'Right, I think we're all set!' she said brightly at 9.58 a.m.

At 9.59 a.m., there was a knock on the door.

'Don't worry. It's probably post or something,' Lily said. She'd ordered a few things online recently and had begun to welcome the morning knock from a postie with a parcel. It was kind of like receiving a present – albeit one you'd paid for.

But it wasn't the postie.

'*Bonjour, mon coeur!*' Frédérique appeared on the doorstep with an enormous bunch of flowers. 'You are looking so very beautiful this morning, eh?' He was smartly dressed in black jeans and a white shirt, his hair glistening with gel.

'Oh, Frédérique,' she said. 'I'm sorry, we're just going...'

He stepped into the house, and held out the flowers for her to take. 'They're beautiful,' she said, giving them an obligatory sniff.

They were freshly cut white lilies, scattered with another pink flower she didn't recognise. 'You really shouldn't have.'

'I don't understand,' he said, his brow furrowing. 'You want that I don't bring you flowers? Per'aps you have *le* hay fever?'

'Oh, no. I was... it's just an expression,' she said hurriedly. 'I love them. Thank you.'

'Ah, but you are welcome, my love.' He looked at her affectionately.

Ty wandered through with his bag, his face visibly dropping when he saw who the visitor was.

'And it is the son!' Frédérique exclaimed. 'He, er, *il s'en va...* leaves, *oui*?'

'Yeah, don't worry,' grunted Tyler. 'I'm off.'

'*Mais non*, I am 'ere not because you are leaving! I am not trying to – how you say – make love to your mother. But to 'elp 'er,' Frédérique said. 'She need transport back from the airport and I can drive, *non*?'

'Oh, it's so kind of you,' said Lily, setting the flowers down on the side and hoping the plastic reservoir of water at the base of the cut stems would be enough to stop them dying while they were out. 'But honestly I'm fine...'

'*Mais non*, what kind of man would I be if I let my lover travel alone?' Frédérique said, smiling fondly and not really getting the hint. 'And I fink too, that Tyler 'e will be 'appy to know that 'is mother is safe, oui? Not on a train alone? It is no place for a beautiful lady.'

'Honestly, I'm perfectly capable of taking a train,' Lily interrupted, slightly affronted.

Tyler's neck had reddened at the use of the word 'lover' but he stayed silent.

'Oh, *mais oui*! Of course! But it is far nicer to sit in a car, eh? To 'ave – how you say – door-to-door service! Today I am not your

lover. Think of me as your chauffeur! I am sure your son will be
'appy for this.'

He looked at Tyler, who seemed preoccupied with the zip on
his bag and said nothing.

Undeterred, Frédérique turned back to Lily with a smile. 'So I
follow you in the car, yes? And zen I can bring you 'ome after? I
take the day off my work to 'elp.'

There wasn't really much to be said.

On route to the airport, Frédérique drove so closely to the
back of the Nissan that every time Lily glanced in the rear-view
mirror their eyes locked. Or at least, it felt as if they did.

She tried to concentrate on her son but it was hard to ignore
the green eyes boring into her from the reflective surface.

'Sorry,' she said. 'Frédérique... well, he's being nice. But I had
hoped it would just be us...'

'It's OK.'

'It's not though, is it?' she said. 'Look, I know Frédérique has
said some... well, some things that sound like we're serious; but
honestly, we've only actually been out once or twice. I mean, I like
him. But it probably won't go anywhere really.' She nearly added
it was just a bit of fun, but realised Tyler might find this just as
horrifying. 'It's the language, I think. We're not... we're not lovers,
not like that. I think... I'm pretty sure it's a translation thing.'

Tyler visibly paled. 'It's OK,' he said. 'Really.'

She briefly lifted her hand from the steering wheel and lay it
on his. He was grown up now, but still very much her child. She'd
read that even when people were well into adulthood, their
parents splitting could stir up all kinds of emotions. She couldn't
put her life on hold to spare him, but at the same time she hated
the fact that something she was doing was making him so
miserable.

It certainly wasn't how she'd have planned to introduce

Frédérique to Tyler. If they'd still been seeing each other when Ty next came, she might have suggested a drink or a meal. Something gradual, subtle.

Frédérique didn't have any children. Perhaps if he had, he'd have realised that barging into their time together right now hadn't been the right call. That seeing her son off was something she'd rather do alone.

Perhaps he could have picked her up from the station if he'd wanted. But following them all the way to the airport felt a bit intrusive. It would have been nice to say goodbye to Ty without an audience. But Frédérique just didn't realise how tricky the situation was for her – her separation from Ben so new, Tyler unused to his mother dating. It wasn't Frédérique's fault that he had made things more difficult than they would have been otherwise.

At least, she thought, as they arrived at the airport and she pulled up in the car hire drop-off point, popping the paperwork and the keys into the designated letterbox, she'd be able to say goodbye and reassure Tyler privately before he left. But the minute they exited the car, Frédérique appeared by her side so instantaneously she wondered for a moment whether he was able to teleport.

'Ah, so 'ere we are,' he said, gesturing with his arms. 'Like a leetle family, eh?'

'I'll walk you into the building,' Lily said to Ty. 'See you off. Say goodbye properly.'

'Nah, you're all right,' he said.

She wasn't sure whether this brush-off would have happened anyway, but suspected it had a lot to do with Frédérique's presence. 'Are you sure?' she said.

'Yeah.'

'Well look,' she said, putting her arms around him and giving him a squeeze, 'I'll miss you.'

'Thanks,' he said.

'And you know... I'll be in touch with... your dad.'

'Uh-huh.'

Tyler was about to turn towards the terminal when Frédérique stepped forward and gave him such an enormous pat on the back, Lily worried he might get sued for assault. 'And,' Frédérique said. 'I only just meet you, but I also will miss you too, eh?'

'OK?'

'And 'oo knows? Per'aps when I marry your mother, I will be your father one day!' he added, delighted with himself. 'You will be my son, huh?'

'Yes, well, that's not happening at the moment,' said Lily quickly, trying to minimise the damage without hurting either of them.

'Ah, but I can dream, uh?' Frédérique continued, unperturbed. 'And I think it is easier for 'im to understand when he know that I am in love, *oui*?'

'Well...'

'*Mais oui, mon coeur.* It is difficult for a boy when 'e think I am just one of 'is mother's lovers. That I am 'ere just to make love to you, to satisfy the desire. Children do not like to think of their mothers making love, huh? But if he think I may be your 'usband one day per'aps it is different.'

'Bye then.' Ty said and sloped off to the entrance, his shoulders hunched.

'Bye, darling! Come again soon!' Lily called after him.

Ty lifted his hand in acknowledgement, but didn't turn around. Lily turned to Frédérique, exasperated.

But his face was so wide-eyed and hopeful and expectant and

innocent that she didn't have the heart to crush him. And there wouldn't be much point in any case – the damage to Tyler's imagination was no doubt already done. She would have to explain, gently to Frédérique that 'lovers' wasn't a term they used quite so much in English normally. That it was too... graphic somehow. Especially when speaking about someone's mother.

'And now, I 'ave you to myself,' he said, with a smile. 'I am a lucky man, eh?'

'Right,' she said.

She followed him back to his car and plonked herself in the passenger seat, grateful, now the exhaustion of the last few days was catching up on her, that she didn't have to seek out the train station.

But despite appreciating the lift, she knew she'd have to find a way to slow things down with Frédérique. She needed time to think, to process the news about Ben; to concentrate, too, on the house; on the business to complete seemingly endless paperwork. She didn't want to end things – if they could really be described as having begun – but keep him at arm's length, just for a while. Just until she knew what she wanted.

'Per'aps we stop *pour dîner*?' he suggested as they drove back towards the city centre. 'I know a restaurant – you will love it.'

She nodded. 'Yes, I think it would be good. To be honest, Frédérique. I think we need to talk.'

In any of her past relationships, uttering those words would be a heads-up to the other person that what came next might not be exactly what they wanted to hear.

But Frédérique, unused to the subtle undertone, smiled at her.

'It will be a pleasure,' he said.

30

'Thanks for popping over,' Lily said, adding a drop of milk to the mug of tea she was making and squeezing the bag a little too enthusiastically. 'Sorry, hope you like it strong.'

'Thanks for inviting me.' Sam grinned, taking the mug from Lily's hands and gulping down at least half. 'God, I needed that.'

'It's just nice to actually drink tea with someone again,' joked Lily. 'I mean, I like coffee, but...'

'I know. My first month here, I didn't sleep a wink.' Sam grinned. 'It took me that long to work out not to just order coffee, but to be more specific.'

'Too much espresso?'

'Yep. Plays havoc with my bowels too.'

'Thanks for sharing.'

They watched through the window as Derek and Claudine rushed around the garden, jumping on the hundreds of molehills that seemed to have popped up overnight. As they watched, Claudine picked up a couple of handfuls of earth and began to pursue Derek with it.

'Uh-oh,' said Lily. 'Shall we go out there?'

'Oh, in a minute,' her friend replied. 'It won't hurt him to get a taste of his own medicine for once.'

'You're the boss,' Lily replied, watching Derek brushing earth out of his hair and turning to chase his sister for revenge. He raced off, laughing, towards the bushes.

'Can I ask,' Lily said, 'why Derek and Claudine? They seem such...'

'Different names?'

'Well, yes.'

Sam laughed. 'Very British and very French – we basically took turns to name the kids and it turned out this way. Still, even "Derek" sounds very continental when Gabriel says it. Sort of "Derique".'

Lily laughed.

'So, you think Frédérique took it OK?' Sam asked, seemingly unaware or unperturbed by the escalating fight happening between her offspring.

Lily shrugged. 'He seemed to,' she said. 'I mean, actually he seemed to take it really, *really* well.'

'Well, that's good, I guess?'

'Maybe.' Lily shrugged.

'Oh?'

'Well, he was *so* OK about it that I began to wonder whether he'd misunderstood me – my French is still terrible, so we rely on his English most of the time and it's hard to know whether I've been clear enough sometimes.'

'Ah, bit awkward then?'

'Yes, and then I began to wonder whether, if he did understand what I'd said, I should feel insulted that he didn't seem a little more bothered.'

'Careful what you wish for?'

'Exactly.'

Yesterday at the restaurant she'd told Frédérique that she needed to take things slow. That she wanted to keep seeing him, but that she wasn't sure how she felt about anything right now.

'So I will see you tomorrow after work, *oui*?' he'd asked when he'd dropped her off.

At first she'd wondered if he was joking, but looking at his face had realised he was deadly serious.

'Oh, no,' she'd said. Then 'I'm busy,' she'd added, to spare his feelings.

'Oh yes? What is it you are doing?' he'd asked, interested rather than interrogative.

'I'm... well, I thought I'd...' She'd racked her brain desperately. 'I think there's some sort of music concert on the beach,' she'd said, remembering a poster she'd seen. 'A band of some sort.'

'Ah, but that sounds lovely. So per'aps the next night?'

'Yes, perhaps.'

This morning, she'd made herself feel better about the lie by ringing Sam and seeing if she wanted to come along. 'It's just a folk band of some sort,' she'd said, 'but I think it might be fun.'

'I'll have to bring the kids – Gabriel's got some sort of cards evening at the local bar.'

'That's fine. The more the merrier!' she'd said.

'So, tell me about this party,' Sam said now. 'Assuming I'm invited.'

'Of course!'

'Glad to hear it. Obviously, I'd have crashed it otherwise.'

Lily laughed. 'I just thought that it might be a nice way to, well, celebrate signing for the house and mark the fact that I've sort of made it habitable... just,' she said.

'Don't forget surviving the *loirs* infestation?'

'Oh yes. And surviving the *loirs*.' She grinned. 'But you know, more importantly to thank everyone who's helped. You know, Dawn and Clive, Chloé, you, Claude. And my friend, Emily, might come from England.'

'Sounds cool.'

'Yeah, I think you and Em will really get on,' Lily said. 'You're very similar.'

'Which is a compliment?'

'Which is *definitely* a compliment.' She smiled. 'Anyway, I just thought I could get a few people round – nothing fancy. Children too. Bit of a buffet. Some wine, of course.'

'Well, that'll guarantee the flat-earthers' society turn up at least.'

'Ha. Well, good. Like you say, it's nice to have connections over here.'

'Even if they are borderline insane?'

'Even then.'

* * *

Two hours later, they set off to the beach, packing themselves into Sam's car, which was full of buckets and spades and sweet wrappers, and smelled of ancient chip fat. 'Sorry about the state,' Sam said, as she brushed a couple of magazines off the passenger seat. 'Keep meaning to clean it, but you know how it is.'

'Don't worry, you should have seen mine back in the day. Kids know exactly where to put their sticky fingers, don't they?'

A few minutes later, they were parked and made their way to the lakeside, settling on plastic chairs in front of the ramshackle kiosk and watching the band set up on a stage that seemed to be made from old, nailed together pallets, painted black for the occasion.

It wasn't quite as she'd pictured it. She'd assumed, French folk music. Maybe a harmonica player. Definitely a beret or two. An accordion. A moustache. Instead, the band, who called themselves Mr Musique, sloped onto the stage looking like three random blokes who'd happened to bump into each other on the way here. They didn't seem to have assembled any kind of 'look' between them. One of them had curly hair and glasses and wore a scraggy red jumper, another was dressed in jeans and an ancient, badge-covered leather jacket. The drummer clearly hadn't changed since work and was wearing a pair of blue overalls, unbuttoned at the front to reveal more chest than seemed suitable for a family show.

When the lead guitarist struck his first chord, the style of music was also unexpected. Instead of some lulling, gentle folk songs, they favoured heavy rock, which the lead guitarist danced to with closed eyes and such commitment to each chord and lyric it was pretty obvious that in his mind he was no longer on a tiny beach in rural France, but striding on the stage at the *Stade de France*, singing to a crowd of thousands.

The curly-haired bloke proved the most entertaining of the three. He'd brought an enormous array of instruments and switched tack for every song, starting with an accordion but rapidly moving to a ukulele, then a clarinet, then picking up an enormous horn-like instrument that reminded Lily of something a snake charmer might play. He played each one with equal commitment, but the spectacle of his extracting each with a flourish from a basket gave them a dose of the giggles that they had to suppress. 'What's next?' whispered Sam. 'A didgeridoo?'

The biggest surprise of all though, was they were actually very, very good. Their energy was infectious and after a while Lily began to lose herself in the experience, letting the music flow through her and nodding along with the beat.

There was a reasonable crowd, most sitting at tables with

wine and chips, leaning up against the wooden wall of the food shack smoking, or sitting on blankets on the sand sipping beers and sharing picnics. Children ran around between tables or played on the beach, sticking their toes in at the water's edge. A couple of the punters had dogs who curled up under chairs as if they were waiting for it all to be over.

Despite the loud music, most people continued their conversations during the show, causing the guitarist to go to greater and greater lengths to try to keep the audience's attention, at one point performing some sort of 'dive' from an enormous speaker, landing on his knees in the sand before limping back to his feet.

Derek and Claudine started the event sitting at the table and picking at *barquettes* of chips, before wandering towards the edge of the lake and dipping their toes in the water. They seemed perfectly content, and excited at the fact it was getting a late and they were yet to go to bed.

During the pause between performances, though, Derek – who'd produced a bucket seemingly from nowhere – filled it at the water in the shallows, then began trying to carry it up the beach. Sam visibly paled when she glanced up and saw what he was up to. 'I'd better deal with that,' she said, just as he began stumbling towards a family's picnic.

'Sure,' said Lily, sipping her wine and enjoying Mr Musique's rendition of Guns N' Roses' 'Sweet Child of Mine' complete with French accent, accompanied by the bloke in the background who was now playing what looked to be the world's smallest flute.

She found her foot tapping as she listened to the familiar song – perhaps not performed to Axel Rose's standards, but one that brought back memories of best friends and tape recorders and school discos and listening to the charts on a Sunday night. She closed her eyes and rocked slightly to the beat.

'The music is beautiful, yes?' said a voice beside her.

'Yes,' she agreed, turning to see who'd sat down at their table. Then jumped. It was Frédérique.

'Frédérique!' she said. 'I didn't know you were coming to this!'

'*Mais non*, I decide – how you say – on le spur of le moment!' he said. 'I stay in my 'ouse tonight, like I say. But I was alone, and I start to dream. And I fink, it will be nice to see my *Madame Buttercup* and listen to some beautiful sounds too, eh?'

Lily wondered briefly whether 'distance' meant the same in French as it did in English. Because surely this went against everything she'd spoken about yesterday. Knowing her luck, Frédérique had misunderstood her plea for a bit of space and thought instead she'd asked him to stay as close to her as possible.

'I thought,' she began... But then she looked at his eyes – so happy to see her, and particularly noughties Russell Crowe like in the fading light – and decided to leave it for another day. He was here now. It was a public place. If he wanted to sit and listen to an overenthusiastic would-be rocker, who was she to argue?

'Would you like a drink?' she asked instead. 'I can get another glass?'

She and Sam had been making their way through a carafe of rosé, although if she was honest, she'd taken the lion's share – *did lions even drink rosé?* – as Sam was driving. It wouldn't hurt to have a third person to soak up some of the alcohol before she ended up in hangover territory.

'*Mais oui*,' he said. 'I will order some more wine.'

'Oh, there's no need,' Lily said. 'Sam isn't drinking this evening really, so it'll just be the two of us getting through that.'

'Sam?' Frédérique raised an eyebrow. 'Who is this Sam?'

'Oh, she's my friend, she's...' said Lily, pointing over to the shore where Sam was chasing Derek in what was either a fun game or a complete nightmare.

'Oh, but she is a woman!' Frédérique said, with a broad smile. 'I fink for a moment that you – how you say – times me by two with another man.'

'Oh, no,' she said. Although, could you actually two-time someone you weren't officially in a relationship with?

Before she could work out whether to say anything more Sam reappeared, red-faced from exertion.

'Sorry about that,' she said as she slid into her seat. 'Think he's getting a bit tired. We'll have to make a move in a bit.'

'Oh, OK,' said Lily. 'It's a bit late for little ones, I suppose.'

'Anyway, who's this?' Sam asked, nodding at Frédérique who had been staring so intently at Lily that he jumped, as if only just realising Sam was there.

'It's Frédérique,' Lily said, pleading with her eyes for Sam not to mention their earlier conversation. Sam nodded, briefly, understanding.

'Oh, *Frédérique*,' she said, 'I've heard a lot about you.' She winked at Lily, who dialled up the eye contact a little.

'It is a pleasure to meet you,' Frédérique said, raising his glass in greeting.

'Yes, you too,' she said, grabbing her own half-drunk glass and lifting it briefly. 'Lily didn't think you'd be along tonight?'

'Ah, yes. But how can I stay away from 'er,' Frédérique said fondly, 'when I am so in love?'

'It's great,' Lily interjected quickly. 'It's lovely to see him.'

Sam's look was subtle, brief, but left Lily in no doubt what she thought about *that* statement. 'We women spend so much time taking other people's feelings into account that we forget about our own sometimes,' she'd said earlier. And she was right. But how did you switch off the impulse to smooth things over when it was part of who you were?

'Ah,' she said. 'How romantic.'

'Ah, but I try,' Frédérique said proudly. 'I am – 'ow you say – I like to do the romantic gestures.'

'Hey, you know what, Frédérique,' Sam said with an almost imperceptible wink at Lily. 'You should see if the band will let you serenade Lily. I think she'd love that.'

'You fink?' Frédérique glanced at the lead singer who was lost in the throes of Def Leppard's 'Animal'.

'Oh, no. Don't...' Lily said hurriedly. 'I think Sam is joking.'

'*Mais* it is *une bonne idée!*' Frédérique said. 'You love music, yes? And I can sing for you. You would like this, I think.'

'Oh, no, please don't.'

'But my love, it will be an honour, no? I know zis man in le band – 'e will let me 'ave the microphone I am sure.'

'Please don't,' said Lily. 'Honestly. It would be... lovely but perhaps too much for tonight.'

'Ah, but she is so modest,' he said. 'She fink she is not worth a song? Per'aps you 'ave not been treated so well in the past. But for you, I would sing all the evening.'

'OK, well, another time, perhaps,' Lily said, trying to keep the blind panic from her voice.

'*Oui*. Another time. If you want.'

'Well, just make sure I'm there too when you do it,' Sam said, with a grin. 'I'd really love to be part of that special moment.'

Lily gently kicked Sam under the table. The last thing she needed was someone giving Frédérique any more ideas. Flowers, she could handle. A public serenade? Well, it might look good in the movies, but she'd probably never recover if it happened in real life.

But just when she was worrying that Frédérique was crowding her too much and trying to work out what to say about it, he reached across the table and took her hand gently in his. The touch of his skin reminded her of their date – the kissing, the fact that her body had fizzed with electricity in his arms. She looked up, their eyes locked and she found her mouth relax into a smile. It had been a trying few days, but it was impossible to ignore that there was something between them.

And she suddenly wondered whether *she* was the one being over-the-top.

She'd spent the last twenty years with a man who seemingly wouldn't step out of his comfort zone for her. Who let her walk away when all she wanted him to do was be there for her.

Now she had Frédérique who, although rather demonstrative, was quite patently *there*. Who turned up, seemed committed, and looked like a Hollywood actor to boot. She'd felt his actions were over the top, excessive. But perhaps she was just used to being treated differently. Perhaps she should be enjoying all the attention, lapping it up rather than pushing it away.

Maybe Frédérique wasn't the one who was being idiotic.

Maybe it was her.

31

'Will you stop fussing? It's only appendicitis,' he said, trying to smile.

'What do you mean, "only appendicitis"? They're going to chop you open!'

'Do you think you could... well, use different words? For a start it's just, ahh, keyhole surgery. And secondly, oouch, that is not a relaxing thing to say to me before they wheel me to theatre.'

'Sorry.' She rested her head against his shoulder. 'But you need to promise me you'll be OK.'

'Of course!'

'Because,' she said, 'if you're not, I seriously, seriously won't ever recover.'

'I tell you what. If I do die, I'll haunt you for eternity, how's that?'

'You joke,' she said, 'but I'm holding you to that, Ben Butterworth.'

* * *

She woke up early, the sunlight shining on her pillow interrupting a dream in which she was being pursued through a crowd by a man who, in turn, would have the face of Ben, then

Frédérique, then Russell Crowe (circa 2006). Her heart was pounding, and her T-shirt clung to her in what she'd have once described as 'all the right places'.

Last night when the concert had ended, she'd been disappointed when Frédérique had waved her and Sam off, and instead of making any sort of move, had begun chatting to a couple of friends. She'd assumed he'd at least ask if he could spend the night, so had been wrestling silently for the last half-hour about whether this would be a good idea or not.

She'd started off deciding that he definitely couldn't stay *yet*. But over the course of the next few songs, feeling Frédérique's touch and glancing at him from time to time, had decided that maybe – just maybe – she'd accept his advances.

So when he'd kissed her gently then wandered off to his friends without even giving it a try, she'd felt rejected. Which conversely made her want him even more. Had he known this? Was it a strategy? Or should she simply be more upfront about what she wanted, get things straight in her mind, before asking for space then feeling put out when she was given it?

This morning she was a little more grateful that nothing had happened. She'd woken up with Ben on her mind. Even though they'd been apart for weeks now, she still expected to see him when she drifted out of sleep each morning. Each morning, she still felt a little lost when she found he wasn't there. If she'd woken up today to find a replacement, she wasn't sure if she'd have felt OK about it – not yet.

She looked at the clock, it was eight o'clock, but would only be seven in the UK. But Ben was an early riser – he'd always set his alarm for six on workdays. She could call him now and catch him before work. Just to check up on him. She'd promised Tyler she'd do that.

She had an hour before Claude was due to come over and

cut the grass, this time with a slightly less industrial-looking mower. She'd meant to get herself sorted with a gardener or a ride-on mower by this point, but the grass had got its act together before she had. If she left it any longer, it would begin to resemble the jungled overgrowth she'd found when she first arrived.

The phone rang twice before Ben picked up with what seemed like a fairly cheery 'hello' for this time on a working morning.

'Hi, Ben. It's just me.'

'Hi, Lily.'

'I just thought I'd catch you, see how you are?'

'Thanks. I'm... well, I'm getting there, I suppose. How are you?'

'Yeah, not too bad,' she said, deciding not to fill him in on the events of the past few days. It wasn't worth it; nothing had happened that he needed to know about.

'Em said you've been on a date,' he said, clearing his throat slightly. 'Did it... was it good?'

'Em said?'

'Yeah, she's been over a bit. Helping... you know. I mean, she only told me because... I suppose I pressed her on it a bit.'

'Oh.'

'You don't have to talk about it. It's just... well, you know.'

'It wasn't really a date,' she said. 'Just... you know, an informal thing.'

'Right.'

'Nothing happened if that's what you're worried about,' she felt compelled to add.

'Oh, OK. Well, good. I mean, well you know.'

'Right.' Part of her was fuming, another part quite pleased that he was at least bothered.

'Because... I mean, I know it's not the right time to talk about it, is it? But you know... I never stopped loving you, Lily.'

She felt her chest tighten. 'I know you didn't. I know if I hadn't left we'd still be together. But, Ben, you made it clear that you didn't love me *enough*.'

'Because I wouldn't come with you?'

'Well, yes. Because you knew I wanted—'

'Lily, stop...' he said. 'You're right. I don't know why I said that. It's not your fault... I know the – well – the break-up was my doing.'

Was this some sort of reverse psychology trick? 'Right,' she said.

'I'm serious. I've been seeing a counsellor – a lot, actually – and I'm trying to be more honest about my feelings. To not be, eh, afraid to talk about them, you know? Because the kind of thing I went through... my... my anxiety I mean; it grows when you don't expose it to the light.'

'Well, that's good. That you're seeing a counsellor.'

'And I've realised a few things... since starting to talk about it properly. And I need to say... I *want* to say that it wasn't just my anxiety that caused all this.'

'Oh.'

'No. Not completely. It was the fact that I didn't *talk* to you about it. That I didn't let you in. We'd been... well, I think we lost a bit of closeness because of that. Because I was keeping myself to myself too much. Maybe drinking too much...'

'Oh, Ben, it wasn't that bad.'

'Well, it wasn't ideal.'

'Well, no. I'll admit. But you know, I suppose I did spring it on you rather out of the blue. The whole eBay thing.'

'Ha. Well, kind of out of the blue. And kind of right in the middle of the blue. It wasn't as if you'd never mentioned France before.'

'No, I think I may have spoken about it once or twice,' she agreed.

There was a silence.

'Anyway, I'm sorry,' he said. 'Because maybe if you'd known I was just... well, clinging on at the time. That I was working from home more and more because sometimes it was too much. Well, maybe things might have been different.'

'Oh Ben...'

She was silent for a minute, wondering if she could take the risk. To actually say it, openly. To risk being hurt all over again. 'Ben,' she said, 'look. It's not too late. You can still... I want you to come here. We can work on your anxiety, we can start afresh. It's beautiful here... lonely, but... Please come.' She felt her palms tingle.

He was silent on the other end.

'But you said you were building a new life,' he said at last.

'Only because I had to, not because I *wanted* to...'

Minutes later, she was on the phone to Emily. 'So I did it,' she said. 'I asked him. Directly. Just like you said.'

'Atta girl! And?'

'And nothing. He barely said a word. It was as if...' Lily drew in a big, shuddering breath '... as if I'd never meant anything to him at all.'

'Oh Lily...'

'No. It's OK, it's OK. Because I know now. At least I have some sort of... ending to it. I don't have to... wonder any more.'

Emily was silent. 'I am so, so sorry,' she said. 'I never should have...'

'No, you were right,' said Lily. 'I was too afraid to ask. And maybe it was because I was scared of the answer. Perhaps I knew all along.'

Another silence.

'So he said no?'

'Worse. He put the phone down.'

'Oh, sweetheart.'

'No,' she said, almost fiercely, rubbing her fist across her eyes. 'That's enough. I can't let him ruin this... I've got to...'

'OK, change of subject,' Emily said, understanding completely. 'Tell me about this party. I want to know everything you're planning for it. When exactly is it? What should I wear? And will the illustrious Frédérique be making an appearance?'

Lily felt better once she'd hung up an hour or so later. There was something wonderful about talking to Emily on the phone – text messages and emails just didn't give her the same lift, and when she did a video call, she just became obsessed with looking at her own face.

She wandered down to the kitchen, still only dressed in her pyjamas, to find a man on a ride-on mower bumping up and down her garden. Claude had obviously decided to seize the day and come over to mow earlier than planned. She raced back upstairs and pulled on yesterday's jeans and a pink fleece, washed her face and tied her hair back neatly. Feeling vaguely human, she walked out of the back door onto the sunny terrace and waved in his general direction.

It took her about ten minutes to get him to notice her over the noise of the mower, but she finally managed to persuade him in for a cup of coffee mid-mow. By the time he arrived at the door, covered in cuttings and smelling of grass and earth and petrol, she was already pushing down the plunger on her *cafetière* and had set out a plate with a couple of *pain aux raisins* for him.

'Oh, I must not,' he said, indicating the pastries. 'I am getting fat, my wife say.'

'Are you sure?' Lily said, helping herself to one. 'Surely these aren't too bad for you?' After all, they contained raisins. It was practically one of her five a day.

Claude laughed and patted his stomach. 'Ah, yes. But my wife she is very careful with my 'ealth.'

'Well, she must love you very much,' Lily said.

'*Oui.*' Claude nodded, rolled his eyes and took a sip of coffee. '*Mais peut-être* a bit too much, eh!' He sat down at the table and eyed the pastries hungrily.

'Sure that's not possible,' she said.

They looked at each other for a moment, then it got a bit awkward.

'I'm having a party on the twenty-ninth,' she said. 'Perhaps you and your wife...'

'Florence.'

'Florence would like to come?'

'*Eh bien, oui, merci.*' Claude smiled. 'I will tell 'er.'

He was almost finished with his coffee and Lily knew she had to strike while the iron was hot – if he disappeared into the garden she'd probably not have another chance to talk to him properly, one on one.

'Actually, Claude,' she said, slipping into the seat opposite, 'I wanted to ask you something.'

'*Oui?*'

'You said about Frédérique... How maybe he wasn't a great person to have a relationship with.'

'I do not remember this.'

'Yes! You said he wasn't always good with the ladies.'

'Ah yes, this. I say this. *Oui.* Poor Frédérique...'

'Well, that's just it,' she said. 'I sort of... well, we went on a couple of dates. And I wondered... was there anything I should know? Before... well, we have another?'

Claude looked at her, then down at his mug. 'I am not sure,' he said. 'Frédérique is my friend... and...'

'But I am your friend, too, Claude,' she said. 'And I'm a bit worried...'

Claude smiled. 'Ah, but, *Madame*, you need not to worry,' he said. 'He is not dangerous, *oui*? He is just... how you say... a little amorous?'

'Well, that's not usually a bad thing?'

He shook his head. 'No, and I am sorry if I worry you. It is just, for some ladies it become a bad thing.'

'How do you mean?'

Claude shifted slightly in his chair. 'I fink it might be better if you speak to 'im, *non*?'

'Look I know you're uncomfortable, but I won't mention it to him, I promise. I'm just... well, I suppose I'm scared of...'

'Of 'aving 'im to break your 'eart?'

'*Oui*, yes.'

Claude shook his head. 'Well, I cannot say that he won't do this, because I don't know the future. But some ladies, they 'ave said Frédérique 'e loves them too much. It is too much for them I think? And Frédérique, *'is* 'eart is broken.'

'Oh, poor Frédérique.'

'Per'aps,' he said. 'But per'aps also 'e fall in love a little too easily. Per'aps he need not to dream so much.'

'Oh. OK.' Lily sipped her coffee. 'Thank you for, well, for speaking with me about it.'

Claude shrugged. 'I 'ope I don't make problems for 'im?'

'No, not at all.'

He nodded, then stood and turned towards the back door.

'Claude?' she said.

'*Oui?*' He turned and looked at her.

'I'm sorry. But you say he falls in love too easily. Do you think, when he says he loves someone, well, is he really *in love*? Can it be real?'

Claude shrugged. 'I don't know,' he said, simply. 'I cannot say if it is real, if it will last. Because things do not last sometimes even when there is love, we know this. But I do know that for 'im, when it 'appen it is very, very real when 'e feel it. Perhaps *trop.*'

'Right.'

'But I 'ave to say, that also when he fall out, 'e fall *out.*'

'Oh.'

'So, 'ow you say, *allez doucement* – be soft, careful,' he said.

'You're a good friend to him,' she said.

He smiled. 'Fank you,' he said, before disappearing back to his mower.

32

She was back in the musty air of the *notaire*'s office, surrounded by files. Outside the weather was hot. Sun streamed through the windows, showing the streaks on each of the individual panels, where a cleaner had applied some sort of product, but failed to wipe it off.

But it was cool in the office, the kind of cool only a stone building can offer without air conditioning. And it was, at last, happening.

'And eef I could ask you to *signez vos initials*, 'ere, 'ere and 'ere,' said Monsieur Berger, indicating the crossed places on the fourth document in a row.

'So, he'd like you to sign your initials at the places crossed on the document,' said Chris in her ear in a low voice, as if imparting state secrets.

Lily avoided the temptation to tell him that with the *notaire* speaking almost entirely in English by this point, there really was no need for his help. But she held back – he'd been really helpful when looking over the electrical report, and it was sort of nice to have someone at her side other than Frédérique, who, as he was signing on behalf of his grandmother, wouldn't have been officially allowed to translate for her. She duly placed yet another set of initials where indicated, her hand aching in protest.

'And 'ere if you could write this sentence, *oui, c'est correct, et vos initials...*' continued the *notaire*, his voice almost a monotone by this stage. Lily didn't envy his job at all, which must consist largely of guiding idiots like her through legalese and getting them to sign their name over and over again.

'Bravo!' he said at last, rising to his feet and sticking out a hand for a shake. '*Madame Butterworth*, you 'ave yourself *une maison!*'

'*Merci beaucoup,*' she said.

'*Bah, vous parlez bien français! Je ne savais pas. Vous n'avez peut-être pas besoin d'un interprète, après tout!*' he replied, speaking so rapidly she could barely recognise a word.

'Um,' she said, looking helplessly at Chris.

'He's congratulating you,' he said. 'On your French.'

'Oh. *Merci,*' she said, blushing.

'*Félicitations, Madame* Buttercup,' Frédérique said once they were outside.

'It's *Madame* Butterworth,' said Chris, his brow furrowed. 'Isn't it?'

'Ah yes! I know this now. But, for me, she is as beautiful as a buttercup, *non?*'

'Oh,' Chris said. 'Yes, of course.' He seemed embarrassed.

'It is OK, *Monsieur*, she does not mind. We are lovers,' Frédérique said with a reassuring pat on Chris's shoulder.

'Well, not exactly,' began Lily, but Chris was so red that she wasn't sure what to say next. 'Look, thank you for your help. I wouldn't have managed without you.'

'No problem,' he said, shaking her hand briefly before hot-footing it to his Renault.

'Well, this is a wonderful day!' Frédérique said, turning to her. 'My grandmother will be very 'appy, and I am very 'appy that the 'ouse is now yours and you will be living 'ere.'

'Thank you. Pass on my best to your grandmother,' she said.

'And I can now buy you a drink?' he continued. 'Per'aps champagne?' He put his hand on her arm and she felt the familiar tingle.

'OK.' she smiled. 'Why not?'

'I know just the place – it is close to 'ere and it is my friend who own it,' said Frédérique. 'You want that you follow me in your car? Or you can leave it 'ere, eh, if you want to 'ave a bigger drink?'

'I'll drive,' she said. She was conscious that as well as celebrating having signed the papers, it was time that they had a proper talk about everything, and this seemed as good a moment as any.

She followed his 2CV as it hurtled around corners, not wanting to lose sight of it, but equally not confident enough on the 'death-drop' road to drive at the same pace. Thankfully, the café/bar he'd earmarked was only a few kilometres away, close to Chloé's *chambre d'hôtes* in *Faux La Montagne*.

She'd passed the entrance before but it had been closed, and thought how small and sweet it looked with its purple painted sign and matching wooden door. Once parked, they walked up the gravelled road and pushed the door open, causing a bell to ring. Inside was a tiny stone-floored room, complete with bar, piano, shelves heaving with books and a single computer on a corner desk offering internet connection for €1 an hour. Local artwork was dotted on the walls, and posters advertised a poetry reading at the end of the month. The room smelt of a mixture of coffee and burnt wood, which reminded her a little of her childhood. They'd had an open fire when she was little and she'd loved to sit by it and warm herself in the evenings, watching cartoons and drinking hot chocolate.

Here, the fire clearly hadn't been lit recently, but years and years of use and the half-burned log lying in the grate ready for winter gave the room its mild, smoky aroma.

'Oh, this is sweet,' she said as she walked in.

'*Oui, j'aime beaucoup cette café,*' Frédérique replied. '*Mon ami,* Marcel, he run it since ten years.'

'Oh lovely,' she said, watching as Frédérique strolled up to the bar and jauntily pinged the little bell for service. He was wearing a cream linen suit which could have been plucked straight from the *A Good Year* film set wardrobe, teamed with sandals – the jury was still out on whether these worked with the overall ensemble – and a light, chequered shirt. The trousers, she noticed, were particularly flattering from behind, accentuating the pert outline of his clearly toned...

'Lily? You would like champagne too, I think?' Frédérique's voice cut through her reverie and she realised she'd gone into a trance-like state.

'Oh, *oui, s'il tu plaît!*' she said, jumping back to attention.

Frédérique raised an eyebrow then looked back at his friend, who had appeared behind the counter. She hoped it hadn't been obvious that she'd been staring at Frédérique – or more precisely, his bottom – lost in thought. For a moment, she expected Frédérique to tell the café owner and the elderly couple at one of the tables that they were lovers, as if to explain why she was gaping at his rear end but for once he kept the (mis)information to himself, exchanging brief conversation before beckoning her over.

She'd spent much of last night thinking about their situation. Frédérique was romantic – that was already patently clear. But a bit of a serial romancer, too. And apparently had the tendency to fall *out* of love as quickly as he fell into it.

At the moment, his falling *out* of love wasn't the problem. It was the fact he'd claimed to be in love with her so quickly, putting pressure on what she'd thought would be a casual date or two. She hadn't wanted to jump into a whole relationship, just have a bit of fun. And now she felt she ought to commit to Frédérique or leave him before either of them got hurt.

But then, should she assume he was going to take whatever their relationship was down the same road he'd taken with others in the past? Or should she allow him a new start – a chance to learn from his past mistakes and enter a relationship with a clean slate? Her own track record wasn't exactly great – sure, she'd been married for twenty years, but she'd also moved to France and left her husband almost overnight. Nobody's love life looks great in the rear-view mirror.

Perhaps all she needed to do was communicate – after all, he'd been really vocal about how he felt and what he wanted, but most of the time she'd simply smiled or said nothing. If she explained to him again, and more clearly, that she'd rather take things slowly - just date and see what happened down the line, hopefully he would understand and go at her pace.

The champagne arrived together with two pretty, engraved flutes. It was pink champagne, and looked expensive. 'Are you sure we should open a whole bottle?' she asked. 'We're both driving for starters.'

'*Mais oui*, we can 'ave a little glass,' Frédérique said, 'and we will leave the rest for Marcel *et* 'is *amis* to drink in our honour later, eh?'

'Oh, that's a good idea,' she said, smiling at Marcel, who looked to be about eighty years old with the kind of weathered face normally associated with a life at sea.

'*D'accord?*' he asked and, as Frédérique gave him a nod, twisted his gnarled fingers on the outside of the cork to pull it free. Frédérique raised his flute ready to catch the first frothy outpouring and save them from being showered with bubbles.

It took an embarrassing amount of time, and rather a lot of huffing and puffing from Marcel for the cork to start moving slightly in the neck of the bottle. '*Mince!*' he said, as sweat began to form on his brow.

Lily and Frédérique both waited patiently with the kind of fixed smiles people get when they're pretending that a situation isn't at all awkward.

'*Ah merde!*' Marcel cried eventually as half a cork came away in his hand.

'Oh dear,' Lily said. 'Never mind. Let's...'

'*Je peux t'aider?*' offered Frédérique. Can I help you?

'*Non,*' Marcel answered, his brow furrowed. He placed the fizzing bottle on the floor and drove the corkscrew into it. Then, holding the bottle steady between his feet, he began to heave at the remnant of cork.

Watching his trembling body flex with effort against the stubborn cork, Lily unconsciously nudged her chair backwards to be further back from whatever terrible accident or explosion might be imminent. Her eyes locked with Frédérique's – equally alarmed – eyes across the table. And then the urge to giggle came over her. She looked away, shoulders shaking with the effort of holding it in, noticing that Frédérique also covered his mouth with his hand.

'*Mais s'il tu plaît, laissez-moi,*' he began. Please let me...

But before he could finish his sentence something suddenly gave and Marcel flew backwards, champagne cork still wedged in his corkscrew, and performed a near backwards somersault, knocking over the heavy bottle - which fizzed and spilled onto the wooden floor - before landing in a heap.

Lily quickly grabbed the bottle as Frédérique rushed to help his friend, who'd managed to clamber to his feet, his cheeks red. He said something to Frédérique in a low, angry tone before limping off to the back room.

Frédérique grabbed a cloth towel from behind the bar and lay it on the wasted pool of champagne. There was still half a bottle. He looked at Lily. 'I think, per'aps he 'as too much pride, eh?' he said, with a twinkle.

'Is he OK?'

'*Oui, oui,* just a little bruised in 'is mind, I fink,' he reassured her. 'We men, we like to be strong, uh? We don't like to find out our *plafonds,* our limits.'

Lily nodded. 'Poor guy.'

'Ah, but 'e will be fine,' said Frédérique, filling her glass. 'And, of course, we must still celebrate. We celebrate for the 'ouse, and for...'

Here it comes, she thought. He's going to say something over the top and romantic.

'... and for surviving this terrible *catastrophe!*' he finished with a wink. 'We could have been killed, eh! We must celebrate we still 'ave life!'

She laughed. 'Yes,' she said. 'I wasn't sure we'd get out of that one intact.'

They sat and sipped champagne and watched Marcel limping slightly behind the bar, muttering to himself in inaudible French. Lily told Frédérique about the house-warming party, and the fact that she felt she was closer to hosting some retreat guests than she'd thought. 'I know I'll need to do some work on the barn eventually,' she said. 'But if I start out small and get all the paperwork sorted I think I could have something in place by the spring.'

'This sounds amazing!' Frédérique enthused. 'I can 'elp you, if you like, with the paperwork. It can be difficult, uh?'

'Oh, *merci*,' she said, clinking glasses with him. 'I'd really appreciate that.'

'But of course!' he said. 'Of course I will 'elp. After all we are lov—'

She instinctively reached across and placed a finger on his mouth. 'About that,' she said. Because if she didn't have the conversation soon, things were going to get out of hand.

'*Oui?*' he said, his lips released. 'There is a *problème* per'aps?'

'*Peut-être*, maybe,' she said. 'But maybe just a problem *avec le langue.*'

'OK?'

'In England, we don't usually use the term "lover" very much. It's... well, it's only really used to talk about someone you have...' she lowered her voice '... sex with. And probably not much else.'

'Ah, but—'

'Hang on...'

'OK.' He looked chastened.

'It just... it makes me feel uncomfortable. It's a language thing. But maybe... well, we could say "girlfriend"?'

'But you are not a girl?' he said. 'You are a woman! It is strange this expression.'

'Yes, I suppose it is,' she said, thinking about it. But they couldn't say 'partner', could they? It sounded far too permanent. 'Well, what other expression could we use?'

'*Peut-être, mon chou?*' he suggested.

'My...' She racked her brain. 'Cabbage?'

'Yes, but we don't fink of it as cabbage, eh? It is short for *choux à la crème*, a delicious cake, eh?'

'Oh.' She shook her head. 'But... no.'

'Then,' said Frédérique, 'I will call you *mon coeur*.'

'My heart?' she said. It was certainly better than being a cabbage. And definitely less graphic than being called his lover.

'*Oui*.'

She nodded. 'I like it.'

He smiled. 'Well, I am glad you can tell me this, eh, *mon coeur*. I do not wish to cause you any pain.'

'*De rien*,' she replied. It is nothing. 'But look, that's not all. I... I'm not sure we're seeing this relationship in the same way.'

'*Oui?*'

'Yes. I want to be clear, from the start. Because... I don't want anyone to get hurt.'

'But of course! I would 'ate for you to get 'urt, my love.'

'OK. It's just you seem... very... well, keen.'

'Keen? What is this keen?'

'Um,' she said, quickly scrolling on her phone translator. '*Désireux?*'

'You want,' he said, his eyebrows bunching together, 'that I love you less? That I am not so pleased to be with you?'

It did seem crazy when he put it like that. 'Not exactly,' she said. 'Just... well, you know, I've only just broken up with Ben. We were together for twenty years. I have a son. It's all new... and I don't feel ready for too much. I need to be slow... careful, you know?'

He nodded. 'I understand.'

'You do?'

'*Oui*, now you tell me, *je comprends!* I know exactly what you wish me to do, eh?' he said, giving her an elaborate wink. 'I am very good, of course, at understanding *les femmes*.'

'Are you sure? Because I mean,' she said, not convinced his

reaction was as she'd expect it to be in the circumstances. 'I can explain... what I'd like is...'

'*Oui*,' he said, and it was his turn to reach across and touch her lips gently to stop her from talking. The fizzing sensation happened again and suddenly she wanted to take her words back and ask him to come to her *maison* and make wild passionate love, get married and never leave her side. Luckily, her head was just about able to overrule her enthusiastic heart.

'I...' she began.

'Shh,' he said, shaking his head fondly. '*Mon coeur*, you 'ad me at "be slow".'

'I...'

'And I know, don't worry, *exactly* what it is I am going to do.'

33

'And you haven't seen him since?' Sam said, pushing the trolley laden with wine, beer, paper plates and cups and a badly balanced cake box along the aisle.

It was lunchtime, and the supermarket had emptied of people as it usually did the minute the restaurants started serving food. Some of the local stores shut up between twelve and two, but the supermarket remained open and tantalisingly unused in the middle of the day. They were making the most of the wide, empty aisles and lack of queues to stock up on party items before the house-warming.

'No, But I mean it's only been a few days, so I'm not worried. He's sent a few texts, and he's coming to the party,' she replied. At first she'd thought she might have upset him, but his replies to her messages had been cheerful and upbeat. He'd just kept a little distance – which is exactly what she'd wanted.

She stopped and examined the vast array of breadsticks, eventually choosing the plain ones and putting six boxes into the trolley.

'Sounds like you got through to him,' Sam said, as they moved off again.

'I really think I did. I was worried, actually, that he might not take it very well. But he seemed to be fine. Maybe a bit too fine.'

'*Too* fine?' Sam asked, making a face.

Lily shrugged. 'I mean, it's a little bit bruising for the ego if he really doesn't feel anything at all, after having professed his undying love.'

'Yeah, I see what you mean.'

'Still, it's certainly less complicated than having him turn up and serenade me at the beach.'

'Definitely. Although having seen Frédérique, I have to say he's a complication quite a few people would kill for.'

'Well, yes, he's a nice guy.'

'Nice? Lily, he's flipping gorgeous! Although don't tell Gabriel I said that,' she laughed, taking a band from her pocket and expertly pulling her red hair into a neat ponytail. 'He's grown a little man belly recently and is totally paranoid I'm going to run off with a muscle-bound farmer or something.'

'Ha. Poor guy. When am I going to meet Gabriel anyway?' asked Lily, changing the subject. 'Can he make it to the party?'

'He says almost definitely,' said Sam. 'Which coming from him is actually pretty amazing.'

'Shy?' Lily smiled.

'Yeah, and socially awkward, but don't tell him I said that.'

'As if I would!'

'Anyway, he's great once you get to know him – just takes him a bit of time to thaw out, you know?'

Lily nodded. 'Basically, the opposite of Frédérique.'

'Yep!' Sam stopped to take in the array of cheese. 'Are we going down the cheese route?' she asked.

'Well, when in France,' said Lily, picking up a few different types. She wasn't a big cheese fan, but she'd lay a bit out with some bread and let people help themselves.

'Anyway, at least you've been upfront with Frédérique,' Sam went on, leaning some of her weight on the trolley and lifting her feet momentarily as it glided along. 'I think he's keen enough to hang around whatever boundaries you set in place.'

'We'll see,' Lily said. 'I'm trying not to put any pressure on it. Just see what happens.'

'Good idea.'

'Don't tell him, but I have actually missed him a bit,' she added.

'Really?'

'It's the first time I've had a chance to, I suppose. I'd kind of got used to him popping up everywhere I went!'

'But,' said Sam, more carefully, 'have you thought any more about Ben? I mean, you said that he'd told you he would have liked to come to France, right? If he'd been feeling OK?'

Lily stopped by a shelf heaving with crisps and picked up a giant packet of ready salted. 'I've been thinking about him more recently – all the stress of buying the house and kind of settling in here, or starting to, sort of put him out of my mind. The way you can kind of switch off a bit from problems when you're on holiday?'

Sam nodded.

'I was surprised I wasn't more... well, heartbroken I suppose when I first got here,' she said, looking at the enormous packet of crisps in her hand.

'Uh-huh?'

'But now that the legal bit is done and I'm sort of getting on with normal life... I'm starting to *notice* that he's not with me. I know that sounds weird – but I think it's finally sunk in that this isn't a holiday. And my normal life... well, he was always part of that. Always.'

Sam touched her shoulder briefly. 'That's tough.'

Lily flicked a tear away. 'It is what it is, I suppose. I mean, it's natural to feel... to miss him.' She put the crisps in the trolley and grabbed a couple of other bags.

'Any regrets?' Sam asked, glancing quickly at her, then back at the food when she noticed Lily's tears.

Lily began to move towards the next aisle. 'Sometimes,' she said. 'Not regrets about being here. Wishing it had been different, I suppose.'

'Yeah, 'course.'

'But there's no point – is there – running back to him. Because I'd have to live with knowing that I wasn't enough, that he couldn't take a risk for me. And I'd be giving up my dream, not just putting it on hold.'

'Oh, Lily.'

Lily shrugged. 'There's no solution; the only thing I can do is move on,' she said, trying to sound nonchalant but failing. 'And I'm here and making a new life. And hopefully in a while I'll be able to move on properly.'

'Definitely,' Sam said. 'It sounds like he doesn't deserve you.' She stopped by the wine boxes and heaved a couple into the trolley.

Lily resisted the urge to snap back in Ben's defence. It was one of those strange conundrums. Lily could say what *she* liked about Ben. But the urge to defend him when anyone else criticised him was almost overwhelming. She knew Sam was just being supportive, but felt incredibly defensive at her words. Ben always *had* deserved her. They'd deserved each other – in a good way.

She'd always felt their relationship was balanced, each of them bending to the other on occasion, rarely fighting. They'd giggle more often than grown-ups ordinarily would, and had never lost their sense of fun.

Then, over the last few months– now she thought about it – they'd begun doing less, going out less. Communicating less. Ben had seemed absorbed in his work – spreading papers across the dining table in the evenings, disappearing into the office or burning the midnight oil in their home study. She'd been preoccupied with getting Ty through his mocks and the pending reviews at her work. Ben had been anxious, suffering, but she hadn't realised.

By the time she'd bought the house in France, they'd drifted apart a little. She'd arrived in France on a wave of anger and self-righteousness that had given her a kind of energy and strength to move forward.

But recently she'd started to think about the whole of their relationship, not just the recent weeks. The day they met in the lecture hall, the moment she'd discovered she was pregnant, their wedding day when they'd fallen into bed too exhausted to consummate *anything*. Their nights out, meals out, days out – always with moments of laughter and the kind of silliness you only really get with someone you've known since you were young and relatively carefree.

They'd evolved around each other like jigsaw pieces, and she could feel the jagged edges left exposed where they'd pulled away from each other. She couldn't imagine finding anyone who fitted her so exactly, because she'd grown to fit Ben and he'd grown to fit her. Perhaps nobody would ever fill the space he'd left.

The shock – and it had been a traumatic, proper, pass-me-some-smelling-salts-no-make-that-a-bottle-of-your-strongest-brandy shock – of discovering that he really would let her walk away had been brutal. But somehow her anger had overridden it at first.

Now the anger had gone and she was left with a feeling of grief. And she knew it was going to take more time and energy to heal than she'd realised at first.

There was nothing she could do about it though, or rather there was something, but it was too much to ask – give up her dream, move back to England, pretend the last part of her life hadn't happened; live with the knowledge that Ben was the reason she'd had to let go of the dream she'd thought they'd shared. The die had been cast and she was here, starting a new life in a new place. She couldn't afford to give in to the feeling of loneliness – either by throwing herself at the nearest twinkly-eyed Frenchman, or collapsing on the floor in a sobbing heap. Not if she wanted to build any kind of future for herself.

Instead, she resolved, she'd buy snacks. Lots of snacks.

'Are you sure that isn't too many snacks?' Sam said doubtfully as they heaved the overflowing trolley to the till. 'Isn't Chloé bringing some quiches as well?'

Chloé had insisted she bring something when Lily had invited her to the party. 'But I must!' she'd said. 'You are my friend, *non*?'

'Yes, but I... I mean this is meant to be a party thanking *you*,' said Lily. 'Thanking everyone. You shouldn't have to work.'

'Pah, it is not work to make a quiche, huh? Especially when it iz for a friend.'

'It'll be fine,' Lily said. 'I'm not a hundred per cent sure who is coming – Dawn and Clive said they'd put the word out, whatever that means. But I can always keep some back for another time. I have a teenage son, remember.'

'Good point,' Sam said as she began to stack packets onto the conveyer belt. 'Perhaps we should get a few more bags.'

Lily smiled. She was lucky to have found a friend like Sam – who seemed to be on her wavelength and knew how to cheer her up, even if she didn't know she was doing it. In fact, what with Frédérique and Chloé and all the other people she had made connections with, she was beginning to feel she'd really landed on her feet here.

Last night, Lily had sent text messages around to everyone she'd met so far.

Party, Saturday, 2 p.m. everyone welcome.

She'd had a host of replies, almost straightaway, including one from the translator, Chris, whom she'd forgotten was still in her 'French contacts' file. He'd seemed very keen and she'd thought – why not? The more the merrier.

She'd spoken separately to Frédérique, not wanting to send something so impersonal out to him. He'd seemed delighted to hear from her. 'Lily, yes, of course I am coming to your wonderful party,' he'd said. 'I would not miss it for the world.'

'Oh, thank you,' she'd said.

'And you would like me to bring some things?'

'No, no. It's all organised.'

'Some music per'aps?' he'd said, undeterred. 'I 'ave *la machine à karaoké*?'

'Well, OK, why not,' she'd said. 'Might be fun.'

'And per'aps I bring some of my 'ome-made wine? I make it from ze plants in my *jardin*?'

'Sounds delicious.'

When scrolling through her wider contacts to make sure she hadn't missed one, she'd paused on the word 'Mum'. Somehow, she'd been unable to delete her mother's number from the phone. She'd even transferred it when she'd bought a new one. It was something about the finality of it; something about the act of deleting a number that at least promised to link her to the woman she'd loved most in the world.

'I wish I could talk to you, Mum,' she'd said.

Mum had always been the one she'd called when the chips were down. She and Ben had been two pillars of strength in her life. Without them, she was wobbling, unsupported. She'd fought the urge to send a text to the obsolete phone. If the number had been reassigned and a stranger answered, it would probably break her.

Instead, she'd poured a glass of wine and read her book on the sofa until her eyes had become so tired she knew she'd drop asleep the moment her head hit the pillow.

* * *

Once they'd driven back and Sam had disappeared to pick the kids up from crèche, Lily sat there again, feeling the silence fill the air around her.

She picked up her phone and thumbed through until she found Ben's number.

It wouldn't hurt to give him a quick call, would it? After all, she had a few questions about Ty's student loans she wanted to ask. And they were still friends and co-parents. She wouldn't tell him how she was feeling or open up to him; but it would be nice to hear his voice anyway.

She clicked on the number and it immediately diverted to his messaging service. She looked at her watch: two o'clock on a Friday afternoon. Perhaps he was driving. She'd try again later.

Emily's phone went to answerphone too. Running out of

options, she looked at David's name. She'd sent a couple of emails since arriving, but it was ages since they'd spoken on the phone. Two o'clock would be ten in the morning in David's life. She pressed the button to call him.

'Hello?' he answered, almost immediately.

'Hi, David,' she said, suddenly wondering why she'd called.

'Hi, is everything all right?'

'Yes, everything... well everything's OK. I just thought I'd call to see how you are?'

'Oh. Well, yeah. We're good, thanks,' he said. She could hear a twang of Australian in his British accent.

'Great. Good.'

'And you're OK?' he said.

'Yes. Yes, I'm fine.'

There was a silence. She'd forgotten just how painfully awkward her brother was on the phone. 'Um, I suppose,' she said, 'I suppose I was just missing Mum, and I thought... well, you know.'

He was silent for a minute. 'I know,' he said at last. 'It's hard sometimes.'

'I wish...' she said, but wasn't sure how to end the sentence.

'Yeah,' he said. 'Yeah, I know.'

'Maybe I should come and see you sometime? It's been ages.'

'Yeah?' He sounded upbeat. 'I'd love that. You know you're always welcome.'

'Thanks.'

'We can help with the ticket if you need?'

'Thanks. I'll let you know.'

Another silence. One she and Ben could have filled with anecdotes, or serious conversation about how they felt, what they were thinking. One she and Mum could have laughed in for hours. She loved David, but felt everything tense when she was on the phone to him, simply because she knew how much he hated calls.

'Well, I guess I'd better let you get on,' she said at last.

'OK. Glad you called,' he said. 'Sorry, I'm... well, you know.'

She snorted. 'It's OK. Maybe we'll try Skype next time.'

'Yeah, maybe.'

'Anyway, see you.'

'See ya.'

And that, she thought, *is why I rarely call him.*

Still, it had been nice to hear his voice.

She tried Ben one last time, but it clicked to voicemail and she didn't leave a message.

To distract herself, she began to put away the party items she'd picked up with Sam. Then, once they were all stuffed in the dresser cupboards or stacked neatly on the table, she decided to sit in the garden for a while.

She'd slept badly the night before – although the new bed had been delivered, the mattress was hard to get used to after an airbed that had gradually deflated but somehow moulded to her body in the night. In the new bed, she was aware of the space around her more – aware that she was alone in a space for two.

And she'd felt uneasy, a kind of free-floating anxiety that she couldn't shake. Something was wrong, but she couldn't put her finger on it.

She poured herself a glass of lemonade, added ice, and stepped into the garden. As usual it buzzed with life – each grassy area clearly filled to the brim with insects. She brushed a few leaves from the cast iron chairs and rested her drink on the table, then settled back, closing her eyes.

She breathed deeply, enjoying the fresh air with its hint of pine from the distant trees. She could hear the sound of an aeroplane passing overhead, but other than that, the insects and the odd rumble of a car, the afternoon was peaceful.

And despite resolving that she would just sit for half an hour, she drifted off to sleep.

34

Saturday morning, she woke with a start, exiting a dream that she couldn't remember but knew had been unpleasant. Sitting up, she steadied her breathing, swung her legs out of the bed and opened the window, before releasing the catch of the wooden shutters and throwing them wide.

Dim light flooded in.

To her relief, the sky outside her bedroom looked clear and there was no hint of the rain she'd worried might arrive despite the clement forecast. *It's today*, she thought, feeling her heart thump with a mixture of nerves and excitement. It was 6 a.m., but there was no chance of getting back to sleep.

It was the first event she'd ever really put on all by herself – she and Ben had had dinner parties back in the day, and had even been known to throw the odd barbecue. But she'd always had backup, someone else to send out for emergency burgers or bottles of wine. Someone to tell her that everything looked OK just before the guests arrived.

Sam had offered to pop over this morning to help her set some of it up, but she'd refused. She hadn't wanted to become a burden to her new friend, who had already gone above and beyond and would also have Derek and Claudine to deal with. 'I'll be fine,' Lily had said. 'You've done so much already.'

Instead, they'd agreed that Sam would come over at 1 p.m. before the party started to ensure there weren't any last-minute disasters. 'We can have a pre-party glass of fizz,' Lily had said, 'and you can keep me from having a nervous breakdown.'

She knew she'd be quite happy once the party was in full swing; the anticipation of it, though, felt a little overwhelming.

She sat back on her bed and pulled the duvet up to her chin, letting the warmth flood back through her body and resting her head on a propped-up pillow. Instead of rushing to get up, she watched the beginning of the sunrise: glimmers of light at the horizon, just below the treeline, flooding up and exposing a hint of blue in the early morning sky.

It was seven by the time she dragged herself out of bed and down the stairs; still seven hours before anyone would arrive – too soon to really start getting anything ready, and she didn't have much to occupy herself with in the meantime. She made a coffee and opened her laptop, firing off a quick email to Tyler with a list she'd put together of things he might need to buy before he moved into halls. 'I'm more than happy to fly over and help,' she offered. 'I'm only an hour or so away.'

She wanted him to know that wherever she lived, she would support him just as much. He didn't have to think of Ben as his 'main parent' and her as someone on the periphery.

Then she switched on her phone which gratifyingly flashed with four messages immediately – nice to be in demand, she thought. The first was from Emily.

Flight arrives at 1, taxi to yours by 3. Mine's a large red. X

She laughed and replied with:

As if I didn't know! Looking forward to seeing you.

The second and third were from Frédérique.

I am sorry I cannot help this morning but I will be there at 2 for your party.

And – sent an hour later.

I can't wait to see you – *je suis excité* 😊 *mon coeur.*

She replied:

Merci! À tout à l'heure.

See you later.

Then she spent a minute or so debating whether to send a kiss or two, or an emoticon with heart eyes, and what kind of impression each might give. In the end she opted for a single 'x'.

The fourth was from Ben. She almost didn't open it – today she needed to stay upbeat and strong, and hearing from him right now might make her wobble. Curiosity though got the better of her, especially when she realised he'd sent it at 1 a.m. – a time of night when text messages are more likely to reveal emotion or truth, due to either exhaustion or alcohol.

She opened it. It said:

Lily, I'm sorry. I can't

Can't what? He'd obviously started to write and pressed send before finishing. Or started to write then decided against it, but accidentally sent it anyway. She was about to send a message in response, then something about the way he'd written it, the time it had been written struck her. Perhaps he was struggling.

She looked at her watch: 7.30 a.m., so 6.30 a.m. in England. She couldn't ring him yet. He'd probably be trying to get a lie in after a busy week – he wouldn't thank her for an early morning call.

It was probably just him telling her he was sorry he couldn't take her call the other day, or that he couldn't remember the password for their online banking. Or couldn't remember someone's birthday and needed to ask. Or something.

But something about the message, in tandem with the strange, unspecific feeling of dread left over from her dream, made it hard to settle.

She made another coffee and wandered into the garden, in the strange half-light that now lingered until almost 8 a.m., marking the fact that time was moving on and the seasons were changing. The morning air was cool, but pleasantly so and her cotton pyjamas gave more than enough protection from the chill. She blew the heat from the top of her mug and took a sip, looking out over the horizon to the glimmer of morning behind the trees. The heat of the hot liquid entering her throat sent a shiver through her body.

She imagined Ben coming out of the house behind her, wrapping an arm around her back. Standing with her to appreciate the beauty of it all; the fact that they'd stepped out of the structure imposed on them in their old life and chosen to create their own. She couldn't shake the feeling that, if he'd only come, he would love it here. His job seemed to consume him at times – but here he'd have the freedom to rediscover who he was, what he really wanted to be. Some financial space – made possible by the lack of mortgage and equity freed up from the Basildon house. Headspace. Natural surroundings. And air that seemed to cleanse with every breath.

The sob came without her realising she was crying; embarrassingly loud in the empty garden. She checked herself and took a breath. It was no use. Because he wasn't here. And it was clear that he never would be.

But the fact they were no longer together didn't stop her loving him, caring for him. And now, worrying about him. Back in their house in that different life she'd walked away from, he was probably sleeping calmly, the text message half sent in the early hours a million miles from his mind.

Yet something within her that she couldn't quite name wouldn't let her forget about it. Because she knew he would never be up at that time unless something was wrong. And contacting her in the night wasn't something he'd ordinarily do.

Had his anxiety overwhelmed him again? Was he finding it hard on his own? Had that little message half written to her phone been some sort of cry for help?

Suddenly, waiting seemed ridiculous. Ben would be up now, and if he wasn't, well, it was too bad. People who send mysterious messages at 1 a.m. didn't deserve lie-ins of any sort. She was going to ring him, she decided, putting her coffee down and racing into the house – as if racing somehow would make a difference when it was almost seven hours since his message had been sent.

Ben's phone wasn't switched off at least. But after eight or nine rings it clicked onto his phone's answering service. She tried again, perhaps he hadn't heard the first time? But once again the call was interrupted by a generic woman asking her to leave a message.

Lily knew he rarely checked his voicemail, always assuming

the person would ring back if they needed to. But left a message anyway.

'Ben, listen. Could you call me, as soon as you get this. Nothing's wrong. I just... I just want to speak to you quickly,' she said, not wanting to alarm him.

She hung up, then dialled Emily. Uncharacteristically, her friend's phone was firmly turned off. Mind you, it was early.

She was probably only worried because it was the day of the party and she had so much nervous energy, Lily reassured herself, dialling Ben again just in case. Ben would answer in a minute then her worry would be replaced with relief and probably a bit of anger.

But again the phone rang out. She'd wait a few minutes and try again. He was probably in the shower or still snoozing and couldn't hear his phone. But once again she couldn't shake the feeling of unease.

Knowing this wouldn't go down well at such an early hour but not completely caring, she rang Ty.

Thankfully, he answered. 'Wha—?' he said, sleepily.

'Ty, love, it's me. Mum,' she said.

He grunted. 'I know. What's up?'

'Nothing. Everything's OK. I know I'm ringing a little... earlier than normal.'

'Uh-huh,' he said, clearly mid-yawn.

'But...' She chose her words carefully, not wanting to alarm Ty. 'I'm trying to get hold of your dad, but his phone's ringing out. I just wondered whether you could give him a nudge for me.'

'A nudge? What, a text?'

'No, Ty,' she said, exasperated, 'I mean get out of bed and just pop along and give him a knock.'

'Mum, I'm at Steve's.'

'Oh.' Steve was Ty's friend and lived fifteen miles away. 'Why?'

'What? Just because!' he said, incredulous that she was asking. Rightly so, too, as he probably slept there almost as much as he did at home these days. But why today?

'OK,' she said. 'Listen, Ty, I'm probably being silly, but when you saw Dad yesterday, was anything... well, was he OK?'

'Why?' he said, sounding guarded.

'Oh, no reason. Just... you know, checking up on him. I mean, I still care about your dad, you know.'

There was a silence.

'He's... well, look,' Ty said. 'He's OK.'

'You don't sound sure?'

Ty sighed deeply. 'Look, Mum, you need to speak to him yourself.'

'I have tried, Ty. I'm not... I just want to know he's OK, that nothing's... going on.'

Another silence in which she felt a spike of anxiety.

'I'm not meant to talk about it,' he said, finally. 'He did tell me... something yesterday. But it was private. He made me promise.'

'Talk about what? Come on, Ty?'

'No, look, I promised, OK?'

'So something *is* going on?'

A sigh. 'Well, yeah. But you know...'

'No, I don't...' She tried to keep the note of panic from her voice. 'Ty, I think you have to tell me. If your dad... well, if something's going on, I have a right to know.'

'I can't,' he said simply.

'Well, tell me if he's OK?'

Another silence. 'Mum, I'm sorry. I just... you need to talk to Dad.'

They hung up moments later, and she immediately dialled Ben's number.

Nothing.

Emily's number.

Nothing.

What had started as a mild concern was blown into something more by the silence; the lack of clarity.

Ty would surely tell her if something was *really* wrong. He'd want her to help. But at the same time, was her eighteen-year-old properly able to recognise if Ben was in a really bad place? Would he really know when it was time to call for backup? It was certainly unusual for Ben to confide something in his son then ask him not to tell anyone else.

Part of the problem had been that she hadn't wanted to alarm Ty. His dad might be ill, or struggling in a way he might not understand. So her questions had had to be vague, and his answers had been just as unfathomable. There were all different kinds of 'OK'.

She rang Ben's phone again.

Nothing.

This was ridiculous. She was working herself up about nothing! After all, Ben had people around him – Emily had been popping over regularly and she'd reported that he was out and about, seeing a counsellor, making it to work but not letting it consume him. That he wasn't 'out of the woods' but well and truly on the mend.

And what? One missed call and she was panicking.

She scrolled through her phone to Ben's mum. But what was she going to say to Maureen? Get her to race over thirty miles because her son wasn't answering a call from his ex-wife?

The feeling of anxiety still thundered inside her, but she tried to put it into context. She'd woken anxious after a dream, she had a big and daunting day ahead. Yes, it was natural to worry about

Ben, but her worry had been overblown by the feeling of fear she was already experiencing.

Maybe he hadn't answered because he just didn't want to speak to her.

He was probably out for the day, or catching up with work and preoccupied with some sort of spreadsheet related conundrum. The text message had meant nothing. He'd probably forgotten he'd even sent it and would think she was crazy for reading too much into it. Ringing him four times? Ringing their son? She was overreacting.

It was just a feeling. It didn't mean anything. Ben would be fine.

It struck her that other than Emily, there was no one else she could really call about this. Nobody whose opinion she'd want to ask. Nobody who knew Ben. Nobody she really felt able to properly confide in.

David, in Australia, might be sympathetic but wouldn't understand. Ty would be frantic if he knew how worried she was, but didn't have the age or experience to help.

Memories of calling Mum in the past flooded her mind – times when she was worried about Ty, or had had a fight with Ben; when she was waiting on medical test results, or stressed about work. Everyone thinks their mum is the best mum, don't they? But to have a mother you could call any time, day or night, who would always seem pleased to hear from you, would always have advice to dispense – perhaps not always the advice she'd wanted to hear, but advice nonetheless - she'd been so, so lucky.

Mum would have known what to do now.

Her eyes began to fill with tears and she coughed them away. This was ridiculous. It was the day of the party – a day of celebration. And what? One text message sent in error and suddenly she was approaching emotional collapse?

The grief for Mum would never leave her, the grief at her and Ben breaking up was still raw too. But this wasn't the time for grief. There was so much to celebrate too. She'd just woken up on the wrong side of bed.

Shaking her head, she put her phone down and purposefully turned over the screen so she couldn't glance at it for a bit. Instead, she made her way upstairs and began to fill the bath. It was going to be a long day, so she should take a bit of relaxation where she could.

'Wine?'

'Ah, yes please,' she said, settling down on the bench in their back garden. 'Fill it up!'

'Long day?'

'Something like that.'

It was bright, but chilly; she pulled her cardigan more closely around her shoulders. 'Just think,' she said. 'When we move to France, we'll be able to do this every evening. Without a cardigan.'

'I think they still have winters in France.'

'OK, in front of roaring log fires too then.'

'Sounds perfect.' They clinked their glasses together and fell into silence.

'Ben,' she asked. 'When do you think we might do it?'

'Not yet,' he said. 'But one day. Definitely one day.'

* * *

She couldn't have hoped for better weather. The garden was flooded with sunlight, but the temperature remained a pleasant twenty-four degrees, meaning she wouldn't have to worry about her lack of sunshades as her guests probably wouldn't feel the need to crowd under the meagre shadows cast by the pine trees at the end of her garden. The weather forecast had predicted showers later, but without a cloud visible in the sky she was pretty confident they were set for the next few hours.

The food – such as it was – was ready. She'd opened packets and jars, tipped salads into plastic bowls, covered pots with cling film and everything was ready to be served. She'd even managed to fit four bottles of wine into the fridge, and there were more lined up ready to replace them once the party started.

Sam's car drew up outside at exactly 12.59, and she opened the door as Claudine and Derek rushed past her legs. Sam, brandishing two bottles of champagne, hurried up the path behind them.

'Oh, you didn't have to bring anything!' Lily said. 'Thank you.'

'You can never have too much champagne,' Sam said, with a wink, handing her one of the bottles. 'Let's crack one open, shall we? Just to make sure it's not corked.'

'That sounds very sensible,' nodded Lily, with mock seriousness. 'Just to protect the guests, of course.'

'Of course!'

'Where's Gabriel?' she asked. 'Did he decide not to come after all?'

'Apparently he'll be along later,' Sam said with an eye roll. 'He couldn't bear the idea of infringing on our champagne and gossip time.'

'Sensible man,' Lily said, as they walked through to the kitchen.

'Wow, it's looking great!' Sam said approvingly.

'Thank you. I mean, it's scrubbed up OK, right?' Lily said, quite proud of the way everything was looking.

'It looks amazing,' Sam said. 'There's just one thing missing...'

'What's that?'

'I don't seem to have a glass of champers in my hand.'

Before she could rectify this, Chloé arrived, an enormous Tupperware container in her hands. She was wearing a navy dress, cinched in at the waist, that fell around her calves in delicate folds and looked – as always – absolutely perfect. '*Les* quiches,' she said, before Lily could say anything. 'I am sorry, I only make three.'

'Wow, thank you,' said Lily, smiling as she took the plastic box. 'It's really kind. And you look lovely.'

'Ah, but so do you!' Chloé said, looking at Lily's strappy dress approvingly.

In the kitchen, she introduced Chloé to Sam. 'Ah, I 'ave seen you at the lake, *non*?' Chloé said.

'Yes, probably. And I think my aunt stayed with you one year when we were renovating?' Sam replied.

Formalities over, they finally popped the champagne cork and sat out on the terrace watching the children run amok in the enormous space. 'So, is your friend, Emily, still coming?' Sam asked.

'Ah, Emily is coming?' Chloé said. 'She is a good friend to come so far.'

'Yes, yes, she is,' said Lily. 'She should be here at three – her plane's in about one,' She looked at her watch. 'I haven't been able to get hold of her today at all.'

'Ah, but she is travelling! It is not easy.'

'She's probably switched flight mode on.'

'Yes.' Lily nodded, still a bit perplexed that none of her messages had been answered. Worse, she still hadn't been able to get hold of Ben and although there was probably no need to worry, she felt a frisson of anxiety in her chest whenever she thought about it. She took a gulp of champagne and felt it fizz coldly down her throat.

'Steady on,' Sam said. 'You'll be legless by the time anyone else arrives.'

'Ah, just calming my nerves,' Lily said. 'Don't worry, I'll slow down.'

'Ah, you don't need to be nervous,' said Sam, brushing her arm, 'it's going to be grand.'

'Thanks.' Lily smiled. She couldn't bring herself to explain to Sam that she was also worried about Ben. Not least because she might well start crying and be streaked with mascara by the time the guests arrived. She was just feeling emotional because of the house-warming and the rite of passage it felt like. It felt like one of those occasions where everyone important in your life should be there, making the ones who aren't loom large in your mind.

'*Bonjour!*' said a voice behind them, and they both jumped, Sam giving a little squeak and spilling a slosh of champagne on her front.

'Frédérique!' Lily said, turning. 'You scared us.'

'I am so sorry, *Mesdames*,' he said, seriously. 'But the door is open and I am carrying thees.' His arms were wrapped around an enormous speaker, from which a microphone dangled on a wire. 'My karaoke machine, uh?'

'Oh, thank you,' Lily said, hoping she wouldn't come to regret her decision to let him bring it. 'Let's put it in the living room for now.'

'The living room?'

'*Le salon.*'

'OK, *bon.*' He disappeared back into the house and Lily got up to follow him.

'You actually let him bring a karaoke machine?' Sam said quietly, grinning.

'I know,' Lily said. 'But it could be fun.'

'Perhaps it's finally time for that serenade?'

'Don't encourage him!'

Lily entered the kitchen and walked through to the living room where Frédérique was in the process of plugging the speaker into the wall. 'Let's leave it for now,' she said. 'We can set it up later, when people are here?'

'As you want, *mon coeur*,' he said, turning and smiling dazzlingly at her. He took her in his arms and planted a soft kiss on her lips, leaving them tingling as always. She leaned in for another, pressing her body against his. What was it about this man?

'Ah, I 'ave missed you, *non*?' Frédérique said as they moved apart. 'I 'av been thinking about what you said – about how you need to be old-fashion... how you want to be slow. But I miss you.'

'I missed you, too,' she said.

There was a knock at the door and she jumped slightly out of his arms as if she were a character in a soap opera caught in a clinch with someone else's husband. 'I'd better get that,' she said, rushing to the door.

''ello love!' Dawn and Clive stood there, clutching a bottle of red.

'Oh hello!' she said, exchanging slightly awkward kisses with the couple before standing back to let them into the hall. 'If you want to go through, and out the back, there are drinks and nibbles waiting.'

'Thanks, love.'

More people began to arrive, and after a while she drifted through to the back, leaving the front door open for any latecomers.

It was a good turnout. Claude and his wife – who was stunningly beautiful, with long black hair caught up in a casual chignon – a few expats she recognised from the party, as well as Dawn and Clive; Chloé, Chris the translator and his wife, who was just as fluent in French as her husband and was soon nattering away to Chloé with such a flawless accent that Lily resolved to book up some lessons as soon as the party was over. All in all, there were nearly twenty people there; most of whom she knew and many of whom had helped her in some way.

She flitted from group to group, making sure wine was topped up, nobody was left out, and felt a little like a bride at a small wedding – surrounded by people who wished her well, who had already become part of her life, or might well be in her life moving forward.

She'd made up a party tunes playlist on her phone and streamed it through a speaker she'd brought out into the garden. Derek and Claudine danced, swinging each other around in a way that looked a bit precarious to Lily, but that didn't seem to bother Sam a bit. Even Gabriel turned up – tall, but with a slightly awkward stoop. He was clearly a little uncomfortable, but greeted Lily warmly. 'So this is the woman who steal my wife!' he joked. 'It is nice to meet you at last, Lily!'

An hour in, and the only fly in the champagne was the fact that Emily still hadn't appeared. But she'd checked the flight times from Limoges and seen there'd been a half hour delay. Her friend would arrive soon, she reassured herself. And probably, any minute, she'd get a call telling her to open some red wine in readiness. It would be fine.

Frédérique was behaving himself, almost too well, and had spent some time speaking to Claude, then Chloé, periodically appearing at her side to make sure she was happy and didn't need anything. It was almost too good to be true.

And, of course, the moment she had this thought, the music suddenly went off.

People glanced around vaguely, not particularly bothered, and went on with their conversations as Lily walked to her phone to check it hadn't drained its battery. But before she could reach it, she heard a noise that made her stiffen.

'*Madame Buttercup!*' it boomed. '*Mesdames et Messieurs*, ladees et gentlemens, may I 'ave your attention, please!' All heads turned in the direction of the terrace, where Frédérique stood, holding a microphone. His speaker had been propped in the living room window and was booming his words out across the garden, and probably to everyone on the beach and beyond.

Lily shook her head and tried to catch his eye. Sam had been right he was going to serenade her! But surely Frédérique realised that it wasn't something she wanted him to do – particularly here?

She braced herself for some gentle French crooning, a little embarrassment that she could laugh off. And hoped now that Emily wouldn't turn up – at least for the five or so minutes it would take her boyfriend to lay down a love song.

Only Frédérique didn't start singing.

'Lily, *mon coeur*, come 'ere,' he said, holding his hand out and flashing his brilliant smile. She walked forward as if on autopilot and he took her hand.

'I just wanted to take a moment for thees wonderful woman, eh?' he said. 'She come 'ere and in no time she change all our life!'

Lily doubted she'd made a difference to the lives of most people here, seeing as she'd only met a few of them once, and others had simply been over to chop down the grass or prevent walls from tumbling down. 'No,' she said. 'I...'

But Frédérique was in full flow.

'And I fink for this wonderful party too, eh, we should be very grateful!' he said. 'And maybe that I will give her the clap. We must all give her the clap – yes?'

The audience dutifully clapped and Lily felt the blush that had started on her neck creep to her cheeks.

'Thank you,' she said. 'Come on, Frédérique, that's enough.'

'Ah but, my love,' he said, still clutching the microphone. Still booming. 'I 'ave something more to say.'

Lily caught Sam's eye and had to look away quickly, not sure whether she was going to burst into tears or catch a fit of the giggles. She felt sorry, too, for Frédérique. However misjudged this intervention, it was sweet that he wanted to make her feel special.

She focused her eyes on him. 'Can't you say it later?' she hissed, keeping her face fixed in a smile. 'I'm really... it's private, surely?'

'Ah bah *non*!' he said, seemingly forgetting he was broadcasting half of a private conversation for an audience. 'This is something I want to say for all your friends, eh?'

There was nothing she could do.

She braced herself for an onslaught of compliments; or perhaps the opening strains of a love song.

But what happened next was far, far more dramatic.

Suddenly, Frédérique dropped on one knee. 'My love,' he said.

She was stunned into silence. Surely, the man wasn't proposing. Perhaps it was just a romantic start to some sort of singing routine he'd worked out.

'A few day ago thees woman she say to me, she want to 'ave a romance that go more *doucement*,' he said, 'more gentle, maybe a leetle more old-fashion, oui?'

'But...' Lily said.

'And for the first day I fink maybe she does not love me, huh? Then I realise what she mean!'

'What I...?'

'My beautiful Engleesh lady, she is not *disponsible* to just anyone,' he said. 'She is my *princesse*, oui?'

For a moment, Lily didn't follow.

'I make love with many, many women,' Frédérique said, addressing her. 'So many, many women. But for you, I know, it is not enough, eh?'

'What?'

'I mean to say,' he said. 'Zat you are more special, *mon coeur*. You say to me, don't call me *lover* we are not *lovers*.'

This was excruciating.

'We are *le* heart of each other,' he said, nodding.

'Well, kind of...'

'And then I know what it is you want!' he said, triumphantly. 'And it is too, what I would want for us, oui? You want that we marry before we make love. To take it old fashion, like in le movies?'

'No, that's not—'

'So I say to you, *Madame Buttercup*. You 'ave come into my life and made the sun shine again. You are beautiful, you 'ave *l'indépendence*. You capture my 'eart so completely, that I am yours forever.'

'Oh.'

'I know we know so little of each other. But please to believe me, my heart, I must tell you that I do not make this proposal just because I want so much to make love with you, *mon coeur*.'

'I...'

'Because, of course, I want your body, so beautiful. But I also want your 'ead. Your mind. My love. I want to be making love to all of you.'

'Oh.'

'I want to be wiv you forever.'

'...'

He drew a box out of his pocket, opening it to reveal a beautiful ring, set with a sapphire surrounded by diamonds. Her engagement ring from Ben had been a simple diamond solitaire, bought when they were too young to afford something bigger. But she'd always longed for a beautiful, antique ring. *One day*, Ben had told her, *I'll buy you one.*

But one day hadn't come.

'I speak to my grandmother, and she say, Frédérique, you must follow your 'eart. She iz the one! And she give me 'er ring and say, do not let 'er go,' Frédérique said. 'And so I must ask you, my beautiful Lily, whether you will put this on your finger and agree to a marriage with me. Because love, when you know, you just know. Oui?'

'But Frédérique,' she started, but he held a finger up to silence her.

'My love, you are alone. And it make me *triste* – sad – each day to think of you like this. You want to make life *la* France, you want to 'ave much happiness, I think? Let me 'elp. Let me be someone by your side. Someone oo never to let you down, or leave you, or let you go from me alone. You deserve a *personne* – a man – oo love you enough. Oo love you like you deserve to be love.'

Lily felt tears suddenly pool in her eyes.

'*Mon coeur*, all you do to me is to say *oui*, and I am yours. And you will never 'ave to be alone again.'

She looked at his face – so handsome and earnest. The ring – so beautiful, and gifted by his grandmother. He was over the top, sure. But maybe after years of half-heartedness, she deserved a little romance?

And he was right. Despite everything. Despite the friends she had already gathered around her. Despite the fact that England was only a short flight away and she had so many ways of staying in touch with people, she often felt completely and utterly alone.

Lily looked at Frédérique's handsome face, his beautiful eyes that crinkled when he smiled. She looked at the expectant faces surrounding them. It was in so many ways the perfect moment. Here in a house she loved, in a country she was coming to know. She could gather up her very own Russell Crowe (circa 2006), her Max Skinner, and she'd be living a long-held dream. Of living a different kind of life; of being loved.

It would be so, so easy to say yes.

She steeled herself for what might come next.

'I'm sorry, Frédérique,' she said, her voice picked up on the microphone in his hand. 'I'm so sorry, but I can't.'

'But...'

'Let me explain,' she said, feeling her heart lurch when she saw his eyes begin to glisten. 'It's not you, it really isn't. You've been... Well, wonderful. And kind. And you've done everything you thought I wanted. It's amazing. To be wanted, to be loved that much. I would love to be able to say yes.'

She knelt down opposite him. 'But I can't. And it's because I'm in love with someone else.' She brushed a little strand of hair from his forehead. 'I shouldn't have come on a date with you in the first place,' she said. 'But I was angry, angry with him. And for a while the anger made me feel that I didn't love him. But I do. I know now that I still do.'

'Your 'usband?'

'Yes,' she said. 'I still love Ben. And it's wretched because I know that he doesn't love me any more. That he doesn't want me *enough*. He's back in England and—' her voice was suddenly thick with tears '—I don't even know if he's OK or not. I can't... we don't even speak.'

The sky, that had been darkening slightly, rumbled as if in sympathy. A single drop of rain fell on the ground between them.

'It's OK,' Frédérique said, his expression kind. 'You do not 'ave to explain.'

'But I do,' she said. 'Because you've done all this. And it's so, so wonderful. And you deserve so much better. But I couldn't say yes to your proposal, or even a proper date, when deep down I know that if Ben was to walk through the door right now, I'd take him back without question.'

There was a silence. Frédérique's eyes became distant as he focused over her shoulder and she wondered whether he was trying not to cry. Her guests, standing taking in the spectacle, broadcast to all over loudspeaker, fell silent too, as if in sympathy. The only noise was from Claudine, grabbing on to Sam's dress and crying 'Mum!' urgently.

Then she heard it – a light step behind her.

'Do you really mean that?' someone asked.

She recognised his voice instantly. 'Ben?' she said, turning and seeing her husband for the first time in weeks. She scrambled to her feet, eyes wide with shock.

He looked thinner, a little pale, rumpled from the journey. But absolutely, 100 per cent *there*. Behind him in the kitchen doorway, she could see Emily, who gave her a small shrug and smile.

'Ben!' she said. 'Why are you... when did you...?'

The rain started to fall more heavily now and Derek and Claudine began to scream and run for cover. The rest of the guests, though, seemed transfixed.

'Lily, I'm so sorry. I've been a complete prat,' he said. 'I didn't talk to you when I should have. I didn't tell you what was going on. I was scared and embarrassed.'

'Oh, Ben.'

'And in doing so, I lost the most important person in my life. The thing I was most scared of in the world happened and it was because of me.'

She shook her head, 'But...'

'No, wait,' he said, his hair beginning to sag under the weight of falling droplets. 'And I thought at first that perhaps it was no more than I deserved. But then, when I began to get better, I realised that you didn't ever really leave me.'

There was a loud scrape as Frédérique got up and put the microphone down. Lily reached to touch his arm and they looked at each other briefly. He nodded, with a sad smile, before disappearing into the kitchen.

She wanted to make sure he was all right, but she couldn't move. Didn't want to move.

'Ben...' she said.

'Please,' he answered. 'Hear me out. All those times when you spoke about moving in the past, I was scared – I'll admit it. But good scared. Excited scared. I wasn't sure whether I'd like it, whether it would work out.'

'But...'

'But I knew that it was something I'd do with you – because it was important to you. I never... in my wildest dreams I'd never imagined I'd let you walk away.'

'Oh Ben.' She rubbed his upper arm with her hand and their faces moved closer together. She looked into his eyes and felt suddenly more at home than she had for months. She felt the jagged edges of her jigsaw piece mould with his until finally everything made sense.

'I was kind of stuck in a rut at work, but also worried about what might happen if I got out of the rut... I dunno. I never really realised I was so... so stuck until you walked away and I just couldn't follow you.'

'It's OK,' she said. 'Really.'

'I thought... I guess I felt like it was too late. And then you said what you said... You said to come. To be with you. And I realised that perhaps it wasn't too late after all.'

She smiled, feeling a mixture of rain and tears on her cheeks.

'I need to ask you to forgive me,' Ben continued.

'You don't have to...'

'Yes, I do. The things I could have said and done, the way I made you feel. That's on me. And I need to know – can you forgive me, Lily?' Rain was running down his face, but she was pretty sure he was crying too.

She looked into his eyes, drinking him in, barely feeling the now driving rain. 'Ben Butterworth,' she said. 'You're already forgiven.'

'You really mean that?'

'You know I do.'

Smiling slightly, his eyes shining, he leaned forward and kissed her mouth softly. And there wasn't the fizz of excitement she'd felt with Frédérique, but a deep connection that rooted her to this man, this moment. Something that wasn't instantaneous but had grown and strengthened from years and years of being together, of being in love.

In the background, she was aware that her sodden guests had begun to clap.

'You should have said "You had me at hello!"' Emily said, as she appeared at Lily's side and gave her a quick squeeze. 'Haven't you watched any rom-coms lately?'

Lily smiled. 'Sorry,' she said, rain saturating her hair, running down her shoulders, turning her dress into cling film. 'But then, we had our happy ending years ago. Then years of real life. And now, well this is something even Richard Curtis couldn't top.'

And going up on tiptoes, she pulled Ben in for yet another kiss.

EPILOGUE

It was 4.30 p.m. and darkness had set in, providing the perfect backdrop for the Christmas lights strung back and forth above the marketplace in the shape of stars and colourful snowmen. Lily opened the car boot and lifted the last of the paper carrier bags inside, before shutting it and walking around to the driver's side.

As she slipped in, she felt the residual warmth of the car's heating against her back. She closed the door and rubbed her hands together quickly to restore some kind of feeling to her fingers before she gripped the wheel.

A light snow had fallen earlier, soon swept aside by tractors dispatched from local farms with snow ploughs attached; but the sky was heavy and full and although she'd always dreamed of a proper white Christmas, she hoped she'd make it home before the bulk of it fell.

She took one last look at the tiny row of shops and the road dotted with blue striped market stalls, taking in the colourful displays, the woman selling mulled wine from an enormous urn;

the last-minute shoppers flitting between craft stalls, laden with beautiful gift bags and paper packages.

Since popping out an hour ago, she'd already bumped into several people she knew – all of whom wished her *bonnes fêtes* and half of whom had leaned in for a hug or kiss as they were doing so. She was getting used to that now – the intimacy was no longer a surprise and she had begun to quite like being greeted in this way.

She'd also seen Frédérique, who'd been in the centre together with a man dressed as Père Noël and someone else in a reindeer costume. They'd been handing out little parcels to local children, who stopped in wonder whenever they caught sight of Santa, despite the fact his costume was fairly basic and the beard made of nothing more than cotton wool.

It was all about wanting to believe, she thought. Wanting to believe the magic and ignoring any evidence to the contrary.

She'd waved and Frédérique had waved back with a smile.

This morning, she and Ben had tried and failed to make home-made mincemeat, so had forgone their usual mince pies for gingerbread, which they'd piped with white icing as best they could. It had been a chance to put their new La Cornue range cooker to the test – something they'd treated themselves with after finishing the kitchen. The renovation had been a real team effort – she'd held cupboards in place while Ben drilled; they'd chosen chalk paint colours together and laughed when she'd kicked over a tin. Somehow any disaster or hiccup they'd faced had seemed trivial, or funny with Ben by her side. She'd thought about how alone she'd felt a few months ago when she'd ripped off the paper – and half the wall – in the hallway. It had seemed like another life.

When they'd finished their inexpert gingerbread, she'd taken a plate to Hermione, the neighbour, who'd been delighted at the gesture. '*Délicieux!*' she'd said, waving the plate. '*Merci et bonnes fêtes.*'

'*Bonnes fêtes,*' they'd replied.

Ben was sleeping better now – Lily had met a local reiki practitioner who'd agreed to work with her on a future retreat and somehow she'd managed to convince Ben to give the therapy a try 'for research, for the guests' as she'd put it. He wasn't fully committed to what he always called 'woo-woo' cures, but even he had to admit he was sleeping better post treatment.

They'd also found someone for him to talk to – a local bilingual psychologist who he'd agreed to see twice a week. There was no magic wand; they both knew that. But Lily was beginning to see more and more of the old, happier Ben and it was wonderful.

Ty had arrived a couple of days ago and spent most of the time in his room, exhausted from his first term. Last night at the table she'd caught him glancing at Ben and her shyly, as if taking in their relationship for the first time. When she'd rung to tell him back in the summer, he'd been pleased; but this was the first time he'd seen them together.

Tomorrow, they would share a small turkey meal – although finding a turkey had been more difficult than she'd imagined – before heading off for a *digestif* with Chloé and her mother. If the weather allowed, they were then going to visit the lake – wrapped up warm against the icy wind that buffeted the water and left cheeks glowing with cold – for a late afternoon walk.

They'd decorated the house – choosing a real tree for the first time in years, one with roots that they could plant out later and bought new decorations from the Christmas markets and the local fairs that peppered the area in the lead-up to the festive season. Yesterday evening Sam and Gabriel had come round with the kids – who were practically bursting with pre-Christmas joy.

It was going to be a wonderful Christmas.

Last night, Ben had given her an early present. 'I just couldn't wait,' he'd said. She'd unwrapped it to find a snow-globe containing a small stone cottage.

'It looks just like ours,' she'd said. 'Where did you find this?'

'In Limoges – at the flea market,' he'd told her. 'As soon as I saw it I thought, I know who'd love that.'

'Well, I do. Thank you,' she'd said, leaning forward and kissing him.

'It's not just that,' he'd said, taking her hand. The candle between them on the worn antique table had flickered as he'd moved. 'It's... I want it to mean something.'

'It does! It's lovely!' she'd said.

'No, not that,' he'd said. 'Although, thanks. I'm glad you like it. But what I'm trying to say, I suppose, is thank you.'

'What for?'

'For waiting. For believing in me.' He'd sighed and looked around the kitchen. 'For all of this really. The dream.'

'*My* dream.'

'No,' he'd said. '*Our* dream. That's what I want you to think when you look at this.' He shook the globe, sending white fluffy pieces tumbling. 'I'm not here just because I love you. Although I *do* of course. I'm here because I want to be.'

'Oh Ben.'

'Wait, there's more,' he'd said, with a small smile. 'I just... I want you to know that all the times we spoke about it – the move, I mean – over the years, well, I wasn't pretending. I loved the idea of it – of being together, somewhere completely new, working for ourselves. Stepping outside all the day-to-day stuff and having an adventure.'

She'd smiled.

'It was only when it came to it – when push really came to

shove, I got scared. I... well, I wasn't well. And it felt like too much, you know? It felt like it would always be too much.'

She'd squeezed his hand. 'I know, it's OK.'

'Anyway, I just wanted to make sure that you know I'm here for the long haul, whatever that turns out to be. Here because I love you. But also here because every day I'm beginning to love this life more and more. I'm... well, happy – happier – I guess. And it's because of you...'

'What, my rogue eBay activity?' She'd grinned.

'No,' he'd said, all seriousness. 'Because you showed me what it meant to have courage; you took the first steps out here for me. And because I discovered when you left that the only thing in life I'm *really* afraid of is having to live without you.'

At that, she'd put the snow globe, with its tumbling flurry, down on the table between them, then leaned forward to pull him in for a kiss.

She smiled at the memory, then reached to turn the key and start the engine. But before she could pull away there was a knock on the window. Frédérique's face smiled at her through the glass. She wound it down, smiling. '*Bonjour*, Frédérique,' she said.

'Bonjour, *et bonnes fêtes.*'

'*Merci, toi aussi.*'

It had taken a few weeks for them to re-establish some sort of friendship. But in October she'd seen him with a woman on his arm, whom he later introduced to her as Frances. He seemed happy, and his happiness had helped her release the last bit of guilt at her rejection of him.

'I think it will snow for your first Christmas in France, oui? It will be very cold. Have you enough fuel?'

'*Oui, merci*, we had a delivery yesterday and we've got plenty of wood.'

'That is good to 'ear,' he said, his eyes crinkling as he smiled widely at her.

'And you? What are you doing for Christmas?'

'Ah, I am seeing my mother and father, but also my grandmother is coming, eh? Per'aps you and your 'usband will meet 'er and tell 'er about the 'ouse.'

'Yes, that would be lovely.'

'So, Merry Christmas to you, *Madame Buttercup*,' he said, with a wink.

'Merry Christmas!' she said.

She wound her window up and began to drive, realising as she did that she was smiling. Never in her wildest dreams had she thought this year could come to a close in such a wonderful way – in a new place, with family and new friends, and happier than she'd been for years.

They both finally had their residence permits, their business was fully registered and in January the website would go live. Although she was a little nervous about actually taking bookings, she was excited too. Somehow on the cusp of things, ready to take a tentative step into something brand new and thrilling.

As she neared *Broussas*, a few flakes of snow began to hit the windscreen and she watched the automatic wipers spring to duty. By the time she pulled up outside the house, it was falling more heavily – highlighted diamond-bright in the glare of her headlights. She turned the engine off and looked for a moment at the house that had begun to feel just like home – only better. Inside she could see Ben, reaching to add another bauble to the tree, his skin reflecting the coloured lights. Ty was there too, holding a box of decorations.

She watched as Ben put an arm around his son and said something, at which they both laughed.

Opening the car door, she stepped out into the cold night,

feeling the flakes against her skin and breathing in the icy cold air. And feeling not the closing of the year, or the sombre mood that sometimes engulfed her when winter's curtain of darkness fell, but that this was the start of things – of possibilities and adventures and years of life ahead in which to live her dreams.

ACKNOWLEDGMENTS

I have so many people to thank for their help both in supporting my writing and generally putting up with me over the course of getting 'A Year at the French Farmhouse' to publication.

The first has to be Ray, my husband, who has read draft after draft of a novel that is probably not his first choice of genre, and never tires of listening to my outpourings of creative enthusiasm or self-doubt (or at least, he never appears to). My children: Lily, Joe, Tim, Evie and Robbie, who have had to keep their distance from my attic office during some of the more intense writing periods despite wanting me to join them on the trampoline or needing my help with their maths homework. Sorry kids.

I'd like to give a special thank you to my agent Ger, of The Book Bureau. I count myself extremely lucky to have her as my agent. She is always on hand to give me feedback, answer questions and generally provide unwavering support. Finding the right publisher for a book can be a fraught process, and she has gone above and beyond to keep me upbeat and positive – which is no mean feat. She is well and truly in my corner and believes in my work, even when I doubt myself. So thank you.

Tara, my editor, has been wonderful too. So enthusiastic about the book, and great to work with. The whole publication process has been delightful from start to finish (yes, even the edits), with clear communication and a real personal touch. The whole team at Boldwood: Jenna, Nia, Amanda, Claire and so many others has been a delight to work with and I've been so impressed with their efficiency, professionalism and great communication.

I'd also like to thank some of the independent bookstores who have been so supportive of my career, despite my living in France and being unable to yet visit in person. Most notably 'The Book Nook' in Ware, 'Heffers' in Cambridge, 'Book Corner', Saltburn and the online indie shop 'Tea Leaves and Reads.'

I've been supported brilliantly online both in my author group 'The D20 authors' – all of whom debuted during 2020 – and in reading groups, most notably 'The Motherload Book Club' and 'The Fiction Café Book Club' – both home to wonderful reading communities and run by amazing admins.

I also need to thank Natalie, a brilliant friend and avid reader.

I am blessed to live in a wonderful village in France with friendly inhabitants and a real community feel. Living here for the past decade has given me so much to draw on, and writing this book has made me fall in love with the country I call home all over again. Thanks to everyone who has made me and my family feel so welcome here.

Finally, thanks to readers who have been in touch, left reviews or shared my books with others. There's nothing more wonderful than knowing my books are being read, enjoyed and shared – and it's always a delight to hear from readers.

MORE FROM GILLIAN HARVEY

We hope you enjoyed reading *A Year At The French Farmhouse*. If you did, please leave a review.

If you'd like to gift a copy, this book is also available as an ebook, digital audio download and audiobook CD.

Sign up to Gillian Harvey's mailing list for news, competitions and updates on future books.

https://bit.ly/GillianHarveyNews

ABOUT THE AUTHOR

Gillian Harvey is a freelance journalist and the author of two well-reviewed women's fiction novels published by Orion. She has lived in Limousin France for the past twelve years, from where she derives the inspiration and settings for her books.

Visit Gillian's Website:

https://www.gillianharvey.com/

Follow Gillian on social media:

twitter.com/GillPlusFive

facebook.com/gharveyauthor

instagram.com/gillplusfive

bookbub.com/profile/gillian-harvey

tiktok.com/@gillianharveyauthor

Boldwood

Boldwood Books is an award-winning fiction publishing company seeking out the best stories from around the world.

Find out more at www.boldwoodbooks.com

Join our reader community for brilliant books, competitions and offers!

Follow us

@BoldwoodBooks

@BookandTonic

Sign up to our weekly deals newsletter

https://bit.ly/BoldwoodBNewsletter